DETROIT PUBLIC LIBRARY

P9-CDS-170

CHASE BRANCH LIBRARY
17731 W. SEVEN MILE RD.
DETROIT, MI 48235
313-481-1580

NOV -- 2017

CH

The Devil
You Know

Also by Mary Monroe

The Lonely Heart, Deadly Heart Series
Every Woman's Dream
Never Trust a Stranger

The God Series
God Don't Like Ugly
God Still Don't Like Ugly
God Don't Play
God Ain't Blind
God Ain't Through Yet
God Don't Make No Mistakes

Mama Ruby Series
Mama Ruby
The Upper Room
Lost Daughters

Gonna Lay Down My Burdens
Red Light Wives
In Sheep's Clothing
Deliver Me from Evil
She Had It Coming
The Company We Keep
Family of Lies
Bad Blood

"Nightmare in Paradise" in *Borrow Trouble*

Published by Kensington Publishing Corp.

The Devil
You Know

MARY
MONROE

KENSINGTON BOOKS
www.kensingtonbooks.com

To the extent that the image or images on the cover of this book depict a person or persons, such person or persons are merely models, and are not intended to portray any character or characters featured in the book.

DAFINA BOOKS are published by

Kensington Publishing Corp.
119 West 40th Street
New York, NY 10018

Copyright © 2017 by Mary Monroe

All rights reserved. No part of this book may be reproduced in any form or by any means without the prior written consent of the Publisher, excepting brief quotes used in reviews.

All Kensington titles, imprints and distributed lines are available at special quantity discounts for bulk purchases for sales promotion, premiums, fund-raising, educational or institutional use.

Special book excerpts or customized printings can also be created to fit specific needs. For details, write or phone the office of the Kensington Special Sales Manager. Attn.: Special Sales Department. Kensington Publishing Corp., 119 West 40th Street, New York, NY 10018. Phone: 1-800-221-2647.

Library of Congress Card Catalogue Number: 2017944859

Dafina and the Dafina logo Reg. U.S. Pat. & TM Off.

ISBN-13: 978-1-61773-810-4
ISBN-10: 1-61773-810-7
First Kensington Hardcover Edition: November 2017

eISBN-13: 978- 1-61773-811-1
eISBN-10: 1-61773-811-5
Kensington Electronic Edition: November 2017

10 9 8 7 6 5 4 3 2 1

Printed in the United States of America

*This book is dedicated to Sheila Sims, Archie Belford,
and Maria Felice Sanchez.*

Acknowledgments

Selena James is an awesome editor and a great friend. Thank you, Selena! Thanks to Steven Zacharius, Adam Zacharius, Karen Auerbach, Lulu Martinez, Robin Cook, the wonderful crew in the sales department, and everyone else at Kensington for working so hard for me.

Thanks to Lauretta Pierce for maintaining my website.

Thanks to the fabulous book clubs, book stores, libraries, my readers, and the magazine and radio interviewers for supporting me for so many years.

To my super literary agent and friend, Andrew Stuart, thank you for representing me with so much vigor.

Please continue to e-mail me at Authorauthor5409@aol.com and visit my website at www.Marymonroe.org. You can also communicate with me on Facebook at Facebook.com/MaryMonroe and Twitter @MaryMonroeBooks.

Peace and Blessings,

Mary Monroe

This is the third and final book in my Lonely Heart,
Deadly Heart series

The Devil
You Know

Chapter 1
Lola

THE MAN I WANTED TO SPEND THE REST OF MY LIFE WITH HAD NOT even proposed yet. But I was so determined to marry Calvin Ramsey I tried on a wedding gown yesterday and I already picked out a name for our first child. After three dates, I was convinced that he was the only man for me.

I didn't care that I had met him on the Internet. Friends with Benefits: Discreet Encounters was an online dating site that had been created for horny adults interested in having casual sex. I'd gotten that and much more when I hooked up with Calvin. In addition to being a fantastic lover and owning his own home in a middle-class neighborhood, he was handsome, had a wonderful personality, and had a good job as a long-haul truck driver. The list of his good qualities was a lot longer, but these were the things I cared about the most.

When I was a girl, I used to fantasize about having a fancy church wedding. I was no longer a girl and I was tired of just fantasizing about being a bride. Too many years and men had slipped away, and so had most of my patience. I had to move fast because my time was running out. I was going to be thirty-three in October, and my biological clock was ticking like a time bomb.

My best friend, Joan Proctor-Riley, had called me at eleven-thirty a.m., ten minutes ago. After we had chatted about a few mundane things, I eased Calvin's name into the conversation. "I know Calvin is going to be a good husband and a wonderful addition to my family, but I hope they never find out where I met him. They'd cook my goose to a crisp."

"I don't think you need to worry about that until he asks you to marry him." Joan snickered. "Besides, I'm the only one who knows where you met him and I'm sure not going to blab, because my goose and yours are in the same oven. In the meantime, don't be in a rush to get married. Once a dude puts a ring on your finger, the party's over. Keep dating other men because you might find a better prospect for a husband. Like that hot army doctor from Uganda you had so much fun with last month."

"And live in the same house with him and his four wives? No thanks." I chuckled.

Joan and I had several dirty little secrets, but being members of an online sex club was the "dirtiest" one of all. Discussing our dates was one of our favorite subjects.

She suddenly began to whisper. "Um, if Reed gives you a call between four and five p.m. today, tell him I'm on my way home. If he asks anything else, make up something. Call me, or send me a text to let me know everything you told him." Joan had already told me that she was going on a date in a few hours and needed me to cover for her. She had told her husband that we were going shopping.

"I've had your back for years. Don't you think I know how to handle your husband by now?"

"You should. But I still like to remind you. A woman can never be too careful. Reed is convinced that I'm cheating on him."

I gasped. "Hello? You *are* cheating on him!"

"Well, I don't have a choice. Sleeping with him is like sleeping with a log. The last time we had sex, he actually fell asleep while he was still on top of me! Dating other men is the only thing that's keeping me from losing what's left of my mind."

I sighed. "Sleeping with a log is one thing I won't have to worry about with Calvin." I got misty-eyed just thinking about the man I was in love with. I didn't have any pictures of him yet, so when I wanted to look at his handsome, bronze-toned face and well-developed body, I visited his online profile and gazed at him until my eyes watered. I couldn't wait to introduce him to my family and everybody else. "Once I get Calvin locked in—as in marriage—I will never sleep with another man again. I plan to be with him until one of us dies. . . ."

Chapter 2
Joan

*L*OLA RARELY TOOK ADVICE FROM ME, BUT I STILL OFFERED IT. WE were the same age, but I was much more mature and sensible. As much as I loved my girl, there were times when she annoyed me with some of her unrealistic goals. She was fantasizing about marrying a man who had never even given her a single reason to think that he was in love with her. This foolishness completely blew my mind.

"You need to be more realistic. For all you know, you may never even hear from Calvin Ramsey again. If you think he's so hot, a lot of other women must think so too. With all those wealthy older women in the club, one just might hook him up to be her boy toy and get him to stop dating other club members."

"What are you trying to tell me, Joan?"

"I'm trying to tell you to slow down and get to know Calvin better. What if he turns out to be like Reed, or worse?" I was in our guest bathroom, where I usually went when I wanted to use my cell phone to have a private conversation. I could hear Reed in the living room talking to somebody on the landline. I cursed under my breath when I heard him say, "Six this evening. I'll make sure Joan makes plenty of gumbo." I had no idea who he was talking to. And I had no desire, or even the ingredients, to make some damn gumbo this evening!

Reed and I had been married for fifteen years and I'd told him hundreds of times not to make plans for us without checking with me first. But he still did it anyway. There was just no telling what kind of bullshit get-together he had agreed to this time. The cookout that he'd dragged me to at his parents' house in Monterey earlier this month had been pure torture for me. Dealing with my obnoxious mother-in-law and some of her uppity friends always put me in a bad mood. It seemed like no matter what I wore around them or how I behaved, it was always inappropriate. It gave Mother Riley another reason to remind me that I was from "the hood." Most of Reed's friends annoyed me just as much. It was no wonder I was leading a double life. It had become complicated, but I was having a good time and that was all that mattered.

"Lola, I have to hang up. It sounds like Reed is cooking up some shit that could derail my plans to get out of the house today," I hissed as I turned off my cell phone. I slid it into my bathrobe pocket and cursed under my breath again before I joined Reed in our elegantly furnished living room. He had ended his call. "Who were you talking to?" I sank down next to him on the couch.

He frowned as he looked me up and down. "Didn't I tell you to dispose of that shabby flannel bathrobe? How come you stopped wearing that silk one I gave you for your birthday?"

"It's too small."

"I'm not surprised. It would still fit if you'd stop going to those greasy low-end restaurants with Lola. You may not care that you're losing your shape, but I do. At the rate you're gaining weight, you'll be as big as the rest of the women in your family by the time you're thirty-five. The sight of flab and cellulite makes my flesh crawl," he said gruffly.

"Oh really? In case you don't remember, your mother weighs almost three hundred pounds," I shot back.

"That's different. At least Mother can blame her weight gain on menopause and other things common among women her age. You can't."

I rolled my eyes and playfully punched the side of Reed's arm. "Who were you talking to on the telephone?" I asked again.

"We're going to play bridge with Dr. Weinstein and his wife this evening. Meg is making spoon bread to go with the gumbo you're going to cook—"

"No," I said, interrupting Reed with my hand up to his face. "I told you last night that Lola invited me to go shopping with her today!"

"So? You should be back in plenty of time. Mitch and Meg aren't coming until six."

"I don't know if I will be back in time. You know how Lola likes to lollygag and drag me into every store in the mall. Besides, we don't have any gumbo mix or crab legs."

Reed looked at his watch and then at me with a shrug. "No problem. I'll go with you and Lola so I can make sure she doesn't drag you into every store. We can stop by the market on the way home and pick up everything you need."

"Look, Reed, you know damn well Lola will not want to go shopping with me if you come," I said, already rising. "The sooner I get up out of here, the sooner I'll be back. I'll let her know that we have plans for later today so she won't expect me to stay with her too long."

"I guess I can agree to that," he muttered.

I sprinted back to the bathroom and took a quick shower. Then I darted down the hall to the master bedroom and applied a minimal amount of makeup and pulled my hair into a ponytail. Since I was supposed to be going shopping, I couldn't make myself look too glamorous. I put on a pair of jeans, a plaid blouse, and a pair of low-heeled, black pumps.

"I'll see you in a few hours," I told Reed as I strutted toward the door with my purse in my hand. I didn't even have to look at him to know that he had a puppy dog expression on his face.

"I sure hope so," he whined. "I don't want to disappoint Mitch and Meg like we did the last time we invited them over."

"Then 'we' need to learn how to plan better." I still didn't look at Reed. I rushed out the door and trotted down the hall to the elevator.

Thirty minutes later, I arrived at the Hyatt hotel in nearby San

Jose where I planned to spend a few hours with John Walden, a club member I hooked up with quite frequently.

John was a handsome and very successful attorney originally from Jamaica. He had resided in England most of his adult life, but now he lived in Phoenix with his Italian wife and their three children. Like me and thousands of other members in the club, he had joined Discreet Encounters for the same reason: to have discreet, no-strings-attached sexual encounters.

John must have been standing in front of the door, because he immediately snatched it open when I knocked. "You're early," he greeted. Before I could speak, he jerked me into the room, wrapped his arms around me, and gave me a quick but very passionate kiss.

"Um, I can't stay but three or four hours," I managed, licking my bottom lip.

"I've heard that before," he complained. "Look, I don't get to see you as often as I'd like to and—"

"John, my husband invited some people over for dinner this evening. If I don't get home in time to prepare it, he'll go ballistic and the night will be a disaster for me. Now, be reasonable. If he starts keeping closer tabs on me, it'll be even harder for me to see you."

"Then I guess we shouldn't waste any time," John said, giving me a hungry look. He scooped me up into his arms and carried me to the bed.

Chapter 3
Joan

*I'*D BEEN WITH JOHN FOR LESS THAN AN HOUR. HE SAT ON THE SIDE of the bed clutching his cell phone as he talked to his wife. In the ten minutes since he'd placed the call, he had told her one lie after another about how bored he was and how much he wished she'd come to California with him. When he stood up and started pacing back and forth, frowning and shaking his head as he talked, I knew it was going to be a long conversation.

We had already made love once, finished a bottle of champagne, and were both still naked. The more encounters I had with John, the more I enjoyed his company. As well as everything else about him. He'd grown a goatee and lost a few pounds since our first date so he was more handsome than ever.

I had clawed his smooth, copper-colored back and left so many scratches, it looked like a road map. But it didn't matter because according to John, his wife was such a prude; she never looked at him when he was completely naked. He winked and threw me a kiss. Rolling his eyes, he told his wife that she was the only woman he loved and that he had never even looked at another woman since he married her. On that note, I rolled off the bed, retrieved my phone from my purse on the nightstand, and slipped into the bathroom. I needed to check in with Lola.

"Thank God you picked up. Where are you?" I said when she answered on the second ring.

"I'm having lunch with Elbert at Denny's."

"Oh. Did I know that?"

"I told you when we talked last night, and I told you when we talked this morning."

"I guess it slipped my mind. Elbert is so easy to forget." Elbert Porter was a nerdy guy who'd attended high school with us. He was the divorced son of one of Lola's stepmother's friends. He was as cute and harmless as a puppy, and he adored Lola. She would never admit it, but I knew she only spent time with him because she felt sorry for him. It was certainly not because he was good in bed. He was so religious, he didn't believe in sex outside of marriage. But with her crazy life, which was probably crazier than mine, she needed a straitlaced man like Elbert to keep her grounded. "Can you talk for a few minutes?"

"Yeah. He's in the men's room. Are you still with John?"

"Yup! He's on the phone with his wife."

"What's up?"

"Did Reed call you?"

"Not yet. And I hope he doesn't."

"I hope he doesn't either. I'm having a great time. Ooh-wee, girl! John is such an amazing man. If you know what I mean." Joan giggled.

"So you keep telling me."

"Are you going to be with Elbert much longer?"

"Nope!" she said quickly and with more emphasis than was necessary. I knew how much Elbert bored her. "After we finish lunch, I'm going straight home."

"Good. I'll call you a few minutes before I leave to let you know where to meet me. You remember our plan?"

"Of course. I went to the mall last night. I have the dummy shopping bags for you in the trunk of my car."

Reed was so suspicious these days; I never came home empty-handed after a bogus shopping trip with Lola. Despite his many flaws, he was not gullible enough to believe that a woman could spend several hours at a mall and not buy anything.

"I know you probably told me already. And if you did, I forgot. So tell me what I bought this time." I giggled.

"A couple of blouses and some sexy lingerie. Will one bag of merchandise be enough? I have three this time. One is full of men's items you can give to Reed so he'll think you were shopping for him too. I bought shaving lotion, half a dozen undershirts, and four pairs of those sissified socks he likes."

"I'll take all three bags. Thanks for looking out for me. I appreciate your help."

"And I'd appreciate you paying me. You know my paycheck from the grocery store doesn't go far when I have to pay for all the high-end stuff you like."

"I'll give you a blank check today. Remind me to treat you to lunch next week. You can choose the place. But puh-leeze, not Denny's, Wendy's, or one of those gut-busting chitlin joints! We gain weight just being near those places. And the next time we really do go shopping, I'll treat you to a Neiman Marcus spree." I laughed.

"You'd better bring one of your high-limit credit cards, because I'm going to make up for the last two times I picked up merchandise for you and never got paid," Lola teased.

"I will. I'll even throw in a few hundred bucks cash as a bonus. Oh! Before I forget, you need to give me all the information about your date tomorrow with that dude from Chicago. I'd like to be prepared in case your nosy stepmother calls me if you don't make it back home in time to pick her up from church."

"I'll e-mail or text it when I get a chance."

"You don't sound too excited about this date."

"I am excited. But I still get skittish before I meet a club member in person for the first time." Lola let out a long deep breath. This was usually a sign that she was about to complain about something, so I braced myself. "I'm having fun and enjoying all the great sex, but sometimes I wish there was just one man in my life."

I groaned and shook my head, something I often did during our conversations. "Well, if you are right about Calvin, you will have just one man in your life soon." I paused because I could no longer hear John talking. "I have to hang up now!" I abruptly turned off my phone and skittered out of the bathroom.

John had stretched back out in the bed. He grinned as his eyes roamed over my body. "Is everything okay, luv?"

"Like that old song says: 'Everything is beautiful,'" I sang in a husky tone as I crawled into his arms. "Let's order another bottle of champagne."

Chapter 4
Calvin

I USUALLY KEPT MY CELL PHONE TURNED OFF WHEN I VISITED MY FI-ancée's house. Too many other women had my number and called or texted me when I least expected it. Sylvia Bruce was the love of my life, but she was as nosy as every other woman I knew. I'd caught her going through my mail one night when she'd cooked dinner for us at my house a couple of days before Christmas last year. "I was just checking to see if you received that cute card I sent with Santa drinking a glass of wine," she claimed. I had received the card and had told her, so I knew she had been snooping.

Whenever Sylvia visited my house now, I made sure my mail and cell phone were not within her reach. And I always "swept" my house before she came over. I had to make sure that there was no evidence of another woman's visit. Some were notorious for leaving a tube of lipstick or a hairpin behind. Whether they did it on purpose or by accident, it was not cool.

Dealing with women had become so tangled I had to be on guard at all times. A man in my position had to be extremely careful because I had some deep dark secrets that I planned to take to the grave. The main one was, I had murdered so many women I'd lost count. I had dumped numerous bodies in vari-ous places such as deserted alleys, ditches, and wooded areas along the interstate routes I drove from one end of the coast to the other. I'd even dropped one nasty bitch down an abandoned well in a remote area near Modesto. So far, only three or four (or was it five?) of the black ones had resembled Glinda. With the exception of a big-ass, pie-faced Native American cow and a couple of Latinas, all the others had been white. And there would be more . . .

My homicidal rampage had started about six years ago. Some details had become so fuzzy over the years, I wasn't even sure of the exact date. Up until then, I had never harmed a woman. As a matter of fact, I had been raised to despise violence. I didn't count the men I'd killed in Afghanistan during my stint in the marines. Killing had come with the territory. After all the bullets and other mayhem I had dodged over there, I'd come home to face my worst enemy yet: my cheating wife and first victim.

When the newspaper reported Glinda's mysterious disappearance, a lot of people didn't even know she was my wife. She had refused to take my last name when we got married because she didn't want to lose her "independence and identity." Well, that was something she'd never have to worry about again. If she had not taunted me and attempted to leave me on our last night together, she would still be alive. But she'd pushed a button that I never knew I had until then.

I had enjoyed taking Glinda's life, but doing it only one time had not been enough. I wanted to relive the experience as many more times as possible. And the only way I could do that was to kill other whores like her until I had satisfied my thirst for revenge.

But homicide was a very risky business. With today's technology, busybody witnesses, and smarter cops, people who had committed murders decades ago were being rounded up in droves. The last thing I wanted to do was spend the rest of my life in prison, so I knew I had to "retire" soon.

I had recently selected my final victim from a source that had become a predator's playground: an Internet dating site. If everything went according to my latest plan (I'd revised it numerous times), Lola Poole would be dead within the next two or

three weeks. I had to get rid of that slut before Sylvia and I exchanged vows in June. The last thing I wanted to do was go on
my honeymoon knowing that that bitch was still breathing.

Yesterday, which was Friday, I delivered some state-of-the-art
appliances to a department store in Bakersfield. I loved being a
long-haul truck driver. Being alone on the open road allowed
me to enjoy my solitude and clear my head. I'd been scheduled
to do another haul on Sunday, but this morning when I called
Monty, one of the best bosses in the world, and told him I'd proposed to Sylvia last week, he gave me up to five days off—with
pay—so she and I could celebrate our engagement with some of
our close friends in Vegas tonight.

It was 1:35 p.m. Our flight was not scheduled to leave for another six hours, so Sylvia had decided to cook dinner for us. I
loved to eat, and she loved to cook. Her mother's family was
from Brazil, and her father and his folks were from Louisiana.
When it came to good food, I got the best of both worlds. Today
it was one of my favorite meals: collard greens, buttermilk corn
bread, blackened flank steak, rice and beans, and yams. We
planned to eat an early dinner so we wouldn't gobble like hogs
at our engagement party.

Our luggage was already in my Jeep Cherokee. Sylvia was taking a bubble bath, and I was slumped on her living room couch.
When my cell phone vibrated, I pulled it out of my back pocket
to see who was calling. I groaned as soon as I saw the caller ID.
The only reason I didn't scream profanity and slam my fist on
the coffee table was because I didn't want Sylvia to hear the
commotion. I answered the call and said in a cheerful but low
voice, "Hello, Lola."

"Hi, Calvin. I hope you're having a nice day," she squealed,
sounding like the pig she was. Every time I heard her disgusting
voice, I flinched.

"Yes, I am. Are you?" I replied, speaking as cordially as I could.

"My day is going okay, but it could be a whole lot better. . . ."

I chuckled. "I'm sure a lot of people feel the same way."

"But I always try to look at things from a positive point of view.
I mean, my day could be going a lot worse."

Why this woman took the time to call me and talk such mundane dribble was a mystery to me. "That's a good attitude to have, Lola." I was just about to tell her I was busy and had to hang up, but before I could get another word out, she sniffed and rambled some more.

"Um, you've been on my mind a lot since our last date, so I just called to say hello."

It had been only a week since our last rendezvous. Before that, we'd been intimate only one other time. "I was going to call you this evening," I lied. "You've been on my mind a lot too." My last statement was true, but painful. This miserable, disgusting whore was on my mind every day.

Glinda's body and my second and third victims—women who resembled her (which was the reason they'd died)—now occupied a large freezer in my garage. It had room for only one more woman, and that was Lola. I had started planning her murder the first time I saw the picture she'd posted on the Internet. Her incredibly close resemblance to Glinda and the fact that she was also a whore had sealed her fate. Before I had stumbled across Lola, I had developed so much rage, it didn't matter whether my victims reminded me of Glinda or not.

Chapter 5
Lola

*I*T WAS SO NICE TO HEAR CALVIN'S VOICE AGAIN. I HAD PROMISED MYself that I would be patient and wait for him to call me, but I'd called him at the spur of the moment anyway. Just hearing him say that I'd been on his mind made me tingle.

"Is this a bad time for you to talk?" I asked. "I was at loose ends and thought I'd give you a call." It had been about three minutes since my conversation with Joan.

"I can chat for a minute or two. I'm glad you called, Lola. What have you been up to since our date last Saturday?"

"Not much."

"Come on, now. Don't tell me you've been sitting around twiddling your thumbs."

"Uh, no, I haven't." I had turned down a date with a computer guru from Chicago for tonight and we'd agreed to hook up tomorrow afternoon instead. I couldn't go out tonight because I had promised my stepmother that I'd help her clean off the back porch. With all the junk we had dumped there, it could take several hours. However, if Calvin asked me to see him tonight, Bertha would have to clean off the back porch by herself! "I do have plans for tomorrow, but I could change them," I threw in hopefully. If he asked me to spend some time with him on Sunday, I wouldn't hesitate to put the computer dude off again.

His response disappointed me. "That's nice. Have a good time tomorrow," was all he said.

I didn't want to take a chance on hearing him say something else I didn't like, so I decided to end the call. "I'll let you get back to whatever you were doing. It was nice talking to you."

His next response didn't disappoint me. "Lola, I can't wait to see you again."

I gasped. "Just let me know when . . ." I stopped talking because I was afraid that if I kept yapping, I'd say something real stupid. And when I recalled some of the stupid shit I'd said to him during previous conversations, I winced. There had been times when I had come off acting and sounding like a giddy teenager. Despite the fact that I didn't look my thirty-two years, it was important for me to present myself as a mature and intelligent woman. Even with all this in mind, I said something stupid anyway! "I hope our next date will be as wonderful as our last one. There are a couple of other tricks I'd like to show you." I held my breath and slapped the side of my head. If I could have kicked my own ass, I would have done that too.

Calvin laughed. "I can't wait. Baby, I hate to cut this call short, but I have to go now."

"Oh, okay. . . ."

"Thanks for calling."

"Bye, Calvin," I said quickly. He didn't say another word. The next thing I heard was silence.

Before I could turn off my phone, Joan called again. "It's you-know-who," she announced. "I'm still with John."

"I figured that," I said dryly. "How much longer are you going to be with him?"

"Well, he's friskier than usual, so it could be another couple of hours or so."

"Where is he?"

"He had to go out and get some more cigars. Reed still hasn't pestered you yet?"

"Nope."

"Good. It's bad enough I'll have to spend this evening with him and the boring-ass Weinsteins, so I'm going to milk this date dry. Are you still with Elbert?"

"Yeah. He was late picking me up and we had to wait thirty minutes for a table. Now I think he's got the runs."

"Why do you think that?"

"He's in the men's room for the second time in less than fifteen minutes."

"Yuck! How unromantic," Joan snickered.

"Bye, woman!" I snapped.

I preferred upscale restaurants, but Denny's was closer so it was a very short ride from my house. I didn't like to spend any more time alone in a car with Elbert than necessary. Joan once referred to him as a "mercy fuck without the fuck" and accused me of "dating" him only because I felt sorry for him. She was half right. I dated Elbert because I felt sorry for myself. I didn't like the fact that I had so many expectations when it came to men. Good sex and socializing in bars were two of my favorite pastimes. Elbert didn't do either one. He told me on our first date back in January that he had not been intimate with a woman since his divorce almost ten years ago. There were a lot of other things I did that Elbert didn't do. He never lied and never said or did anything to hurt another person's feelings. And he was as devoted to his mother—who lived with him in a big house he owned—as I was to Bertha. She was crazy about him because his mother was one of her closest friends. And he managed a meat market so he gave her all the free meat she wanted and that made her very happy.

"Lola, you get better looking every day," Elbert told me right after we had ordered our burgers and fries. Because of his handsome features, well-groomed shoulder-length dreadlocks, and toned body, I didn't mind being seen in public with him.

"Thank you," I muttered before I sipped from my water glass. "The same goes for you."

"I'm so glad you had time for me today," he went on. He dipped his head and gave me a shy look as he stirred his tea, the strongest beverage he ever drank. "It means a lot to me and it makes me feel better about you not being able to go with me to the hot air balloon race. . . ." I swallowed the lump that had suddenly formed in my throat. It took so little to make Elbert happy. I was so glad that my presence meant so much to him, especially since that was all he wanted.

"Well, I did have to move a few other things around so I could have lunch with you and we'll go to the balloon race some other time. I can't stay too long because I have to help Bertha clean off the back porch when I get home."

The main reason I had agreed to have lunch with Elbert was because I had canceled a date to go to the bingo hall with him last Saturday so I could spend a few hours with Calvin. I knew it had hurt him and I had not given it much thought at the time, but afterward I'd felt guilty. Spending time with him today was my way of making it up to him.

"Oh! Before I forget, I have some good news and some bad news," he said with an excited look on his face.

"What's the good news?" I turned my head so that I was gazing at him from the corner of my eye.

"They sold raffle tickets at the bingo tournament you canceled out on last Saturday. I bought the ticket that won first prize: a ride for me and a guest in a stretch limo from my house to San Jose, dinner, and tickets to a comedy show."

"What's the bad news?"

"Everything's been scheduled for Saturday after next."

"Oh. Well, I'll be your guest if you want me to," I said quickly.

Elbert scratched his neck and gave me a serious look. "Uh . . . that's the other part of the bad news. I didn't think you'd be available, so I promised Mama I'd take her. One more thing— it's on the same day as that outdoor gospel concert you said you'd go to with me, so we won't be able to do that either."

"That's all right, Elbert. I understand." I was already feeling down in the dumps because Calvin had not been able to talk to me for more than a few moments when I'd called him earlier. Now I was feeling even lower. I prayed that I would find out soon where my relationship with him was going. If he decided to get serious with me, I'd stop going out with Elbert because I was tired of disappointing him. It was not fair to him, or me, to continue such a dead-end relationship too much longer. Just as I was about to say something else apologetic to Elbert, he spotted one of his friends on the other side of the room.

"Lola, I don't mean to be rude, but I have to go talk to Vernon for a few minutes. He approached me with a real sweet business deal last week, and I need to get more information from him." Elbert didn't give me time to respond. He leaped out of his seat and walked briskly over to the table his friend occupied.

Less than ten seconds later, my cell phone rang again. I expected to see Reed's name on the caller ID, Bertha's, or Joan's. I almost choked on my tongue when I saw Calvin's name! I pressed the answer button so fast and hard, the tip of my finger felt like I'd stuck a pin in it. "Hello," I said, answering halfway through the first ring.

"Lola, I'm sorry I couldn't talk to you longer when you called earlier. Are you busy?"

"Um, kind of."

"Oh, I'm sorry. Then I won't even bother to tell you why I called. . . ."

"Don't hang up!" I hollered, forcing myself not to sound too frantic. "I'd really like to know why you called." Of all the men I'd ever known, Calvin was the only one who made my heart skip a beat and the rest of my body tingle whenever I heard his voice. *He had to be my soul mate.*

"I wanted to know if you could meet me somewhere as soon as you can. I have a really busy schedule, but I'm free for the next couple of hours."

"You want me to meet you *right now?*" I wailed. The Tuesday before last when Calvin asked me to meet him at the spur of the moment, I had taken off early from work to do so. That's how badly I had wanted to be with him. I'd enjoyed our first sexual encounter, and I'd enjoyed the second one when we got to-

gether last Saturday. As much as I cared about him, I was not about to disappoint Elbert again by running out on him before we even finished lunch so I could go have sex with Calvin—if that was what he wanted. I loved him, but I had to draw the line somewhere. I didn't want him to think that I'd be at his beck and call, any time he wanted me.

"If you can't make it . . ."

"I can't make it today. I'm having lunch with a friend at the moment."

Calvin hesitated before he responded. "I see. I'm sorry, Lola." I could tell from his flat tone that he was as disappointed as I was! "I don't know what I was thinking. Ever since I talked to you earlier today, you're all I've been able to think about. I thought it would be nice to enjoy your company before I go back on the road tomorrow. A lot of things are coming up with my work, so I might have to spend more time down South this week than I usually do after a run."

"I understand. I know your work keeps you very busy. I hope your invitation for me to spend your birthday weekend with you in Frisco is still on. . . ."

"I still want you to spend my birthday weekend with me, but July is so far away. Oh well. Do you think you'll have some time for me in the next week or so?"

"Uh-huh." I tried to sound as nonchalant as possible. I didn't want Calvin to know just how anxious I was to see him again. What I really wanted to do was jump up on the table and do a happy dance. "I'll even take off a couple of days from work and we can spend as much of that time together as possible," I offered. There was no way in the world I'd ever tell Joan that I'd made such a bold suggestion. I hadn't even told her that I'd tried on a wedding gown and picked out a name for my first child with Calvin.

"Baby, you just made my day."

I saw Elbert shuffling back to our table. "Uh . . . same here. I have to hang up now. Bye." I turned off my phone and slid it

back into my purse. "I hope you had a nice conversation with your friend," I said when Elbert sat back down and dragged his chair closer to mine.

"I did, but I didn't want to waste too much time with him as long as I have you all to myself for a little while." Elbert sniffed and looked at me like I was something good to eat.

"Oh," was all I could say.

Chapter 6
Calvin

"**W**HO WERE YOU TALKING TO?" SYLVIA ASKED, ENTERING HER LIV-
ing room with nothing but a towel wrapped around her slender
body. She stopped in front of me with her hands on her hips.

She rarely busted me, so I didn't have much experience in
wiggling my ass out of tense situations. When Sylvia got in my
face—and it was almost always for something as petty as my not
putting the toilet seat back down—I apologized. When she got
on my case about something more serious, like me eyeballing
other women when we were out in public, I got loud and defen-
sive. I was not in the mood for any drama, so I decided to go easy
on her this time by playing dumb and innocent. "Huh?" I
paused and cleared my throat. "Who, me?"

"Yes, you," she snapped, pursing her lips into a self-satisfied
smirk.

"It was nobody." My response was pretty stupid because she
had obviously overheard me talking on my cell phone. I prayed
that she had not heard too much of my end of the conversation.

"Nobody? That's strange. I heard you tell 'nobody' you couldn't
wait to see them again."

I was edgy, but I didn't show it. "It was one of my coworkers.
You remember that goofy, fat white dude named Roger?"

"Oh, I'll never forget him and his three chins." Sylvia laughed.
"I can still picture that snaggle-tooth hillbilly gnawing on eight
chicken wings, three plates of collard greens, two huge pieces of

corn bread, and three servings of sweet potato pie last month when we invited him to dinner. Then he had the nerve to load up a plate to take home."

I nodded. "He had such a great time; he said he can't wait to have dinner with us again. I told him I couldn't wait to see him again too."

Sylvia plopped down into my lap. "I hope he doesn't eat like a hog at our engagement party in Vegas tonight."

"That was another reason he called. He won't be able to make it. His son was arrested this morning for breaking into some-body's house. Roger has to stay in town to deal with that."

Sylvia let out a loud sigh and rolled her big brown eyes. "Kids. Every parent I know is having one problem or another with their kids." She gave me a pleading look while she massaged my shoulder. "But they are still a blessing, and I can't wait to be a mother. I'm glad you agreed we could start our family right away. Even then, we'll be well into middle age by the time our kids reach their teens, so we'll really have our work cut out for us."

"Baby, don't you even start worrying about us having prob-lems with our kids," I said as I stroked her hair. "Everything is going to be just fine."

"I know it will be, Calvin. As long as we work together and trust and believe in one another, we'll have a wonderful mar-riage and family."

I was relieved because Sylvia had dropped the subject of my telephone conversation. No matter what I did, she didn't like to ruffle my feathers, so we rarely squabbled. I couldn't get over how lucky I was to have found such an amazing woman. I would have married her even if she looked like a baboon. But I was glad she had an attractive face and a nice body. I puffed out my chest as I looked around her living room. The brown leather couch and matching love seat she'd purchased two months ago still smelled and looked brand new. She was an excellent house-keeper. There was not a speck of dust or clutter anywhere in sight. Sylvia was the only person I knew who organized the dozens of books in her bookcase in alphabetical order by title. I

often asked myself how come I had waited five long years to propose to this well-rounded woman. She gave me a quick kiss and
excused herself to go get dressed.

Fifteen minutes later, she returned wearing a denim jump-
suit. She sat down next to me and squeezed my crotch. "We have
time if you want to get busy before we leave for the airport," she
told me in a husky voice.

I definitely wanted to "get busy," but not with Sylvia. I wanted
Lola. "Baby, you must have read my mind." I stood up and
reached into my pocket for a condom. Before I could even open
the wrapper, the landline on the end table rang. I shook my
head and gave her an exasperated look. She answered it anyway.

"Oh, hi! I'm so glad you called. I wanted to check in with you
before we left for Vegas," she said with a huge smile. A split second later she frowned and then she remained silent for about a
minute. "Shit! I forgot all about it! I'll be there in ten minutes."
She hung up and gave me a sad-eyed look.

"Who the hell will you be seeing in ten minutes?" I asked
hotly.

"That was Sonia. Remember the lawsuit she filed after she got
hit by that bus when she visited our grandmother in Brazil last
year?" Sylvia and her three younger siblings had been born and
raised in the States, but their mother had been born in Brazil,
where most of her family still resided.

"Yeah. What about it?"

"The lawyer who's handling her case sent her a stack of docu-
ments she needs to read and respond to. Everything is in Portuguese, and I need to go translate."

"What the fuck?" I yelled, waving my hand. "Why would a
lawyer send her something in a foreign language instead of English?"

"Baby, English is a foreign language to some people. I promised
Sonia yesterday that I would do it, but I got so busy today, it completely skipped my mind."

"Your sister speaks Portuguese and so does your mother," I
pointed out. "Why do you have to translate?"

"Mama's on a retreat with her church group. And, yes, Sonia speaks the language, but she can't read or write it that well. She needs to get the papers completed, then notarized and back in the mail by Monday morning." Sylvia gave me an apologetic look, but I was still pissed off, and horny as hell.

"Well, go on so you can get back in time for a little fun before we leave for the airport," I said gruffly, waving her toward the door.

"Honey, we'll make love as soon as we check into our hotel. We'll have a little time alone before the party starts."

"Aw, shuck it! I can't wait that long!" I poked out my lower lip and pouted.

"Baby, calm down. You're behaving like a two-year-old." It was hard to tell which one of us was more exasperated. Sylvia blinked hard and wrung her hands. I sucked in a ton of air and shook my head as she continued. "I'm going to be with Sonia at least a couple of hours, so I doubt if I'll be able to get back in time for us to fool around before we leave." She looked around the room and then back at me. "Why don't you go out and have a drink with one of your neighbors or one of your friends? I don't want you to sit here by yourself."

"Yeah," I mumbled. "I just might do that." I still had an erection and I had to get it taken care of soon—not *hours* from now.

Five minutes after Sylvia left, I dialed Lola's number. She picked up right away, and I wasted no time asking her if she could meet me somewhere ASAP. She claimed she was having lunch with a friend, so getting a piece of tail from her wasn't going to happen today, but I was not worried about her. I practically had this nasty heifer eating out of my hand, so I knew I'd get ahold of her sweet little ass again real soon.

When we entered the lobby at the Venetian, one of the most exclusive hotel/casinos on the Vegas strip, I got agitated. For one thing, it was more crowded than usual, and I hated crowds. They made me paranoid and nervous. "Is there a big convention or something going on?" I asked the young clerk when we finally got up to the registration counter after standing in line for twenty-five minutes. It was a few minutes before ten p.m.

"Yes, a couple. We also have several A-list celebrities on board this week, and they're all traveling with a mob of assistants and bodyguards," he told us.

"Oh," I said dryly. One thing I didn't want to deal with was the kind of chaos that followed big-name celebrities when they came to Vegas. The last time we stayed at the Venetian, the celebrity guest list had included Kim Kardashian and Kanye West. Grim-faced security guards, photographers, and drunken patrons hogging the elevators and acting crazy had turned that visit into a nightmare for us.

I didn't plan on gambling much or hanging out in the clubs. I wanted to get the party over with so I could focus on other things. Despite the fact that Sylvia was over-the-moon happy, and a couple of my former marine buddies had driven all the way from Sacramento, I felt sad. I cared about her, but I didn't love her the way she thought I did. Because Glinda had mistreated me so brutally, I would never trust or love another woman. However, Sylvia made me feel special and as comfortable as I'd felt with a woman since Glinda. The main reason I was marrying Sylvia was because I wanted to live like a "normal" man. I wanted to be free of the painful anger that I'd been carrying around for so many years. I was tired of killing women, and I was more than ready to be a father. I was also getting married because I didn't want to grow old alone. Sylvia didn't look her age, but she was nearly five years older than me, which meant she was pushing forty. I could understand why she was so anxious to have her first child.

I was convinced that she had never cheated on me, and never would. I couldn't say the same about myself. I still believed that it was unnatural for a man to be happy with just one woman, but after we got married, I would be faithful to Sylvia for as long as I could.

"Honey, you don't look too happy," she noticed. We had just entered our suite.

"I'm fine, baby. I . . . I . . . just had a mild flashback on the way up in the elevator," I explained as we started unpacking.

"That's what I figured. It must have been a bad one, because I've never seen such a hopeless look on your face like the one I saw a few moments ago. I hope that someday you can forget about the hell you went through in that damn war in Afghanistan."

"I'm sure I will. I'll be just fine after a few drinks," I said, forcing the biggest smile I could manage. "It would take something stronger than a flashback to ruin tonight for me."

Flashback my ass. Sylvia truly believed that because of my experience in Afghanistan, I suffered from a mild case of post-traumatic stress disorder. It was the lame excuse I used whenever she noticed me looking sad or distracted. The truth of the matter was, I rarely thought about the war and the few nightmares I'd experienced because of it. I had to focus on the real source of my distress: Lola. She was currently my only and *worst* nightmare. Killing that miserable, whorish, stupid, disgusting bitch was going to be even more pleasurable and exhilarating than killing Glinda.

Chapter 7
Lola

IT WAS ONLY FOUR-THIRTY P.M. AND I COULDN'T WAIT FOR THIS PAR-ticular Saturday to end. I cussed under my breath as I dug through some of the junk on our back porch, breaking two nails and almost dropping a heavy Crock-Pot on my foot.

All kinds of thoughts floated around inside my head. Turning down a date with Calvin because I was with Elbert was the main thing on my mind. I couldn't understand why Elbert was so interested in me. He could have dated so many other women and probably be married again by now, but it seemed like the more I put him off, the more he pursued me. I knew that he would not give up as long as he thought there was a chance for us to have a serious relationship.

Bertha had told me that she and I would clean off the back porch together, but she hadn't lifted a finger so far. When I had almost finished stuffing all kinds of junk into boxes that we would transfer to the garage, my forty-four-year-old stepsister, Libby, came out to the porch. "Didn't you hear me calling you?" she snarled.

I turned around with a forced smile. "I'm sorry, but I didn't hear you." Even though she almost always spoke to me in a harsh tone, I went out of my way to sound pleasant most of the time. "Do you need something?"

Libby stood in the doorway with her hands on her double-wide hips. She and her twin brother, Marshall, had mistreated

and abused me since my late daddy married their mother, eighteen years ago. Like Bertha, Libby was plain and overweight but
she carried herself as though she had been crowned Miss Universe. "Joan's husband is here. He's got some crazy notion that
she's been shopping with you since she left home this morning.
I told him that you didn't leave this house until Elbert picked
you up for lunch a few hours ago and you've been home ever
since he dropped you off."

As soon as Libby twirled around and went back inside, I
snatched my cell phone out of my blouse pocket and dialed
Joan's number. When she didn't answer, I called the operator at
the Hyatt and told her to ring John Walden's room. He answered right away.

"Uh, I'm a friend of Joan's," I began. My heart was beating
like a drum. This was the first time I'd called Joan while she was
with a date. I didn't know how much she had told John about
me, but she'd told me a lot about him. He was a very successful
attorney who lived in Phoenix with his wife and their three kids.
Joan had this man so whipped, he had asked her several times to
leave Reed and move to Arizona to be his mistress. He'd offered
to buy her a house or a condo, put her teenage son in a private
school, give her a generous allowance every week, and let her
pick out any vehicle she wanted. So far, she had turned him
down, but whatever she was doing to the man, it had to be damn
good. Every time he came to the Bay Area on business, he made
a date with Joan. He had come a couple of times just to be with
her. Once he'd even left a safari in Kenya three days early so he
could spend the rest of his vacation with her.

"And you are, luv?" he asked. Joan had not told me that John
had an English accent, but I should have guessed. He was originally from Jamaica, but he had lived in London for years.

"I'm Lola. I apologize for disturbing you, but I need to speak
with Joan about something very important," I said quickly with
my eye on the door. Libby was so sneaky, I had to stay alert at all
times. I didn't even let down my guard when I was in my own
bedroom. One night last month, she'd entered my room while I

was in a chat room having a steamy conversation with a club member in anticipation of a date. I'd abruptly signed off in the middle of my last sentence. When Libby left a couple of minutes later, I tried to resume the chat, but the dude ignored me. There was no telling how she would react if she returned to the porch and overheard what I was talking about now. I lowered my voice and continued. "I'm a member of Discreet Encounters too and I . . . uh . . . well, she'll know why I'm calling. Is she still with you?"

"Indeed she is." John had such a deep sexy voice, it was no wonder he had Joan acting like a fool. But a nice voice and tons of money was not all he had going for him. I had seen a selfie that Joan had taken of them a few dates ago. He looked as handsome in it as he did in his profile picture on the club's website. Because of his good looks and suggestive club screen name, which was "LongJohn," he was very popular. A lot of club members who'd been with him—including Joan—had rated him five out of five stars on the club's review board.

The next voice I heard was Joan's. "What's up?"

"Your husband is here!"

"What?" Joan shrieked. "What did you tell him?"

"I didn't tell him anything yet. I'm still cleaning off the back porch. Libby just came to tell me he's here." I swallowed hard and looked at the door again, glad to see it was still closed. "She already told him that the only time I left the house today was when Elbert picked me up to go to lunch!"

"Shit! Look—tell him that before we went shopping, Elbert badgered you to go to lunch with him. Around the same time, I got a call from Liza Mae and she wanted me to come over and do some things for her."

Liza Mae was a bogus friend that I had created to throw Bertha off when I needed a good excuse to be away from the house to go on a date with a club member. I used it when Joan couldn't be my alibi. It was such a good lie, she used it too. The story was, Liza Mae had attended high school with us. A couple of years ago a drunk driver hit her and she'd been in a wheelchair ever since. Joan and I took turns going to help her out because she had no family and only a part-time caregiver. Bertha and Reed had believed the ruse from day one, and still did. We had even given them a dummy telephone number, which was an independent voice mail service account I'd opened. Bertha and Reed had dialed the number several times, but because their calls always went straight to voice mail, and Liza Mae never returned any, they rarely called now.

"Okay. I'll hold Reed off as long as I can, but I advise you to get back home as soon as possible."

"Thanks, girl. Next time we get together, drinks are on me."

I turned off my phone and put it back in my pocket. Then, holding my breath, I went inside and shuffled to the living room where Reed had joined Libby; her handsome husband, Jeffrey; their brooding teenage son, Kevin; and Bertha. Libby and her family were temporarily staying with Bertha and me because their house was being renovated. Jeffrey was a very nice man. He and I got along real well, so I didn't mind his presence, but Libby and Kevin were two of the most mean-spirited people I knew. Just hearing their voices made me cringe.

Reed stood in the middle of the floor. Libby and Jeffrey occupied the couch, and Kevin and Bertha shared the love seat. The way Bertha was kicked back with a bottle of beer in her hand, it looked as if helping me clean off the porch was the last thing on her mind.

"Hello, Reed," I greeted weakly, dragging my feet and wiping my hands on the sides of my jeans.

"Hello, Lola," he muttered, giving me a guarded look. I blinked and glanced at the other faces. Bertha looked dazed. Libby looked amused. And Kevin, who had inherited Libby's dumpy body and homely features, was so involved with his cell phone he didn't even bother to look up. There was a puzzled expression on Jeffrey's face. With his shaved head, well-developed body, smooth bronze skin, and penetrating black eyes, next to Calvin Ramsey, he was one of the handsomest men I knew. I couldn't say the same about Reed. He had been very handsome and well-built once upon a time. I assumed marriage had taken a toll on him, because a few years after he'd been married to Joan, he let himself go to the dogs. The thick, curly black hair he'd once had was mostly gray now and looked like a burning bush. He was only ten years older than Joan and me, but he had dark circles around his eyes, lines on his face, and a belly that looked like it contained a four-month fetus. He narrowed his tired eyes, glared at me, and folded his arms. Dressed in a plaid shirt and shabby jeans, he looked more like one of the OGs from the hood than a prominent dentist.

"What did you want to say to me, Reed?" I asked dumbly.

"Where the hell is my wife?" he asked in a gruff tone.

Chapter 8
Lola

"*D*IDN'T SHE CALL YOU?" I BLINKED AND BIT MY BOTTOM LIP AS my mind struggled to come up with the next thing I should say to Reed.

"No, she didn't, and she's not answering her phone. Libby told me you went to lunch with Elbert, not shopping."

"I did, but Joan and I had planned to go shopping. She didn't want to have lunch with Elbert and me."

"I see." Reed shifted his weight from one foot to the other and gave me a guarded look. "If Joan didn't go shopping with you, where the hell did she go? She left home several hours ago."

"You remember Liza Mae, the invalid Joan and I help out from time to time? Her nurse had a family emergency, so she won't be able to see Liza until later tonight."

"So Joan is with this Liza Mae woman?"

"Uh-huh." I sniffed. "I would have gone myself but I had to come straight home after my lunch with Elbert and help clean up the mess on our back porch. Do you want me to call Liza Mae's house and see if Joan is still with her?"

Reed shook his head and gave me a weary look. "What's this woman's address?"

"Her address?" I gulped. The ruse about Liza Mae had always been flimsy at best. I found it hard to believe that an educated man like Reed was still buying it, and that he had bought it in the first place.

"Joan gave me that woman's phone number and I've called it several times in the past. All I ever got was a voice mail recording. It's time for me to meet this woman, or at least know where she lives."

"Let me call her first. I don't think it's a good idea for you to just show up at her house without notice. She's got this thing about people she doesn't know having her address," I managed, pulling out my cell phone again.

"Try Joan's number first. Maybe if she sees your name on her caller ID, she'll answer!" Reed said harshly.

"O . . . kay." I brought up Joan's number from my contact list and hit the call button. I was so relieved when my call went straight to voice mail. "Hi, Joan. I know you're probably not able to take my call, but when you get my message, please get back to me as soon as you can." I sniffed and looked at Reed. "I'll call Liza Mae's number now."

"If that woman answers her telephone this time, which I doubt she'll do, I'd like to speak to her myself," Reed said firmly.

"Um, yeah, sure." I punched in the telephone number and got the voice mail that I had set up, with Joan disguising her voice so well, even Reed couldn't tell it was her. "Hello, Liza Mae. This is Lola," I began with caution. From the corner of my eye, I could see Bertha and Libby staring in my direction with anxious looks on their faces. "I hope you are doing well today. I just wanted to let you know that Joan's husband is here and he wants me to give him your address. Please call me back as soon as you get my message and let me know if it's okay to give it to him. I'm sorry I couldn't come with Joan this time, but I'll see you again real soon. Have a blessed day. Bye." I hung up and blinked so hard a few times, my eyes ached. "Reed, you know how funny some people, especially women, are about somebody giving out their personal information."

"Sure I know." Reed gave me a cold gaze for a few moments. Then he shook his head and looked at his watch. "I've wasted enough of my time trying to find Joan. I have other things to do. If you hear from her before I do, remind her that we are entertaining Dr. Weinstein and his wife this evening. She needs to get her tail home so she can get dinner started."

"I'll do that," I mumbled as he gave me a skeptical look. "I guess I should go finish straightening up that porch."

I breathed a sigh of relief when Reed rushed out the front door. Despite the curious looks I was getting from Libby and Bertha, I ignored them and returned to the back porch. Just as I was about to pull out my cell phone and call Joan again, Bertha stumbled out the door with that curious look still on her face. "That Joan. She ought to be ashamed of herself, running around like she doesn't have a care in the world. She's a married woman and should act more like one. I don't know why Reed has not kicked her to the curb by now! Oomph, oomph, oomph!"

"She's always been a free spirit," I defended.

"Free spirit, my booty! She's a selfish, spoiled, inconsiderate floozy who doesn't appreciate all the good things in her life. I don't care where she goes, she needs to let her husband know where she is at all times. I never made a move without telling your daddy. Even when I was only going to the corner store or the beauty salon. I hope you behave better than that wild woman when you get married. If Reed doesn't get Joan under control soon, next thing we know she'll be fooling around with other men."

I ignored Bertha's comments and started digging through another one of the piles of junk.

She hopped over one of the boxes I'd already emptied and moved closer to me. "Ooh-wee. Things are looking real good, Lola Mae. I'm glad we didn't put off doing this unpleasant chore too much longer. This porch hasn't looked this organized in years," she swooned. "There's not much left for us to do." She shook her head and grinned. "Now, don't work too hard. You already look kind of tired."

"I'm not tired, Bertha, but you look tired. You can go back inside and I can finish up by myself."

"Okay, sugar. We'll clean out the kitchen closet and tackle the garage next."

"Yeah, that's fine," I said as she skittered back inside.

I didn't even bother to dial Joan's cell phone number this time. I called the hotel and had the operator ring John's suite again. I was glad he answered on the first ring. "Yes!" he snapped.

"John, this is Lola again," I said in a low voice.

He let out a loud sigh before he hollered, "Holy moly!"

"Um, I'm sorry. I know you're busy and I hate to keep disturbing you, but I need to speak to Joan."

"Can she call you back, luv? She's sitting on the crapper taking a leak." I could tell from his impatient tone that I was annoying him. "I'll have her ring you when she's finished."

"If you don't mind, I'll hold. It's really important for me to speak to her now," I insisted.

"So be it," John snarled.

About half a minute later, Joan came on the line. "You again? Well?" she said.

"Well what?"

"Well, what did you tell Reed? Is he still there?"

"I told him you were with Liza Mae because her nurse had to cancel at the last minute so she called you. He asked for her address this time."

"Address? How did you get around that one?"

"I made a bogus call in front of him and left a message for Liza Mae to get back to me and let me know if it's okay to give out her address. He didn't push the issue after that. We'll have to revise this Liza Mae thing if we're going to keep using it. And I think I know a way. There is this shady woman who comes in the store several times a week. Last year she spent time in jail for identity theft, so she's had experience posing as other women. If we give her a few bucks, I'm sure she'll pretend to be Liza Mae. She lives alone, so we could use her address and rent a wheelchair—"

"Now you stop right there. I don't want to involve anybody else in any of our schemes."

"Joan, I don't want to do that either, but we have to do whatever is necessary if we don't want people to know our business.

And you just have to be a lot more careful from now on. Sooner or later, your luck is going to run out," I warned.

"Humph! Don't get too smug, Sister Poole. Your luck could run out too!"

"Yeah, but I don't have a husband to answer to. You're the one with the most to lose. The worst that could happen in my case is that Bertha and Libby could find out I belong to a sex club and talk trash to me—which is something Libby has already been doing since the day I met her. I have nothing else to be concerned about." A split second after my last sentence, a premonition of doom entered my head and I got an instant headache. I blamed it on the stress brought on by my turning down a date with Calvin and lying to Reed.

Chapter 9
Calvin

I HAD LET SYLVIA MAKE ALL THE ARRANGEMENTS FOR OUR ENGAGE-ment party, and she'd wasted no time. The day after I'd proposed last week, she started making plans. She'd used phone, e-mail, and text to contact everybody we wanted with us to help celebrate. I was glad we agreed to keep the list short. Not everyone could change their plans or afford a trip to Vegas on such short notice, so only eight of the dozen folks we'd invited confirmed their attendance. The only member of my family on the guest list was my husky, sad-eyed older brother, Ronald. He was my only relative who communicated with me on a regular basis. But there were some limitations. His wife had a beef with me because Glinda had slept with the dude she'd been with before she married my brother. Like several of the women I knew back then, relatives and friends alike, Ronald's wife had made it clear that she had no use for my wife and didn't even want her to set foot in her house. Because of that, even after Glinda disappeared, I didn't visit my brother as often as I wanted to. My older sister, Vickie, sent me cards on my birthday and at Christmas, but she never invited me over, and vice versa. Her husband was also one of the men my wife had fooled around with before I married her, and a few times afterward.

I missed spending time with my family. A few cousins still called and came around, but that was usually only when they wanted something. I had nieces, nephews, and other young relatives I had never met. Glinda was responsible for the turmoil between my family and me. None of them had accepted her and flat-out told me that if I married her, I'd be sorry. I found out after I'd fallen in love with her—which was the same night we met—that she had been the town tramp for years. Since she and I had moved in different circles, information about her shameful reputation came to me too late. My mother told me she'd never speak to me again if I brought such a slut into our family, but I'd married her anyway. It was the biggest mistake I ever made, and it looked like I was going to spend the rest of my life paying for it.

Sylvia was going to be a good wife. Even though she was not drop-dead gorgeous like Lola, and could stand to gain a few pounds, she was attractive and smart. With my looks and brains, hopefully she and I would produce some cute and intelligent children. Even though I was practically beating women off with a stick, Sylvia was the best choice for a long-term relationship.

The engagement party we had thrown together so quickly started off with a bang a few minutes before eleven p.m. Before we checked in, the casino host had had our suite decorated with green and white balloons and white roses, and they tacked a huge banner above the door that said **CONGRATULATIONS SYLVIA & CALVIN**! in bold print. Room service delivered several platters of snacks and enough complimentary champagne to fill a bathtub. One of my coworkers had brought his iPad with wireless speakers so we had music to dance to. Despite all the fun our guests were having, they were anxious to get to the casino floor to gamble. I didn't protest when they all began to slink out the door after only a couple of hours. My brother was the last to leave.

"Bro, I wish Mama had lived long enough to meet Sylvia," he told me, clapping me on the back. Then he turned to Sylvia and said, "You're the kind of woman my mother would have been proud to have for a daughter-in-law. My wife's father is from Brazil, so you and she have something in common."

"Thank you for saying that. I hope I get to meet your wife soon," Sylvia said with her voice cracking.

"I'm going to make sure you do." Ronald winked at me and added, "I think it's time for folks to let bygones be bygones. Nothing is more important than family." He turned back to Sylvia. "I'll do all I can to make sure you get a warm welcome into the family."

"Thank you. I'm going to do my best to make Calvin happy," Sylvia said with a nod.

Ronald gave her a big hug and me another clap on the back. "You two enjoy the rest of the evening," he said before he left.

As soon as I closed the door, Sylvia immediately told me, "Baby, I have bad news. I feel my period coming on early, so we won't be able to celebrate our engagement tonight like I wanted to."

"Oh shit, sweetie," I complained. "And I'm as horny as a big dog in heat."

"Well, I can't control Mother Nature, but I do have some good news."

I squinted and gave her a guarded look. "And the good news is?"

"Since I've gotten older, my periods last only two or three days. We might get a chance to get busy before we leave Vegas."

"I certainly hope so. I'd like to have some real fun tonight," I whined. My dick was so hard it was throbbing. And I was going to do something about it. Sylvia was not into oral sex that much. She balked every time I asked her to give me a blow job, so I couldn't even fall back on that. I had only two choices: I could masturbate or find another woman. I didn't want to masturbate . . .

I followed Sylvia to the bed, and we sat down at the same time. She heaved a heavy sigh and gave me a pitiful look. "Honey, I am sorry our timing was so off. I really wanted to make serious love to you tonight."

"Don't worry about it."

"I know you don't want to go to a show or stay in and watch movies like I'm going to do, so why don't you go down and gamble."

"I think I will do just that," I mumbled. "I'm feeling kind of lucky this evening."

I avoided my brother and our other guests at the blackjack table and walked briskly in the opposite direction. I didn't stop until I got to the garage where I had parked the rental car I'd picked up.

I needed a woman and I didn't care what I had to do to get one. Not only did I need her for sex, I needed her to help get Lola off my mind for a little while so I could concentrate on Sylvia.

It wouldn't be hard to find sex in Vegas. Escorts advertised their services on the sides of shuttle buses, and scruffy people lined the Strip's sidewalks passing out "business cards" with hookers' working names and telephone numbers. I didn't care what tonight's woman looked like—as long as she wasn't too plain or fat. I didn't even care how much money she wanted. I'd give her every dollar I had on me, because she wouldn't live long enough to keep it anyway.

Chapter 10
Joan

*F*OR THE PAST THREE OR FOUR YEARS, REED HAD BEEN TALKING about buying us a big house in the hills, having more children, and taking month-long vacations in some of the most glamorous countries in the world. A few months ago, he abruptly stopped talking about his big plans for our family. And it was just as well. As far as I was concerned, our marriage was over. Unfortunately, he didn't think so.

One reason we still lived under the same roof was because I was literally afraid to leave him. I was not afraid that he would hurt me physically, because he was not the violent type. And he knew better. For one thing, he was well aware that my three older brothers, my stepfather, or some (or all) of my other ferocious male relatives would never let him hurt me and get away with it.

We were still together because I was afraid that he would hurt himself if I left. "I will not live without you, Joan." He had been singing the same song for years. A couple of years ago when he realized our marriage was in big trouble, he'd attempted suicide. No matter how many times I tried to get his parents to talk some sense into him, they refused to believe there was anything to worry about. "Just be good to him and he'll be fine," his mother told me each time. "Don't do anything to upset him," his father added. I eventually stopped bringing up the subject with them.

Mama and my stepfather, Elmo, were even less supportive. They constantly reminded me that I was doing so much better than any of the other women in our family because I'd married one of the most successful dentists in town. One of their favorite "tunes" was, "We didn't raise no fool so we know you ain't going to walk away from all that prestige, not to mention all that damn money."

Reed's constant whining, suicide threats, and accusations of my seeing other men made me so miserable, I wanted to kill him myself. However, I had found another way to comfort myself: online dating. It involved a lot of maneuvering and lies, but it was worth it. Besides, it was the only way I could stay married to Reed and not go off the deep end.

I'd started searching for love on the Internet a couple of years ago. Most of the men I encountered were looking for somebody they could have an exclusive relationship with. Some were even looking for wives. One married businessman I met on Plenty-OfFish fell hard for me after only two dates. He wanted to marry me so badly, he offered to commit bigamy. I was willing to do a lot of stupid things, but marrying another man while I was still married to Reed was not one of them.

It didn't take long for me to get tired and bored with guys who wanted more than sex. One lonely night while I was randomly Googling for sites that catered to people who were interested only in casual relationships, I discovered Discreet Encounters. It was a dream come true. And not just for me. Lola eventually joined. I had no idea how much longer she planned to remain a member, but I had no desire to end my membership anytime soon.

After only three encounters, John Walden had become my favorite date. We had a good thing going, and I wanted to keep it going. I had never seen him even remotely annoyed until today. Lola's telephone calls had upset him as much as they'd upset me.

"Next time we get together, don't let your friend know the name of our hotel," he snarled when Lola and I ended our second conversation.

"I won't," I mumbled. I placed the hotel telephone back into its cradle, and John immediately pulled me into his arms again. We were still in bed.

"Is everything okay, m'dear?" he asked as he raked his fingers through my tangled hair. "Your friend sounded thoroughly distressed. What seems to be the problem?"

"It's Reed," I mumbled.

"Again? For the love of Jesus H. Christ! What a bloody bummer!" John grumbled.

"He went to her house looking for me and asked all kinds of nosy questions in front of her whole family. They already think I'm crazy, and so there's no telling what kind of rumors they'll start spreading about me now. That man has turned my life into a nightmare!"

John let out a loud groan and abruptly sat up. "Then why don't you end your nightmare and start a new life in Phoenix with me. You can pick out a smashing new condo, a set of wheels, a completely new wardrobe, the most exclusive private school for your boy that my money can buy, and more. I keep telling you that my offer is still open."

"And I keep telling you that I can't end my marriage and move to Phoenix. I've lived in California my whole life, so it's not that easy for me to pack up and move to another state. Besides that, I don't know if I would like being the other woman."

John gasped so hard he choked on some air. "What? You are 'the other woman,' my dear! And not just with me. A lot of other chaps fancy you and vice versa. I read the club reviews on a regular basis, so I know what a busy little bee you are!"

I dropped my head and stared at my hands for a few seconds. When I looked back at John, he had the most pitiful look on his face I had ever seen.

"In spite of our relationships with other people, I love you, Joan. We've been open and honest with each other since our first encounter. So is it fair for me to assume that you trust me?"

"I guess," I said with a shrug. "I trust you as much as you trust me."

John rolled his eyes. "That's a can of worms I'm not ready to open yet." He laughed. Then he got serious again. "The thing is, I'd do anything in the world for you."

"Anything but leave your wife."

"That is absolutely out of the question. Don't even think about that." John had told me from the get-go that he would never divorce his wife. For one thing, he was in love with her. Breaking up the marriage would devastate her, not to mention the impact it would have on his children. He had admitted that a major reason he couldn't leave his wife was because she was from a powerful Italian family with a shady reputation. It had taken years for them to accept a black man into the family. I didn't ask for any explicit details, but I had a pretty good idea what he was up against. "You know how much you mean to me, and I never want to give you up."

"And you don't have to. We'll just have to keep working around my husband. Ooooh! Sometimes he makes me so angry I wish he'd just disappear!"

"I can arrange that. . . ."

This time I gasped. "I don't even want to think about what you mean by *that*!" I boomed. I suddenly felt so uneasy, I couldn't remain still. I literally jumped off the bed. "Um, I need to get home. We have guests coming this evening." I skittered across the floor to the dresser where I had dropped my clothes. "I'm going to take a quick shower and then be on my way. Call me when you get back to Phoenix."

"You can count on that." John leered at me until I closed the bathroom door.

Chapter II
Calvin

*T*HE ONLY THING I HATED ABOUT LAS VEGAS WAS DRIVING ON THE Strip after dark. With so many lanes and bumper-to-bumper traffic, it was a nightmare. It took forty minutes just to get from my hotel to the freeway, less than a quarter of a mile away.

I didn't want to waste too much time, so I exited after about two miles and stopped at the first gas station I saw. It was in a pretty rough-looking neighborhood. I handed the attendant on duty a twenty and asked him where to find the street hookers. He directed me to an area four blocks away, and I took off like a rocket. The closer I got to my destination, the seedier the surroundings looked, so I didn't expect to find any beauty queens.

Surprisingly, the girls on this particular stroll were quite attractive and frisky. They began to grin and wave at me as if I were the only trick who had approached them all night. I felt like a kid in a candy store.

It didn't take long to make up my mind. I saw what I wanted right away. She was one of the most innocent and fragile-looking females I'd ever seen, and the only Asian sharing a corner under a streetlight with half a dozen other hookers. I parked at the curb, lowered the window on the passenger side, and gave her a nod. She approached with a huge smile on her small, heart-shaped face and poked her head in the window. She was very tiny, so I could control her with one hand tied behind my back.

My rage was increasing with each second, but I smiled back. "What's your name, cutie?" I asked.

"Tell me yours first." She sounded even younger than she looked, and she was obviously still in her teens.

"You're very sexy, but you look kind of young to be out here." Despite the monster I had become, I still had a few scruples. I refused to victimize pregnant women and minors. Even though Glinda had claimed to be pregnant the night I killed her, she had told me too late.

"I am kind of young, but I'm old enough for whatever you have in mind. Now, what's your name?"

"My name is . . . um, James."

"Yeah, right. And my name is Snow White. Look, sweetie, I don't care what your real name is. The only man's real name I care about is Mr. Benjamin Franklin. For a homely man, that old dude sure makes a hundred dollar bill look pretty." The hooker wagged her finger in my face. "But I'll accept smaller bills with other men's mugs on 'em too, as long as you give me enough." She paused and gave me a pensive look. Then she added in a very dry tone, "My name is Hyeon."

"That's a pretty name." I kept the smile on my face as I caressed my chin and squirmed in my seat. I wanted to look as awkward and nonthreatening as possible.

"In Korean it means *virtuous*."

This was the first time I had come across a virtuous whore. I had to hold my breath to keep from laughing. "I like you a lot, Hyeon. Are you pregnant?"

"Huh? That's a weird question! What the fuck difference does it make if I'm pregnant or not?" She didn't look so fragile and innocent now.

"Please don't bite my head off, baby," I protested with my hand in the air. The only reason I didn't grab this pit bull by the throat now was because I wanted to fuck her first, and because those other whores were still looking. "I was just asking a simple question. My last date was with a pregnant girl, and she couldn't do all the things I wanted her to do."

"I ain't pregnant and never will be if I can help it. I hate kids! Now, do you want to buy some pussy tonight or what, dude?" she yelled.

I shrugged. "Yeah, I do." I snorted and looked her up and down. She wore a plaid miniskirt and a white blouse with the tails tied into a knot up under her perky breasts. In addition to her four-inch heels, she had on a pair of white ankle socks.

Hyeon suddenly looked back toward the other women. One motioned with her finger for Hyeon to rejoin the group. She ran back to the curb and they had a brief, animated conversation. A few seconds later, she returned to the car with a concerned look on her face. She looked around before she poked her head back in the window. "You a cop?"

"Nope. Do I look like one?"

"Honey, looks ain't got nothing to do with it. I know cops who look like priests. My homegirl was just reminding me that I have to ask. I ain't been working the streets long, so I'm still learning the ropes."

"Oh? Then you don't have much experience, huh?"

"*Pffft!*" Hyeon gave me a dismissive wave and an exasperated look. "I've had ten dates since I got on the block at noon, and the night is still young! I've been getting paid since I was fifteen. I used to work in a brothel near Reno until another bitch ratted me out to the head honchos that I was underage. They fired me on the spot. But you don't have to worry, I turned eighteen last week."

"I'm glad to hear that."

"Do you mean to tell me you wouldn't deal with me if I wasn't of legal age?"

"Something like that."

"Honey, you got some nerve worrying about what's legal. In case you didn't know, buying pussy off the street ain't legal in this state." Hyeon snickered. To put her more at ease, I snickered too. "Anyway, I'm new at doing my business outside of a brothel, that's what I meant. Now let's stop yip-yapping about bullshit nonsense and talk business."

"Why don't you get in and we can talk while I drive."

I couldn't rent a motel room—which was the reason I had not called an escort service—because I didn't want to leave a paper trail. I drove toward the outskirts of town.

"What do you want?" Hyeon asked. "I can take it up the butt if that's what you're into, and I give a mean blow job. A lot of my black tricks like shit like that."

"Not this black man." I gave her a mild frown. "Just straight sex will do tonight. How much?"

"The more you give me, the better time I'll show you."

"Don't you girls generally have a set price?"

"I don't do nothing 'generally' when it comes to my money, but like I just told you, the more you pay me, the better time I'll show you. Now I could sit here and ask you for five hundred bucks but—"

"That's fine."

Hyeon's jaw dropped. "Five hundred bucks! Woo-hoo! Dude, I was just talking off the top of my head. I wasn't going to ask for nothing even close to that, especially if all you want is straight sex. Are you one of them rich black celebrities, or a drug dealer or something like that?" She narrowed her eyes and stared at the side of my head.

"Nothing like that. I'm just a plain old waiter." I chuckled.

"You're just a *waiter*? Shiiiit! Honey, you must make some damn good tips if you can afford to pay big money like that for a piece of ass."

"Oh, I do quite well. I serve some of the most famous celebrities in the world."

"That's what I figured. Guess what? I 'serve' some of the most famous celebrities in the world myself." We bumped fists and laughed at the same time. "You must work in one of the Strip casino restaurants."

"Yup. Now if you don't mind, can we cut to the chase?" I glanced at my watch. "I have to get to work soon."

"Okay then. Point-blank, for five hundred bucks I'll fuck you inside out. You got a room?"

"Oh, no," I said quickly. "I don't take long to get off, so we don't even need a room. I'll find a spot where we can have some privacy."

"I know a cool place not far from here. Just me and a couple of other girls know about it. We do most of our quickies there."

I looked at my prey again. She was still staring at the side of my head. Less than a minute later she said, "Turn right at the next street and pull behind that old building at the corner and stop."

"What? Did you change your mind?"

"No, I didn't change my mind. I just want my money now. This is the place I was talking about."

I pulled behind the dilapidated building and parked, and then I took out my wallet. Hyeon gave me another smile when I handed her five crisp hundred-dollar bills. She hummed as she stuffed the money into her bra. "We don't even have to go into that dusty old warehouse. Your backseat will do."

"That's fine with me," I muttered. I pulled out a pack of condoms from my back pocket.

Before I could even unzip and get a condom on, Hyeon crawled into the backseat, removed her panties, and stretched out on her back. She lifted her skirt and spread her legs open. With my door still open and the interior light on, I got a good look at her almost bald little pussy and got excited even more.

"I'm good," she whispered as I climbed on top of her. She was so tiny, it felt like I was mounting a pillow, but once I got my equipment in place and started slamming into her, I realized I was with a well-used, well-experienced woman. She probably had sex with more men in a day than some women had in a lifetime! I came in less than a minute, which was unusual for me. I could hump a woman for an hour or longer if I wanted to, but I needed to do my business and be done as soon as possible because I had other plans for this bitch.

"Oh my God," I croaked. "Baby . . . that was so damn good." I shuddered and took a deep breath. My adrenaline felt like it was about to burst out of my veins.

"See. I told you I was good." Hyeon gave me a smug look. Her legs were still wrapped around my waist. "I make all of my other tricks come real quick too." It was the last thing she said before my hands went around her throat.

Chapter 12
Calvin

I LEFT THE RENTAL CAR'S INTERIOR LIGHT ON, EVEN THOUGH IT wasn't necessary. The light coming from the moon was bright enough for me to see what I was doing.

I had come to Vegas dozens of times, but this would be my most unforgettable visit. It was nowhere near the big city people thought it was. I was only about three miles from the Strip, but I could still see the bright lights that lit up the casinos and hotels. I couldn't think of any location in the world that deserved to be nicknamed Sin City more than Las Vegas. It was a damn shame how some of the millions of people who came here ended up losing not only their money and dignity but their lives too.

The average person had no idea how complicated murder was. I didn't know any killers personally, so I didn't know what their experiences were like. Mine varied from one victim to the next.

The things I liked the most were a challenge and a deserving victim. I enjoyed having sex with a seasoned whore like Hyeon. Because of her "career" choice she deserved to die. She was as easy to overpower as a paper doll, so the challenge was a major letdown.

"You picked the wrong trick tonight, bitch!" I screeched as I straddled her. She gave me a surprised look, but didn't say a word, scream, or even struggle. It seemed as if she'd been expecting me to kill her.

When she stopped breathing, I dragged her limp body out of the car and dropped her to the ground like a sack of garbage. She landed facedown, so I squatted and turned her onto her back. This made it easy for me to slide my hand down into her bra and retrieve my five hundred bucks. I chuckled when I saw that the little whore had stuffed her bra with tissue paper and a small change purse. It contained a set of keys, a tube of lipstick, her ID, a wad of hundred-dollar bills, and an unopened package of condoms. More trophies to add to the collection I stored in my attic. Just thinking about my treasure trove excited me. I had collected enough goodies to have a pretty good yard sale some-day. The thought of that made me chuckle again.

Hyeon's cash, a total of $1,800, was exactly enough to pay off what I still owed on the engagement and wedding rings I'd pur-chased for Sylvia. The only other items I decided to take were her keys and the lipstick. I wiped my fingerprints off everything else I had touched with the sleeve of my shirt and left those things on the ground next to her.

The sky, which reminded me of a black blanket I once owned, looked almost close enough to touch. There was a full moon, and it looked downright eerie, but that didn't bother me. I didn't be-lieve any of the hogwash I'd heard about how a full moon im-pacted some people's actions and made them do crazy shit. I was just as likely to kill a woman on a night during a half moon as I was when there was a full moon. I had done so several times already.

A creature started howling, and I got spooked. I couldn't see it, but I could tell that it was too close for comfort. I had to haul ass before I became its victim. I shuddered when I thought of how ironic it would be if a coyote or a wolf took me out.

I gazed in the opposite direction toward the desert, which was not too far away. It was no secret that it contained the remains of a lot of bodies, but I was not familiar with the desert, and I didn't have a shovel to dig a grave for Hyeon, so she was already in her final resting place. The ground was littered with half a dozen empty beer bottles and a few other pieces of debris, but there was nothing I could use to hide the dead girl's body. Then I remembered she had removed her skirt and panties inside the car. I retrieved both and dropped them on top of her stomach. I was about to leave when I noticed sand and a few leaves on both legs of my pants. I brushed myself off, looked around to make sure I was not leaving behind any evidence, and then I jumped back into the car and sped off.

It was an uncomfortable ride back to the Strip. I made a couple of wrong turns and the drive took longer than it should have, so I didn't bother to stop in the casino and do any gambling. Tonight's kill had been too quick and easy, so there had not been enough of a thrill to satisfy me. I scolded myself for not choosing one of the other whores, a bigger bitch who might have put up a good fight. I had learned to take the good with the bad. I would make sure that the next woman would be more of a challenge.

When I finally made it back to my hotel room, Sylvia greeted me with a toothy grin. Before I could even close the door, she shot across the floor and wrapped her arms around my waist.

"All right, all right," I said, as I kicked the door shut. "How much did you lose?"

"I haven't been out of this room. I'm just so happy to see you. Did you win a jackpot?"

"Ha! I wish!" I complained as we strolled hand in hand toward the bed. "I might go back down later tonight when it's not as crowded. I might even try my luck at another casino."

"Guess what?" Sylvia didn't give me time to respond. "I had a false alarm."

"A false alarm about what?"

"When my stomach churns the way it was doing earlier, it usually means my period is about to start. This time it didn't mean that. I should be good to go for at least another three or four days." She winked and began to take off the baby blue negligee I'd given her for Christmas last year.

I looked into Sylvia's eyes and gently pushed her down on the bed. I was still disappointed that Hyeon had been such an easy and quick kill, so I was hyped up. Downright antsy was one way to describe how I felt. I couldn't believe how high my energy level was. I felt like a dude half my age. I had to find a way to release that energy. I still hadn't decided on a date for Lola's execution. In the meantime, I had to kill again, and *soon.*

I removed my clothes, climbed on top of Sylvia, and pried her legs open with mine. I plunged into her so hard, she whimpered and her entire body shuddered. "Calvin, take it easy," she managed, tapping the side of my arm.

"I'm sorry, baby. I didn't realize how turned on I was," I panted. I had not made love with so much vigor since my last romp with Lola. I closed my eyes and imagined she was the one I was with. One of the things I planned to do just before I killed her was fuck the hell out of her.

Chapter 13
Joan

*I*T WAS FIVE P.M. WHEN I GOT BACK HOME FROM MY DATE WITH JOHN. I had a feeling Reed was going to get all up in my face, but I was ready for him. I knew he was pissed off because I hadn't responded to any of his messages and had changed my plans without letting him know. I was just as pissed off about him making plans for me to cook dinner and entertain the Weinsteins without checking with me first. Now that I'd had most of the day to think about it, the full impact had sunk in, so I had a chip on my shoulder when I opened the door to our luxurious eighth-floor condo. I took a deep breath and strutted into our living room.

Reed's reaction surprised me. "Good news," he greeted with a toothy smile.

He'd caught me off guard and I didn't know what to think. "What's the good news?" I set the shopping bags I had picked up from Lola on the coffee table and casually walked toward the couch, where he sat with his legs crossed.

"It'll be just us tonight," he announced. "And I'm glad. We don't spend enough quality time alone, but I'm going to make sure we do in the future."

"Oh," I said, stifling a groan. "What about the Weinsteins? Did they cancel on us?"

Reed shook his head. "They had to take a rain check. There were some serious complications with one of Mitch's patients so he had to rush over to the hospital and sort that out. Poor Mitch.

I'll bet he curses the day he chose to practice gynecology. The female body is as volatile as a land mine. Anyway, I suggested that we all get together in a couple of days, but Meg is having her nose done on Monday, so we'll have to wait until she's healed. I hope you're not too disappointed."

Disappointed? Not hardly. I couldn't think of anything more exasperating than entertaining Reed's dull friends, especially Mitch and Meg Weinstein. I tolerated them and Reed's other friends because it was one of the few things I did that made him happy. "I'm not disappointed." I sighed with relief and sat down next to him. "Where's Junior?"

"He decided to visit your mother for the rest of the weekend. I made sure he'd finished his homework. I gave him an advance on his allowance—plus a little extra—and told him he could spend it on anything he wants as long as it's okay with his grand-mother."

"Well, I hope he cleaned his room before he left." I looked around, frowning at the numerous medical magazines and news-papers scattered all over the floor and the black glass coffee table.

"He did that too, and I didn't even have to tell him. I'm going to order some takeout so you don't have to cook this evening."

I held my breath because I knew he would eventually bring up my not being where I told him I'd be today. I was anxious to ad-dress the subject so we could get it over with. We didn't speak for about half a minute. The silence was so awkward, I was glad when Reed finally spoke again.

"How was Liza Mae?" he asked, caressing the side of my arm.

"She's fine," I said quickly with my heart beating about a mile a minute. "Today is the anniversary of her accident, so she was really depressed. Her nurse had planned to take her to the park and then out to lunch this afternoon, but when the nurse had to postpone her visit, Liza Mae called—"

Reed held up his hand and interrupted me. "I know. Lola told me you went to that woman's house."

"I should have called to let you know I'd changed my plans, and I'm sorry I didn't. Then Elbert invited us to have lunch with him. Lola went for it and I would have, but I knew he really wanted to be alone with her. I was glad Liza Mae called when she did." I stopped talking because Reed looked like he wanted to say something. When he didn't, I continued. "I went to her house right away. After I gave her a sponge bath, I fixed her a snack. After that, she started dropping hints about all the other things that needed to be done. I swear to God, taking care of an invalid is so much hard work. I don't know how that nurse does it. Since I only do it every now and then, I really shouldn't be complaining." I couldn't ignore the skeptical look on Reed's face. "Why are you looking at me like that?"

He took a deep breath and narrowed his eyes. "Aren't you leaving something out?"

I blinked and remained silent.

"Joan, where else did you go today?"

"What? Didn't I just tell you?"

He shook his head. "Why don't you just give it all up? I already know more than you think."

I blinked some more. "Are you accusing me of something?"

"The only thing I'm accusing you of is not telling me the whole truth about where you went today. I want you to fill in the blanks."

"I am not going to sit here and listen to any more of your bullshit!" I attempted to rise, but Reed grabbed my arm and pulled me back down.

"Joan, I know where you went today and why."

I froze. "Huh?" was all I could say. "How did you find out?"

He laughed, and that scared me. I knew he had a few loose screws rolling around in his head, so nothing he said or did surprised me anymore. "Never mind how I found out. No matter what you do, at the end of the day, I forgive you, baby." The more he talked, the more he confused me. "Life is too short and I am not going to let the little things bother me too much. After I left Lola's house, I paid your mother a visit. I know exactly what you've been up to."

I was speechless. I sat stock-still because I had no idea where Reed was going with this conversation.

"Your sister broke down and told me that last Saturday and the Saturday before that, you took her, your mother, and your cousin, Too Sweet, on a shopping spree. You've burned through thousands of dollars this month buying things for your family."

All I could do was stare at Reed's face and wonder when and if he was going to bring up my visit to John's hotel room.

"Besides Junior, your sister was the only other one in the house when I got there. Elaine wouldn't admit it, but I know you were not with Liza Mae as long as you want me to believe. I know that Elbert picked up Lola from her house, and you were not with her. Maybe you caught up with her later and spent a few minutes with her. Who knows? I do know that for the time you were MIA, you were with someone else." If he knew I'd been with another man he sure was confronting me in a round-about way.

"Is that what you think?"

"It's not what I think, it's what I know."

"Well, if you know so much, you must know who I was with!"

Reed nodded and pursed his lips. He turned his head to the side and peered at me from the corner of his eye. "After you and Lola parted—if you were actually with her in the first place— you couldn't have spent much time with Liza Mae, so you went shopping with somebody else." He gave me the kind of look I used to get from Mama and Elmo during my teens when they caught me in a lie. "Honey, you know I don't care how much you spend on your family, so there is no reason for you to hide it from me when you go overboard. You spent most of today at the mall with some of your relatives spending my, excuse me, *our* money on them, right?"

"Uh, maybe I did . . ."

"I wish you hadn't lied about it. I'm the one person you should always be honest with. And by the way, I tried to get an address for that Liza Mae woman from Lola, but all she did was beat around the bush."

"Why do you need Liza Mae's address?"

"Joan, I know where every one of your other friends live. Don't you think it's strange that I don't know where Liza Mae lives after all this time? I've never even seen her in the flesh, nor have I ever spoken to her. I've left her numerous voice mail messages in the past couple of years and she's never returned a single one." Reed laughed and rubbed the side of his head. "If I didn't know any better, I'd swear she didn't even exist."

My mouth dropped open. "That's the most ridiculous thing I've ever heard!" I hissed. "I have no reason to make up stories about people who don't exist. And if I did, I wouldn't choose an invalid. Why don't I invite her to have dinner with us? I can pick her up and bring her here." Lola's outlandish suggestion that we hire a woman to pose as Liza Mae didn't seem so outlandish now. I was willing to do whatever it took to keep the wool over Reed's suspicious eyes. "How soon do you want to meet her?"

"*Pffft!*" Reed dismissed my bluff with a dismissive wave. I was glad, because if Lola and I needed to revise our ruse it would require time, careful planning, and some new lies. "I'm sure she's a nice lady and we should have her over for lunch or dinner, but I'm in no hurry to meet her. Let's stop talking about her for now." He leered at me in a way that made me feel naked. "I can think of something a lot more fun for us to do. . . ." He winked and slid his tongue across his bottom lip. I gulped and moaned under my breath when he poked my crotch with his fingers. "You're looking mighty sexy in those skinny jeans, baby."

"Thanks," I mumbled, and stood up.

"Where do you think you're going?" he snickered.

"I'm going to put away all the new stuff I bought today."

"No, you're not. Bring your cute little ass here," Reed ordered. Before I could resist, he grabbed my arm, pulled me back to the couch, and started unzipping my jeans.

Chapter 14
Lola

*E*VEN WITH ALL THE MEN ON MY ROSTER NOW, MY LIFE HAD BE-come routine. It was nine p.m. Saturday night and I was doing what I normally did when I didn't have a date or something else on my agenda. I was in my bedroom stretched out in my bed with a copy of *Brides* magazine in one hand and a bag of chips in the other. Because I had eaten such a huge burger at Denny's for lunch, along with a banana split for dessert, I was still too full to eat the dinner Bertha had prepared. If she hadn't cooked chitlins again—the second time in five days—I probably would have scarfed down something just to keep her happy. She loved to cook and watch people eat whatever she'd prepared. Other than those two activities and church, she still clung to me like I was some kind of security blanket. I was determined to wean her as soon as I could.

I was about to open my second bag of potato chips when a call from Joan came in five minutes before ten p.m. "You still awake?" she asked dumbly.

"No, I'm talking to you in my sleep," I snapped.

"I'm at the drugstore down the street from your house. We ran out of Tylenol again. Can I come over for a few minutes?"

"Sure. Is everything all right?" We hadn't spoken since Joan had called me from the hotel several hours ago. I had left her a voice mail message and sent a text since then. I was surprised that she was just now getting back to me.

"I guess. Where's the family from hell?"

"Bertha's varicose veins were bothering her so she went to bed early, and Libby and her crew are downstairs watching TV."

"I'll be there in five minutes."

When I heard Joan's car pull up, I opened my door and stood in the doorway until she entered the house and stomped up to my room. "Libby didn't even speak when Jeffrey let me in," she complained.

"So what else is new?" I groaned. I closed my door, and she shot across the floor and plopped down on my bed and crossed her legs. She immediately started looking around the room. "How come you never have anything in here to drink when I come over?"

I sat down in the chair in front of the desk facing my bed. "I had a couple of wine coolers a little while ago. I would have saved you one if you'd let me know you were coming."

Joan blew out some air and gave me a sorry look. "I guess you're waiting to hear what happened when I got home this evening."

I nodded. "How did dinner go with the Weinsteins?"

"They had to cancel. Something about Mitch having to go to the hospital to check on one of his patients." Joan shook her head and gave me a weary look. "Girl, you wouldn't believe what Reed put me through a few hours ago. We had sex on our living room floor. It was as lame as always."

"I'm sure it's the same old story, so skip over it and tell me everything else."

She exhaled and uncrossed her legs. "After he left your house, he went over to Mama's. To make a long story short, he thought I was out shopping with some of my relatives spending money on them. He laughed and basically told me he didn't care about that, but he cared about me lying to him. That clueless asshole had no idea where I really was!" An extremely smug look crossed Joan's face. Each time she pulled the wool over Reed's eyes, it inflated her ego even more. "Anyway, he got real nosy about Liza Mae. He fussed about her never returning his calls and her being the only one of my friends he's never met. For a minute, I thought he was going to force me to take him to her house today. I dodged that bullet when I offered to have her join us for dinner one day."

"Hmmm." I folded my arms and gave Joan a thoughtful look. "It sounds like our Liza Mae ruse is getting too risky for us to keep using without providing any evidence that she even exists. The last time I told Bertha I was going to visit her, she wanted to go with me so she could pray with her and offer to be of some assistance herself. Bertha is deathly afraid of cats, so when I told her that Liza Mae owns eight, she changed her tune. But Libby has been making noise about meeting her too. Do you want me to talk to that woman I mentioned about her posing as Liza Mae? I'm sure she'd do it for a couple hundred bucks. She's so down on her luck, she eats some of her meals at a soup kitchen and the Rescue Mission. She could use the money, and I know she'd enjoy a nice free steak and lobster dinner with you and Reed."

"Not yet. Let's see what happens in the next few weeks. For my future dates, I think I'll fall back on my bogus book club alibi more often."

"That's even weaker than the Liza Mae story. Reed might start pestering you for book club members' names and the location of the meetings."

"Oh well." Joan groaned and cleared her throat. "My life is becoming so complicated. Can we have lunch tomorrow? If I have to sit around the house tomorrow with Reed, I'll go crazy."

"I'd love to, but I'm going to be tied up."

An annoyed look appeared on Joan's face. "What's going to tie you up, or should I ask who?"

"I have a date tomorrow afternoon."

"With Elbert?"

"*Pffft!* Puh-leeze! I'm in no hurry to see him again any time soon. Especially since I had to turn down a date with Calvin today because I was in the middle of lunch with Elbert when he called."

Joan's jaw dropped, and she leaned back so far on the bed I thought she was going to fall. "He didn't!"

"He wanted me to meet him somewhere, like within the hour."

She started fanning her face with her hand. "That's the hottest thing I've heard all week. You talked to Calvin about going on a date with *him* right in front of Elbert's face? Girl, you've got more nerve than Kanye West. I'm impressed. Even *I* wouldn't do something that bold."

"Calm down. It was not like what you think. When Calvin called, Elbert was talking to one of his friends on the other side of the restaurant. I hung up before he got back." I sighed and gave Joan a pensive look. "Poor Calvin. He sounded so desperate."

"What's wrong with you, girl? He's one of the best-looking men in the club. And according to numerous reviews other women have posted, he's as good in bed as he looks. Why would he be desperate? He probably called you because you're so close by."

"There are several women in the club who live in the Bay Area. He could have called one of them, but he called me."

"So? How do you know he didn't try to hook up with another member before he called you? That would explain him calling you at the spur of the moment."

"If he did, I don't want to know. All I care about is that he wanted to be with me. I hope I'm available the next time he calls for a date. But . . ." I stopped talking and held my breath.

"But what?"

"This is the second time he's called at the spur of the moment for a date. I hope he's not going to make it a habit, because there will be other times when I can't drop whatever I'm doing to meet up with him. I don't want him to think I'm a pushover."

"I thought you loved Calvin." I detected a hint of sarcasm in Joan's tone. I ignored it because I didn't want our conversation to get more tense than it already was.

"I do, but I want to be taken seriously."

I also ignored Joan's dismissive wave and the incredulous look on her face. "*You* want to be taken seriously? By a man you've already set the tone for? *Pffft!* I'd say you're a month late and ten dollars short."

"It's not too late! Calvin and I are still getting to know each other!" I hollered. "You're supposed to be my best friend, so I wish you would cut me some slack."

I sulked for a few seconds and then Joan quickly backpedaled. "I'm sorry. Please don't pay me any mind. You know I'm just talking out the side of my mouth."

"Out your ass would be more like it. That's why I'm not going to let what you just said bother me," I quipped. We laughed.

"Oh well. Moving on, who is your date with tomorrow?"

"That painter I told you about last month. His screen name is "HotLips." I hope his whole body is hot. Oooh!" I said with a tremor in my voice.

"Oh yeah! The blond dude from Canada. The one who said he's going to paint a portrait of you. According to the reviews, he's as hot as they come. And unless he slid a cucumber into his shorts when he took his profile picture, he's got a nice package between his thighs."

"Tell me about it. I read the reviews and Googled him too. His work is on display in museums all over the world. He's in California for some fancy event in San Francisco."

"Yum yum. He sounds delicious. It'll be a long date if he's going to paint your portrait too."

"Uh-uh. I don't even have to pose in person. He's going to use my profile picture. If the painting looks good enough, I'm going to hang it on Bertha's living room wall. With all those grim mugshots of Libby and Marshall, it would definitely brighten up the room."

"You're wearing a string bikini in your club profile picture. You know damn well Bertha is not going to stand for a cheesecake shot on her wall. Not to mention Libby and Marshall. It rattles them to see you parading around in tight shorts and low-cut blouses, or anything else that shows off your curves. Libby, because she's jealous. Marshall, because it turns him on."

"I know that. I told Evan—that's his real name—that I want him to paint my face the way it looks in my profile picture but to put me in a cute dress or a nice blouse and skirt. He promised to make me look ten pounds thinner and at least five years younger."

"I can't wait to see it. If I like it, maybe I'll make a date with him and let him paint my picture. . . ."

"Go home to your husband, Joan." I laughed and stood up. After a long hug, she left. I got back into bed and picked up my *Brides* magazine again. My eyes almost popped out of their sockets when I flipped to a page with a black model wearing a gown that looked like the one Princess Diana wore when she married Prince Charles. A *black* model wearing the same type of gown I'd always fantasized about getting married in had to be a sign that I was moving in the right direction! I made a mental note to visit the bridal salons in the next few weeks. I was not going to wait for Calvin to propose. I'd buy my gown and hide it until he did.

South Bay City, where Joan and I resided, was one of the most interesting locations in California. It was a small city, but with Silicon Valley and San Jose in the same vicinity, there were always high-tech electronic and medical conventions or conferences going on around us. Most of the attendees from out of town who belonged to Discreet Encounters were always looking for a good time. Joan and I were having a lot of fun spending intimate time with some very interesting men. And it was all legal. Our dates didn't give us money to sleep with them, so this was not a thinly disguised version of prostitution like I had thought it was when Joan first turned me on to the club almost two years ago. Except for Calvin Ramsey, a long-haul truck driver, we dated only the club's doctors, lawyers, executives, and members in other high-income brackets. Dates with men at their level meant that venues for the sexual encounters would be posh hotel suites and include a lavish meal, champagne, and sometimes very expensive gifts. Conversations with the elite were a lot more interesting than chitchatting with a janitor or a cab driver and shacking up in a Motel 6 or a trailer. Joan and I received requests for dates with men in those dreary professions on a regular basis.

We didn't even consider dating any of the club's low-income members. However, I'd been tempted a few times because some of them were pretty hot. I wanted to have a good time, and good times were not cheap.

A potential date's looks were more important to some club members than the source of income. It didn't bother our high-end dates that I was only a cashier in my neighborhood grocery store living from paycheck to paycheck and that Joan was only a housewife. At thirty-two, we were not as young as a lot of the club's female members, but we were among the best looking. One of the first things we heard from a member was how beautiful we were. We were confident that as long as we kept up our looks and kept our bodies in shape, we'd have no trouble attracting attention.

But all that still wasn't enough for me. I wanted Calvin Ramsey to be the only man in my life.

Chapter 15
Calvin

SYLVIA HAD LAIN IN MY ARMS GRINDING HER TEETH, DROOLING ON my shoulder, and snoring like a drunken sailor. We'd made love half an hour before. She had put her negligee back on, but I had still been naked.

I'd lain on my back staring at the ceiling and reliving the sexing and killing of Hyeon three hours earlier. Just thinking about the terrified look on her face as I strangled her had given me a rush. I'd smiled when I recalled how her eyes had crossed and then rolled back in her head before she stopped moving. I finally dozed off and didn't open my eyes again until nine a.m.

"You must have really been tired," Sylvia commented when she came out of the bathroom. I sat up and she joined me on the bed, sitting so close I could feel her breath on my face.

My throat felt like butterflies were flying around in it. My mouth tasted like pig shit and probably smelled even worse, but Sylvia didn't even flinch when I kissed her. "Good morning, precious."

"Good morning, Calvin. Are we going out for breakfast, or is room service okay with you?"

"Yesterday was very hectic, so I'm in no hurry to get up and go out," I replied, caressing her cheek. She had already put on her makeup and a bright green sundress. "Have room service bring up some coffee." I cleared my throat and sat up straighter.

"Is that all you want? I wouldn't mind having some bacon and eggs or some pancakes and sausage."

"Just coffee and wheat toast for me." I gave Sylvia a quick, sloppy kiss. This time my foul breath did make her flinch, but I pretended not to notice.

While she was ordering room service, I piled out of bed, stumbled to the bathroom, and closed the door. I stood in front of the mirror and smiled at my reflection. "You are one blessed motherfucker," I told myself in a low voice. I was thoroughly convinced that because of my upcoming wedding and Lola's pending murder, I'd be on cloud nine for the rest of my life. I winked at myself and rinsed out my mouth.

After a quick shave and a hot shower, I whistled as I put on my bathrobe. I was still whistling when I returned to bed a few minutes later and stretched out on my back. The only thing I wanted to do now was relax and think about my future and all the wonderful things I had to look forward to. Marriage and fatherhood should have been at the top of my list, but they were not. They would be once Lola was out of the picture, because my killing spree would be over (I hoped . . .). I wouldn't be mentally and emotionally free to enjoy my life until then.

Sylvia opened the shades, and the bright sunlight streamed into the room and warmed my face. The heat felt so good. To me, this was an indication that the day was going to be pleasant.

Our suite included a great view of the Strip. It looked almost as chaotic this morning as it had last night. My brother, and the rest of the folks who'd attended our party, had already left Vegas, but Sylvia and I were going to stay three more days. She moved away from the window and sat at the foot of the bed with the TV remote in her hand. "I don't know what this world is coming to," she said, shaking her head. There was a look of distress on her face.

"What are you talking about, sweetheart?" I asked as I nudged her butt with my foot. I was surprised that I didn't have a hangover or a bellyache. I had drunk a lot of champagne and gobbled up a lot of cheese, crackers, salami, and fruit the evening before. The only things aching on my body were my wrists. Hyeon had gripped them during the struggle, but not hard enough to leave handprints or bruises, so I was not concerned.

"The local news just reported that some homeless people collecting cans and bottles this morning behind an old warehouse found an unconscious young Asian woman."

My heart picked up speed, and I took a very deep breath. "Oh? What happened to her?" *Was it Hyeon?* I wondered.

"There's just no telling. She was a hooker with a long arrest record. Lord knows those women put themselves in danger every time they get into a stranger's car. The cops didn't find any money on her, so whoever attacked her must have robbed her too."

It had to be Hyeon! My brain suddenly felt as if somebody had set it on fire, but I remained cool and calm. "Maybe she pissed off one of her tricks, or tried to rob him. Some of those hookers are pretty ruthless."

"It doesn't matter how ruthless she is. She's only eighteen. That monster had no right to try to kill her."

"Oh?" I said again, this time listening with more interest. "Somebody *tried* to kill her?" I couldn't believe my ears. That deceitful little bitch had pretended to be dead!

Sylvia dropped the remote onto the bed and scooted closer to me. She draped her arm around my shoulder and exhaled. "Baby, I'm so glad we lead such normal lives. Reading about crime or watching it on TV is as close as I ever hope to get to any of it."

"Was she able to tell what happened?" My body was gradually falling apart, one piece at a time. My stomach felt like a mule had stomped on it with all four hooves, my eyes were burning, and my ears were ringing.

"She just regained consciousness a couple of hours ago, but she is so traumatized she can't remember what happened. All she was able to tell the cops was that she'd been picked up around midnight last night by a black man in his thirties. The police have two witnesses though."

"Two witnesses?" I bleated. By now, my heart was thumping so hard it was difficult to breathe.

Sylvia nodded and gave me a curious look. "What's the matter, honey? You look like you just saw a ghost."

"Wh—what do you mean?" I stammered.

"You sound and look as if you're in pain. Did you just have another flashback?"

"Uh . . . yeah. But it was a mild one and it lasted only a couple of seconds."

"Well, the way the blood suddenly drained from your face, I thought you were having one as bad as the one you had last night."

"It's nothing to worry about, baby."

"I do worry about it, Calvin. When we get home, I'm going to make an appointment for you to see someone."

"Okay. Let's forget about it for now." I rubbed my nose, which was also causing me some discomfort now because the insides of my nostrils were burning. Then I gave Sylvia a concerned look. "I feel sorry for that young hooker. I hope she's going to be all right."

"I hope so too."

"What did the witnesses tell the cops?"

"Not much. Hookers don't like to talk to cops, but they both admitted they'd been doing drugs for hours when they saw that young girl get into a car with a black man. That's all they told the cops."

My heart rate slowly returned to normal, and I breathed a huge sigh of relief. But I was still not out of the woods. "Hmmm. Did they write down a license plate number or tell the cops what kind of car the dude was driving?"

"Honey, the only thing whores care about is making money. Unless they're trying to set somebody up, why would any of them write down license plate numbers or care about what kind of a car a trick is driving? Sometimes you say the craziest things." Sylvia gave me an exasperated look and shook her head. "Oh— I know you didn't ask for anything to eat except toast, but I ordered you a Denver omelet anyway." She exhaled and stood up with her arms folded. "What do you want to do today? Are you going to gamble some more?" I was so glad she'd suddenly changed the subject I wanted to kiss her again.

"I might try my luck at a few slot machines, but not in Vegas."

Sylvia gulped and gave me an incredulous look. "You're not making much sense. I think you drank too much champagne last night. You want to gamble but not in the gambling capital of the world?"

"It's too damn crowded. Maybe we ought to drive over to Laughlin and spend the day kicking back on the beach and riding around on those water cabs."

"I know that'd be a lot of fun, but Laughlin is at least a ninety-minute drive from here, one way. And it's probably just as crowded as Vegas. Are you getting bored?"

"Kind of. I'll be glad when we get back to San Jose."

Sylvia giggled and gave me a thoughtful look. "I didn't want to admit it, but so will I. Vegas has become too hectic for me."

"I hear you. I'm glad we're on the same page."

"We should have stayed home and celebrated there. I'm sorry I badgered you to come here. If you don't mind, I'd like to leave today if we can change our flight."

"I don't mind."

Ominous thoughts suddenly crossed my mind: What if the Korean hooker regains her memory and gives a detailed description of me? If she remembers the make and model of the car and tells the cops, they might nose around until they figure out it was a rental. And if they fiddle around long and hard enough, they might come up with a list of names of all the people who rented the same make and model, and my name would be one of them. Shit! Words could not describe how anxious I was to get out of Vegas now.

I immediately called the airline. They charged me a pretty penny to change our reservation so we could be on the next available flight to San Jose, but I didn't care what it cost.

* * *

As soon as I dropped Sylvia off at her house, declining her offer to spend the night with me, I rushed to get home. I turned into my driveway on two wheels. I was in such a hurry to get inside, I didn't even bother to take my luggage out of the trunk.

I clicked on my living room light and looked around, trying to recall where I had left my laptop. I spotted it on the coffee table, then sprinted across the floor and turned it on. Google brought up four links about Hyeon. I clicked on the first one and found everything I needed to know. Not only had the bitch recovered, she'd already been released from the hospital! I became as frightened as I had been earlier. Why had I not checked to make sure she was dead? I would *never* be that lax again. There was no way I was going to let my next victim play possum on me. I would make sure she was dead, even if I had to dismember her.

I set my computer aside and turned on my cell phone to check my messages. I was surprised to see nothing from Lola, but I had a feeling I'd be hearing from her again real soon. The slut was probably in a hotel room with some joker fucking his brains out. I went back to my computer and pulled up her profile. As soon as her picture appeared, bile rose in my throat. "Bitch! Slut! Cow! Whore! You won't be grinning like a damn hyena when I get through with you!" I screeched with my jaw twitching. The sight of her face enraged me so much, I hawked a wad of spit at the monitor. I grinned when it landed right between her eyes.

Chapter 16
Lola

I WOKE UP SUNDAY MORNING AT NINE A.M. I WAS SO DROWSY I wanted to go back to sleep and, I hoped, dream about Calvin. I probably would have if somebody hadn't started pounding on my door five minutes later. I sat bolt upright. Before I could respond, the door swung open and Bertha strutted in. "Lola, you have company," she announced, clapping her hands as she pranced in my direction. She stopped at the foot of my bed. "Get up and come downstairs and show your visitor some hospitality."

"Who is it?" Other than Joan, I couldn't imagine who would come to visit me on a Sunday morning.

"Elbert." There was a dreamy look on Bertha's face. She had already dressed for church in her favorite beige tweed suit, black pumps with low chunky heels, and some of her most gaudy jewelry. She had her makeup on and one of several wig-hats she wore when she didn't feel like fussing with her own hair.

"What is he doing here? I just had lunch with him yesterday," I wailed.

"Lola, you don't have to get so upset. I wish you'd wipe that scowl off your face," Bertha complained.

"I can't help it," I defended. "I'm just . . . well, I'm just waking up and I am not in the mood to entertain company."

"Not even Elbert?"

"Especially Elbert."

Bertha folded her arms and gave me a critical look. "I don't know what's wrong with you, girl."

I rolled my eyes, and this time the scowl on my face was for Bertha. "There is nothing wrong with me."

"There must be. No woman in her right mind would look a gift horse like Elbert in the mouth. I'd be thrilled to pieces if a man like him wanted to see me two days in a row. Humph! I just adore him to death. He's as sweet to me as he is to his mama," Bertha swooned. "He looks so dapper in his blue suit today. Even though he looks like Medusa with those outlandish dread-locks hanging off his head, he's still a very handsome young man. Does that truck driver you think you're in love with wear those nappy things on his head?"

"Calvin's hair is short and neat. It looks very becoming on him, but if he ever decides to grow dreadlocks, he'd still be very handsome too," I said.

"I'll see for myself when and if you ever bring him to the house." Bertha paused and gave me a thoughtful look. "I like what you told me about him praising you for looking out for me. I hope he and I will get along."

"You'll get along with Calvin as well as you do with Elbert," I insisted.

"He sounds perfect, but I always thought truck drivers were loud, slovenly, alcoholic buffoons with half a dozen tattoos." I was tempted to tell Bertha that she had just described her son, Marshall.

"Calvin drinks occasionally and he doesn't have any tattoos," I declared with a proud sniff.

"Hmmm. I can't even picture Calvin. Do you have a photo of him?"

"Not yet. I'm sure I'll be bringing him to the house to meet you and everybody else real soon." I was already working hard to lock Calvin into a more secure position in my life. It looked as if I would have to work even harder, especially since Bertha had "accepted" him as a potential mate for me. "Tell Elbert I'll be down as soon as I get dressed."

When I got downstairs, he was slumped in a chair at the kitchen table eating grits and some of the beef bacon he'd given Bertha last week. When I started dating him, he promised us that we could have all the meat products we wanted for free as long as he managed the neighborhood meat market. His generosity was another reason Bertha "adored him to death."

"Hi, Elbert," I muttered, shuffling into the room. "I didn't know you were coming."

"I didn't know I was coming either. But last night I remembered Bertha had told me yesterday morning that she was almost out of beef bacon and asked me to bring her some as soon as I could," he said, all in one breath. He paused and wiped his greasy lips with the back of his hand.

"Well, it's good to see you again. I really enjoyed our lunch yesterday. And by the way, you look real nice in your blue suit," I said, offering him a tight smile. Bertha stood next to me beaming like a lighthouse.

"You should see me in my black suit. I'll wear it next time we go out," he said excitedly. "If you're not too busy today, you want to go to the park with me?"

The park! This man couldn't get any duller if he tried. I had something much more interesting to do than going to the park to watch a bunch of elderly people feed bread crumbs to the pigeons. I had a date with a very interesting man, and I couldn't wait to get to him. One of the reviewers on the club website claimed he was a fantastic lover and the most charming man she had ever met. Two other club members raved about the portraits he'd painted of them.

"Uh, I can't go today. I already have plans to do something else," I explained. I was beginning to sound like a broken record. Except for yesterday, the last three times Elbert asked me out, I told him I had "plans to do something else." I dreaded the day I'd have to tell him I couldn't see him at all anymore. That would be the day I committed myself exclusively to Calvin Ramsey.

"Oh." He looked as if he was going to start crying. "I told Mama you'd probably have something else to do today," he added glumly. "I really enjoyed having lunch with you yesterday. I wish we could get together more often."

"Maybe we can go see a movie one day next week," I threw in.

"I sure hope so. It's getting harder and harder for me to see you these days," Elbert complained.

"I've been very busy. And I'm probably going to get even busier," I said firmly.

"Oh well. I'll keep trying anyway." He hunched his shoulders and stood up. There was a weak smile on his face.

I smiled back. "I hope you will." The words slid out of my mouth before I could think about what I was saying. I was pleased to know that Elbert was not ready to give up on me.

"I'll give you a call next week." Now there was a slightly woeful look on his face as he turned to Bertha. "You need a ride to church, Sister Bertha? Mama rode with Sister Becket this morning, so I sure would like some company. . . ."

"Yes, I would," she replied without hesitation. She sounded and looked just as disappointed as Elbert. "What plans do you have today, Lola? I was hoping we could finish cleaning off the back porch so we can start on the kitchen closet."

"I'm having lunch with a woman who used to work at the store with me. After that, we're going to get our nails done. I haven't seen her since she got married and moved to Reno a couple of years ago. I'm sure we'll do something else after we leave the nail salon, so I'll be gone quite a while." I took a deep breath and smiled at Elbert. To make him feel even better, I threw in a wink. "I'll talk to you later," I told him, already backing out of the kitchen. I didn't wait for a response. I whirled around and rushed back to my room to get ready for my date.

Bertha liked to attend the morning service, so she and Elbert left a few minutes later. I was glad I didn't have to look at the sad expression on his face again, or the disappointed one on Bertha's, before I left to go meet up with my date.

I took a quick shower and dressed as fast as I could. I wanted to be long gone before Libby and her crew returned from Denny's, where they ate brunch almost every Sunday morning. I was in a good mood and I didn't want her to spoil it.

Chapter 17
Lola

*I*T WAS EXACTLY ONE P.M. WHEN I ARRIVED AT THE HOTEL WHERE Evan McCoy had booked a suite. I had lost count of how many encounters I'd had, but there were still times when I got paranoid. I was concerned that the people who worked at the hotels I frequented would begin to suspect that I was a hooker, so I tried to look as conservative as possible. This time I wore a plain blue sleeveless blouse and a pair of black slacks. I wore stilettos or sexy sandals when Joan and I went to bars, but I wore a pair of low-heeled black pumps on my dates—the same ones I wore when I went to church or out with Elbert. With my hair pinned back and very little makeup, I appeared so prim and proper I looked more like a schoolteacher or a librarian than a sex club member.

"My God! You look so different in person!" Evan exclaimed when I entered his suite. He closed the door, grabbed my hand, and twirled me around. Then he held my hands in his and squeezed. We stood stock-still and gazed into each other's eyes for a few seconds. Evan had a wife and a teenage daughter, and he had made it very clear that he was a happily married man. Like several other married club members I'd been with, he claimed wifey was great in bed but that having sex with the same person year after year was no longer exciting. I didn't care what I had to do when I got married, I was going to keep my marriage fresh and exciting. And I hoped the man I married felt the same way, because a married woman could cheat just as easily as her husband, and for the same reasons. I shook my head to send away the negative thoughts. I wanted to give all my attention to Evan. "You are a total surprise!" he hollered, still gazing at me.

"In a good way, I hope," I cooed.

"Honey, it's better than good. You are absolutely stunning. Perfect face, body to die for. I didn't expect you to dress . . . um . . . well, I expected a woman with a body like yours to dress a bit more provocatively."

I laughed. "I usually do. I own some really sexy outfits, but I don't think it's a good idea for me to wear them into a hotel. I don't want to draw attention to myself."

"Well, I have news for you, baby. Women as gorgeous as you are will attract attention no matter what they wear."

"Thanks, but I still like to look conservative. I don't want the hotel employees to get the wrong idea about me. . . ." I let my voice trail off.

Evan gave me a curious look as he hunched his shoulders and raked his fingers through his thick blond hair. He had a nice, trim body and a deep tan. With his shabby jeans and sleeveless shirt, he looked more like a middle-aged surfer than a well-known painter. "I get it!" he hooted, slapping the side of his head. "You don't want to be mistaken for a working girl, right?"

I nodded.

"Sweetheart, I wouldn't even worry about things like that. I'm not a trick and you're not a hooker. We are simply two consenting adults who happen to belong to a sex club, and there is nothing illegal about that. Now that that's out of the way, let's get acquainted. Okay?"

"Okay," I said, nodding again.

"My God!" he exclaimed, rearing back to look at me some more. We were still standing in front of the door. "You are a beautiful woman. I can't wait to *go at it.* I can see why 'BrownSugar' is your screen name. You definitely look sweet enough to eat."

I had no idea why Evan thought "HotLips" was a good screen name for him. Like some of the other white dudes I'd dated,

Evan hardly had any lips at all. When he hauled off and kissed me, it felt as if I was kissing the rim of a plate, but I acted as if I'd just received the kiss of a lifetime. I swooned and gave him a knowing look. "I am good enough to eat," I teased, speaking in the sexiest tone I could manage. I had updated my profile two weeks ago and included a new picture. I was proud of my body and liked to show it off in sexy outfits like the silver string bikini I wore when I had Joan take a new picture for me to post. "You look good enough to eat too. . . ."

"In that case, I hope your appetite is as big as mine."

I looked around the room and was pleased to see two bottles of wine on a tray by the bed.

"Make yourself comfortable, sweetheart." Evan waved me toward the bed, but he remained standing in the same spot with his hands on his hips. "I can't get over what a vision of loveliness you are."

"Thank you, Evan," I said shyly. I cleared my throat and gave him one of my biggest smiles. I set my purse on top of the dresser, then sashayed across the floor and plopped down on the side of the bed. He had a nice body for a forty-five-year-old man. He had told me that he worked out six days a week and he took all kinds of vitamins. And, without me even asking, he had admitted that he took Viagra too. That didn't bother me at all. I'd been with a few other men his age who also took Viagra, claiming they didn't need it yet but that it enhanced their performance. "Have you started painting my picture yet?"

"Oh! Your portrait!" He slapped the side of his head again and looked at me with his eyes open wide and his mouth hanging open. Then he darted to the closet and removed a large, pizza-shaped box. "I want to apologize in advance. I did an exquisite job of immortalizing you, but even the old masters—including Rembrandt and da Vinci—could never have done you justice." He sat down next to me and gently placed the box in my lap.

Like a child on Christmas morning, I began to open my present as fast as my hands could move. "You painted my picture already?" I was impressed and glad. Because if this date flopped I wouldn't have to see Evan again to get my portrait.

When I saw what was inside, I almost fainted. I abruptly pushed the box off my lap. "I . . . I can't accept this," I stammered. I slid it farther to the side and stood up, wringing my hands. They felt as if I'd just held them over a campfire. There was a horrified look on Evan's face. My lips were moving, but I was having a hard time getting more words out. "Get that damn thing away from me!" I screeched.

Chapter 18
Lola

*I*COULDN'T IMAGINE WHAT WAS GOING THROUGH POOR EVAN'S HEAD. He looked like a frightened rabbit, and I felt like one. "I'm so sorry," I wailed, still wringing my hands. My stomach was in knots and my head was spinning. I was also sweating and shifting my weight from one foot to the other. What did I get myself into? It looked as though this was going to be the date from hell. "I shouldn't be here!" I hollered.

"My God! Is the portrait that bad?" he asked. He rose off the bed, rushed over to me, and put his hands on my shoulders. By now my entire body was trembling.

"No, it's not bad," I managed, shaking my head and blinking so hard my eyes ached.

"Then I must say that I am more than a little bewildered."

"I should leave," I choked, already moving toward the dresser to get my purse.

"What?" Evan hollered, sprinting over to me. "What the hell for? Is it because you think the portrait is too unflattering?"

"You did a good job. I'm glad you put me on a beach. And the setting sun in the background looks so serene." I dropped my head, and when I looked back up at Evan, I had tears in my eyes. I blinked hard to hold them back. "It's the dress you painted on me. It's yellow," I said hoarsely. Calvin was the only other man I'd told about my irrational fear of yellow clothing. He'd been so sympathetic and understanding, I knew I could tell him anything. There were so many other things I planned to share with him. One was that I didn't want to spend the rest of my life alone. Another one that had recently begun to haunt me was my fear that I'd develop some serious health problems. My parents had died fairly young, and because I had no contact with any other blood relatives, I didn't know if bad health was in my DNA. I tried not to think about such things too often, and I certainly didn't like to talk about them with anybody except Joan and Calvin. But Evan was not going to let up.

"Then what the hell is the problem?"

"I *never* wear anything yellow," I explained.

"Huh? Well excuse me, but I don't know you well enough to know the type of clothing you find acceptable. But what's so offensive about a yellow sundress? With your beautiful bronze skin tone, it looks marvelous on you."

I held my breath for a few moments. And then I said the words that made me cringe. "I have this premonition that if I wear something yellow, I'll die in it."

Evan looked at me as if I was speaking in tongues. "And how did you come up with such an ominous conclusion?" he asked with both eyebrows raised.

"My mother was laid to rest in a yellow dress," I said stiffly. "The same shade as the dress you painted."

"I see." He blew out some air and gave me a pitiful look. "And seeing yourself in one brought back a painful memory. I'm sorry. If you don't mind telling me, what makes you think you'll die if you wear yellow?"

"There was a picture taken of my mother at her funeral. I thought it looked like me lying in that coffin. Other people thought the same thing."

"Jeez. I don't—"

I held up my hand and interrupted Evan. "Let me finish." I sucked in some air first. "I didn't think much about it for a while, but a few years later, a friend of mine took a picture of me lying on her bed. We were teenagers and always acting crazy. She snapped the picture just as I closed my eyes. I had on a yellow blouse that day. As soon as I saw that picture I recalled the one of my mother in her coffin in that yellow dress. From that day on, I was convinced that if I ever wore yellow again, I would die."

"So you're superstitious, eh? Well, if it'll make you feel any better, I'm terrified of vampires, even though I know they don't exist. When I was a kid, I saw one vampire movie too many. Before I knew it, I was so terrified of those fanged creatures, I couldn't even stand to look at a picture of one. The phobia intensified as I got older. In college, I secretly slept in a necklace made out of garlic."

"What about now? Do you still have that fear?"

"Not at all. I realized it was ruining my social life. After a few months, I smelled like garlic even without the necklace. Long, hot baths with industrial strength soap and the strongest aftershave I could find couldn't mask the unholy stench of garlic. Because of that, girls lost interest in me after the second or third date."

"Do you still sleep with garlic around your neck?"

"No, and I haven't done so in twenty years."

"How did you get over your fear?"

"One night after downing enough beer to fill a large bucket, I slept in such a clumsy position the damn necklace got tangled and almost strangled me. I never wore it again. To my surprise and relief, from that day on I was no longer afraid of vampires. Being strangled to death was a lot more frightening—especially accidentally by a necklace."

"Or strangled any other way," I said, feeling my own neck.

Evan put the portrait back into the box and returned it to the closet. "If you would still like me to paint your picture, in a different color outfit, just let me know."

"I'll do that," I said. "And I'm really sorry for ruining things," I mumbled.

"Don't worry about it." Evan exhaled and folded his arms. There was a smile on his face, so I knew he wasn't mad. He licked his lips, snapped his fingers, and widened his eyes, as if a great idea had suddenly come to him. "Well, since you're al-

ready here and we had planned to spend a couple of hours together, are you still up to having a little fun today?"

I answered with a smile.

After two glasses of champagne, we got cozy in the bed.

Evan was a fantastic lover, but because of that picture, I was so
flustered and distracted, I didn't enjoy the experience at all.

Chapter 19
Calvin

*I*T WAS HARD NOT TO THINK ABOUT THE INCIDENT IN VEGAS WITH the Korean hooker. My thoughts ran from one extreme to the other. One minute it didn't seem like such a big deal, the next minute it did. With these thoughts swirling around in my head, I was preoccupied for the next couple of days. Every crazy thought I could imagine haunted me. First I was worried about the cops finding Hyeon's DNA in the car I had rented, but I didn't worry about that long when I realized what a far-fetched notion it was. With the thousands of people renting cars in Vegas, what was the chance of the cops finding out that Hyeon had been in the car I'd driven on the same night she'd been attacked? I had not bothered to wipe her fingerprints off the spots she'd touched, because as far as the cops were concerned, she could have been in that car with one of her previous tricks since she'd been work-ing the streets. When I realized how unlikely it was that I'd ever be linked to Hyeon, I stopped spending so much time thinking about it. But I couldn't put it completely out of my mind until I was sure I was out of the woods.

On Thursday, four days after Sylvia and I returned to San Jose, I decided to go back to work, even though my supervisor had told me I could take off two more days. I hoped the distrac-tion would help clear my head and squash the little bit of fear I felt about my latest crime. And it did.

I drove south from Sacramento for about four hours before I decided to pull into a truck stop to gas up, use the restroom, and pick up a snack. It was nine p.m., and I was on my way to a fitness center in La Jolla to deliver some state-of-the-art gym equipment. While I sat in the cab of my rig munching on a ham sandwich, a hitchhiker lugging a bulging backpack approached me. She was a cute, skinny blonde who looked to be in her early thirties. "You going South?" she asked in a flat tone.

I took my time answering. I swallowed the last bite of my sandwich first. "I'm going to La Jolla," I grunted.

"Can I hitch a ride as far as Fresno?"

I didn't like the deadpan expression on her face, her dry tone, or her Southern accent. As a matter of fact, I didn't like her. But because it was the day after April Fool's Day and I had laughed at some of the pranks a few of my coworkers had pulled, I was still in a fairly good mood, so I decided to be cordial. "Get in."

"I'm Melanie," she said.

"I'm James."

"Nice to meet you, James. Um . . . no offense, but I was afraid to ask a black man for a ride," she told me less than a minute after she'd crawled into my cab and plopped her flat ass down so close to me that her knee touched mine.

"Then why did you?" I asked gruffly. I snorted and moved my knee away from hers. She wore a pair of dingy brown jeans and a white T-shirt. The weather was fairly cool, so I was surprised she didn't have on a jacket or a sweater. "I'm sure you can hitch a ride with one of the white truckers."

"Well, I'm in a hurry and you're the only one sitting out here alone. Today is payday for some of the truckers, so it's a real busy night for the lot lizards. The hookers who work these places can get real mean if you interfere with their business."

"So I take it you're not a hooker?"

"Hell no! I ain't never sold my tail and never will. I'm just down on my luck and needed to get out of town for a while. Me and my husband just moved out here two months ago from West

Virginia, and I can't stand this place. I told him I was going back home, with or without him. So I'm on my own now. My sister lives in Fresno, so I'm going to stay with her until I scrape up enough for a plane ticket back to West Virginia. My husband gambled my whole paycheck away yesterday, so I didn't have enough money for a bus ticket." Melanie paused, and after giving me a critical look, she continued. "No offense again, but even if I was a hooker, I couldn't see myself having sex with a black man."

"To each his own," I said with a shrug.

"Do you mind if I smoke a joint?"

"Yes, I do. If I get stopped by a highway patrolman for some reason and he smells that shit, I could lose my job and get arrested."

"Oh well. Just thought I'd ask. I haven't been high all week and it's beginning to get to me." I glanced to the right and was surprised to see a grin on Melanie's face. "Anyway, James, I don't have anything against black folks, or any other people of color. I just don't believe in race mixing. It causes all kinds of problems. One of my cousins in San Francisco had a baby by a Chinese man, and that little boy is the most confused child I know. Not to mention his weird looks. Know what I mean?"

I nodded. "I know exactly what you mean. Thanks for being so up-front and honest. Just so you know, I would *never* have sex with a white woman. No offense."

Melanie seemed surprised to hear such a statement, especially with so much emphasis put on the word *never*. "Oh. Well, now that we got that out of the way, we don't have to discuss it again. If you want something for giving me a ride, I'd be happy to treat you to a meal when you make the next stop. It has to be a real cheap meal though."

"That won't be necessary," I said, looking at my watch. "I have to get going, so if you want to change your mind about riding with a black man, you need to do it now."

Melanie rolled her eyes and let out a loud breath. "Beggars

can't be choosers." I was surprised to see a smile on her narrow face. "So you wouldn't have sex with a white chick, huh?"

"Only if I didn't have a choice." I turned on my motor and eased back out onto the freeway.

"Is it because you don't think we're pretty or sexy enough? Or, are you . . . a racist?"

"That's not it. I've seen a lot of sexy white women, and I have several white friends. I'm just not attracted to white women."

"I bet if you ran into the right one, you'd change your tune."

I chuckled. "Maybe I would. And if you ran into the right black man, you would too."

We laughed at the same time.

"You seem like an interesting man, so I don't think you'll bore me along the way. I enjoy talking with you, so I'm glad I caught a ride with you." Melanie paused and stared at the side of my face. "I don't care if you are black. You look pretty safe."

If this racist bitch didn't have it coming, I didn't know who did.

I enjoyed chatting with Melanie for the next thirty miles. She was actually more intelligent than she looked. "I voted for Obama." After a heavy sigh, she added, "But only because my old man made me."

When we approached a sign announcing the next rest stop, she asked me to take a break so she could use the restroom and pick up something to drink.

I gassed up my rig, took a bathroom break, and purchased a bottle of water. When I returned to my rig, Melanie had already popped open a can of beer. "Since you won't let me smoke no weed, this beer will give me a buzz so I can sleep better."

After she had guzzled her fourth can of Budweiser, she dozed off. About twenty miles down the road, her head wobbled and ended up on my shoulder. It stayed there until she woke up fifteen minutes later. When she reached over and started caressing the side of my face, I assumed she was tipsy, disoriented, or dreaming. "You sure have some nice smooth skin."

"You mean for a black man?" I teased.

"Oh, stop being such a crybaby. You're making something out

of nothing! Why is it you people always have to play the race card?"

"Baby, you dealt the first hand."

"If I ever do make it with a black man, I hope he's as handsome and nice as you."

"I hope he is too." I snickered. I was glad when she leaned her head back and closed her eyes. Within minutes, she dozed off again. I let her snooze with her head on my shoulder until we reached a spot that I had become familiar with a few years ago. I looked in my rearview mirror to make sure no vehicles were behind me. The coast was clear, so I stopped and turned off my motor. This was the same wooded, deserted stretch where I had dumped a Paris Hilton clone and another bitch on previous runs. I wondered if their remains had ever been discovered. With all the coyotes and other creatures in the area, it was unlikely.

When my hands went around Melanie's throat and started squeezing, her eyes flew open. "Huh? Mister, what the fuck are you doing? You must be out of your fucking mind!" she exploded. Her eyes were as big as saucers, and she was trembling like a leaf in a windstorm. Her voice dropped to a whimper. "You . . . you don't have to force me! You can do whatever you want for free!"

"That's exactly what I'm doing, bitch!" I growled as I squeezed her throat harder.

"Oh God!" she screamed. And then she started kicking the dashboard and clawing the sides of my arms. I was glad I had on a thick shirt and a jacket to keep my DNA from getting underneath her fingernails. Her last words were, "You can fuck me all night if you want to! You don't even have to pay me a plugged nickel!"

"Me fuck *you?* Ha! No offense, Melanie, but I would never have sex with a white chick."

She was still kicking and clawing. I squeezed harder so she couldn't say another word. All she could do was gasp for air as she prepared to meet her maker.

I could not slip up the way I had in Vegas. I Googled several times each day to follow up on that incident. As of last night, the hooker had not been able to recall anything more than what she had already told the cops. When I checked again this morning, the report was that one of her concerned relatives had come over from Korea and talked the little whore into going back to live with her. Case closed. I was out of the woods.

I had to make sure Melanie was dead. I twisted her neck until her head was on backward.

Chapter 20
Joan

*L*OLA DIDN'T RESPOND TO THE TEXT I SENT HER TUESDAY MORN-
ing inviting her to have lunch with me. I showed up at her work
a few minutes before noon anyway. I needed to pick up milk and
bread, so I had two reasons to go to Cottright's, the mom-and-
pop grocery store where Lola had been working as a cashier
since we got out of high school.

It was a warm day, so I wore a tank top and a pair of skinny
jeans I had purchased a few days ago. I had to park at a meter
three blocks away, but I didn't mind. Since I hadn't worked out
in a while, I needed the exercise. Besides that, every man I
passed stared at me, smiling and flirting. I enjoyed the attention
and it felt good to know that I was still a very attractive woman.
Especially after Reed's recent complaint about me "losing" my
shape.

Lola was happy to see me.

"When did you start reading minds?" she asked when I approached her counter. I was glad the store was fairly empty. Even
so, old man Cottright peeped from behind a potato chip rack
and gave me a dirty look. "I was hoping you'd call or come by,"
Lola added. "I really need to talk."

"I need to talk too. Can we have lunch?"

"Yeah, but I haven't cashed that check you gave me and I'm
down to my last few bucks until payday, so we'll have to go someplace real cheap."

I shook my head. "It's on me," I said, holding up my hand. "I owe you a lunch, remember?"

We walked to Jenny's Kitchen, a popular soup and sandwich establishment two blocks away. It was one of the places we patronized so often, the waitress didn't even bother to give us menus. We always ordered the same thing: ham and cheese on rye bread, potato salad, and diet lemonade. There were several other businesses and a junior high school in the vicinity, so there was always a crowd for lunch. The only available seats were at the counter, and we grabbed them right away.

"How was your date on Sunday?" I asked after the server had taken our orders.

"He was nice enough, I guess, but I won't be seeing him again."

"Uh-oh. What was wrong with him?"

"Nothing was wrong with him. He wasn't bad looking, and he was a pretty good lover, I guess."

I rolled my eyes. "What's up with this 'I guess' shit? And what about the free painting he promised to do of you? The one you were so anxious to get your hands on."

Lola blinked and gave me a weary look. "He painted me wearing a yellow dress."

I knew all about Lola's fear and had advised her to get professional help. So far she had not taken my advice. I had quite a few yellow outfits in my huge closet, but out of respect for her, I never wore any of them when we were together.

"What did you do when you saw the picture?"

"I freaked out, and it almost scared poor HotLips to death." Lola let out a dry laugh. "I told him why I never wore anything yellow, and he was very sympathetic and understanding. The painting was very nice, but I refused to accept it. I even offered to leave his room right away to give him enough time to hook up with another date. He wanted me to stay."

"Hmmm. From that dreamy-eyed look on your face now, I have a feeling he made it worth your while."

"He did, but like I just said, I'm not going to see him again."

"Why don't you ask him to do another portrait of you in a different color outfit?"

"He asked if I wanted him to do another one, but I told him I didn't." Lola paused and gave me a hopeless look. "Every time I go on a date with a happily married man like Evan, it just reminds me how anxious I am to get married and have a family."

I shook my head and let out a mighty sigh. "What makes you think marriage and a family will make you happy? How many happily married couples do you know?"

Lola gave me a blank look. "I know lots of married couples. Your mama and Elmo and almost all of the girls we went to school with. What about Shirelle, my daddy's ex-mistress? And her niece, Mariel?"

"How many of them are *happy*?"

"How would I know? I don't know what goes on behind people's closed doors, Joan. Why did you ask such a stupid question?"

"You know what goes on behind *my* closed doors. You know what a joke my marriage is. And for the record, I can't count the number of times Mama has said she wished she'd never met my stepfather. I am so sick of Reed, I left the house running this morning before he even left to go to his office."

"Uh-oh. What stupid thing did he do or say this time?"

"He told me this morning, while he was on top of me sweating like a fucking ox, that I'm not nearly as good in bed as I used to be."

Lola's eyes got big, and her mouth dropped open. "You're kidding! Have you ever told him just how lousy he is in bed?"

"No, but I will someday. He criticized my bedroom skills and told me that I was no longer as cute as I was when he met me. I was only seventeen then. Just being that young is cute!"

"Humph. Tell that pot-bellied gremlin I said he's not as cute as he used to be either."

"Tell me about it. I was tempted to tell Reed about all the good times I have when I'm in bed with LongJohn. Not to mention all the rest of my hookups! He's going to rent some adult movies for us to watch so I can get back on track because he thinks I've forgotten what real sex should be like!"

"He said all that this morning?"

"Yes!"

"If you were that lousy in bed and losing your looks, Reed would have done something about it by now. Like most men who say shit like that, he'd have a mistress."

"Don't even go there. He wouldn't cheat on me to save his soul." I gave Lola a pensive look. "He's as obsessed with me as you are with Calvin."

"Be careful now," she warned. "Don't say something you'll regret."

"I'm just messing with you. Speaking of Calvin, have you heard from him since that last text you told me about?"

"No, I haven't. I sent him another one last night, but he hasn't replied yet. I know I'm on his mind, because he tells me all the time that he can't wait to see me again."

"For your sake, I hope it'll be soon."

"I have a feeling it will be." That dreamy-eyed look was on Lola's face for the rest of the meal.

Chapter 21
Calvin

SYLVIA AND I WERE GOING TO CELEBRATE HER BIRTHDAY ON JUNE 12 and exchange vows on the same day.

Since she'd waited so long to get married, she wanted a fancy church wedding with all of our friends and relatives in attendance. Her mother and some of her other family members were planning to throw us a lavish reception and had already reserved one of the most popular venues in town. We had also booked a suite in a five-star hotel in Rio de Janeiro, Brazil, for our honeymoon.

I was extremely pleased that she wanted me to move into her house. For one thing, it was in a much more convenient location than mine. It was closer to the local branch of the trucking office where I had to check in from time to time. And it was a great area to raise children. She lived two blocks from one of the most prestigious elementary schools in San Jose. I planned to sell my house, but I couldn't do that until I made a few home improvements. The roof leaked in the dining room, the plumbing in the kitchen and in the bathroom needed some repair work, and the water heater had been acting up lately. Most important, I had to get rid of that freezer in my garage. The last time I took a peek inside, which was just two nights ago, the three women in it looked just as freshly dead as when I killed them. Glinda was on the bottom, so when I wanted to look at her cheating face, I had to rearrange the other two. That was

not easy, because those frozen bodies were very difficult to ma-
neuver. I didn't mind all the hard work I had to perform, because my mission would be over soon.

It had been half an hour since my encounter with Melanie,
and now I was back on the road cruising along as if nothing had
happened. My only regret was that I had not spent more time
with that bitch so I could have enjoyed killing her even more.
Her racist comments had pushed me too far too fast. Her al-
leged feeling about not wanting to have sex with a black man
was the only reason I hadn't raped her before I killed her. I
would never put my dick in a place where it wasn't wanted.

I had attacked two women in less than two weeks. That gave
me a rush I could not describe. My careless fuckup in Vegas had
suddenly begun to bother me again. It was the reason that another disturbing thought slid into my mind, and it chilled me to
the bone: What if Lola survived my attack and was the one who
fingered me? If that happened, I would never be able to forgive
myself. The thought was so unspeakable, a sharp pain that felt
like a spear shot through my chest. It was so excruciating, I
thought I was having a heart attack. I pulled into the next rest
area and parked so I could compose myself. Wheezing like an
old man, I remained in my seat and rubbed my chest for several
minutes before I felt well enough to get out and stretch my legs.
There were no bars nearby so I could have a few drinks to calm
my nerves, but there was a convenience store. I decided to grab
some Advil and a few energy drinks.

The weather was dreary and much cooler than it had been
when I picked up Melanie. It was the kind of night when people
ventured out only if they had to. There were plenty of lot lizards
slithering from one trucker to the next. I was horny, but not one
woman was even remotely attractive. A cross-eyed redhead with
half of her front teeth missing approached me when I exited the
convenience store. "They call me Gummy. For twenty bucks I
can show you why they call me that." She grinned and opened
her mouth as wide as she could, making a slurping noise. Her

gums looked like raw chicken. The thought of this wall-eyed snagglepuss giving me a blow job didn't appeal to me at all.

"I think I already know," I told her with a laugh and a dismissive wave.

Immediately after she took off and headed toward another trucker, a woman on crutches hobbled up to me. She was almost old enough to be my mother. I didn't give this hag the chance to proposition me. I shook my head, rushed back to my rig, and locked my doors.

I popped open a can of Red Bull and pulled out my cell phone to check my messages. I was surprised that Sylvia hadn't left any. Usually when I was on the road, she called every few hours. I assumed that now we were engaged, she didn't think she needed to check in with me as often as she used to.

I almost threw up when I saw that the only other message on my phone was a text from Lola. It was just as annoying as all the others she'd sent.

> **Hello, Calvin. I hope all is well with you. I can't wait to hear from you again.**

That silly bitch. Since she was not going to be around much longer, I thought it would be nice to make her final days a little more enjoyable. It was almost midnight, so I assumed she'd be in bed and wouldn't see my response until she got up the next morning. I texted her back:

> **Can't wait to see you again too. I'm on the road and will call you in a day or so.**

I was horrified when the stupid cow texted me again a few moments later!

Chapter 22
Lola

MY FINGERS WERE MOVING AT LIGHTNING SPEED ON MY CELL phone keyboard as I typed:

Hello Calvin! Thanks for responding to my message. Have a blessed night!

It was after midnight, but I stayed up another hour hoping he would reply before I went to sleep. He didn't, and I was not too disappointed. I knew that he would have, if he had been able to. He had always been up-front with me about how "busy" he often was. And I never doubted him. With his weird work schedule and his activities as a member of Discreet Encounters, there was no telling what all was going on with him. For all I knew, his cell phone battery might have died or been too low for him to text me back right away.

I finally turned off my phone. After a trip to the bathroom, I padded downstairs to get a glass of milk. I returned to my room and glanced at a few pages of *Brides* magazine.

I soon fell asleep and had the most ominous nightmare I'd ever had. I saw my dead body lying in a coffin. And somebody had dressed me in a yellow shroud. There were a lot of people in black outfits standing nearby, but the only face I recognized was Calvin's. He was dressed in black too as he hovered over my coffin, *laughing*. The dream was so disturbing it woke me up. My gown was saturated with sweat from top to bottom. "What the hell was that all about?" I asked myself out loud. I had dreams almost every night, and most of them were very pleasant, but every now and then I had one that made no sense at all. Among the stack of books on my nightstand was one entitled *How to An-alyze Your Dreams*. It had helped me interpret some of my previous dreams, but it didn't help this time. I scrambled out of bed and opened my window to cool off and get some fresh air. I fanned my face with my *Brides* magazine for five minutes. I wasn't in the mood to read anymore, so I went back downstairs to get something else to drink. After a shot of vodka, I went to bed and prayed that if I had another dream it would not be a bad one. My prayers were answered. I had a very erotic dream.

When I woke up before daylight, I couldn't remember all the details of my last dream, but I could remember that I'd had multiple orgasms with Calvin and he had asked me to marry him. I forgot all about the bad dream. Now I was in a very good mood. If a dream about him proposing to me sent me to cloud nine, I wondered how I'd react when he actually did do it.

"Why are you smiling so much this morning, Lola?" Libby asked as I joined the family at the breakfast table a few minutes past eight.

"What's wrong with me smiling?" I cleared my throat and kept my happy face. There was a platter of grilled ham and beef bacon, a coffeepot, a huge bowl of grits with steam rising above it like a smoke signal, and a tray with a stack of toast on the table. The only empty seat was the one next to Libby. As usual, her appearance was very hard on my eyes. She wore a ratty terry cloth bathrobe, and there was a doo-rag wrapped around her knotty head. The scowl she often displayed was on her face. It didn't even faze me this time.

"Let me give you some advice, Lola," Jeffrey said with a wink as he stirred his coffee. "Smile and the world smiles with you, cry and you cry alone."

"Amen," Bertha said, giving me a pensive look. "Lola, Elbert called a little while ago."

I sighed, rolled my eyes, and said, "Again?"

"Yes, he called 'again.' And you ought to be thanking the good

Lord that he keeps calling. A normal man would have given up on a woman who always seems to have other things to do almost every time he calls," Bertha added.

"Humph! Then Elbert Porter must not be normal," Libby said with a smirk.

"I guess he's not." I smirked back. "I told him from the get-go that I had other men friends, and I remind him of that all the time."

"Then how come one of your other men friends ain't married you yet? And how come we never see your other men friends?" Kevin asked with a snicker. "Elbert is the only one who's been here to see you since we moved in. Your other boyfriends must be hella ugly."

Before I could respond, Jeffrey jumped in. "Boy, finish your breakfast so you can get your ass to school. And don't ever let me hear you talk to a grown woman the way you just talked to Lola. Do you hear me?"

"Yeah, Daddy," Kevin mumbled with his head bowed.

Libby picked up where Kevin left off. "Since we are already on the subject, how come Elbert is the only man friend of yours who ever comes to the house, Lola?" she asked. "What happened to that truck driver you told us about?"

"I've been meaning to ask you that same thing myself," Bertha eased in. "Did he run off already?"

My chest tightened. I wanted to cuss out everybody except Jeffrey, but that would have been out of character for me. Instead, I just shrugged and said, "No, Calvin didn't 'run off' already. He's just been real busy lately. Um . . . he told me that things will slow down for him in a couple of weeks. I'll invite him to dinner and I'm sure he'll be glad to come over and meet everybody." If Calvin didn't accept my invitation, I had to come up with a real good lie. I couldn't save face if I said he was no longer interested in me or that he didn't want to meet my family. The only lie I could come up with that would prevent them from giving me a hard time was to say he had suddenly died.

Chapter 23
Calvin

SYLVIA AND I ATTENDED A WONDERFUL EASTER SERVICE AT CHURCH yesterday, and we had lunch at Olive Garden. She suggested a movie afterward. She was a huge Vin Diesel fan so I took her to see *Furious 7*. We spent the rest of the evening at her place kicked back with a bottle of wine. It had been a long, hectic day, so when I went to my place I was so tired I didn't turn on my TV or computer.

When I got up this morning and checked my messages, there was one from Lola that she had sent yesterday with a dancing Easter bunny attached. In response to that bunny bullshit, I sent her a text with nothing except one of her favorite symbols: ☺ You would have thought that I'd sent her a picture of my dick. She immediately responded back: ☺☺☺☺. That Lola. Was there no end to her foolishness? I didn't want her to think I had time for childish games but no time to hook up with her, so I decided to wait a few days before I got back to her.

I didn't have to worry about Sylvia riding my back too much since she was so busy planning our wedding. She was very busy at the drugstore pharmacy, where she had recently been promoted to senior pharmacist. She also liked to spend time with her family and friends. That didn't bother me at all, because my plate was just as full as hers. In addition to work and other activities, I liked to play poker, fish, and attend ball games with some of my buddies. And, because I was so popular with some of the

Discreet Encounters babes, my sexual encounters took up a lot of my time.

Five days after Lola's multiple smiley face text, I had still not responded to it. A few minutes after six p.m. I grabbed a beer and flopped down on my living room couch. I turned on my laptop and went to the club's website to check out the recent blogs and reviews. I got a kick out of reading about some of the other members' dating adventures. Some of the new posts were so steamy, my crotch started throbbing and I had to do something about it. I checked the availability of a few local members to see if we could get together in the next hour or so.

None of the women I was interested in were free, so I kept browsing. The ones in the next batch weren't available either, so I gave up. It looked like I wasn't going to have another discreet encounter for a while. I decided to check my club in-box to see if any new messages had come in since I'd checked an hour ago. I couldn't believe my luck! I had received a date request from a club member just a few minutes prior. She lived in Tijuana, Mexico, and her club screen name was "RedHot." And she was definitely on fire. Maria Gonzalez and I had dated several times. She worked as a tour guide for a big travel agency in Tijuana, so she could take free trips. We usually hooked up when I had to make hauls to businesses close to the border. But one time I'd wanted to be with her so badly after I'd delivered merchandise to a department store in San Diego, I rented a car and drove to Mexico. The following month, she'd flown to Long Beach to spend the night with me. This woman was amazing. Each time with her was better than the last. It had been a month since we had communicated, so I was glad to hear from her. Her message was short, simple, and sweet:

Hola, RamRod! I will be in the States on the 21st of this month and would love to get together so you can cool me off. RedHot

"Damn!" I said sharply. I slapped the side of my computer monitor. Sylvia was going to be on vacation for a few days that same week and wanted to ride shotgun with me on my run down to San Ysidro to drop off some patio furniture. I had already told her it was okay. One reason I had agreed to her request was that I didn't want to pick up another hitchhiker. I had enjoyed the last kill so much, I wanted to do it again real soon—but not too soon. I needed to cool off for a while. I wanted to wait at least another week or two before my next murder. I hoped it would also be the last one: Lola. She was going to die before the end of the month!

In the meantime, I had to settle for something a little less fulfilling. I didn't know how I was going to swing it, but I had to figure out a way to see Maria when I got to San Ysidro. I grabbed my phone and pulled up Sylvia's number.

"Hey, baby," she cooed. "I was just thinking about you."

"I was just thinking about you too. Are you still planning to accompany me to San Ysidro?"

"Of course! I hope we get a chance to spend some time at the beach and do some shopping. And we definitely have to treat ourselves to a romantic dinner. I've always heard that when a Mexican restaurant in the States is close to the border, the food is more authentic and the margaritas are to die for. I'll Google some restaurants and check their ratings so we can go to the best one."

"Baby, we won't have time to do all that. After I complete my delivery, I have to meet with one of the district managers. I just got off the phone with him."

"Oh, Calvin. I was really looking forward to riding down the coast with you and hanging out at some of the fun places along the border. We'll only be in San Ysidro overnight, now this. What's the meeting about? Is something wrong?"

"Oh, it's nothing like that. Mr. Donnelly just wants to go over some new contract bullshit. This dude is so long-winded, he'll tie me up for hours. He likes to drink, so after our meeting he's taking me to his favorite bar."

"Didn't you tell him you had already made plans?"

"Baby, I couldn't do that. When he called, he had already reserved one of our district offices for the meeting. The company recently came up with all kinds of new stuff that I have to be brought up-to-date on. Union rules for one. Not to mention information regarding my retirement benefits and other necessary shit."

"What about your coworkers?"

"What about my coworkers?"

"Why don't you get one of them to take notes and share them with you?"

"This is a one-on-one meeting. Since I'm a senior driver, I'll be taking notes to share with some of the new drivers."

"That sure is one hell of a tacky way to do business. If this new information is so important, they should have all the truckers attend this damn meeting at the same time."

"I agree with you completely. Trucking is a tacky business. That's the way of the blue-collar world, baby."

"Well, I still don't like it. Can we do something before or after your meeting? I don't want to go to the beach or to dinner alone. And I sure don't want to sit around in a hotel room and twiddle my thumbs while you're at that meeting."

"It can't be helped this time. I love my job and I want to keep it. Besides, my performance review is coming up in a couple of weeks, so I need to be on my best behavior. The last thing I need to do is cancel an important meeting so I can run up and down a beach and suck up margaritas. If you don't want to go to a restaurant alone, you can get something to go and eat it in our hotel room."

"Okay. All right then. I don't care how late you get out of your meeting; I want to do at least one fun thing. We can have a late dinner and a few drinks before we leave, I hope. And we can give our hotel bed a real good workout. Otherwise, there is no point in me riding in that damn truck all the way down there." I bit my bottom lip because that was exactly what I was thinking. I held my breath and hoped she'd cancel. "But I promised you I'd go, and I know how much it means to you."

"Sure, sweetheart. We'll figure out a way to do something

after my meeting. I need to give a call to my supervisor now to see if there's anything he wants me to bring up in the meeting. I'll talk to you later."

"Don't hang up yet!" Sylvia ordered. "I have something I need to ask."

"What is it?"

She hesitated for a few moments. "Do you really love me?"

I shook my head and rolled my eyes. I answered immediately. "You know I do."

"Sometimes I wonder about it."

"Well, you need to stop wondering about that. I love you, Sylvia. Happy?"

"Uh-huh. Can you come over and spend the night? Since our upcoming trip is not going to be what I expected, I'd like to spend some quality time with you now. Besides, I've been feeling kind of sad all day."

"Oh? Did something happen?"

"Not to me. Remember that newspaper article we read a while back about those three missing black women?"

"Vaguely. Why? Do the cops have any leads yet?"

"Not a one. It's like those women vanished into thin air. Anyway, they were mentioned again on the TV evening news yesterday. The brother of one of the women came into the pharmacy today to get a prescription filled."

"How did you know who he was?"

"I waited on him. While I was ringing him up, he identified himself. The medication he was picking up was for his severe depression. Not knowing what happened to his sister is slowly destroying his family. The mother was having such a hard time coping, she cried herself to sleep one night last month and never woke up."

"Hmmm. That's a sad story, but you can't let other people's problems get to you. This is a crazy world and it's going to get even crazier. If you let every tragic thing you hear about bother you, you're going to end up needing medication yourself."

"You're right, baby. Forget I brought it up."

"Would it make you feel any better if I spent the night?"

"It sure would. That's why I asked you to."

"All right. I'll see you in a few."

I hung up and dialed Maria's number. She didn't answer, so I left a voice mail. "Hey, *mamacita*! I can't wait to see you so I can put out that fire between your legs. I won't get down there on the twenty-first until around five or so. Just let me know what time and where to meet you."

Chapter 24
Joan

*I*DIDN'T KNOW IF IT WAS JUST MY IMAGINATION OR IF REED WAS TRY-ing to change for the better. I was so curious and concerned about his behavior, I called his office at ten o'clock this morning to see if he wanted to have lunch with me. I wanted to monitor him more closely for the next few days so I could determine if there was something for me to worry about. After a long pause, his receptionist told me that he had called in sick two hours earlier.

"He called in sick?" I asked. I was so taken aback, I held the telephone away from my ear and looked at it for a few seconds before I continued. "This is his wife," I said firmly.

"I . . . I . . . know . . . know it's you, Mrs. Riley," the receptionist sputtered. "Would you like to leave a message?"

"No, I don't want to leave a message!" I hollered. I had to pause and catch my breath. "Beverly, I'm sorry. I didn't mean to yell at you," I apologized. "Reed left home this morning at his usual time and he didn't say anything to me about being sick."

"Maybe he felt better after I spoke to him and he changed his mind and went someplace else," she offered. Beverly had been with Reed longer than any of his other staff. She was so dependable and loyal, there was no doubt in my mind that she would lie to protect him.

"Did he sound sick?"

"Not really. But like I said, maybe he felt better after he spoke to me."

"Maybe he did," I mumbled. "Can you do me a favor?"

Beverly took her time answering. "Um . . . yeah."

"Don't tell him I called."

"I won't."

I hung up and called Lola. She didn't answer, so I left a voice mail message. "As soon as you get a chance, call me back. Reed is acting very mysteriously."

She returned my call when she took her lunch break at noon. "Reed is acting mysteriously? Please don't tell me the man is on another one of his suicide missions," she said. She sounded even more concerned than I was.

"I don't know what he's up to, but something is not right."

"When did you notice?"

"I first noticed it a few weeks ago. Lately I've been noticing it more and more. When he left to go to his office this morning, he was in an extremely jolly mood for him."

"So?"

"So, that's out of character. Especially early in the morning. He usually leaves for work looking and acting like a pallbearer. I called his office a couple of hours ago to see if he wanted to meet me for lunch. His receptionist told me he had called in sick. What I want to know is where he went if he didn't go to his office."

Lola remained silent for a few moments. "Hmmm. Have you tried to reach him on his cell phone?"

"Yes, and my call went straight to voice mail."

"What about his answering service?"

"I didn't think to call her, and I won't. If he's somewhere he shouldn't be, she wouldn't know. I told his receptionist not to let him know I called. He'll think I'm checking up on him, and that's the last thing I want him to think."

"Joan, you *are* checking up on the man. And it's about time. He's been 'checking up' on you for years."

"This is the first time he's ever done anything out of the ordinary," I defended.

"This is the first time that you know of."

I swallowed hard and considered Lola's words. "Now that I

think about it, he's been doing a few other things out of character for several weeks now. Reed used to hate going to his office
before nine a.m. and staying later than five p.m. He's been
doing both now, one or two days a week, for the past couple of
months. He's also been going out for drinks with people I've
never heard of. And one night last week after we had gone to
bed, I woke up around midnight and he was nowhere in sight.
When he came home an hour later, he claimed he'd gone to the
drugstore to get something to help him sleep. The one we usually go to is only two blocks from here. When I called him on it,
he claimed he had left his wallet at his office and had to go pick
it up because he didn't have any money or credit cards on him.
I didn't give it all that much thought until today."

"Hmmm. I don't want you to think I'm defending Reed, but
that doesn't sound too suspicious to me. I've gone out in the
middle of the night to pick up something, and I've left my wallet
at work before. You don't have a lot to go on, but I can understand you feeling the way you do. What do you think he's up to?"

"Oh no!" I yelled. My heart skipped a beat, and blood rushed
to my face.

"What's the matter?"

I had to gulp some air before I could continue. "Right after
his suicide attempt, I read several articles on the subject. One
said that shortly before some people commit suicide, they go
through a period of elation. They have mood swings from one
extreme to the other."

"You mean they become bipolar or something?"

"I don't know if being bipolar has anything to do with it. And
as far as I know, Reed is not bipolar. The article said that when a
person decides to end his or her life, they might get slaphappy
because they know that when they die, they will no longer be in
pain. So leading up to that moment, they go around looking
and acting happier than ever."

"And Reed's been doing that?"

"Yeah," I managed in a low, nervous tone. Then I got loud.
"Oh shit! Lola, I don't want the man to die! What if he checked

into a hotel today to do it? One thing he promised me after his first attempt was that if he ever does it again, he would not do it at home where his son might be the one to find him!"

"Don't get hysterical yet. I'm sure it's not what you think. Have you called his parents? What about some of his friends?"

"I haven't called his parents. That's the last thing I want to do. They'd drive up here in a flash, and you know I can't stand my mother-in-law. Hold on! Somebody's coming in the door." I wobbled up off the couch, with my eyes on the door. I breathed a sigh of relief when Reed walked in. "It's him. I'll call you back." I set the telephone on the coffee table and put my hands on my hips. "Where the hell—" I stopped talking when I saw a large bouquet of red roses in his hand. "Where have you been? And what's this about you telling your receptionist you were sick?"

"That's what I told Beverly to tell you," Reed said gently as he strolled over and handed me the roses.

"Why? And what are these roses for?"

"I know how much you like roses, and the last time I gave you some was on Valentine's Day." He sighed and rubbed the side of his head. Then he put his arms around my waist. "Honey, I know I've been acting like a damn fool lately, and I'm sorry. With work and my parents complaining about their health every time I talk to them, I had a lot on my mind. I just needed a little time to myself, that's all. I drove around for a while, went to the museum, and then I took a break for lunch."

"And you couldn't tell me that?"

He gently pulled me to the couch, and we sat down at the same time. I set the bouquet on the coffee table. "On top of everything else that's bothering me, I've been feeling like shit ever since I told you that you were losing your shape and looks and needed to sharpen your bedroom skills."

"So you didn't mean any of that?" I snarled.

"Well . . . I . . . you used to give me some mean blow jobs!" he boomed. "Now after a few half-ass slurps, it's all over. And you don't move the way you used to. If you want to keep me happy, you're going to have to work at it. You're too young to be going through some kind of female-related issue that would cause you to lie there like a blow-up doll when we make love. So there's got to be another reason. . . ."

My heart dropped and my stomach turned. All kinds of outrageous thoughts began to float around in my head. It was on the tip of my tongue to tell Reed how many other men I'd been with in the past few months who couldn't stop telling me how good I was in bed! "Are you going to accuse me of cheating again?"

"No, I know you're not cheating on me. I just think you're bored with me, that's all. I know I'm no ball of fire like some of your other boyfriends probably were before we got married. And I never will be. But starting today, things are going to be different. I won't badger you about all the time you spend away from home, and I won't do or say anything inappropriate."

"Until the next time."

Reed shook his head. "There won't be a next time. You can go shopping with Lola and your relatives, play nursemaid to that invalid woman, have drinks with Lola, and go to book club meetings. I think we should give each other more space and spend more time doing things with other people."

I gave Reed a skeptical look. "So you'll be spending more time at the golf course and the country club with some of your colleagues and friends, right?"

"Uh-huh. As a matter of fact, Dr. Weinstein invited me to go hiking this coming weekend. I hope you don't mind."

This time I gave him a curious look. He had never shown any interest in hiking. He hated gnats, mosquitoes, and every other creature associated with the outdoors. "I don't mind. I think Junior would like to go too."

"Don't you remember? Junior wants to spend this weekend with my parents."

"I forgot about that. Well, with you two boogers out of my hair, I can get some chores done that I've been putting off."

"You can start by putting your flowers in a vase." Reed stood up and glanced toward the door. "Um . . . I forgot to pick up the newspaper while I was out, so I'm going to go do that now."

When he left, I called Lola again. "I think Reed's going through a midlife crisis," I told her with a chuckle when she answered.

"Why? And where did he go if he didn't go to his office today?"

When I told her everything Reed had told me, she laughed louder than I did.

Chapter 25
Lola

*I*T HAD BEEN THREE DAYS SINCE I'D LAST TEXTED CALVIN, AND HE had not responded. He was busy, but because of the things he'd told me and the way he'd made love to me, I knew he wanted to be with me as much as I wanted to be with him. He was the man I hoped to spend forty or fifty years with, so I told myself to be patient. But it was not easy.

It was nine p.m. Sunday, and I was in my room for the night. Whenever I had spare time, I read the blog on the club's website to see what other members were up to. Every now and then somebody reported a bad encounter and wanted to warn the rest of us. But most of the club members liked to boast about previous or upcoming encounters. I didn't see anything of interest to me this time. Just as I was about to click on another page, a comment from a Latina in Tijuana, Mexico, caught my attention. Her screen name was "RedHot," and she was "into Black men," so I got real curious. I immediately clicked on her profile so I could check out her picture. I expected to see a middle-age, plump, plain Jane who worked in a sweatshop or on a pig farm. I couldn't believe my eyes. Not only was she the most beautiful female I'd ever seen, she was only twenty-one. And if that wasn't bad enough, that heifer bragged about an upcoming date she had scheduled with RamRod. That was Calvin's screen name! My ego suffered a massive blow.

I could hardly contain myself, but I did. I had to. Whomever

Calvin slept with was his business, not mine, and vice versa, but that wasn't enough to keep me from getting jealous. I knew he spent time with other women. I just didn't want to read about it. One reason was, it made me want him even more. I thought that if he read about one of *my* upcoming hookups, he would feel the same way. The only problem was, I didn't have any new dates scheduled.

I clicked on my club in-box and was pleased to see that I had received three date requests since I'd checked three hours ago. The first one was from a man in Gary, Indiana, who claimed he owned several apartment buildings. He was in his late sixties. I had never seen a man in his age group that I wanted to sleep with, but I pulled up his profile anyway. When I saw his lanky body, gray beard, and long horse face, I knew I didn't want to spend any time with this man. The second one was a much better prospect. Jason "HappyPants" McFarland was a thirty-five-year-old banker from Charleston, South Carolina, who was in California on business. In his lengthy message, he raved about how hot I looked. He was not nearly as handsome as Calvin, but his looks were passable. And the reviews that other members had posted about him were spectacular. I Googled him anyway. He was not just a banker, he was the president of the bank he worked for. I replied right away. He responded about an hour later and included his cell phone number and the name of his hotel. I called him immediately. His deep, sexy voice and cute Southern accent gave me goose bumps, but what he said half a minute into the conversation turned me off.

"You're real pretty for a black woman," he told me, speaking in a serious tone. I'd been with lots of men—black, white, and everything in between—and this was the first time one had said something so ignorant and offensive to me.

"For a black woman?" I shot back, with my ears burning. "Can you explain what you mean by that?"

"I sure enough will, sugar. White women are the most beautiful and desirable women on the planet. From the beginning of time, envious women of other races have tried to imitate them.

Like all the sisters and Latinas running around with fake blond hair looking like clowns and whatnot. Know what I'm saying?"

"Sure, I know exactly what you're saying, *brother*," I replied with my voice dripping with sarcasm. I rolled my eyes and shook my head so hard my brain felt as if it had shifted. "Well, if you're a black man into white women, why in the hell are you trying to get a date with a *black* woman?"

"It's been a long time since I dated one, and my family—straight-up country folks—keep getting on me about turning my back on my race since the bank made me president. I love my family, and lately I've been feeling guilty about disappointing them. Eventually, I hope to meet a black woman suitable enough for me to settle down with. I want to get my folks off my back. I thought it was time to reacquaint myself with sisters and get back in the groove by going on a few dates with a woman like you."

"A woman like me?" This was the second stupid thing a man had ever said to me, and all in the same conversation!

"I think the best way for me to get back in the swing of things with black women, bedroom-wise, is to hook up with a few who specialize in such activities."

"Maybe I shouldn't say this, but it sounds like you'd do a lot better calling an escort service."

"An escort service? *Pffft!* I've never paid for sex before in my life!"

"Then maybe you should try another sister in the club." Silence followed for about ten seconds. "Are you still there?"

"I'm still here. So you're saying you don't want to spend any time with me?"

"That's right," I said gently. "Maybe if—" Before I could finish my sentence, I heard him click off.

I was determined to arrange a date, so I responded to the only other request in my inbox that sounded remotely interesting. Lester "HotDog" Mitchum was a real estate tycoon from Columbus, Ohio. He had come to California to scope out some property for one of his clients. And, he reminded me of the model, Tyson Beckford, one of the hottest black men on the planet, in my book. I Googled Lester and was impressed with his background. He was divorced; had two sons in law school; and his family owned property in Ohio, New York, and Florida. A friend had turned him on to Discreet Encounters, and he couldn't rave enough about all the "great fun" he had experienced so far. Despite all he had going for him, the reviews that had been posted about him were only average. I sent him a message anyway, and we set up a date for next Friday night.

I immediately posted the information on the club's blog. Calvin had told me that he read the comments a few times a week, so I knew he'd see it in the next day or so. I wanted him to know that I was still going strong.

Chapter 26
Lola

*I*HAD NOT SPOKEN TO JOAN SINCE OUR CONVERSATION ABOUT REED'S mysterious behavior. We'd been playing phone tag, leaving voice mail messages and sending texts ever since then. I was anxious to see or talk to her again.

Today was like every other Friday at the store—busy and so boring I couldn't wait for five o'clock to arrive so I could rush home and get ready for my date.

At eleven, I gave Joan another call, and this time she answered. I invited her to have lunch with me because I had something funny to tell her. "Can't you tell me over the phone?" she asked.

"I could, but I won't. I'd like to see the look on your face when I tell you."

She met me at Jenny's Kitchen at noon. Before we started eating our ham sandwiches, I bragged about the date I'd set up with the real estate mogul. She howled with laughter when I told her about the banker and what he'd said about me being pretty "for a black woman."

"Thanks for alerting me about that jackass. There's a message in my in-box that he sent last night."

"Humph! I see he's not wasting any time trying to hook up with a black woman. I'm surprised he waited this long."

"That's probably because he's tried every other black woman in the club already and they turned him down."

"Unless you're hard up for some action this weekend, I advise you to ignore that fool."

"Don't worry. I already have something lined up with one of my regulars, but I'm not sure I'm going to go. I'm not really in a dating mood right now." These were words I never expected to hear from Joan.

"*You* aren't in a dating mood?" I snickered. "I guess hell must have frozen over."

"Please don't tease me," Joan said with a pout. "I get enough of that from my family." She bit into her sandwich and started chewing like a cow. I took a plug out of mine and did the same thing.

I waited until we had both swallowed our food and sipped some lemonade before I spoke again. "I'm sorry." I cleared my throat and gave her an apologetic look. "Which regular? And why do you think you might not go?"

"DrFeelGood is back in town and according to him, he's 'dying' to spend a few hours with me again." "DrFeelGood" was Ezra Spoor, one of the most prominent plastic surgeons in the state of Florida and Joan's frequent sex partner. "I would love to spend some time with him, but I'm worried about Reed. I don't know if it's a good idea to leave him alone for a few hours Saturday afternoon."

"So he's still acting peculiar?"

"Uh-huh. Last night he said something that really disturbed me."

"What?"

"He told me that he's enjoyed being married to me. Then he babbled on about how much fun we *used* to have. . . ."

"What's so disturbing about that?"

"He was talking about us in the past tense. As if one of us is not going to be around much longer."

"I wish you wouldn't talk like that. Like I said before, I think you're making something out of nothing. If Reed is in a more cheerful mood than he usually is, like you told me the other day, enjoy it while you can. I really don't think you need to be too concerned about him committing suicide."

"You're right. I should know by now not to jump to conclu-sions when it comes to Reed. I think I will keep my date with the good doctor. At least it'll be a distraction so I won't have to think about Reed." Joan gulped and said in a loud and happy tone. "Oh shit! I just remembered that Reed's going hiking with Dr. Weinstein this weekend!"

"That's even better. You can spend even more time with your 'nothing but A-list celebrity clients plastic surgeon' from Palm Beach." I laughed. "I'll give you a call tomorrow and we'll have a long chat about the date I'm going on tonight. That is, if Bertha's not breathing down my neck all day."

"She does that every day," Joan said impatiently.

"Some days she does it more than others. Especially lately. She's been riding my back all week about cleaning out the ga-rage and doing a bunch of other chores around the house. Last night after work when I stopped off at the mall, she called my cell phone twice. When I didn't answer, she called the stores I had told her I was going to. If I tell her I'm going to be with you tonight, she might bug you, or even come to your house the way Reed did the last time you told him you and I were going shopping. I told Bertha this morning that I was going to visit a winery with Lana Brooks this evening."

Joan finished her lemonade and let out a mild burp. She ex-cused herself and gave me a puzzled look. "I just remembered something. Lana married that hot Italian musician two years ago and moved to Rome. She hasn't been back here since. Why are you using her as your alibi instead of me?"

"With you being so worried about Reed, I didn't want to add to your load right now. There is no way Bertha can track Lana down. God, how I wish it was Calvin I was going to see tonight. I'm going to go crazy if I don't find out soon where our rela-tionship is going."

Joan rolled her eyes and gave me an exasperated look. "I was hoping we'd have a conversation that didn't include him. The man you need to focus on is that hot real estate tycoon you're going to be with later. This morning I read what you posted on the club's blog about your upcoming date with him, so I checked out his profile. He's better looking than Calvin and he has a lot more going for him. Calvin is . . . well, I'm sure he's a nice person, but after all, he is only a truck driver."

"He's 'only a truck driver' to you, but he's a lot more than that to me, Joan!" I snapped. "It's been years since I cared about a man half as much as I care about Calvin." I stopped talking because I'd almost lost my breath. I composed myself and continued, speaking in a sterner tone. I wanted to make sure Joan knew she'd pushed the wrong button. "I could say a lot more, but I won't. You've heard it all before, so I don't have to keep telling you how much I want to be with Calvin. A woman who lives in Mexico bragged on the blog about her upcoming date with him, so I checked out her profile. Girl, that horny Latina is barely out of her teens. And she looks like Salma Hayek, Jennifer Lopez, and Sofía Vergara all rolled into one."

"Ouch! That's so painful! I saw her post this morning and I checked out her profile too. I agree with everything you just said. If she was a hurricane, she'd be a category five. I was waiting for you to bring her up." Joan sighed and squeezed my hand. "Look at it this way—at the end of the day it's not a big deal. In the first place, we're in a sex club and hooking up with other members is what we all do. You know from the reviews that a lot of women have slept with Calvin—and will continue to do so as long as he's in the club. If it bothers you, stop obsessing over him and look for a soul mate who is *not* in a sex club."

"I wish I could. Some days I wish I'd never answered his first message. But I'm glad I did, because in spite of everything, I still think he's the one for me."

Chapter 27
Calvin

*I*T WAS AMAZING HOW MUCH A WOMAN COULD CHANGE IN JUST A FEW weeks. Since I'd proposed to Sylvia last month, she had lost at least ten pounds—which she could not afford to lose—and she was beginning to show her age. Despite her body looking like a beanpole now, and the new lines on her face, she was still attractive and had a lot to offer a man like me. She was from a good family, but they were some of the most annoying people I knew. I tolerated them because they catered to me almost as much as Sylvia did. I also liked that she made good money as a pharmacist. She loved her job, so I didn't have to worry about her giving it up anytime soon and leaving all our financial responsibilities to me. It was hard to find a woman with more going for her than Sylvia. I often told myself, and other people told me as well, that I couldn't have chosen a better woman to marry.

But Sylvia was still not enough for me.

I couldn't wait for Tuesday to come so I could get my hands on RedHot Maria.

It was Friday evening, a few minutes past seven. I was in my bed with my head propped up on two pillows, and my laptop was in my lap. I was browsing news links on recent crimes along the interstate. Other than a few road rage incidents and several accidents that had been caused by drunk or careless drivers, there was nothing of interest to me this time. So far, there had been no mention of any nosy hiker or busybody road worker stumbling across Melanie's body.

Sylvia had stopped by on her way home from work and we'd made love an hour ago. As usual, she had already dozed off. She looked so peaceful lying next to me with locks of her thick hair covering one side of her round face.

One of the few things I didn't like about Sylvia was that she had become a light sleeper in the last couple of years. When I coughed to clear my throat, she abruptly opened her eyes and mumbled some gibberish. She sat bolt upright and looked at me with a dazed expression on her face. "I'm sorry, honey. I forgot where I was," she slurred.

"Well, thanks a lot," I mock whined. "I guess I've lost my touch if you can forget I'm in the same bed with you after all we did a little while ago. Did you forget about that too?"

"*Pffft!*" Sylvia gave me a dismissive wave and a harsh look. "Oh, don't be such a crybaby. You know when I go to sleep, I'm off in another world. That's what you get for letting me drink three beers in a row." She kissed my cheek and squeezed the soft bulge between my legs. "You're still fiddling around on the Internet? How come you've been doing so much of that lately? What's up?" she asked, squinting as she glanced at my monitor screen.

"Nothing's up, baby. I missed the evening news on TV today and a couple of days last week. With so much going on in the world these days, I like to stay informed. One of my coworkers got robbed at gunpoint at a truck stop on his run down to Encino last week."

"That's a damn shame. Was he hurt?"

"Nope." I waved my hand as I logged off and closed my computer. "The same dude was involved in a road-rage incident with a carload of drunken punks a few weeks before that."

A concerned look crossed Sylvia's face. "Honey, I know you enjoy your work, but do you ever think about doing something different? Being a long-haul truck driver is not like it used to be years ago. It's bad enough that you don't work regular hours and days, but it's getting more and more dangerous out there too. Yesterday, I read that a woman's body was found along the side of the highway south of Sacramento. And she's not the first one! A few months ago, some campers found the skeleton of another woman in a ditch in the same area. That's one of your routes! I had no idea it was so dangerous!"

"Dangerous for women, maybe; but I've never had any trouble."

"Anyway, the killer didn't rape or rob this woman I read about yesterday, but he took her engraved class ring. That maniac was so vicious, he didn't just strangle that poor woman; he twisted her neck and turned her head completely around. The cops said it was the most bizarre thing they had ever seen. They even called in the FBI because they think a serial killer might be on the loose in that area."

"Why do they think that?"

"According to the FBI profiler they interviewed, most serial killers usually don't start out doing something too extreme to their first few victims. Especially something as gruesome as twisting a person's head all the way around. He thinks that the maniac who killed the hitchhiker has killed before and will do it again if he's not stopped. With the FBI involved, it's just a matter of time before they catch that bastard. And when they do, I hope they send his ass straight to death row."

I gulped and silently cursed myself. I *was* slipping. First, the careless shit in Vegas and now something that had attracted the goddamn FBI! If I had not twisted that bitch's head around, it would have looked like just another run-of-the-mill strangulation, something that anybody could have done. I was so glad I had almost completed my mission. Lola's murder would definitely be my *grand* finale. "Hmmm, I read the paper almost every day. I wonder how I missed that story."

"I almost missed it myself. It was just a paragraph at the bottom of page four."

"I'm surprised that I haven't come across anything about it on any of the news sites I've been Googling lately."

"Well, I guess you didn't look long or hard enough." Sylvia yawned and scrambled out of bed. "I'm going to fix myself a sandwich. You want a snack? You look hungry. I can fix you something before I leave."

"Yeah. I guess I could use a bite or two. If you don't mind, could you make me a BLT on rye?"

"Calvin, you know I don't mind. As long as you don't mind waiting a few minutes for me to cook the bacon."

"Take as much time as you need," I said.

As soon as Sylvia left the room, I got back on my computer and went straight to Google. This time I searched using words that were more to the point than ones I had previously used: murdered woman found with head turned completely around. A link popped up right away, and I clicked on a report that was only two paragraphs long. My eyes burned as I read about my latest crime. I was pleased to know that the cops had no leads and the FBI agents were baffled. I was surprised that those grandstanding show-offs would admit being "baffled." The article went on to say that a lot of crimes committed on the highways rarely got solved. The victim, thirty-three-year-old Melanie Crukshank, had a lengthy criminal record. She had outstanding warrants in three states for everything from armed robbery to attempted murder. She had even been arrested for allegedly smothering a meddlesome elderly neighbor to death. The case had been dropped on a technicality. Now I knew I didn't have to worry about the cops spending too much time trying to find Melanie's killer. She had probably committed more crimes than I had! I'd done the world a favor by getting rid of her. I chuckled and rubbed my hands together.

I glanced toward the door. I could smell the bacon cooking and I could hear Sylvia in the kitchen humming some silly tune. I logged onto the Discreet Encounters website. I grinned when I saw that Maria had left a post on the blog about how excited she was about our upcoming date. My grin turned to a grimace when I saw a post that Lola had left about a date she had scheduled for tonight. "Stay busy, bitch," I whispered as I glared at her stupid, rambling post. "The more dudes you fool around with, the better. When they find your skanky body, the list of suspects will be so long, the cops will have to work overtime."

Chapter 28
Lola

MOST PEOPLE WHO WORKED WEEKDAYS LOOKED FORWARD TO Friday, but I didn't. Since Libby moved in, it had become my least favorite day of the week. Spending the weekend in the house with her was torture. I was so glad I had a date for tonight. If I had a good time, it would be easier to get through Saturday and Sunday.

When I got home from work that evening, Libby was stretched out on the living room couch watching a game show. She was still in her bathrobe. Several beer cans and a McDonald's bag were on the coffee table in front of her. I smiled and greeted her as I walked by, but all she did was shrug her shoulders. She didn't even look up at me. What Jeffrey saw in her was a mystery to me. He had everything going for him, so I couldn't understand why he had settled for a frump like Libby. Not only was he good-looking and pleasant to everybody, he made good money as a firefighter and he eagerly helped with the household bills. He also did a lot of maintenance work around the house, and he was useful in other ways. Libby and Kevin were two of the biggest, laziest deadweights I knew. Not once had Bertha asked them to help us clean out the garage, or anything else for that matter. I had cleaned off the porch all by myself, and I couldn't understand why Bertha kept talking about "us" doing this and doing that when I was the one doing it all. She had so many other things on her plate, I never said a word about her not lifting a finger to help me clean off the porch. I had a feeling I'd be the only one cleaning out the garage, the kitchen closet, and all the other places she had been complaining about for the past few months. I didn't mind doing so many chores by myself, but only if I could do them when I felt like it. And this Friday evening I did not feel like it.

Other than wondering when I was going to see or talk to Calvin again, the main thing on my mind now was the date I was about to get ready for. Lester and I had agreed to get together at seven p.m.

Bertha was cooking one of my favorite meals: collard greens and deep fried chicken. It was a wonderful break from the chitlins and pigs feet that she had been cooking several times a month since I was a teenager.

"That sure smells good," I commented as I entered the kitchen.

"Thank you, sweetie. After dinner, we can get to work cleaning out the garage or the kitchen closet," she told me. She looked so serene standing over the stove in her heavily starched apron stirring butter into the cooking oil heating up in the deep fryer.

"Uh, I won't be eating dinner at home this evening," I said, giving her a quick peck on the cheek. Despite our ups and downs, she meant a lot to me and I wanted to do all I could to help her enjoy her golden years. She had been good to me, and I still went out of my way to be good to her.

Bertha whirled around, an extreme look of disappointment on her face. "And why not?" she asked sharply, wiping sweat off her face with the dishrag.

"Um, I'm taking the train to visit a winery with one of my former classmates. Don't you remember I told you that before I left for work this morning?"

"No, I don't remember you telling me that." Bertha gave me a sulky look, but a few seconds later, she smiled. "Well, that's nice, and I'm sure you'll have a good time. We can do some more cleaning tomorrow, but just make sure you get back in time to give me a perm tonight. You told me the other day you would. I'll save a few pieces of chicken for you anyway."

"I just gave you a perm last month. I used one of the strongest relaxers the beauty salon had, so your hair should be okay for at least another three or four weeks."

"Yes, you did relax my hair last month, but my bald spots are itching, and the hair I have left doesn't cover them the way they should so that means it's time for me to get a touch-up."

"Okay, but it'll probably be too late when I get home tonight. I'll do it in the morning."

Bertha shook her head. "Uh-uh. Tomorrow morning won't do. Sister Hightower is picking me up at eight, so we can catch the bus to that new casino in Rohnert Park." The pout on Bertha's face was so severe, I was tempted to give in, but I was not going to this time.

"Well, I guess we'll have to get up early enough for me to do it. I usually get up before seven on weekends. That would give me enough time." I was getting impatient, and from the look on Bertha's face, I could tell she was getting mad.

"What in the world has gotten into you, Lola Mae? Have you been drinking?"

"No, I haven't been drinking."

"Then what else is wrong with you, girl?" Bertha moved closer to me and started sniffing around my mouth. I shifted my weight from one foot to the other. "Hold still and let me smell your breath." I shook my head and groaned. It was hard to believe that Bertha still treated me like a teenager.

"Look, Bertha," I snarled, moving a few feet backward as she continued to sniff. "I already rearrange my life too much for your benefit. Now I have plans for this evening and I am not going to change them to stay home just so I can do your hair. Why don't you just wear a scarf or one of your wig-hats tomorrow? Or maybe you can get somebody else to give you a perm." I glanced over my shoulder toward the living room. Libby remained silent but glared at me.

"I wish you wouldn't sass me, girl," Bertha whined. She started blinking hard and wringing her hands.

"I'm not sassing you—"

"Girl, I advise you to watch your step. You are way out of line this time," Libby snarled as she stomped into the kitchen. "You don't talk to my mama like that!"

Jeffrey and Kevin heard the commotion and galloped down from upstairs and into the kitchen.

"Is everything all right down here?" Jeffrey asked, looking from me to Bertha, then Libby.

"This idiot is down here disrespecting my mama, and I am not going to stand for it!" Libby screamed, looking at me like she wanted to wring my neck. "And after all Mama has done for her *motherless,* cheesy black ass, she ought to be ashamed of herself!"

Bertha rubbed her chest with both hands and sat down hard into one of the chairs at the kitchen table. Her head was rolling from side to side and the rest of her body was jerking. Words could not describe the terrified look on her face. "I . . . I . . . don't feel so good. It's my chest . . . my chest . . . ooooh . . . I don't feel so good," she swooned as her eyes bucked out.

Kevin went up to her and put his hands on her shoulders. "Take it easy, Grandma. We'll take real good care of you," he said gently. Then he turned to me and snapped, "You need to stop upsetting my grandmother, because it ain't cool!"

I was so exasperated, I didn't know what to say next. I didn't even want to remain in the room, trying to defend myself in a battle I had lost a long time ago. I shook my head, turned around, and headed toward the staircase. I ran up the steps two at a time, and I didn't stop running until I was in my bedroom.

Instead of taking a shower or one of my hour-long bubble baths, I took a quick bird bath in the bathroom sink and put on fresh makeup. To save even more time, I decided to wear the same plain blue blouse and black pants I had worn to work. I was not going to be in my clothes for long after I got to the hotel anyway, so it didn't really matter what I wore.

Everybody was in the living room when I crept quietly back downstairs with my car keys in my hand. Bertha was stretched out on the couch. Libby stood over her, fanning her face with a magazine. Kevin hovered nearby. I could hear Jeffrey in the kitchen talking to one of his friends on the telephone. He was apologizing about having to cancel a poker game because he had to stay home and help his wife look after his mother-in-law. Jeffrey ended his call when he saw me standing in the doorway with a worried look on my face. "Lola, you go on and meet your friend and don't worry about Bertha. Everything's under control. You know how dramatic she can be sometimes. She's just having a bad day," he assured me.

"I didn't mean to upset her. . . ." I stopped talking because Jeffrey held up his hand and waved me toward the door.

"Go on and meet up with your friend," he insisted. And then he literally marched me to the door and pushed me out. "I hope you have a good time."

I did have a good time. Lester's lovemaking skills were only average to me. I didn't care, because I liked his looks and great personality. However, I couldn't stop thinking about Bertha. But after a prime rib dinner and two glasses of wine, I was so relaxed I didn't give her tantrum another thought. For the first time, I was glad Libby and Jeffrey were staying with us. She was their problem tonight.

I enjoyed Lester's company so much, when he asked if he could see me again in the near future, I told him yes. "But only if I'm not married by then."

"Oh? Are you engaged?" He sounded and looked disappointed.

"Something like that." I didn't know how much longer I could stand to live with Bertha. If I didn't reel Calvin in soon, I was going to lose my mind.

"I'll keep in touch anyway," Lester said with a sigh. "If I'm lucky, I'll get at least one more date with you."

After one more glass of wine he walked me to the door, pulled me into his arms, and gave me a very passionate kiss. His lips stayed on mine so long, I had to push him away. He grinned. "Whoever dude is, he's very lucky."

"So am I," I said. I was not sure when, or if, I'd even hear from Calvin again, but I still thought there was a chance that he would marry me.

Maybe I'd already lost my mind. . . .

Chapter 29
Calvin

WHEN SYLVIA LEFT AN HOUR AGO, I MOVED FROM MY BED TO THE living room couch. I lay on my side, staring at the wall, wondering why I felt so restless and sad all of a sudden when there was really no reason to be. Now, on top of everything else on my mind, I was concerned about my mental state.

I hoped that if I was going insane, it wouldn't happen until after I'd completed my mission. I was more eager than ever to wrap my hands around Lola's throat. I wanted to see her as soon as possible. Not to kill her—I still had a little more planning to do before that happened. With my mind being so frazzled, my hormones were all over the place. The only reason I suddenly wanted to see her was to sleep with her. The strange thing was, having sex with Lola hadn't even crossed my mind today until now. Even after sexing Sylvia earlier tonight, and a date with a hot little Mexican cutie coming up on Tuesday, Lola's body was the one I wanted tonight.

I dialed her cell phone number and my call went straight to voice mail, so I sent her a text:

> **Can we meet at Sal's Pizza Den in South Bay City on Montgomery Street in an hour? ☺ Sorry for another last-minute request. Would like to see you before my run on Tuesday, and this is the only night I can do it.**

I couldn't believe that I had begun to sound almost as immature and giddy as Lola, but I'd do whatever it took to keep her thinking I was the man she thought I was.

I sent the message and expected to hear back from her right away. Ten minutes passed and she still had not responded. Twenty passed, then half an hour. What was wrong with the dizzy bitch? Had she passed out, been abducted, or lost her phone? With her, there was just no telling. I suddenly remembered that shit she'd posted on the club's blog about a date she had arranged for this evening! That nasty buzzard was probably holed up in a hotel room fucking her brains out. BITCH! SLUT! WHORE!

Instead of calling her or sending another text, I turned off my phone. But I was so horny, I couldn't sit still. I didn't feel like picking up another woman off the street, because she may have ended up dead. Besides, all I wanted tonight was a piece of ass. None of the local Discreet Encounters members were available, so I had to go to plan B: a random escort service I'd used several times over the years. With all the free sex I was getting from club members these days, I didn't mind paying for a piece every now and then. I would have preferred an encounter with a black woman, an Asian, or a Latina, but none of the ones I wanted were available. I was okay with the slender blonde who knocked on my door an hour later.

Her name was Heidi. In her ad, she claimed to be in her midtwenties, but this bitch was thirty-five if she was a day. She had a pretty face, stringy blond hair, bad breath, and one hell of a potbelly for such a skinny woman. I was willing to overlook her flaws because I was interested only in what was between her legs.

"You have a real nice place," she said, looking around. "You live alone?"

"I have a couple of roommates. They'll be home soon so let's not waste any time." There was no way I was going to tell a hooker that I lived alone. I took her hand and led her to my bedroom.

"That's fine with me. I'm anxious to get home so I can rest and give my pussy and my mouth a break. I've been fucking and sucking all day. Can I have a drink before we get down to business?" Heidi plopped down on my bed. "Booze helps me get in the mood quicker."

"If you do this all the time, shouldn't you always be in the mood?" I quipped.

"Well, this is just a job to me, so the only man I'm always in the mood to fuck is my fiancé." She gave me an impatient look and started removing her clothes.

I kept a straight face, but I shook my head. This woman was engaged to be married and here she was selling her body to a stranger. She was no better than Glinda!

"I hope you have something real strong. Anything except tequila. That shit is even too strong for me." She was completely naked by now.

"Sorry, baby. All I have is beer."

"Then I guess that'll have to do."

I backed out of the room, trotted into my kitchen, and took one can of Budweiser out of my refrigerator. I had already drunk four in the last hour, so I needed to take a piss before I got busy with Heidi.

I couldn't have been away from her for more than three or four minutes, but when I got back to my bedroom, that crazy bitch was leaning over my nightstand rifling through my wallet! "Aw shit!" she hollered when she whirled around and saw me.

"Oh hell no!" I yelled, sprinting across the floor. I dropped the beer onto the bed and snatched my wallet out of her hand. "Bitch, what the fuck are you looking for?"

"When we made our date, you said you could only afford to pay me a hundred bucks. I was checking to see if you were lying. You've got almost half a grand!"

"What difference does it make? You agreed to a hundred!"

"I don't like liars," she hollered. She walked casually over to my dresser, where she'd left her clothes and shoes, and immediately started putting them back on. I was right behind her, boiling with rage.

"Well, I don't like thieves, so I advise you to get your flat ass up out of my house while you still can, BITCH!"

Heidi gasped and gave me a stunned look. "Look, I'm a Catholic. I don't like to hear cuss words or use them, but you are one lying *asshole*. I hope—"

I didn't give her a chance to finish her sentence. Before I could stop myself, I lunged at her and wrapped my hands about her throat. "Aaarrrggghh," she screamed as she clawed at my hands. I didn't have a tight grip on her, so she was able to pry my fingers away. "Please don't kill me. I'm pregnant," she whimpered. "If you don't believe me, I can show you the prescription I got from my doctor the other day for my prenatal pills."

Having a baby in her belly explained Heidi's potbelly, and it was one of the reasons I chose not to kill her. I didn't really want to kill anybody tonight anyway. Besides, I didn't know if she had told somebody where she was going. And I had called her, so my cell phone number was in her phone's log history. As pissed off as I was, I managed to control myself. I backed away and wagged my finger in Heidi's face. "Get out of my house!"

Without another word, she ran as if she had just had an encounter with Satan. And, in a roundabout way, she had.

This unexpected turn of events had suddenly cancelled my urge to have sex. My erection fizzled out so fast, my dick felt like a deflated balloon. I didn't think I'd be able to perform at all again tonight, but I still wanted to be in the presence of a woman for a couple of hours, just to keep me company. The problem was, there was no way I was going to solicit another woman from an escort service right then, especially just to have her come over and watch TV and have a drink with me. And I had no desire to see Sylvia again tonight. I had a couple of ex-girlfriends who would still jump through hoops for me. Unfortunately, they both knew Sylvia, so I couldn't invite one of them over. Besides, there was only one woman I really wanted to be with tonight: Lola.

I took a few deep breaths and strolled over to my dresser and checked my cell phone. Lola had responded. My eyes burned as I read her message:

Calvin my phone battery had died so I just saw your message a little while ago after I charged my phone. If it's not

too late and you still want me to meet you at that pizza place, just let me know.

I didn't send a text. I dialed her number but the damn call went straight to voice mail. I started talking right after I heard that annoying beep. I couldn't believe my own words. Here I was telling the whore who was at the top of my shit list that I wanted to see her tonight *just to talk*. On top of all the other issues I had to deal with, now I was worried that I was losing some of my manliness.

Chapter 30
Lola

*I*DIDN'T SEE THE TEXT MESSAGE FROM CALVIN UNTIL I GOT BACK TO my car in the hotel parking lot after I'd left Lester's hotel suite. He had sent it more than an hour ago—around the same time I had been wallowing in bed with Lester! I couldn't believe that this was the second time he had requested a spur-of-the-moment date when I was already with another man! Since my date with Lester had ended, and the night was still young, there was no reason for me not to see Calvin too.

Before I could reply, my battery fizzled out! As long as I'd been using cell phones, I was still lax about making sure my battery was always fully charged. I had a charger in my car, so I started charging my battery immediately. It was almost half an hour before there was enough juice to use my phone again. When I read Calvin's message again, it brought tears to my eyes and it made my heart flutter. That sweet man! He just wanted somebody to talk to tonight.

When I called him I got his voice mail, so I sent him a text. I wanted to wait in the hotel parking lot until I heard back from him, but when a security guard started giving me the fish eye, I left.

It made me feel good to know that Calvin was so anxious to see me tonight. His pending rendezvous with that Mexican woman next week didn't bother me as much now, and I put it on the back burner. A lot of other women had previously posted reviews about him. I wasn't too concerned about them because they were older, fatter, and not nearly as attractive as I was. I was much more concerned about that frisky, gorgeous, young *chica* who was also one of his regulars. I told myself not to feel too threatened, because she lived in Mexico and I lived just one city away from Calvin. Since he only wanted somebody to talk to tonight, that convinced me that I was more to him than just another piece of ass.

After I stopped to get gas, I drove around for a while before I parked in a Burger King parking lot and dialed Calvin's number again. He answered on the second ring. "Calvin, I'm sorry. I didn't reply right away to the text you sent a while ago because my battery had died. I charged it, and that's why I'm just now getting back to you," I explained.

"Oh?"

"Um . . . I've been out all evening and I was not near a land-line," I said in a small voice. "Do you still want to see me tonight?"

"I'd really like to."

"I can meet you at that pizza place you mentioned in your text."

"Are you sure? I know you don't like to be out driving by yourself after dark."

Bertha suddenly crossed my mind. I hadn't given much thought to her panic attack—or whatever it was—especially since she had several people in the house with her. I didn't know what I'd have to deal with when I got home, and I wanted to get as much enjoyment out of tonight as possible. "Don't worry about that. I'm feeling kind of brave tonight." I giggled. Even though he'd said he only wanted to talk, I held my breath and waited for him to tell me what hotel he wanted to take me to after the pizza.

"I can't tell you how glad I am to hear that, Lola. I promise I won't keep you out too long. I'm sure we can finish off a pizza and a couple of beers in an hour or two."

"I'm sure we can." My ego took a hit, but I was glad he didn't want to sleep with me tonight after all. As much as I wanted to feel his body close to mine again, I didn't like sleeping with two men in the same day. "Calvin, you can keep me out as long as you want," I cooed, sounding like a vixen on the prowl.

"I'm going to leave now. If traffic is not too heavy, I'll see you in about twenty-five minutes."

When I arrived at Sal's Pizza Den, it was so crowded, it took five minutes to locate Calvin in a back booth near the kitchen. When he spotted me, he stood up and started walking in my direction. As soon as he got close enough, he pulled me into his arms and kissed me so passionately, I was surprised I didn't melt into the floor.

"I'm so glad you could join me," he said with a tinge of sadness in his voice. "I know it's been only a few weeks since we were together, but it seems like a few years." He was more sensitive than I thought! It was another point in his favor on my imaginary scoreboard. "Some mail for my late uncle was forwarded to me today. I really miss him, and every time something happens that reminds me of him, I feel kind of gloomy. I didn't want to be by myself tonight, and I enjoy talking to you as much as I enjoy everything else about you."

This was more confirmation that sex was not the only thing he wanted from me! Of all the people he knew, I was the one he wanted to be with when he was sad. I couldn't think of anything else this man could do or say that would make me love him more.

We ordered a large pepperoni pizza and a pitcher of beer. For the next two hours, Calvin talked about his late uncle and how much fun they used to have when he lived in Chicago. He also told me more about his experiences in the military and some of his work-related adventures. His corny jokes were not the least bit funny, but I still howled with laughter. The most important thing he said was, "You are the most intriguing woman I've ever met. Not to mention the most beautiful and the sexiest."

Calvin's assessment of me was so endearing it restored my ego. I wanted to leap across the table and rip his clothes off, but since he was not interested in me only for sex, I didn't want him to think that it was my main interest in him. Somehow I managed to control myself. "Thank you," I said shyly.

After he finished the beer and the last slice of the pizza, he glanced at his watch and then he gave me a pensive look. "Lola, this has been a wonderful night, but I guess I've bored you long enough."

"Yes, this was a wonderful night. I hope talking to me made you feel better." I stood up because he had dropped a generous tip onto the table and already had his car keys in his hand.

"I do feel better. Much better." He put his arm around my shoulder and kissed my cheek. "Let me walk you to your car."

When we got to my dusty old Jetta, Calvin wrapped his arms around me and kissed me long and hard. When I felt his erection pressing against my stomach, I stiffened. He suddenly released me and backed away. "You feel so damn good!" he mouthed.

"So do you," I mumbled. If he had changed his mind and wanted to have sex with me tonight after all, I was ready, willing, and able. All he had to do was tell me. I checked my watch. "It's not that late and I'm in no hurry to get home. Um . . . what do you want to do now?" I asked dumbly.

He gave me a serious look. "I really hate to leave you, but I do have to get going," he told me in a casual tone. I was about to pucker my lips because I thought he was going to kiss me again, but all I got this time was a quick pat on the shoulder before he told me, "Take care of yourself. I'll be in touch, baby." Then he spun around and trotted across the parking lot to his Jeep.

When I pulled into my driveway ten minutes later, I was surprised to see all the lights out in the house. Libby's car was in the driveway, but Jeffrey's was not. When I got inside, I was even more surprised to see that nobody was home. Wherever they had gone, they had left in Jeffrey's vehicle and taken Bertha with them.

I went to my room and got into my nightclothes. I didn't want to check my e-mail and other messages because I didn't want to be disappointed if Calvin hadn't sent me another one yet. I scolded myself for even thinking about something that silly. I had just left the man a few minutes ago, so he would not have had time to send me another message. Since I had had such a wonderful time with him tonight, I was in a good mood and I wanted to stay in it.

I had no trouble falling asleep because of all the beer I'd drunk, but I woke up suddenly about twenty minutes later. Jeffrey's car was still not in the driveway, and I was still the only one in the house. I got so concerned, I put my clothes back on, went downstairs, and started pacing the living room floor.

I tried to call Jeffrey, but I got his voice mail. I didn't want to hear Libby's voice, so I didn't call her. When I heard the loud muffler on our elderly next-door neighbor's fifteen-year-old Chevy, I rushed outside.

"Mr. Fernandez, can I talk to you?" I yelled, running toward him waving my arms. He parked and piled out with a frightened look on his molelike face. "Did you see my family this evening? They're not home and I don't know where they are. Bertha *never* stays out this late."

Before Mr. Fernandez answered, he made the sign of the cross. I braced myself because, under the circumstances, this particular gesture was not a good sign.

Chapter 31
Lola

"*T*HE AMBULANCE TOOK BERTHA TO THE HOSPITAL A FEW HOURS ago!" Mr. Fernandez told me, raking his gnarled fingers through his wiry white hair. "Libby rode in the ambulance with her. Jeffrey and Keven followed in Jeffrey's car."

I gasped so hard I almost lost my breath. "Something's happened to my stepmother?" I asked dumbly.

Mr. Fernandez, a retired plumber and a very religious man, crossed himself again, gave me a pitiful look, and nodded. He and Bertha had been neighbors and close friends for more than forty years. She had taught all four of his children and their children. They lived in Texas and Mexico now, but every year they sent cards to Bertha for Christmas and Mother's Day. I could see that Mr. Fernandez was just as worried as I was. There were tears in his eyes and sweat all over his face. "The way Libby was screaming, I think it's something *real bad*. I already lit a candle for Bertha. You need to go and be with her now!" Mr. Fernandez whirled around and trotted up to his front door mumbling in Spanish, crossing himself again, and shaking his head.

Bertha had been in my life longer than either of my parents. We had had a lot of ups and downs, and despite all her health issues, real and imagined, she had scared me only one other time. About twelve years ago I'd had a relationship with a man I thought I loved. Bertha had gone out of her way to break us up. She made fun of his large nose and said mean things about him to his face. When she found out he had asked me to marry him, she got so upset she ended up in the hospital. The relationship ended shortly after that, and Bertha quickly recovered, but the possibility of my running off and marrying a man was not the case this time. I couldn't believe that my refusal to postpone a date so I could perm her hair was responsible for whatever had happened to her. But apparently it was.

I ran back inside and dialed Jeffrey's number again, and he still didn't answer. Then I tried Libby's, and she didn't answer either. There was only one hospital in South Bay City. I immediately called the admissions desk to get her room number so I could go check on her.

It was only a ten-minute drive to the hospital, but it seemed more like an hour. I prayed all the way that Bertha's situation was not too serious. I couldn't even imagine what my life would be like without her. Even though she had been driving me up the wall for years, I still cared about her.

My mind felt like confetti by the time I pulled into the hospital parking garage. I walked on wobbly legs and had a headache so severe, my vision was blurred. I had to blink hard so I could focus well enough to keep from bumping into other visitors and walking into a wall.

What I saw when I got off the elevator, which was a few feet from Bertha's room, made me stop dead in my tracks. Reverend Clyde, the new preacher who now presided over the church Bertha belonged to, was entering her room. I stood stock still and held my breath for a few moments. I couldn't think of anything more ominous than seeing a member of the clergy entering a loved one's hospital room holding a Bible.

I exhaled. Then I held my breath some more and stood still for another four minutes. My chest tightened and my stomach turned when I finally started moving toward Bertha's room. When I reached the door, I gently opened it and shuffled in. Reverend Clyde, Kevin, and Bertha's doctor stood on one side of the bed. There was a grim expression on each face.

Jeffrey and Libby stood on the other side of the bed. Libby

was crying and stroking the side of Bertha's face. Nobody noticed me until I cleared my throat. That was when Libby glared at me and roared, "YOU LOW-DOWN, FUNKY BLACK BITCH! YOU FINALLY KILLED MY MAMA!"

"What?" I croaked. My legs buckled and I almost crumbled to the floor. Somehow, I managed to remain standing. I didn't know what else to say or do.

"Lola, I am through with your rotten, useless, self-centered ass!" Libby shrieked as she shook her fist in my direction. Jeffrey had his arms around her waist, but the way she was bucking and rearing, I knew that if she got loose she would really hurt me. Or maybe even kill me. She didn't even let the presence of the preacher and the doctor stop her from ranting. "I HATE YOU! I HATE YOU! I HATE YOU!"

"What . . . what happened?" I whimpered. Even though Libby was mad as hell at me, I still approached the bed. When I attempted to touch Bertha's face, Libby pushed my hand away. The next thing I knew, she slapped my face so hard I saw stars. I didn't hit her back, because I had too much respect for Reverend Clyde and Dr. Wilcox to act like a savage.

"What do you care? You've got some nerve coming here! If you don't get out of my sight, I'm going to do more than slap your face!" she screamed.

"I have just as much right to be here as you!" I countered as I massaged the spot where she'd hit me. "She was my mother too!"

"She was your *stepmother*, bitch! And you treated her like trash! Now you get the hell out of this room before I kick your ass!"

"Libby, you need to calm down," Dr. Wilcox said in a gentle tone. "This is a sad occasion and I won't tolerate you causing such a ruckus—"

"Don't you tell me what I can do, Wilcox! Mama would have been better off with a witch doctor than a jackleg quack like you! If you had taken better care of her, she'd still be alive!"

"Libby, that's enough. This is not the time or place to vent your anger," Reverend Clyde said gently, holding up his hand.

"Don't fuck with me, preacher man! I will kick your holy ass too!" she screeched. I had never seen a man's jaw drop as fast as Reverend Clyde's did. Libby had crossed one line too many. Insulting one of the most respected doctors in town and threatening to beat up a preacher was as low as a person could go.

I started backing out the door.

"Libby, you've made your point," Jeffrey said, giving her a stern look as he released her. From the expression on her face I thought she was going to slap him too. Kevin, who was crying as hard as Libby, wrapped his arms around her and held her in place. Jeffrey strode over to me. "Lola, let's go outside," he said in a shaky tone. I moved like a zombie when he put his arm around my shoulder and led me out of the room. We didn't stop until we reached the end of the hall.

"Jeffrey, I hope you don't blame me for what happened to Bertha," I whimpered. "You told me to go on out because everything was under control."

"You are not responsible for anything." He gave me a bear hug and rubbed my back for a few seconds. When he leaned back and looked at me, his eyes were full of tears.

"What time did she die?" I sniffled. I had already shed a few tears, but I knew I was going to shed a lot more.

"She died about two minutes after Reverend Clyde arrived. She went peacefully. And she was lucid enough to tell us all good-bye."

Jeffrey's last sentence really tugged at my heartstrings. If anybody should have been present for Bertha to say a final good-bye to, it was me. And if I had not wasted those *four* minutes standing outside her room, I could have. "I . . . I wish I'd been with her," I sobbed.

"I'm so glad she held on until Reverend Clyde had enough time to pray for her one last time."

"If only I had not upset her this evening—"

"Lola, listen to me and listen good. What's happened tonight is what it is. And we can't change a thing now."

"But Libby thinks it was my fault!" I wailed.

Jeffrey held his hand up to my face and shook his head.

"Bertha died because it was her time. Forget about what Libby said. You let me deal with her. The next few days are going to be pretty tense for everybody. Now you go home and get some rest—in your room. When I bring Libby home tonight, don't come out unless I tell you to."

"You think she's planning to get violent when she gets home?" I wailed, balling my fists because by now I was just that angry. If Libby attacked me when she got home, all hell would break loose because I would defend myself. And I didn't care who witnessed it.

"I don't know what she's planning to do, but let me worry about that. We'll talk about this tomorrow after we've all tried for a good night's sleep and when Marshall comes to the house."

"Oh God. Then both he and Libby will gang up on me! Jeffrey, you better stay close, because if either one of them touches me, there will be one hell of a bloodbath up in that house." My whole body was trembling and my fists were still balled.

"Nobody is going to gang up on you, and there is not going to be a bloodbath, tonight or any other time. I'll make sure of that."

My legs felt so weak, I had to lean against the wall to keep from falling.

"You look terrible, so I want you to leave now. We'll take care of everything here, so don't worry about a thing."

After Jeffrey hugged me again, I stumbled into the elevator. It felt as if I were having an out-of-body experience, because I couldn't even feel my feet moving as I headed to the parking garage.

I couldn't stop the tears from gushing. Everything seemed so surreal; it was hard to believe what was happening.

I sat in the parking garage another ten minutes before I called Joan.

Chapter 32
Joan

I WAS SO GLAD IT WAS FRIDAY. IT HAD BEEN A CRAZY WEEK FOR ME, and I was happy it was about to end.

I had spent most of the evening with Junior and three of his friends. After a soccer game that they had won, I treated them to dinner at Red Lobster and two hours at their favorite video arcade.

Junior had a lot of friends. He liked to spend time with them without me breathing down his neck, so I gave him a lot of space. Unlike some of the other teenagers I knew, my son was damn near perfect. I was so proud to be his mother. As far as I could tell, he had never experimented with drugs and he didn't associate with a bad crowd. He loved school and was an honor student. He was also a good-looking boy, so he had more than his share of girls chasing after him. Reed and I had had several conversations with him about sex. He didn't know that I'd found a package of condoms (with two missing . . .) in his pocket last week when I was about to do the laundry. I hadn't mentioned it to him or Reed, and didn't plan to anytime soon. I was just glad that my son was being responsible.

While the boys played video games, I visited the mall across the street. Even though I had more clothes and everything else I needed, shopping was still one of my favorite pastimes. Since I'd grown up pinching pennies and shopping in discount stores, going hog wild in some of the most upscale stores in town gave me a rush. I surprised myself when I purchased only four pairs of shoes and a new bathrobe. I surprised myself again when I got home and saw that I had already purchased the same bathrobe a few days ago. It, as well as several other items I'd bought in the last few weeks, still had the price tags attached. I made a mental note to go through my wardrobe before my next shopping spree so I wouldn't duplicate items.

A few minutes past ten p.m., I poured a glass of wine and curled up on the living room couch, happy to be alone. Reed had left to go hiking with Dr. Weinstein about four hours ago, and Junior was in bed.

Five minutes later, just as I was about to turn on the TV, my cell phone rang. I snatched it off the coffee table, glad to see Lola's name on the caller ID. I was anxious to hear about her date.

"It's me, Joan. Can you talk?" She sounded distressed. I was glad I had placed the wine bottle close by, because something told me I was going to need it.

"Sure. My in-laws picked up Junior a little while ago, and Reed's going to be gone for the whole weekend. Hallelujah!"

"Oh? Where did he go?"

"He and Dr. Weinstein went hiking at Point Reyes."

Lola remained silent for a few seconds. "Oh yeah. You told me about that. Humph. Reed's more of a dark horse than I thought."

"What do you mean by that?"

"Other than playing golf and harassing you, I didn't know he had interests besides his work. Especially something like hiking."

"I didn't know he was interested in hiking either. I just found out the other day." I cleared my throat. "Okay, don't beat around the bush. I know you called to tell me about your date, and he must have been pretty bad if you're taking your time to get to him."

Without preparing me, Lola announced, "Bertha's dead."

Those two words made my jaw drop. "What?" I got so light-headed a feather could have knocked me over.

"And it's my fault."

"What the hell are you talking about? *Did you kill that old woman?*" I had to take a long drink from my wineglass.

"You know I would never put my hands on Bertha."

"Then how is it your fault?"

"She wanted me to delay my date tonight so I could give her a perm. That would have taken at least a couple of hours and I didn't want to put Lester off that long. I refused to do so. She tried to guilt me into letting her have her way. I didn't do it this time, and she got real upset. Since everybody else was in the house, I went back upstairs to get ready for my date. When I got back downstairs and saw Bertha lying on the couch, moaning and groaning, I almost changed my mind about going out. Jeffrey assured me that she was only being dramatic, as usual, and he told me to go on out because everything was under control. So I left. I thought she was having a panic attack, like that time she thought I was going to run off and marry that marine. Anyway, this time Bertha had a heart attack. She died before I could get to her hospital room after I left my date." Lola choked. "I . . . I . . . didn't get a chance to say good-bye to her."

"Oh my God!" I exclaimed as I rose up off the couch. "Where are you now?"

"I'm still sitting in my car in the hospital parking lot. I'm so damn nervous, I'm afraid to drive. My hands are shaking and I can barely feel my feet."

"Oh, girl, I am so sorry. You must be frantic! Do you want me to come pick you up?"

"No, you don't have to do that. I just need to sit here a few more minutes until I calm down. I had a bad feeling when I got home and saw all the lights out in the house. When Mr. Fernandez told me that an ambulance had taken Bertha to the hospital, I knew then that she had to be in pretty bad shape."

"Lola, don't you blame yourself for what happened. It was not your fault."

"Libby thinks it is. When I got to the hospital, she cussed up a storm and accused me of killing Bertha. The next thing I knew, she slapped my face so hard I saw stars. And right in front of

Reverend Clyde and Dr. Wilcox. She even said some nasty shit to them when they tried to calm her down. I don't know what she's going to do or say when we get back to the house. If Jeffrey hadn't been there to keep her off me, you probably would have read about me in tomorrow's newspaper."

"Listen to me. You don't have to deal with her tonight. I'm more afraid for her than I am you because I don't want to see you behind bars for beating her ass. Calm down and come over here. My liquor cabinet is full, there is plenty of food in the refrigerator, and you can even spend the night if you want to."

"I'm on my way."

Chapter 33
Joan

*I*T HAD BEEN HALF AN HOUR SINCE I'D SPOKEN TO LOLA. I STARTED pacing my living room floor, and every few seconds I checked my watch. I was so anxious to see her, I called her number just to make sure she was still on her way. "What's up, girl? Where the hell are you?"

"I got stuck behind a stalled car on the freeway and the cops closed all but one lane, so that slowed me down. I just turned onto your street. I'll be there in a couple of minutes," she told me.

After a quick trip to the bathroom, I returned to the living room. Just as I was about to pour myself another drink, Lola rang the buzzer. I let her into the lobby and waited for her in my doorway. When she stumbled out of the elevator there was a look on her face that was so sad, it made me want to cry. She practically fell into my arms.

"I have a drink ready for you," I said with my arm around her shoulder as I led her into my living room to the couch. Wine was too mild for this occasion. I had set two glasses of rum and Coke on the coffee table because we both needed a strong buzz tonight. Lola dropped her purse onto the table and snatched her drink before she even sat down. I remained standing for a few moments, looking at her and shaking my head. She looked more despondent than she had the night her daddy died.

"Lola, everything is going to be just fine." I sat down at the other end of the couch and reached for my drink. I took a long pull before I continued. "I'm sorry Bertha is gone, but this could be a blessing in disguise," I said with a heavy sigh. "You've been under her thumb so long, you may have a hard time adjusting to a real life."

Lola looked at me and blinked. "If you don't think my life is not already real, what is it?"

"First of all, you haven't been able to do a lot of things most women our age do. The way Bertha controlled you, it was more like you were her hostage. Now you can come and go as you please without making up a bunch of lies. And you can finally get married and have the family you've been wanting all your life—when you meet the right guy."

Lola dropped her head. "I already know who the right guy is, and you know too."

"Calvin," I said, giving her a pathetic look. "Before we talk about him and Bertha again, tell me how your date went tonight."

Lola looked away for a few moments. When she returned her attention to me, there was a mysterious smile on her face. "I had a marvelous time. They were both nice."

"Both? Oh shit! I'm scared of you. Since when did you start doing threesomes?"

She exhaled and gave me a strange look. "I don't do threesomes. After I left Lester's hotel room, I checked my messages in my car. There was one from Calvin. He wanted me to meet him as soon as possible." She paused and took a quick sip. And when she put her glass down, she stared straight ahead and remained silent.

"Go on," I prodded, nudging her with my hand.

"I had a really nice time with Lester. He was real cool and charming and even cuter in person. He showed me such a good time I told him I'd see him again."

"You don't have to give me all the details about how good he was in bed. You can tell me that later. I want to hear what happened with Calvin."

"To make a long story short, before I could get back to him my cell phone battery conked out. I sat in the hotel parking garage and charged it enough for me to use my phone again. I called him and told him why I hadn't responded to his message right away and I asked if he still wanted to see me tonight. Of course he said yes."

"What hotel did you go to?"

"We didn't." There was such a glassy-eyed look on Lola's face, when she blinked she reminded me of an owl. "He didn't want to have sex. He just wanted to spend some time with me. I met him at a pizza parlor and all we did was share a pizza, drink some beer, and talk."

"Oh? I'm surprised to hear that a sex machine like Calvin only wanted to see a . . . uh . . . sex machine like you just to talk." Joan cackled. "I guess Reed's not the only dark horse we know, huh?"

"I guess not. I can't wait to sleep with him again though. I can't tell you how happy I was to hear that he is interested in more than just sex from me." The glassy-eyed owlish look was still on Lola's face. "I think the man's in love with me."

I was amazed to hear her make such an outrageous statement with nothing to back it up. I didn't want to add to her distress, so I decided to keep my comments to myself for the time being. "I'm glad you think that." I couldn't think of anything more neutral to say, but there were all kinds of thoughts dancing around in my head. One was, if Lola had convinced herself that Calvin was in love with her, she was going to be even more love-struck than before. Despite what I thought, I was happy for her. Especially now that Bertha was out of the picture. "Did you tell him about Bertha?"

"I left him a voice mail a few minutes after I talked to you. He hasn't replied yet. I am so sorry he never got to meet Bertha. After all I had told her about him praising me for taking care of her, she was as anxious to meet him as he was to meet her." Lola paused and her eyes suddenly got big. The look on her face was so serious, it scared me. I was not prepared for what she said next. "It's time for me to let Calvin know how I feel about him, and I need to know how he feels about me. And the sooner the better. I'm going to talk to him about it within the next week or so." She gave me a hopeful look. "What do you think?"

I didn't have the nerve to admit what I really thought. I couldn't believe what she'd just told me—with a straight face—she was going to do. "If you think he's in love with you, why do you need to ask him?"

"I just need to hear him say it."

"What if he's not in love with you and doesn't even want to be in a serious relationship?" I asked, squeezing Lola's hand.

She gave me a thoughtful look before she answered. "If he tells me that, I'll be disappointed but I'll live. At least I'll know that I have to keep looking for Mr. Right and put Calvin on the back burner. Now that Bertha is gone, I'm going to have to make some serious decisions about what to do with myself now. Especially about Calvin."

"It's about time," I said as I squeezed her hand even harder.

Lola gave me a sharp look and snatched her hand away. "It's about time for what?"

"It's about time for you to look at your obsession with Calvin from a different point of view. You saw that message the Mexican woman posted about her upcoming date with him, so you know he's not sitting around biding his time, or fantasizing about living happily ever after with you."

"So what if he's going to hook up with that woman from Mexico? I'm still going strong with other club members too. We're all in the same game, remember?"

"And some of us lose," I said, giving Lola a woeful look.

"Tell me about it." I was happy to see her smile. "But I'm going to be okay, Joan."

"Well, this has been one hell of a night for you. You hooked up with two men, Bertha died, and Libby cussed you out, accused you of killing Bertha, and slapped you. What's your next move?"

"I'm not sure. I'll go home and face Libby tomorrow. We'll probably lock horns big-time, but whatever happens, happens." Lola's voice turned harsh. "If she puts her hands on me again, I will fight back like I did that time she attacked me when she thought I was having an affair with Jeffrey." She stretched her arms high above her head and yawned. And then she chuckled. I was glad to see that she was not too broken up about Bertha. Her eyes were red and slightly swollen, so I knew she had already shed a few tears, and I knew she'd be shedding a lot more in the next few days.

"What's up with you and DrFeelGood? Is your date with your Jewish honey still on for tomorrow? Between him and John Walden flying in and out of town, they must have racked up thousands of frequent flyer miles by now," Lola teased.

"Yes, our date is still on. I need to stay on good terms with him if I want to get those free breast implants and any other surgery I may need someday. I'm going to meet up with Ezra around two. With Reed gone until Sunday night, I plan to take full advantage of that. I told Ezra I'd spend the whole night and part of Sunday." I swallowed hard and squeezed Lola's shoulder. "But I can postpone my date if you want me to." I held my breath. Lola was my girl. Whenever she needed me, I went out of my way to be there for her. I wouldn't trade my relationship with her for all the men on my roster put together.

"Don't change your plans on my account. Go have yourself a good time tomorrow and don't worry about me. Now if you don't mind, I'd like to get some rest. I'm going to need all of my strength tomorrow when I face Libby."

Chapter 34
Calvin

*A*s much as i despised lola, i had actually enjoyed her company tonight. Just being in her presence and looking at her miserable face reinforced my belief that killing her would set me
free. This bitch was the main source of my pain, so her murder
would be even more grisly than the others. "Lola, thank you
so much for allowing me to cry on your shoulder tonight," I'd
told her.

"Calvin, I want you to know that any time you need to see me
only to talk, or because you need some company, just let me
know," she'd answered. She had already scarfed down three
slices of pizza and was eyeballing the one I had in my hand. That
was another thing about the bitch. She was a damn glutton! I
had never seen a woman suck up as much food and beer as this
one and still have a decent body.

I had kissed her passionately before we'd parted, and she had
felt so good in my arms. By the time I got home, my desire to
have sex had returned. I couldn't let Lola know how weak I was
by calling her again and asking her to come back out and meet
me at a hotel so we could have sex after all. She was a dingbat
and probably would have done it, but I was afraid that if I saw
her again too soon, it would be the last time she'd ever see me,
or any other man. I would see her soon enough, so I was determined to stick to my plan. Until then, I had to rely on other
sources for my pleasure.

I sat in my driveway for only two minutes before I knew what I had to do next. I didn't even bother to call up Sylvia to let her know I was on my way to her house. It was past midnight, and we'd already spent intimate time together earlier, but I knew she'd be glad to see me again.

When I opened my eyes Saturday morning around nine, I was naked and had an erection that was as hard as blue steel. I was ready to start humping again already, but not with Sylvia. The more I thought about the good time I was going to have with Maria on Tuesday, the harder I got. As a matter of fact, during my romp with Sylvia a few hours ago, I had imagined it was Maria's luscious body I was on top of. I smiled just thinking about her.

My sudden appearance at Sylvia's house in the middle of the night had surprised her, but she'd been happy to see me. I had had two intimate sessions with her in less than twenty-four hours, and that was enough for now. I had not planned to use her as a crutch to hold me up until Tuesday when I'd meet up with Maria, but that was exactly what I'd done. If I had taken Lola to a hotel last night for sex after our pizza break, there was no telling what I would have done to her, because her presence had enraged me more than I'd expected. I had to keep telling myself that I needed to stick to my plan. After being with her last night, I knew then exactly when I was going to kill her: *She would die the very next time I saw her.*

Sylvia was in the kitchen. I could smell bacon cooking and hear her talking to her sister on the telephone. My future sister-in-law was long-winded. I knew she'd keep Sylvia occupied for a while, so I pulled my cell phone out of my pants pocket to check my messages.

There was a voice mail from my jackass cousin Willis. He wanted to know if he could borrow three hundred bucks. I rolled my eyes and deleted his message. I was not even going to answer it. Dude already owed me a grand, and each time I mentioned it to him, he told me one tale of woe after another and that he would repay me "whenever" he could. I had money problems like everybody else I knew, but I was generous even when I couldn't afford to be. Last month when my brother Ronald asked to borrow half a grand to get his car fixed, I didn't have the cash to spare at the time, so I borrowed it from my boss. My brother was good about paying me back, so I always came through for him. The second message was from him. He wanted to know if it was okay for him to put the money he owed me in an envelope and slide it under my door or leave it in my mailbox. I immediately texted him and told him to hold on to the money until I was able to see him in person. There was no way in the world I would allow him, or anybody else, to snoop around my property when I was not present. A few weeks ago, my neighbor Robert told me that while I was on a haul, he'd seen Ronald peeping in my living room window one night. When I confronted my brother, he claimed he had been doing a welfare check because I hadn't responded to his last three messages. Now whenever he left one, I got back to him right away.

The only other voice mail had come from that damn Lola. I held my breath as I listened: "Hello, Calvin. This is Lola. I have some bad news to share with you. While I was out tonight, my stepmother had a heart attack. She passed away a few minutes before I got to her hospital room after I left you. With her funeral and everything else I'll have to deal with, things will be hectic for me for a while. I thought you should know, because I might not be reachable or able to respond to messages in a timely manner. I'll talk to you soon. Bye."

I listened to her message twice, wondering how this new development was going to impact my plans for her. I wanted her dead before my wedding. And if things went my way, she would be. I didn't want to call her back, because I couldn't stand the thought of hearing her annoying voice. I sent her a text:

> **I am so sorry for your loss. If there is anything I can do, give me a call. Let me know when things return to normal so I can see you.** ☹

I made a mental note to send her some flowers at her work, but I dismissed that notion right away. For one thing, I didn't want her to know that I knew the location of that pooh-butt grocery store she worked for. I couldn't send flowers to her home address, because she had no idea that I already knew where she lived. Before our first sexual encounter, I had discreetly cased her house and "stalked" her from afar. Then, in a clever disguise, I had visited the grocery store and watched her work.

Right after I sent the text, I turned off my phone. "Bitch, the next funeral you attend will be your own," I said under my breath.

Chapter 35
Joan

WHEN I ROLLED OUT OF BED AND ENTERED MY LIVING ROOM AT seven a.m. Saturday morning, Lola was already up and dressed. "Did you sleep well?" I asked, joining her on the couch.

She nodded and offered a weak smile. "Your guest room is so comfortable, I didn't want to leave."

"And you don't have to leave until you are good and ready."

"I need to change clothes and . . . I need to go to the house and get whatever is going to happen between Libby and me over with so I can move forward." Lola looked at her watch and began to rise. "I guess I should be on my way. I know you have to get ready for your date with DrFeelGood."

"*Pffft!*" I waved my hand. "I won't be seeing him until this afternoon, and so what if I'm late. I didn't tell him to come back out here again so soon in the first place." I was so glad Reed was out of my hair for the whole weekend. I could really relax on my date and spend more time with Lola. Even though she claimed she had slept well, she looked tired and beaten down. And she probably was. Losing Bertha and having another run-in with Libby was enough to wear even the strongest person down to a frazzle. "You should at least have some breakfast. I know you don't want to deal with Libby on an empty stomach, now, do you?"

"It wouldn't matter whether my stomach was empty. Dealing with a pit bull like her under any circumstances would be bad."

Lola paused and gave me a frightened look. "Something tells me I won't be living in Bertha's house too much longer."

"Hold on, now." I held up my hand and gave her a stern look. "Don't get too far ahead of yourself. Libby and Jeffrey will be moving back into their house when all the renovations are done, and that should be in a few weeks or a few months at the very most. Bertha's house is completely paid for and it has been your home since middle school. You don't need to move out now, because you won't have to deal with her mess anymore."

"That's true. And I have every right to continue living there. Humph. I paid the property taxes, the monthly home owner's association dues, and the landscaping and other maintenance expenses for the past twelve years all by myself."

"That's all the more reason for you to stay on there. Not only that, it's a nice house in a nice, safe neighborhood. And keep in mind that you'd still be living rent free. Once Libby and her crew get their asses out of there, that place will be paradise."

"All that sounds good, but I don't know if I want to stay in such a big house by myself."

"You don't have to. You can rent out the other two bedrooms and make a profit to boot."

Lola looked at me like I was crazy. "Yeah, right. Libby and Marshall would never allow that to happen. If I do decide to stay, I'm sure they'll make me start paying rent. And they'll probably charge more than I can afford, just to force me to move out."

"I hadn't thought about that, but you're right."

"There's another thing to think about: Those two greedy hogs will probably want to sell the house, so I wouldn't be able to stay on there even if I wanted to."

"You're right about that too, I guess." I gave Lola a pitiful look and sucked in some air. It seemed like the more I tried to say things to make her feel better, the worse she looked. "I'm going to go take a quick shower and put on some clothes."

"While you're doing that, I'll fix breakfast," Lola said, forcing a smile.

"Cool. I won't take too long." I started removing my bathrobe and walking back to my bedroom.

Lola cooked grits, bacon, biscuits, and eggs and made a pot of coffee. I ate like a pig, but she left more than half of her food on her plate. "You know you can stay here until I get back from my date. The liquor cabinet is full, so you can drink all you want. It'll give you more courage when you go home to face that cow."

Lola took a deep breath and shook her head. "I'd love to stay here a couple more hours and get wasted, but I don't want to be drunk when I go home. That'll give Libby something else to bitch about," she said with a frown. "And I don't want to get busted for drunk driving. Bertha used to warn me about that all the time. She said if I ever got my name in the newspaper for drunk driving it would embarrass her so much, she'd never get over it."

It was eight-thirty a.m. when we left my place. We hugged, and I assured Lola that everything was going to be all right. But I had a feeling that nothing was ever going to be all right for her again.

I didn't like to call Ezra Spoor by his screen name, DrFeel-Good, but he certainly liked to call me by mine. "Hellooo, HotChocolate!" he greeted when I arrived at his suite in the Courtyard San Jose airport hotel. I set my overnight case on the floor. He closed the door and then wrapped his arms around me and led me to the king-size bed. "What's this, our tenth or eleventh date?"

"This is our thirteenth date," I said firmly.

"Thirteen and counting. Boy, am I glad to see you again!" He was already tugging at the zipper on my jeans.

"Ezra, please control yourself and slow down," I scolded, slapping his hand as I pulled away from him.

"But I'm so happy to see you, I can't help myself," he said with a sulky pout. He wrapped his arms around me again and we eased down on the bed at the same time. We kissed, and he fondled and caressed my body until I abruptly stood up.

"There is no need for us to rush into anything. I can stay all night this time."

"Super! And it's about damn time. How did you manage that? Is what's-his-face in a coma or something?" Ezra stood up and started groping and caressing me some more.

"He went hiking with one of his colleagues," I explained.

"Hmmm. That's a damn good place for him. Let's hope he gets lost, devoured by a mountain lion, or falls down a ravine." Ezra guffawed like a hyena.

Despite how disgusted I was with Reed, even more so by now, I didn't like it when my lovers talked about him in a negative way. That was my job. And when it came to bashing Reed, I preferred to do it with Lola. "That's not funny!" I pinched his hand and gave him the most exasperating look I could manage.

"Just kidding," he snickered.

"I told you to have a steak and lobster lunch ready when I got here and I don't see it," I complained as I looked around the room. "You know how I like to feed my face."

"I'll order lunch and a couple of bottles of their finest champagne straightaway. In the meantime, get your little fanny out of those clothes so I can feed my face too. . . ."

Chapter 36
Lola

I WAS SO NERVOUS ABOUT FACING LIBBY, I DECIDED TO PUT OFF GO-
ing home until I felt better. I couldn't go to a bar for a drink, so
I stopped at the first Starbucks I saw instead. I sat at a table and
nursed a large latte for an hour before I returned to my car.

My heart rate doubled when I turned onto my street. I was
pleased to see that Libby's car was not parked in front of the
house. Nor was Jeffrey's. I parked in the driveway and slowly
dragged my feet to the front porch steps. When I got to the top
step, I saw something that made me freeze. There were several
large, black garbage bags stacked in a clumsy pile on one side of
the porch. Every bag looked as if it had been tossed onto the
pile by somebody in a big hurry. I couldn't believe that Libby
had already begun to dispose of some of Bertha's belongings.
Her body had barely had enough time to get cold! Libby and
Marshall were so cold-blooded and greedy, the next thing I expected them to do was have a yard sale to get rid of the rest of
their mother's stuff. The thought of them being that callous
turned my stomach.

My hands were shaking when I reached into my purse to get
my house key. When I attempted to unlock the door, the key
didn't work. I figured it was because I'd used the one to the back
door. The keys looked similar. I tried the other one, and it didn't
work either. I ran off the porch to the back of the house. When

I couldn't unlock the kitchen door, reality hit me like a ton of bricks: The locks had been changed!

I returned to the front porch and decided to see what was in the garbage bags. The first one contained some of my clothes and my collection of DVDs and CDs. I was dumbfounded. I didn't even bother to check the other bags. I loaded them into the trunk and backseat of my car. With my blood boiling, I got back into my car and sat there for a few minutes, trying to decide what to do next. I didn't want to call the hotel where Joan was with DrFeelGood, especially since I had interrupted her rendezvous with that love-struck lawyer the last time she was with him. My mind was in such a tizzy, I didn't even realize what I was doing until it was too late. I pulled my phone out of my purse and dialed Elbert's number.

He had called me dozens of times, but this was only the seventh or eighth call I'd ever made to him. "God, please let him answer," I prayed, something I never thought I would resort to.

He picked up on the third ring. "Lola, praise the Lord it's you! I was just about to call you myself! I just heard about Bertha a few minutes ago!" he yelled. "Reverend Clyde stopped by the house this morning and told me and Mama all about the mean and evil way Libby talked to you when you went to the hospital last night. I couldn't believe my ears! That was a sin and a shame, but don't worry, because God's got His eye on that woman!" Elbert snorted and softened his tone. "I've been sitting here worrying myself to death thinking about you. Are you all right? Where are you?"

"I . . . I'm sitting in my car in Bertha's driveway because I can't get into the house."

"Did you lose your key?"

"No."

"Libby won't open the door for you?"

"Nobody's home. After Libby chased me out of the hospital, I went to Joan's place and that's where I spent last night. I may have to sleep in my car tonight because Libby had the locks changed. That's why I can't get into the house. I can't go back to Joan's place because she's away until tomorrow evening."

"Bless your soul! I don't know what to say. I always knew Libby was a bad egg, but I didn't know she was rotten enough to behave in such an ungodly way. Lola, I have plenty of room and you're welcome to stay with Mama and me for as long as you need to."

I considered Elbert's offer until I heard what he said next. "You know I've been very fond of you for a long time. I'm sorry it took a tragedy to bring you to me. . . ."

"I think I'd like to be by myself for a little while, so I'm going to check into a motel."

"Well, when you do, give me a call and let me know which one. You need any money? I can give you a couple of grand, more if you need it. And you don't have to worry about paying me back."

"I have enough on me to pay for a room for at least a few nights. I can go to the ATM if I need more, but thank you so much for the offer."

"Do you need anything else? Fresh clothes and whatnot?"

I had to swallow hard to get rid of the lump in my throat. "Libby stuffed most of my belongings into garbage bags and left them on the front porch."

"That no-good, no-neck, funky black bitch!" I had never heard Elbert use profanity, or any harsh words, so I was surprised to hear him refer to Libby in such an unflattering manner. "I'll pray for you, Lola. And please keep in touch. Did that wench put your laptop in one of those garbage bags?"

"I don't know. I haven't checked all of the bags yet. If she didn't, you can get in touch with me by text or call me on my cell phone."

"Lola, I meant what I just said. I've always been fond of you and I want to help you."

"Thanks, Elbert. I'll . . . um . . . I'll be in touch."

I checked into the Stanton Street Motel and paid in advance for three nights. I broke down and cried as I hauled the garbage bags into a neat but musty-smelling room. I had a lot of clothes and shoes, so I knew Libby had not packed up all of my stuff. I couldn't believe how she had balled up some of my best outfits and stuffed them into the same bag with my shampoo and toiletries. A large shower gel bottle had leaked and left stains on three of my most expensive dresses. I had a desktop computer in my bedroom as well as a laptop. She had not packed either one. Also missing were the photo albums that contained pictures of Mama, Daddy, and me, and other sentimental items I'd stored in my dresser drawers. I was going to get the rest of my belongings even if I had to have the cops escort me back into the house!

I couldn't believe how drastically my life had changed in less than twenty-four hours. I stopped crying, stretched out on the squeaky bed, and stared at the cracks on the ceiling until my cell phone rang ten minutes later. It was Jeffrey.

"Lola, are you all right?!" he asked in a distressed tone. "Mr. Fernandez told me he saw you loading the trash bags off the porch into your car."

"I'm fine," I mumbled. It was hard not to break down and start crying again, but I managed to remain somewhat composed.

"Where are you? Where did you go last night?"

"I stayed with Joan. You can tell Libby she didn't have to change the locks to keep me out of the house. All she had to do was tell me to get out and I would have packed my stuff myself."

"Well, she's really pissed off. I was with Marshall at the funeral home when she packed up your stuff and had the locks changed, so I couldn't stop her."

"Jeffrey, I need to get the rest of my stuff. Can you help me? I hope you can so I won't have to bring the cops to the house."

"Don't worry about your stuff. I'll make sure you get it all within the next day or so. Where are you now?"

"I'm at the Stanton Street Motel in the room right next to the office."

"Oh hell no! What are you doing in a rat-infested flophouse like that? That place is nothing but a glorified crack house!"

"It was the cheapest one I could find. I'm going to have to stay here until I figure out what to do next."

"The first thing you need to do is check into a safer, cleaner motel. I can get you a room at the Dawson Motor Inn across from my work station."

"No, Jeffrey. I may need your help later. Until then, let me do as much as I can on my own. I've been using other people as crutches long enough."

"Well, you've never used me and I want to help you. That cheap dump you're in will get real expensive if you stay more than a few days. Do you need any money?"

"I'm fine, Jeffrey. Thanks for asking. I will let you know when and if I need your help." I paused and took a deep breath. "Have the funeral arrangements been made yet?"

"The service will be held at Second Baptist Church this coming Wednesday at eleven a.m. We would have scheduled it for sooner, but it took a while to get in touch with all of Bertha's relatives in Mississippi, and some of her friends and former students."

"Thanks for giving me that information. I'm glad I didn't have to wait to read it in the newspaper obituary column. Libby didn't pack all of my stuff. I really need the rest of my clothes and my computers. Can you bring those things over here by tomorrow?"

"You can relax. I'll be there in about an hour if not sooner."

Jeffrey arrived exactly one hour later. I helped him haul in my belongings. He had been kind enough to put everything in moving boxes instead of trash bags.

After he set down the last box, he glanced around the gloomy room, frowning and shaking his bald head and narrowing his dark eyes. Jeffrey was a handsome man, but the frown on his face now was so severe, he looked beastly. I flopped down in the wobbly chair by the side of the bed, and he stood in front of the scarred dresser with his arms folded. "Lola, you were very good to Bertha and I'm sure she appreciated everything you did for her. She would not have lasted as long as she did without you. I don't know anybody else who would have tolerated her antics as long as you did."

"She was good to me too. She drove me up the wall, but I'm still going to miss her."

"Everybody is going to miss that sweet woman. She touched a lot of people's lives." Jeffrey paused and gave me a sympathetic look. "Um, I guess you know she left an impressive estate. Libby showed me the amended will for the first time this morning. She and Marshall had badgered Bertha for weeks to change it, and she finally did back in January. Her house is worth four times the amount she paid for it forty years ago. Her bank accounts include that huge settlement she collected back in the seventies from Uncle Sam when her brother died in that freak accident in Vietnam. In addition to that, she's still got money left over from the insurance your daddy left her, which has been collecting interest for years in another one of her bank accounts. And there is a one hundred thousand dollar life insurance policy she took out on herself." I was surprised when Jeffrey abruptly stopped talking. He bit his bottom lip and started blinking.

I narrowed my eyes and stared into his. His sudden silence and the way he was still blinking confused and scared me. "Please finish telling me what you started," I prodded. "Are you going to tell me something bad?" With my stomach in knots, I stood up and put my hands on my hips.

"Yes, I am. I'm about to tell you something bad," he warned with his voice cracking. "Something *real* bad. . . ."

My mouth dropped open and my blood pressure shot up so high, I was surprised I was still conscious. "Oh Lord. I think I know what it is!" I wheezed, and then I started blinking too. "Libby and Marshall are going to make a big fuss about whatever Bertha left me. I just know it!" I angrily waved my hand in the air and gritted my teeth. "Knowing those two boogers, they're going to go out of their way to keep me from getting it and—" I stopped talking when Jeffrey shook his head again.

"Bertha left several thousand dollars to her church and a couple of her favorite charities, but Libby and Marshall will inherit everything else." Jeffrey paused and gave me a woeful look. "She didn't leave you a plugged nickel."

It felt as if somebody had knocked the wind out of me, but it took only a few seconds for me to recover. "Oh," was all I could say at first. "I'm disappointed, but thankful that I got to live rent free in such a nice house as long as I did."

"I know it probably won't make you feel any better, but I want you to know that Bertha had originally planned to divide everything between you and Libby and Marshall."

"She did? Well, what . . ." I didn't even bother to finish my question because I already knew the answer. I was glad Jeffrey confirmed it.

"Two months before she died, Libby and Marshall ganged up on her and practically forced her to change her will and not leave anything to you. I didn't find out about it until after they'd done it. I went behind their backs and tried to talk Bertha into leaving you something. She told me she would do so, but she kept putting it off because she was afraid of what Libby and Marshall would do when they found out. Unfortunately, she put it off too long."

"Thanks for letting me know, Jeffrey." I felt somewhat better knowing that Bertha had intended to do something nice for me. Despite all the turmoil she'd caused me, I was happy she'd been such a huge part of my life.

Chapter 37
Calvin

"**Y**OU'RE BETTER THAN YOU WERE THE LAST TIME. YOU EVEN SEEM *bigger*." Maria giggled and stroked my dick as we lay in bed in the hotel suite she'd booked for our rendezvous in San Ysidro. It was eight-thirty p.m. Sylvia and I had arrived four hours ago. Shortly after I'd tucked her away into our hotel, I headed out to the bogus meeting that Sylvia thought I had to attend.

I'd been with Maria ever since. We'd already made love three times and finished a whole bottle of tequila. I planned to stay only one more hour. That would give me enough time to take Sylvia out for a drink and a late snack.

"You're better than you were the last time we were together too," I told her, sliding my tongue across my lips. She had sat on my face so long and left so much love juice, my lips felt like a glazed donut.

"Um, there is something important that I need to tell you." Her tentative tone made me nervous. Glinda had been the last woman who had spoken the exact same words to me just before she told me she was carrying my baby.

"Oh? And what is that?"

"I'm getting married in a couple of months."

I breathed a sigh of relief. "What a coincidence. I'm getting married in a couple of months myself."

"I don't love the man, but he's got a lot of money and he's real nice. The man I wanted to marry is poor and he spends a lot of time in jail. I have to be smart and look out for my future and the children I plan to have." She stroked my dick some more. "What about you?"

"What about me?"

"Do you love the woman you're going to marry?"

"Yes, I do. I love her very much." I squeezed Maria's hand.

"You love her enough not to cheat on her?"

"Cheat? Baby, what we do is no more cheating than jacking off. You know as well as I do that most of the club members are married," I snickered.

"I'm sorry to hear that you think making love to me is the same as 'jacking off,'" she pouted. Her body stiffened and she stopped stroking my dick.

I pulled her closer and tightened my embrace before I kissed the top of her head. "I'm sorry. That was a stupid thing for me to say. What I meant was, I don't think what we do is really being unfaithful. We're only in it to have a good time and enjoy the company of people we like. And of all the women in the club, you're the one I enjoy being with the most."

"Thank you, *papi*. You just made me feel so much better." Maria sighed and started stroking me again. "Then we'll still get together even after we marry other people?"

I hunched my shoulders and kissed the top of her head again. "Honey, married or not, we will continue to get together as long and as often as we can."

"I have never even made love with my fiancé, so I don't know what I'm getting."

"Why have you not made love with the man you're planning to spend the rest of your life with? Doesn't he want to?"

"Yes, he does, but I don't." Maria shuddered and let out a loud breath. "He's fat and hairy and old and ugly. And he smells like a burro."

"Shit, baby! I feel sorry for you, but once you marry this creature, you won't have a choice. And because you made him wait, he'll probably want to hit it two or three times a night."

"I know. He's taking me to Spain for our honeymoon for a

whole month. If he's not a good lover, I'll be climbing the walls by the time I get back home. In case he's not good, I need something to hold me over until the next time I can see you. I'd *die* for another session with you before I get married."

I laughed. Had I not liked Maria so much, I probably would have killed her a long time ago. "Honey, you don't have to do something that extreme to be with me again. I'm thinking about driving down to Baja in a couple of weeks to do some fishing. If I do, you can meet me there. And I will cool you off so well, you'll think I stuck an icicle between your legs."

"That would be the best wedding present you can give me!" she squealed.

Her cell phone lay on the hotel nightstand right next to mine. One rang, and she thought it was hers so I didn't move. "That's your phone," she told me as she scrambled up and trotted into the bathroom.

I rolled over and checked the caller ID. LOLA! Since the clock was ticking on her life, I decided to give her a few moments of my time. I took a deep breath and hit the answer button. "Lola, how are you?" I began, speaking in a low voice.

"I've had better days, Calvin," she bleated, sounding like a sick sheep.

I sat up and held the phone closer to my ear. "I hope I can brighten your day, sweetie. What's the matter?"

"I hope you don't mind me calling, but I really needed to talk to somebody. My best friend is unavailable and you . . . well, you're one of the best listeners I know. You care about people's feelings, so you're the only other person I wanted to talk to."

"Lola, I haven't completed my run. I'm still in San Ysidro. I'll probably be back in the Bay Area by tomorrow evening or Thursday morning. It depends on traffic and whether or not I take a motel break along the way."

"Oh. Well, is this a bad time for you to talk?"

"I can talk for a couple of minutes. I was thinking about you and your stepmother's passing. I hope she died peacefully."

"She had a massive heart attack. I know that had to be painful, so I doubt if she died peacefully."

"I am so sorry to hear that. That's what took my uncle out a few weeks ago."

"She and I argued Friday evening, and she got real upset. I think she had her heart attack around the same time I was with you. She died minutes before I made it to her hospital room, so I didn't get a chance to tell her good-bye. If only I had made it there sooner!"

"So if you hadn't been with me, you might have made it in time to say good-bye to her." My voice was full of genuine compassion. I actually felt for this cow.

"Calvin, don't say that. Don't make me feel any worse. You shouldn't be blaming yourself for anything any more than I should. My stepmother had been in bad health for years, so it was just a matter of time anyway."

"How are you holding up?"

"My stepsister is blaming me for causing the heart attack. When I walked into that hospital room, she lit into me like a blowtorch. I was afraid to go home when I left the hospital. I had to spend the night with my friend, Joan. When I went home Saturday, the locks had been changed and she had packed some of my stuff in garbage bags and left them on the porch."

"Goddamn! Where are you now?"

"I'm in a motel."

"Oh. Well, I'm glad you have your cell phone with you. How long are you going to stay in this motel?"

"I'll probably stay here until I find a place to live that I can afford. Even if my stepsister calms down and lets me back into the house, I don't want to stay there now. I took real good care of my stepmother for years. Just like I promised my daddy I would. But apparently she didn't think so."

"Why do you say that?"

"My stepsister's husband came to the motel and brought some more of my stuff. I only need to get my bedroom furniture now. He told me that my stepmother didn't leave me anything in her will. She left the house, her money, and everything else to her no-good daughter and son."

"Shit. Do you mean to tell me that after all you did for that woman, she left you high and dry?"

"That's right. I didn't expect to inherit the house or any of the profits from it if her children sell it, but I never expected to be completely forgotten. My stepsister's husband also told me that my stepmother had planned to leave me something until her kids talked her into changing her will. Shortly before she died, she told him she'd meet with her lawyer and put me back in it and not let her kids know, but she put it off until it was too late."

"I guess you didn't know her as well as you thought you did."

"Tell me about it."

"Let's give the lady the benefit of the doubt. Maybe she thought you were so smart and self-sufficient, you didn't need anything from her. From what you've told me about her children, always borrowing money from her, they don't sound responsible at all. So maybe their mother just wanted to make sure they'd be in good shape financially when she died."

"That could be true, but it doesn't make me feel any better." Lola snorted and then she laughed dryly. "But I'll be just fine."

"I know you will, and I'm going to do whatever I can to make sure you are." I heard her gasp. Knowing her, she was probably jumping for joy too, but I didn't give her time to respond to my comment. "Lola, let's plan on getting together in the next week or so. But that's only if you feel up to it. And we don't have to do anything but talk and maybe have a few drinks. I really do care about you."

She gasped again. "Thanks, Calvin. I was reluctant to call you, but next to my stepsister's husband, you're one of the nicest men I know. And no matter what happens in the future between us, you will always have a special place in my heart."

Lola's last statement almost made me gag. If this goofball slid any closer to the bottom of my hip pocket, I'd need a shoehorn to get her out.

"You will always have a special place in my heart, too, Lola." I wanted to add, "You will always have a special place in my freezer, too, bitch." This was one of the many things I'd tell her just before I killed her though. "I have to go now so I can get up and get back on the road."

"Bye, Calvin," she mumbled.

"Bye, Lola," I whispered because I heard Maria open the bathroom door. I turned off my phone and held open my arms as she sashayed back to the bed.

Chapter 38
Joan

*I*ABSOLUTELY HATED FUNERALS. SHORTLY AFTER I MARRIED REED, I told him to his face and in writing that if I died first, I wanted to be cremated and I did not want a funeral. I didn't want anybody gawking at me lying in a coffin. The only thing I agreed to was a brief memorial service. I'd told my family the same thing in case Reed and I got divorced, or if he died before I did.

Bertha's funeral was the saddest one I had ever attended. She looked so pitiful lying there with her hands folded across her chest. I was pleased to see that the funeral parlor people had done such a good job on her hair. They had hidden the bald spots that she had always been so self-conscious about. Her hair was in the same curly, bubble-looking do that Lola used to style for her. It was so ironic that this latest nightmare had started because Lola had refused to delay a date and stay home so she could do Bertha's hair.

Every single pew was filled to capacity, and dozens of people had to stand. Bertha's children and some of the relatives from Mississippi sat on the two front pews. Mr. Fernandez and about a dozen of his relatives occupied the two behind them. She had been one of the most beloved teachers at our elementary school. I counted at least thirty of her former students, the retired principal, and several teachers who had worked with her. The guests also included her last three doctors and the Jewish family she used to clean house for when she was in college. The only person missing was Lola.

"Mama, how come you made me come to this dang funeral for some old lady I hardly knew and Lola's not even here?" my impatient son, Junior, whispered. I sat between him and Reed in the middle of a pew a few rows from the front.

"I talked to Lola this morning and she will be here. She's just running late," I whispered back as I glanced toward the back of the room. We had arrived only fifteen minutes ago, and Reed had already dozed off. I jabbed his side with my elbow. His body jerked, and he turned sharply to look at me. "Will you please stay awake? You know you snore like a damn moose, and I'm not going to let you embarrass me in front of all these people."

"Then you shouldn't have made me come," he grumbled.

"Reed, show some respect. If this was your mother's funeral, Lola would be here," I said before I suddenly started boo-hooing.

"Get ahold of yourself, Joan," he ordered in a low voice. "You're worried about me embarrassing you? I'm more worried about you embarrassing me."

Right after Reed stopped talking, I looked toward the back of the room again. Lola had finally arrived. She looked so sad in her navy blue dress and her hair pulled back into a ponytail. I waved to her, but she didn't see me as she moved slowly toward the pews closer to the front and sat down on the third one, right next to Elbert Porter and his mother. He kissed her cheek and draped his arm around her shoulder. I liked Elbert, but I didn't like the fact that he wanted to be more to Lola than just a friend. I had told her more than once that going out with him was sending him the wrong signals about their relationship. I also warned her that he could become obsessed and maybe even start stalking her, but she assured me that Elbert would never do anything to hurt or upset her.

"Isn't Lola supposed to sit in the same pew with Libby and Marshall?" Junior asked as he chomped on a wad of gum. He stopped chewing when I glared at him, took a napkin out of my purse, and held it in front of his mouth.

"Yes, she should, son. But you can see how crowded that pew is," I replied as Junior spat his gum into the napkin and I stuffed it back into my purse. Then I turned to Reed. "Baby, I'm so glad you took a couple of hours away from work this morning to come with us."

"I had Beverly reschedule the rest of my appointments for today, so I'll be taking the rest of the day off as well," he said dryly.

"I'm glad to hear that. It'll be nice to have you home on a weekday." I hated telling a lie in church, but I made an exception when it involved Reed.

"Um . . . I'll be spending the rest of the day helping Dr. Mansfield prepare his speech for that three-day conference in L.A. that he and I will be attending the first weekend in May."

"Oh? This is news to me."

"Didn't I tell you?"

"No, you didn't. Since when does Dr. Mansfield need help preparing a speech? He's been doing it on his own for years."

"He's in his late sixties now, and since he had that mild stroke last year, he's not as sharp as he used to be. He needs a little help now and then."

"But he's still sharp enough to practice medicine?"

"Yes, but only a few days a month. After this conference, he's going to retire. He's already referred most of his patients to other doctors. He was one of my mentors, and he's been like a father to me for years. I'd like to do all I can to make his golden years comfortable. He got real excited when I agreed to help him write his last speech."

"Well, it was nice of you to agree to help him, honey." In spite of all the aggravation Reed caused me, I was proud of the fact that he was so caring when it came to his friends and colleagues. Even so, I was glad to hear that he was going to be out of my hair again so soon. A club member from New York was going to be in California the same weekend in May and wanted to spend some time with me. He was fairly new, so only two women had posted reviews about him. According to one, he was a ball of fire in the bedroom. All the other one said was that she couldn't wait to see him again. I hadn't responded to his date request yet, but now that I knew Reed was going to be gone for another whole weekend, I made a mental note to accept the date as soon as I got home.

"You know how much I love L.A., so I'm looking forward to the conference."

"When did this come up? You always tell me weeks ahead of time when you have to attend a conference."

"I found out about it last month. I thought I told you."

"Well, you didn't tell me, but that's all right. I have a feeling Lola's going to need my shoulder to cry on for the next few weeks, so I'll be pretty busy myself."

"Poor Lola. For her sake, I hope she stays as far away from Libby and Marshall as possible. It's a good thing that looks can't kill, because Lola would have dropped dead as soon as Libby spotted her," Reed said under his breath.

The next thing I knew, Jeffrey got up and rushed over to Lola and whispered in her ear. She promptly rose, and he led her by her arm to the back of the church. There was a look of disbelief on her face when she passed our pew.

The service was so long, I almost dozed off myself. Reed did go back to sleep. I cried into my handkerchief as his head bobbed against my shoulder. When he started snoring, I jabbed him in his side again with my elbow until he woke up.

I was tempted to bolt when Libby leaned on the pulpit and went on and on about what a great mother Bertha had been to her and Marshall. "If God made a more righteous woman, He kept her to Himself," she swooned, fanning her face with a white handkerchief. "Mama, I love you! Please continue to be the guardian angel you were to me in life!" That bitch. Her croco-dile tears didn't fool anybody, because I'd overheard several mourners talking about how she had mistreated Bertha. When we'd arrived, I'd spotted her outside drinking from a can of Red Bull and on her cell phone yip-yapping and *laughing*!

What Marshall had to say was even more incredulous. "My mama was my best friend and the only person I could always count on. And she could always count on me whenever she needed assistance of any kind. She will be missed," he babbled.

All of a sudden, he closed his eyes and began to sway from side to side. He looked like a penguin in his black suit and white shirt. He even walked like one when an usher rushed up and helped him back to his seat. But then he did something that stunned everybody. He pushed the usher away, waddled back to the pulpit, and continued. "Mama had a lot of friends, but like Jesus, she also had a lot of tormentors. Since she is no longer here to say it, I'll say it for her." He paused and looked directly at Lola. "As sweet a woman as my mama was, she was still the victim of wolves in sheep's clothing! Every single one of them will suffer!" It didn't take a genius to know that one of the wolves he was talking about was Lola. Marshall stood there and wept and wailed like an old woman. He stumbled and fell, and three ushers ran to assist him. They helped him up and escorted him back to his seat.

Not only did my jaw drop, so did Reed's. Almost every other person gasped and prayed out loud. Most of them knew how selfish, greedy, and mean-spirited Bertha's children were. And the same people knew how devoted Lola had been to her. Libby and Marshall were behaving like buffoons at their own mother's funeral! From the horrified expressions on almost every other face present, including Reverend Clyde's, it was obvious that they knew the "wolves in sheep's clothing" who had tormented Bertha. I turned around again. I was pleased to see several elders standing close to Lola. One old sister had her arm around her shoulder.

"I can't believe my ears! The nerve of Libby and Marshall. Those two jackasses treated their mother like shit," Reed snarled. "Well, what goes around comes around." There was an amused look on his face. "If there is an afterlife, I'm sure Bertha won't miss them borrowing money from her." I had shared with Reed some of the things Lola had told me about Bertha's relationship with her children, but not everything. I had never told him about how often they borrowed money from her and how disrespectfully they treated her. But the busybodies had such long tongues, their gossip eventually reached people they didn't even know. Even Reed.

"I didn't know you knew about them hitting Bertha up for money all the time," I said, giving Reed a guarded look. "What else have you heard?"

Reed let out a long, deep sigh and shook his head before he answered. "Plenty. I heard that Lola is not the Goody Two-shoes she appears to be."

I held my breath. "Meaning what?"

"For one thing, people say she's got men coming out of her ear. One recent Saturday afternoon, Mother spotted her prancing out of a hotel elevator with a married man, and they were obviously more than friends, if you know what I mean."

"How did Mother Riley know the man was married?"

"She asked one of the clerks at the front desk about him. He told her that this same man, who was from out of town, often checked into one of their suites *with his wife.*"

"So what? Lola's single, so she could have men coming out of her ass if she wanted to. I know she has a lot of men friends, and a few of them could be married. But that's her business." I shifted in my seat and focused on the next speaker. From the corner of my eye, I could see Reed looking at the side of my head. I could only imagine what was going through his mind about my knowledge of Lola's lifestyle and what influence it had on me.

Chapter 39
Joan

REVEREND CLYDE WAS DELIVERING THE CLOSING REMARKS, SO I thought the funeral was almost over. I was wrong. Right after he finished, Libby got up again and skittered back to the pulpit. Reverend Clyde looked at her as if she had lost her mind, but he graciously stepped to the side. "I have a few more things to say," she said with a sniffle. She fanned her sweaty face with a hand fan and dabbed at her nose and eyes some more with her handkerchief. "I know Mama is looking down from heaven with a big smile because she's so happy to see that so many people came out to pay their respects. But the main reason she's happy is because she's with the Lord." Libby paused and looked up toward the ceiling. "Mama, you sit tight up there and keep an eye on your loved ones until we all join you."

"I don't believe the nerve of that hypocritical wench," I said to Reed in a low voice. He didn't hear me because he had fallen asleep again.

When the service finally ended, everybody headed downstairs to the dining area. There were four long tables, and on top of each one were bowls and platters of everything from fried chicken to collard greens to tacos and lox and bagels. Mama had brought six sweet potato pies, and I'd brought four dozen dinner rolls and three large bowls of black-eyed peas.

"I hope you didn't season them peas with no pork. We have to show respect for them Jews and Muslim mourners that came,"

Mama said when I approached her. She hovered over a table looking like she wanted to eat everything in sight.

"I seasoned the peas with smoked turkey necks, Mama," I said, rolling my eyes.

Everybody except me had already descended on the food like vultures. Lola was the last person to enter the dining area. She stood in the doorway looking like a deer caught in a car's headlights. I immediately joined her. "I am so glad you made it," I told her, giving her a big hug. Her body was so stiff it felt as if I had wrapped my arms around a lamppost.

"I . . . I'm glad I made it too," she sniffled. "I almost changed my mind at the last minute. Now I wish to God that I had. As soon as I sat down, Jeffrey came over and told me that Libby and Marshall didn't want me sitting anywhere near the family and instructed him to escort me to the back of the room."

"I saw that," I said, so angry my cheeks throbbed. "You had a close relationship with Bertha, and you meant a lot to her. You have as much right to be here as—" Before I could finish my sentence, two stout ushers headed in our direction, marching like soldiers on their way to a battlefield.

"Sister Lola," one of them began, looking sad and apologetic at the same time. "I know this is a unhappy occasion for all of us, but we have to ask you to leave," he added.

Lola and I gulped at the same time. I thought I was going to lose the cookies I'd eaten earlier. "Why?" she asked.

"It's the family's request. Your presence is causing them even more grief," the other usher said. "I'm so sorry, sister." He looked just as sad and apologetic as the other one.

"I have to leave right now?" Lola asked in a high-pitched voice. From the look on her face, I could tell that she was twice as stunned as I was. Somehow she remained civil, but her voice shook when she spoke again. "Some of my former teachers and classmates are here and I'd—"

The first usher held up his hand and shook his head. "You can fix a plate to take home, but you have to get up out of this church lickety-split. Otherwise, Libby and Marshall might make this situation real ugly."

"Humph! They've already made this situation real ugly!" Lola shot back. The next thing I knew, she spun around and headed toward the exit. Mourners close enough to hear everything gasped and shook their heads as she plowed through the crowd, and I was right behind her. Reed and Junior stared at me in slack-jawed amazement.

"I'll get a ride home with Lola," I yelled to them. I didn't bother to wait for a response. Under the circumstances, my best friend needed me more than my husband and my son.

I climbed into the front passenger seat of Lola's raggedy old Jetta and then she shot off down the street. We didn't speak until she stopped at a liquor store parking lot a block and a half away. "Make sure you get something real potent," I hollered when she opened her door and got out.

"I will. And I'll buy the biggest bottle they have," she added in an angry tone I rarely heard her use.

"I hope I never have to be near Libby and Marshall again as long as I live," Lola seethed as she poured rum into one of the motel's flimsy paper drinking cups. I had already mixed myself a rum and Coke. Lola was so anxious to get a buzz, she didn't even dilute her drink with Coke. "I could kill them both!" she hollered. I sat down on the lumpy bed; she started pacing the floor. "Those motherfuckers!"

"I say good riddance to them both. Be glad they are finally out of your life."

Lola stopped pacing and gave me a hopeful look. "Now I can really focus on having a life of my own without a bunch of complications. I don't have to sneak around and make up stories about bogus friends and all that other shit I had to do when I had Bertha breathing down my neck."

"What about the club?"

"What about it?"

"Are you going to keep dating club members?"

"I will until I meet somebody special, I guess." A tight smile crossed her face. "Or until I know for sure where my relationship is going with Calvin. He's anxious to see me again."

"He called you?"

"No, I called him last night. He was on a run down to San Ysidro. He told me he'd like to see me when he gets back up here."

"I'm glad to hear that. He'll be a nice distraction for you until you get your bearings back." I gave Lola the most endearing look I could manage. "I've said it before and I'll say it again: I hope Calvin is the man you seem to think he is."

"I hope he is too." There was a gleam in her eyes that I had not seen since we were teenagers.

I knew that things were eventually going to work out for her. Now I had some new concerns about my own situation. For the past couple of weeks, Reed had been doing some pretty weird shit, even for him. He'd left his computer on one morning, something he rarely did. While he was taking a shower, I checked his monitor. The link he had opened was an article about people who believed in life after death. When I asked him about it, he shrugged and claimed he was "just curious" about the subject and told me to stop being so nosy. He usually read the newspaper at the breakfast table every morning, but last Thursday it was the Bible. When I asked him why, the only response I got was a mysterious smile.

Last Monday after we had gone to bed, around midnight he nudged me with his knee to see if I was asleep. I was awake but I played possum. A few minutes later, I heard him crying! The next morning when I asked him if everything was all right, he gave me a strange look at first and then he said, "No, but I'm working on it." His peculiar behavior had begun to scare the hell out of me. I hated the vague responses he gave when I tried to get him to open up to me, but I didn't know what else to do for him. I was at my wit's end.

Reed's parents continued to believe that he was fine and that his suicide hints were nothing to be concerned about. They were convinced that if he really wanted to take his own life, he would have done it by now. No matter how many times I offered to make an appointment for him to talk to a professional, he refused. He told me that if anybody needed professional help, it was me.

I prayed that I wouldn't have to attend *his* funeral next.

Chapter 40
Lola

AFTER WE FINISHED TWO DRINKS EACH, JOAN DECIDED TO HANG out with me at the motel for a while. She gave Reed a call to let him know. He expressed his concerns about her being in a dump like the Stanton Street Motel and offered to bring us some Chinese takeout since we had not eaten at the funeral reception, but we had already picked up some rib dinners from Beanie's, the soul food restaurant in the next block. Reed also told Joan that he, and almost everybody else at the church, was appalled about what had happened to a sweet person like me.

I was touched when she told me some of the things he'd said. "He called me 'a sweet person'? I never thought Reed would ever say something like that about me," I said. We occupied the same side of the bed with the Styrofoam plates that contained our rib dinners in our laps.

"Tell me about it. I don't know, Lola. I don't know if I should be concerned about him or not. Sometimes his behavior scares me to death. Especially lately."

"Do you still think he's in that state of euphoria some suicidal people go through before they . . . you know?"

"I don't think that's the case now. It's been going on too long. From what I read, suicidal people generally kill themselves either the same day of their euphoria or within a day or two."

"The man is one for the books, but maybe he's trying to make up for all the misery he's caused you."

I was about to give Reed more benefit of the doubt when he showed up at the motel anyway with a stupid look on his face. We had just finished our dinners and the rest of the rum and Coke. "I was in the neighborhood and thought I'd check to see if either one of you needed anything," he said when he strolled in, frowning at the empty rum bottle on the dresser. "Or did somebody else already take care of that? I noticed a lot of cars in the parking lot. . . ." What he did next happened so fast it took us a few moments to process it. We watched in stunned disbelief as he darted to the bathroom, leaned in the doorway, and looked around inside. He did the same thing with the closet, which was so small a man would have to be a midget to fit in it. I was surprised he didn't look under the bed to see if we were hiding a man there.

Joan looked totally disgusted. "Dr. Riley, can't you do better than that? Do you honestly think that we'd leave the funeral of my best friend's mother and shack up with dudes in a dump like this the same day? You saw how Lola was booted out of the church. How could you even think she, or I—"

I cut Joan off. "Let it go. It's all right."

"Now there you go, jumping to conclusions and putting words in my mouth like you always do," he protested. "I was just being funny."

"You were just being a damn fool!" Joan boomed. Reed lowered his head and started fidgeting. I could tell he was sorry he'd said and done something so ridiculous, but Joan didn't let up. She gave him one of her meanest looks. "By the way, I might spend the night here with Lola."

Reed remained silent for a few seconds and there was a steely look on his face. He snorted and blinked hard as he gazed from Joan to me and back. "That's fine with me. Junior left the church with your folks, and he'll be spending the night over there. Your sister said she'd bring him home in the morning in time to get ready for school," he said. He cleared his throat, narrowed his eyes, and continued talking in a slow, tentative manner. "I . . . um . . . so you're not coming home at all tonight?"

"Didn't I just tell you that I was spending the night here with Lola?" Joan hissed. "And don't expect to see me in the morning in time to make you breakfast. As for today, I suggest you pick up some Chinese takeout and eat that for dinner yourself."

Reed waved his hand and snickered. "Don't worry about me. I talked to Mitch a little while ago and he invited me over for a drink. I just might stay for dinner."

"You're going to Dr. Weinstein's house to have dinner? A little while ago you said you were going to go help Dr. Mansfield prepare a speech today," Joan said with her arms folded, and looking even more disgusted.

"Huh? Oh yeah! I am. I'm going to Mitch's place after I do that."

"Good! Start stepping!" Joan gave Reed a dismissive wave and pointed toward the door.

I was not the least bit surprised that she was being so abrupt. He'd been in the room less than three minutes and had already annoyed me, so I could imagine how unbearable living with him was for her. He scratched his head and glanced at his watch. "I see I'm running late, so I'd better get going," he grunted. He backed toward the door, snatched it open, and left without saying another word.

Joan and I looked at one another and shrugged. "At least he didn't insist on spending the night here so he could keep an eye on you." I giggled but I was dead serious.

"Don't be surprised if he sneaks back and hides behind a tree across the street or between parked cars so he can spy on me," Joan said with a groan. "I swear to God, he's beginning to act stranger by the day."

I shrugged again. "How can you tell the difference?"

"Oh, I can tell the difference in his recent behavior."

"I know you don't want to hear this, especially from me, but I think you're overreacting."

"I don't think so. There is something different about Reed these days and I should be concerned."

I hunched my shoulders and gasped as if a lightbulb had suddenly been turned on inside my head. "I just thought of something. Maybe there's a reasonable explanation for Reed's behavior."

Joan gave me a sideways glance. "Keep talking. I'd like to hear what that explanation is," she prodded.

"He's in his forties, so he's probably going through something as normal as a midlife crisis. Since we're on the subject, do you still think he has suicide on his mind?"

"Yes, unfortunately, I do. I read an article about a man who had attempted to kill himself when he was twenty-two. He lived a normal life for the next thirty years. His family and friends thought he was happy until the day he came home from work and blew his brains out."

"Damn. Let's not even go into that right now. I'm depressed enough already."

"I'll do all I can to bring you out of your depression, and you'll probably have to throw me a lifeline any day now. With me having to deal with whatever Reed's going through, I'm sure I'll be depressed again very soon." We laughed at the same time.

After we'd chatted a few minutes more about the incident at the church, I turned on my laptop and started browsing rental sites. I was even willing to settle for a private residence where I could rent a room. My search was very disappointing. Most of the apartments and houses were in areas I wouldn't be caught dead in, and others were way out of my price range. I scanned the listings until something caught my eye that made me do a double take.

"Joan, look at this: Laurel District house: one story, three bedrooms, two bathrooms, and pets allowed . . . five hundred and fifty a month. That's a real nice neighborhood. And rent is only *five hundred and fifty bucks* a month. Oh, this has to be a typo."

"Either that or the place is haunted. Some of the studio apartments in that neighborhood rent for over fifteen hundred bucks a month."

I read on. "Partially furnished, utilities included." Joan and I looked at each other at the same time. "Something is definitely not right."

She widened her eyes, whipped out her cell phone, and dialed the number listed with the ad. "Hello. I'm calling about the house on High Street. Is the rent really only five hundred and fifty dollars a month?" She listened to the person on the other end for about two minutes before she thanked them and hung up. There was an incredulous look on her face.

"Well?" I said, heaving a sigh.

"It's not a typo."

My jaw dropped. I was shocked and suspicious. "If the house is not haunted, there's got to be something else wrong with it. Mold, termites, mice . . ."

Joan shook her head. "The landlady swears that there's nothing wrong with the place."

"Then why is the rent so cheap?"

Joan blew out some air and gave me a hopeless look. "You don't want to know."

"Tell me what she said," I insisted.

Joan coughed to clear her throat first. After a long breath, she continued. "A couple of years ago somebody bought the building next door and turned it into a halfway house for ex-convicts. The family that had lived in the house for ten years moved two months later. The next tenants left a month after they found out they'd moved next door to a bunch of ex-cons."

"I don't blame those people! I wouldn't want to live next door to a bunch of convicted felons either," I said sharply.

"Give the dudes the benefit of the doubt. They've paid for their crimes.

The landlady said none of them have committed any crimes against any of the other residents in that neighborhood. She said that last year, a woman and her two teenage daughters lived there for six months. The convicts didn't bother them at all."

"Why did they move?"

"The woman's fiancé lived in L.A. When they got married, she and her girls moved down there."

"Hmmm. I can't afford to stay in this motel too much longer and maybe it'd be okay to stay in that house until I find another place I can afford. That shouldn't take more than a few months, and maybe not even that long. What do you think?"

"I think you should decide what's best for you." Joan paused and gave me a hopeful look. "Me, personally, I wouldn't have a problem living next door to some ex-cons. I have a few ex-cons in my family and they've never bothered me. I'd take a chance on that house."

Maisie and Samuel Cottright, the elderly couple who owned the grocery store where I worked, offered their employees some damn good benefits. In addition to paid vacation and holidays, they allowed us to take off up to three days with pay to attend a family member's funeral. I didn't know what I was going to do with myself for the next two days. And I certainly didn't expect Joan to babysit me. She did enough for me already. I decided to spend the rest of my time off looking for a place to live. And I told myself it wouldn't hurt to check out the place next door to the halfway house. I decided to sleep on that thought first though.

Around midnight, we returned to the liquor store and bought another bottle of rum. After we finished it, we decided to turn in for the night. I gave Joan one of my nightgowns and she went to sleep almost immediately. I was glad the room had a king-size bed, because she was the kind of person who tossed and turned and flailed her arms throughout the night. Even with all the space between us, she kicked me so many times I slept in spurts.

Joan was still asleep when I got up at nine a.m. Then minutes later, she scrambled out of bed yawning and looking around with an amused look on her face. "Damn! I really am in a cheap motel," she snickered. "I thought I'd had a nightmare."

I rolled my eyes and ignored Joan's remarks. "I'm going to check out that house you called about yesterday," I told her. I was surprised when she insisted on going with me.

We showered and left half an hour later. After coffee and

some pastries at a nearby coffee shop, we went on our way. When we got to High Street where the house was located, I suddenly felt an extremely cold breeze on my face even though it was April and the temperature was in the midseventies. "Joan, did you feel that?"

"Feel what?" she asked, giving me a curious look.

"That cold air that just blew through here. Didn't you feel it? It was so icy it made me shiver." All of my windows were rolled up and I had not turned on my air, so there was no explanation for the temperature in my car to suddenly drop to what felt like a below-zero level.

"I didn't feel any cold air. I think you had one rum and Coke too many last night and now—stop the car. It's that house on the right."

I parked and looked to my right. What I saw made me shiver even more, even though I could no longer feel the mysterious cold air I'd felt only a few seconds ago. I held my breath and began to tremble. "It's . . . *yellow.*"

"I can see that. Hey, this place is not half bad. Shit. I wouldn't mind living over here myself!"

"Joan, I can't live in a house *that* color," I whimpered.

"Girl, puh-leeze! I can understand you being afraid to wear yellow clothing, but living in a yellow house is a whole different ball game. If you don't get over that insane fear, you're going to miss out on a lot of things in this life."

"I know that."

"I think you should at least consider this place before somebody else grabs it."

"Yeah . . . but a house with three bedrooms and two baths? What would I do with all that space?"

"You could make an office out of one of the bedrooms and a guest room out of one of the others. I can crash with you whenever I need a break from Reed instead of going to my mother's house."

"Well . . ."

"'Well', nothing. I know you don't like people telling you

what to do, but this time I hope you will take my advice. If this lady is willing to rent to you, go for it. And I'll even pay your first month's rent."

"I wonder how much the security deposit is."

"Oh! I forgot to tell you that the lady said she's not charging a security deposit."

I gave Joan an incredulous look. "Damn. She really is desperate to rent this place."

"And you're desperate too. Look, you're not going to find a deal better than this one. If you don't take this place, I will. I'll make it my home away from home." Joan laughed.

I laughed too. And then I gave the landlady a call.

Chapter 41
Calvin

*I*T WAS ELEVEN P.M. WHEN I ENDED MY RENDEZVOUS WITH MARIA. She didn't want me to leave, and I didn't want to, but with Sylvia waiting for me to return from my important "meeting" and spend some time with her, I had no choice.

"I thought that damn man would never stop talking," I complained when I let myself into our hotel room. Sylvia lay crossways in her nightgown on the king-size bed.

"How did your meeting go?" she asked dryly.

I stomped across the floor waving my arms. "It was boring as hell. He went over the same bullshit so many times, I could repeat everything he said! And the dinner I had to suffer through with that punk was even worse." I flopped down on the bed. "Baby, I am so sorry I couldn't make it back before now. Do you want to go out for a snack? There's a fish place a couple of blocks from here."

"That's okay, Calvin. I had a pizza delivered," she said. I ignored her whiny tone and the sad look on her face. Pulling her into my arms and giving her the most passionate kiss I could manage perked her up right away. When I released her, there was a glow on her face. "I hope you're not too tired," I whispered.

"I'm not," she said quickly. "I'm never too tired for you."

I was still fired up from my fuckfest with Maria. All I had to do to perform like a porn star with Sylvia was pretend I was still with Maria.

* * *

After I dropped Sylvia off at her house a few minutes past five p.m. Thursday, I rushed home and literally fell onto my couch.

Around six p.m. I sent Lola a text:

Hello, beautiful. I'm back from my San Ysidro run. Can't wait to see you.

I had a feeling I'd hear from her soon, but I never thought it'd be less than a minute later. That silly bitch probably walked around with her phone in her hand day and night. Her text was just as annoying as all the others:

I would love to hook up with you again real soon! I attended my stepmother's funeral yesterday and I have a few things to take care of before I can see you. Let's talk soon. Love, Lola

How soon? I questioned. I didn't have that much time left, and neither did she. I needed to dispose of this beast before I married Sylvia next month. I wanted to go on my honeymoon with a clear mind and return to begin my new life as a "free" man.

I poured a shot of vodka and flopped back down on my living room couch. All I wanted to do for a while was think, and I had a lot to think about. I still wanted to have sex with Lola at least one more time before I put her out of her misery, but with the unexpected changes in her personal life, there was no telling when I'd be able to see her. I had to revise my plan again. If I didn't get to sleep with her before I killed her, I'd be disappointed but I'd get over it.

An hour after the text from Lola, I drank more vodka and passed out on my couch. When I woke up at six a.m. Friday morning, I watched the local news, made coffee, and called Lola an hour later. She answered two seconds into the first ring. "Hello, Calvin!" Her shrill tone irritated my ears like fingernails scraping down a blackboard.

"I'm sorry to be calling so early, but I wanted to catch you before you left for work," I began.

"I have today off. My employers give us up to three days be-reavement leave when a family member dies so we can attend the funeral and have a little time to grieve."

"How was the funeral? I'm sure you're glad it's behind you."

"It was real sad and I'm so glad it's over. But it was a mess. My stepsiblings were so mean, they had me kicked out of the church right after the service ended."

"You're kidding!"

"No, I'm not, but in a way I was glad. I didn't want to be near either one of them. Anyway, I found a house and I'll probably move in either today or tomorrow." She paused, but before I could respond she started up again in the same shrill tone. "Calvin, I'm still mourning the loss of my stepmother, but I'm moving forward and everything seems to be working out just fine."

"I'm glad to hear that. I hope you found a nice place."

"I did. The landlady showed it to me yesterday and I told her I wanted to move in right away. I signed the lease on the spot. It's a real cute little house with a nice front and backyard, and a garage. There's a convenience store directly across the street with a Laundromat next to it, a strip mall two blocks away on the same street with some of my favorite discount stores, and an Ital-ian restaurant." Lola sighed. "Even though the rent is only five fifty a month, they haven't been able to get a new tenant since the last one moved out months ago. I thought that because of the low rent, the place was haunted, but it's not. There is some-thing else I'm concerned about though."

"Oh? Do you want to tell me about it?"

"There's a halfway house next door at the corner, where some ex-cons live."

"Hmmm. I can understand why people would be skittish about moving next door to a bunch of ex-cons, and that's some-thing you should be concerned about. So this house is in a rough neighborhood, huh?"

"Not really. It's in a nice, quiet area. The police department is only a quarter of a mile away. The landlady shared quite a bit of information with me about the other neighbors. There's a duplex on the other side of the house I'm moving into. Two middle-age gay men have lived in one of the units for almost ten years. A retired secretary and her disabled husband have lived in the other one for twenty-two years. The landlady also said that none of the neighbors have had any trouble with the ex-cons since they moved in two years ago. I did a Google search anyway. Except for a drunken snow cone truck driver rear-ending a school bus, I couldn't find anything on any crimes, big or small, committed on that street in the past five years."

"Well, with all the other positive things about the area, I wouldn't worry too much about the dudes in that halfway house."

"I guess I won't, but . . . the house is *yellow*. I told you why I don't like yellow, remember?"

"Yes, I remember that quite well, but I thought that fear applied only to yellow clothing."

"That's what I thought until I saw that yellow house, a real bright shade at that." Lola laughed. "I'll probably never wear yellow clothing again, but I don't think I have to worry about anything bad happening to me because I live in a house that color. I have to draw the line somewhere."

"Lola, it sounds like you're making some progress with your fear and I'm happy to hear that. Would it be possible for us to get together in your new place once you get settled?"

She let out a loud gasp. "Um, you mean instead of a hotel?"

"We can still have a little fun in a nice hotel room from time to time. I just thought it'd be nice for me to help you get comfortable in your new home at least once. Especially since you no longer have those stepsiblings from hell all over you." I laughed. Lola did too. "Is the house located in South Bay City?"

"Uh-huh. I don't have the ad nearby and I don't remember the address off the top of my head."

I silently prayed that she'd reveal enough vital information so

I wouldn't have too much trouble locating her. She didn't disappoint me. The only thing she didn't provide was a bull's-eye on her neck. "But it's the only yellow house on High Street in the block between Franklin and Webb. And it's the only house on that block with an orange tree in the front yard." I almost wished that I could delay her murder so I could savor my exhilaration a little longer, but it would also mean that I'd still be in pain, and even more women would have to die. "It's on the other side of town, so I'll have to drive my raggedy old car to work. I don't mind though. My credit's pretty good, so I don't think I'll have a problem getting my bank to finance a new car."

"I am so happy to hear that you're moving on with your life, Lola. You're one of the few women I've met in the club that I'd like to . . . uh . . . see more frequently, and I hope you feel the same way about me."

"I am so glad to hear you say that, Calvin," she swooned.

"Well, I'll let you go. I know you have a lot on your plate right now. We'll hook up when you're ready."

"Calvin, I told you that I can cook a mean pot of collard greens. When you come over, that's what we'll have for dinner."

"That's something to look forward to."

"The place needs a little maintenance work, but the handyman just went on vacation yesterday to visit his relatives in Mexico for two weeks. I insisted on moving in right away because I can't afford this motel much longer. It's only a couple of minor things that need to be fixed anyway. The kitchen faucet leaks, and the lock on the back door doesn't work."

"So, you'll have to live for two weeks with a door you can't lock?"

"Yup! And the leaky faucet."

"Thank God it's nothing major. Uh . . . I hate to rush off, but I really need to get going. My brother is coming by and I think he just pulled up. Have a good evening, Lola."

I hung up and started laughing. I had to rub my ears because I could not believe what I'd just heard. Lola was the poster girl for idiots! "Bitch, you just told a man you hardly know where you're moving to and that the place has a broken back door lock that won't be repaired for at least a couple of weeks!" I yelled through clenched teeth.

I couldn't take a chance on the landlady hiring someone else to do the repairs before the handyman returned. Lola Poole had only *days* to live.

Chapter 42
Lola

*T*HE HOUSE I WAS GOING TO MOVE INTO HAD A DECENT-LOOKING couch in the living room, a coffee table, some matching end tables, and kitchen appliances. I still had to get my bedroom furniture and a few other things left in Bertha's house.

In the last two days, I had left Libby several messages asking her when I could arrange for somebody with a truck to collect the rest of my stuff. She had not responded yet. Friday morning at seven-thirty, I called Marshall's number and got his voice mail. I left him a message, but I didn't expect him to return my call either. Finally, a minute after I'd left the message for Marshall, I caught up with Jeffrey and told him I wanted to get my stuff. I scolded myself for not calling him first. "I'll take an early break and meet you at the house in about an hour. I'd like to be there to keep Libby in line," he told me.

I was in a much better mood now because of my conversation with Calvin. I felt stronger and more relaxed, so it was going to be a little easier for me to return to Bertha's house to get the rest of my property. I was glad Jeffrey was going to be on the premises to prevent another confrontation between Libby and me, but it was still difficult for me to drive in that direction.

It was eight-thirty when I turned onto the street where I had lived most of my life. Two blocks from the house, I pulled over because I felt as if I was about to have a panic attack. After taking several deep breaths and drinking half a bottle of water, I felt fine so I drove on.

Libby's car was in the driveway. It had been a little over an hour since I'd spoken to Jeffrey, so I thought he'd already be at the house when I got there, but he had not arrived yet. I parked and got out anyway.

It saddened me to see a For Sale sign already in the front yard. I took several more deep breaths before I had enough nerve to approach the front door. When I knocked, nobody answered. I could hear the television blaring, so I knew somebody was inside. Suddenly, the living-room window curtains parted and I saw old Mr. Fernandez's scraggly face. He gave me a pitiful look and then he abruptly disappeared. I knocked some more, but nobody answered. A few moments later, the curtains parted again and Libby's pug-ugly mug appeared. She gave me a dirty look before she disappeared. I didn't even bother to knock again. I returned to my car and called up Jeffrey again. I was glad he answered right away.

"Lola, I was just about to call you. I'm stuck in a major traffic jam on Interstate 880 and I'm not sure when I'll make it home," he explained.

"Libby and Mr. Fernandez from next door are inside, but they won't let me in. I just need to talk to her about when it'd be convenient for me to bring somebody over here to help me pick up the rest of my stuff."

"Well . . . uh . . . that's another thing."

"What's another thing?"

"When I called home earlier and told her what you wanted to do, she hung up on me. I knew Mr. Fernandez was there to check out some of the junk in the garage to see what he could use. I called his cell phone, and he told me that right after Libby hung up on me, she called somebody to come haul away everything you left behind."

My head started throbbing so hard, it felt like I'd been dropped on it. Tears flooded my eyes. I was so angry that if Libby had been close enough, I would have beaten her to a pulp—and that could still happen when and if she opened the door. I could barely speak, and when I did my words oozed out of my mouth like mud. *She gave my stuff away?*

"Uh-huh."

"To Goodwill or the Salvation Army?"

Jeffrey cleared his throat. "Something . . . like . . . that." I could tell from the slow way he was speaking that this conversation was as uncomfortable for him as it was for me. "She called a junkman. The dude and a couple of his workers rushed over and picked up everything."

"Wait a minute. Are you telling me that Libby had my stuff hauled to the *junkyard?*"

"I'm afraid so. I tried to get there in time to stop her, but I couldn't. I'm going to read her the riot act when I get home. And if it'll make you feel any better, I'll replace everything myself. One of my poker buddies works for Sears, so I can get a good deal on whatever you need."

"Jeffrey, I really appreciate your offer, but you don't have to buy me any new furniture or anything else. I can pick up a few things from Goodwill." I paused because I had a couple of things I wanted to say and I didn't know which one to say first. "You've always been good to me, and I wish you nothing but the best. But after all Libby and Marshall have done to me, I never want to see or speak to either one of them again as long as I live. And you can tell them what I said! I hope you and I stay friends and can get together for drinks or dinner every now and then."

"I'm going to make sure of that. I can't wait to see this new place you're moving into."

"I . . . I—" I stopped abruptly. "Bye, Jeffrey." I decided not to tell him the other thing that was on my mind . . . yet.

After I ate breakfast and drank three cups of coffee at a nearby coffee shop, I decided to visit Kandy's House of Beauty to get my nails done. I had been neglecting them since the day Bertha died, so they looked pretty shabby. As soon as I walked through the front door, Kandy, the sixty-year-old muumuu-wearing blabbermouth who owned the salon, waved me to a chair. She started yip-yapping like a magpie right away. First she complained about how bad my nails looked. Then she told me how sorry she had felt when she saw me get booted out of the church after Bertha's funeral. "Libby came in today to get her nails done. She left about fifteen minutes ago. She bragged up a storm about how she'd locked you out of Bertha's house and how she had the junkman pick up your stuff a little while ago," Kandy reported with a horse-like snort.

"And she said she wished she had kicked your ass more that time when she thought you were screwing her husband," said the beautician working on the hair of a woman in the seat next to me.

"Lola, if I was you, I would kick that cow's ass," the woman getting her hair done added. "Don't let that bitch get away with disrespecting you like that!"

"I am not going to stoop to Libby's level," I said in a strong voice.

"Girl, you need to fight fire with fire. There must be something you can do or say about Libby that would knock her fat ass off the high horse she's been riding all her life," Kandy told me. "If you take her to small claims court for getting rid of your stuff, you might get on the *Judge Judy* show. You could make mincemeat out of her in front of millions of folks."

I didn't want to sue Libby, because I didn't even want to be in the same courtroom with her, especially one on national TV, but I *had* to do something to get back at her. "You're right. There must be something I can do to get back at her and I know I'll figure out what it is real soon." I turned around so Kandy could see my face. When I winked, she smiled and gave me a thumbs-up. I already knew what that "something" was, but I didn't want to share that information with the beauty salon posse yet. They would all hear it soon enough. I had a "weapon" that could cause Libby more pain than a bullet between her eyes. It was time for me to tell Jeffrey the one other thing that I had almost told him during our conversation earlier. I knew that when he heard what I had to say, all hell would break loose and Libby would finally get what she deserved.

When I strolled out of the beauty salon and returned to my car, I immediately called Jeffrey's number again. I didn't even wait for him to greet me before I started talking. "I'm sorry to bother you again so soon, but I have something to tell you."

"Oh? Can it wait? I'm in the middle of a crisis right now."

"I'm sorry to hear that. What I have to tell you will probably cause another crisis, so call me back as soon as you can. Today if possible before . . ." I didn't finish my sentence on purpose because I wanted to pique Jeffrey's interest enough to make him want to stay on the line.

"Before what?"

"Before I lose my nerve."

"I'm listening but I have only a few minutes to spare right now. Libby and I are still discussing that little stunt she pulled on you. She's very sorry she got rid of your property and she promises to make up for it. She even attempted to retrieve everything, but it was too late. She's sitting right here crying her eyes out. Would you like to hear her apologize yourself?"

"No, that won't be necessary. I'm not ready to speak to her again yet, so I hope you don't mind asking her a question for me."

Jeffrey hesitated before he replied. "What's the question?"

"Ask her if she's still fucking Greg."

Jeffrey let out a loud, very painful-sounding gasp. "Excuse me?" he said in a raspy voice.

"I'm sorry to be the one to break the news to you. You're the last person I'd want to hurt. I promised Libby I would never tell you that I caught her with another man."

"Now you hold on a damn minute, Lola! What the hell are you talking about?"

"It happened on a Sunday several weeks ago. I was in the house alone when Libby showed up with a man I'd never seen before. They had sex on Bertha's couch and then she brought him upstairs. I overheard her tell the dude that she didn't want to have sex in the same bed she shared with you but they could use my bed. She didn't know I was in the house. I saw and heard everything."

Jeffrey cussed under his breath. "Why didn't you tell me this shit before now? How do I know you're telling me the truth? For all I know, you could be making this up to get back at Libby. And I don't blame you. But this is way—"

"Jeffrey, we've known each other since I was a little girl and I've never lied to you. I have nothing to gain by causing problems between you and Libby. I'm telling you because it's time for her to stop causing me so much pain without having to deal with any consequences."

Jeffrey cussed under his breath again. "Lola, what's the dude's name again?"

"Greg is all I know. She told me that he was only the second handsome man since you who'd shown any interest in her. That made me feel sorry for her, so I promised her I would never blab. Anyway, not long after that day, she told me she was not going to see that man again."

"Greg, huh?" Right after Jeffrey repeated the man's name, I heard Libby in the background boo-hooing like a baby and no doubt scrambling to avoid the bus I'd just thrown her under. "Thanks for sharing this information with me. When you get a chance, send me a text with your new address. I'll come over to visit when it's convenient for you."

When I turned off my phone, I felt like a cat that had swallowed a giant canary.

Chapter 43
Joan

*L*OLA CALLED THIS MORNING AT TEN TO TELL ME SHE HAD JUST left the beauty salon and would stop by to have a drink and chat for a little while. I had a glass of wine ready for her when she arrived. We sat down on the couch and she gave me an amused look. I took a sip of wine, then set my glass on the coffee table and gazed at her. "All right now. I know what that look means. Don't beat around the bush and you'd better tell me everything," I prodded. She crossed her legs and drank from her wineglass, almost draining every drop in one pull. And then she started talking so fast I had to tell her twice to slow down. What she said made me gasp and shake my head the whole time. I couldn't believe that Libby had her bed and the rest of her stuff hauled to the dump. And I was glad to hear that Lola had finally told Jeffrey about Libby's affair.

"I wish I could have seen the look on her face when she realized I'd blown the whistle on her," Lola sneered. "With what I had on her, she should have been licking my butt to keep me from blabbing. She went out of her way to push my buttons."

"Humph! As mean and nasty as that bitch was to you for so many years, you were too nice to her—for way too long. I would have told Jeffrey on her a long time ago," I snickered. "Keeping shit that scandalous a secret is too stressful anyway."

"You're right. I feel so much better now. Oh, by the way, I'll be moving into that house on High Street this evening. The gas, water, and electricity are already on, and I made an appointment for the cable guy to come out and install my landline, TV, and Internet service."

"I'm glad Jeffrey brought some of your stuff to you before Libby dumped it. Did he bring over any of your linen?"

"No, he didn't." Lola got quiet. "Other than some of my clothes and a few other personal items, I don't have much, so I'll have to replace a lot of things. I'll pick up whatever I can from Goodwill later today. And if I have time I'll swing by the Salvation Army and a few other thrift shops."

"No, you're not."

"No, I'm not what?"

"You are not going near any of those places. You deserve something much better than a bunch of used, soiled, tacky items from secondhand stores! Yuck!"

"Joan, I don't want to buy any used merchandise, but I don't have much of a choice. I'm on a budget—"

"Well, I'm not on a damn budget. I'm going to go to Macy's and Nordstrom and pick up some linen, cookware, and everything else you need. Give me a call and tell me when to meet you at the new place. Then we'll go to the market and pick up a few groceries and some liquor."

Two minutes after Lola left, I called Reed's office to let him know I'd be out shopping for a few hours.

"Again?" he said in a nasty tone. "With *who* this time?"

"I'm going to go shopping alone," I smirked. "Lola's moving into a house this evening and she needs just about everything to get started. I told her I'd pick up a few things for her." I had already told Reed that Libby had evicted Lola.

"What about all the stuff she had before? Didn't she take any of it with her?"

"Libby didn't give her a chance to get it all. She stuffed some of Lola's clothes and other things into garbage bags and set it all on the porch. Lola got those things, but Libby had a junkman haul away her bedroom furniture and everything else to the city dump before Lola could arrange to have somebody pick it up," I said hotly. "That's pretty low, even for a mean bitch like Libby."

"I won't argue with that! She makes the typical bitches I know look like Mother Teresa!" Reed exploded, which surprised me since Lola was not one of his favorite people. "I heard that Libby and Marshall had a yard sale the day before Bertha's funeral. Those greedy devils sold her things instead of donating everything to charity or Goodwill like normal people."

"That's a damn shame. Lola lost family mementos and other sentimental things that she can never replace. And Libby knew that! I didn't know she hated Lola enough to give her stuff away instead of selling it so she could make money like she did with her own mother."

I was so glad Reed felt the same way I did about Libby. "Libby will get what she deserves someday," he said hotly. "It's hard to believe that she's married to a nice guy like Jeffrey. Knowing her, she'll eventually put him in a trick bag too."

"Tell me about it," I agreed. I almost blurted out the news about Libby's affair, but I'm glad I didn't. With all the skeletons in my closet, infidelity was a subject I avoided with Reed.

"Baby, spend as much as you have to, and if Lola needs any financial assistance, be generous. When she feels up to it, let's invite her over for dinner."

"Thanks, sweetie. I guess I should get going. If I'm not here when you get home, you and Junior can either order some takeout or heat up some of the chicken and rice left over from yesterday. Don't worry about me."

"Um . . . I may be home a little later than usual today," Reed informed me.

"Okay," I said with a shrug. I had so many other things on my mind, I didn't bother to ask why he was going to be late, and he didn't offer to tell me. He had not been badgering me so much about my frequent absences lately, and I didn't want to rock the boat by asking him about his. I knew that by the time I got Lola situated, I'd be ready for a big date—and I prayed that a hot, new club member would put in a request or that I heard from one of my regulars.

For the next few hours, I did some serious shopping. The only reason I stopped when I did was because my feet started aching.

I didn't get back home until six. I left everything I'd bought for Lola in the backseat and trunk of my car because I planned to take it to her in a little while. Junior was home alone, holed up in his room doing the homework he should have completed hours earlier. "Where is your daddy?" I asked as I entered his untidy room, picking up smelly socks, clothes, and fast-food containers off the floor as I approached him at the desk facing his bed.

Without looking at me, Junior shrugged and mumbled, "I dunno."

"Didn't he tell you where he was going?"

"Nope. He got home at five-thirty, and a minute after he walked in the door, his cell phone rang. He told the person on the other end, 'I'm on my way' and he took off again."

"Hmmm. It was probably Dr. Mansfield. Reed's been helping him prepare the speech he's going to give in L.A. at the medical conference they're going to next weekend."

Junior looked at me and shook his head. "Dr. Mansfield came by here and dropped off Daddy's golf clubs a few minutes after he left. He said he was on his way out to dinner with his wife and her parents and would call Daddy tomorrow, so Daddy can't be with him."

"Well, I'm not going to worry about which one of his boring friends he's with." But I was worried about who Reed was spending so much time with these days. And I was sure I'd find out who it was soon.

Chapter 44
Lola

"*I* TOLD YOU THE PLACE HAD A COUCH BED I CAN SLEEP ON UNTIL I get another bed, so you didn't need to buy a sleeping bag—and a Spider-Man sleeping bag at that," I said when Joan arrived a few minutes before seven Friday evening. We had just unloaded everything from her car and set it onto the living-room floor of the house where I'd just signed a month-to-month lease. She had purchased everything I needed, from a small flat-screen TV to the sleeping bag.

"A *used* couch bed," she reminded with a dramatic neck roll. "There is no telling what kind of germs the previous tenants left on that damn thing. And reusing something that personal is so not cool!"

"Do you know how many other people have wallowed on the same hotel beds we've been—"

"Shut up! That's different!" Joan laughed and wagged her finger in my face. "Anyway, it was my money and I wanted you to have some really nice, new stuff. And the sleeping bag looked so cute, I couldn't pass it up," she defended.

"I don't know how long I'll be here, and I don't want to have too much stuff to move into another place," I said, looking around at all the shopping bags and boxes of new merchandise. Everything had come from some of the most expensive stores in town, even the toilet paper.

"I know how addicted you are to chips, so I picked up a

bunch. There's bread and stuff to make sandwiches in one of those bags. I forgot to pick up mayonnaise and other condiments though."

"We can get some from the convenience store across the street and have dinner and some wine."

Joan looked at her watch. She frowned and shook her head. "I'll have to take a rain check. Today is Mama's birthday. My stepfather, and Junior and I, are taking her to dinner at that new Japanese restaurant on Morgan Street this evening."

"I had promised to take Bertha to the same place for her birthday in August. . . ."

"Lola, I know it's hard, but you need to forget about Bertha. One thing you should never forget is that she left you out of her will!"

"Libby and Marshall made her change it. If they hadn't, she would have left me something," I defended.

"For once in her life, Bertha should have stood up to her rotten-ass children."

"I'm sure she changed her will because she didn't want them to get mad at her."

"*Pffft!* The way they treated that poor woman, it sounded like they'd been 'mad at her' all their lives. I wouldn't—"

I held my hand up and cut Joan off. "I am over it, so let's change the subject. In spite of what Bertha did, or didn't do, for me, it's not easy for me to forget about the woman who practically raised me."

"I'm sorry." Joan gave me a hug and a pat on my shoulder. "I need to keep my big mouth shut more often." She tilted her head and gave me a solemn look. "Uh, I know you have a lot on your mind lately, but you haven't mentioned Calvin today. Does he know everything that's going on?"

"Most of it. He was very sympathetic."

"Are you going to see him anytime soon?"

"I sure hope so. Until then, all I can do is think and dream about him."

"Sweet dreams," Joan quipped. I gave her a tight-lipped smile and shook my head. I could tell it made her uneasy, but her unnecessary remark had done the same thing to me. She checked her watch and abruptly stood up. "It's later than I thought. I'd better get over to Mama's house before she sends somebody to look for me. I'll call you," she said on her way out.

I fixed myself a sloppy ham sandwich for dinner. Joan had bought some wine but no cups or glasses, so I drank it straight from the bottle. By eight p.m. I was tired and too buzzed to do anything else but go to bed.

Two of the three bedrooms were in the back part of the house. The one directly across the hall from the living room was the smallest, but it was the one I chose to sleep in. That night, I slept like a baby.

When I crawled out of that silly sleeping bag around eight a.m., I checked my cell phone for messages. I had requests for dates from three men I had previously been with. Because of all the stress and chaos I had endured since Bertha's passing, I was anxious for some male company, but I was more interested in spending time with a man I *really* wanted to be with. And there was only one: Calvin. I prayed that he would get back to me before I decided to accept a date with another club member. Elbert had also sent me a text:

> Jeffrey told me all about that fleabag motel you checked into. I told you that you're welcome to stay with me as long as you want to—rent free. Love, Elbert.

There was no way in the world I was going to live under the same roof with Elbert. Not even on a temporary basis. His mother, Alma, was another version of Bertha. What would be the point of me moving into another house where I'd probably end up being another needy old woman's caregiver? One of the few times I'd accompanied Elbert to his house, Alma had practically coerced me into giving her a back rub and a perm, and she'd dropped all kinds of hints about things I could do for her on my "next visit" to her house. In addition to all that, when I went to the bingo hall or some church event with Elbert, if Bertha didn't tag along, Alma did.

I had no desire to see or talk to him any time soon. I decided to text him back and let him know I was doing just fine so that he would stop inviting me to move in with him and his mama. I would never be anything more to Elbert than a friend. I knew that it would be better for him, and me, for us to stop going out together, because it was only giving him false hope. I planned to ease out of our relationship altogether, but not until I had locked Calvin into something much more secure than what I had now.

In the meantime, I was going to do all I could to get over the pain Libby and Marshall had caused me. One of the things I wanted to do was visit Bertha's grave and put flowers on it. There were two cemeteries in South Bay City. At ten minutes to two, I gave Jeffrey a call and asked which one she had been buried in. "Um . . . neither one," he muttered.

"What?" I wheezed. "Bertha didn't want to be cremated and she made sure everybody knew that. Is that what they did with her body?"

"Yes and no."

"Did they or did they not?"

"Lola, this is a ghoulish subject, especially for a Saturday afternoon. Do you want me to come to your place later today, or would you like to meet me somewhere and we can discuss this then?"

"I can't wait that long. Tell me now," I insisted.

Jeffrey sucked in some air and groaned. When he started talking again, his voice was so low I could barely hear him. "I hope you have some alcohol, because by the time you hear what I'm about to tell you, you'll need some."

"I have plenty. Do you think I should have a drink before you tell me?"

"Yes. I think you'd better do just that. This is not going to be easy on you, or me."

I put Jeffrey on hold, ran into the kitchen, and fixed myself a tall glass of rum and Coke. I took a long pull on my way back to the living room. "Jeffrey, I'm back." I drank some more and then I dropped down onto the couch. Jeffrey proceeded to share information with me that was about to make my blood boil.

"An hour before Bertha took her last breath, Marshall called up one of his friends whose father is connected to a med school. People donate bodies to them for scientific research. To make a long story short, he and Libby wanted to dispose of their mother's remains as cheaply as possible."

So many things happened to me in the next few seconds, I was surprised I was still lucid enough to form my next sentence. I gasped, my jaw dropped, my heart skipped a beat, and a pain shot up my spine like a dagger. "Are you telling me that they wanted to sell their mother's body to science?" The words left such a foul taste in my mouth, I had to finish my drink in one gulp. The kick it gave my brain was nothing compared to the kick of what I'd just heard.

"I don't know if there is a profit to be made in these situations, but according to a website I visited, the donation program usually covers the cost of burial. So I guess you could look at that as a profit."

"Wait a minute. I'm not following you. I thought you said they didn't have her buried."

"Let me finish. They didn't have her buried. The program also does the embalming and they cover the cost of cremation after they're done with the body. Libby and Marshall got downright giddy when they heard how much money they could save by donating their mother's body to science."

"What about that big funeral? Didn't they have to pay for that?"

"Lola, Bertha's funeral was nothing more than a dog and

pony show. And it didn't cost Libby and Marshall a plugged nickel."

"Who paid for it? Bertha's church?"

"I'll get to that in a moment. Anyway, I tried to talk them out of it, but it did no good. Later that night when I got in touch with Bertha's folks in Mississippi and told them what Libby and Marshall were planning to do, her cousin Melvin and his wife boarded the next available flight. When they arrived less than twelve hours after I'd called them, they made such a ruckus, Libby and Marshall changed their tune. They still balked about having to pay for a funeral. Melvin offered to pay for it, so they agreed to let him take Bertha's body back to Mississippi so she could be laid to rest closer to her parents and other family, people who really loved her. Melvin was so angry, he didn't want his cousin to be near her children any longer. Not even in death."

I was in tears by the time Jeffrey stopped talking. "Bertha must be rolling over in her grave. I didn't realize just how selfish, stingy, greedy, and evil Libby and Marshall really were until today," I said as I wiped tears off my face. "I'm glad I'll never have to deal with them again."

"I feel the same way. I'm sorry it took so long for me to see them for the monsters they really are. I still have feelings for Libby, and we'll be forever connected because we have a child together, but I'm done with her." Jeffrey gave a snort of disgust. "Do you still want to meet somewhere for a drink? I'm not busy right now, so I could meet you right away. Today is half price beer at the Green Rose bar."

"No, I'm doing fine with what I have. I just want to sit here and think about everything you told me."

"Lola, don't do that. It'll only make you feel worse. I didn't even want to tell you about this, because I knew it would hurt you, but I'm glad I did. Reverend Clyde and a few other people know about it, and they are just as outraged as I am. I knew that you'd eventually hear about it, and I'm glad you heard it from me."

"Thanks, Jeffrey. Please keep in touch."

"I will. Now, you go on with your life. You've been looking for someone special to share it with for a long time, and I know you'll find him soon."

"I know I will too," I said.

Chapter 45
Joan

THIS FRIDAY STARTED OFF LIKE ANY OTHER DAY IN MY CRAZY LIFE. I didn't expect anything out of the ordinary to happen, but I would soon find out how wrong I was.

I made breakfast for Junior and Reed, and the minute they left, I turned on my computer and ordered a few items off Amazon. I was in a pretty good mood, and one of the reasons was because Lola was feeling so much better. She had been in her new residence a little over a week, and things were really looking up for her, and for me. Reed was leaving to go to L.A. with Dr. Mansfield later tonight, so I'd have another whole weekend break away from him and I was really looking forward to it.

It was only eight a.m., but I was feeling horny. The way Reed had been looking at me the past couple of days, I knew it was just a matter of time before I had to endure another one of his clumsy minute-long trysts, and that would not be enough to hold me over until I could get some real sex.

I had a message from my lawyer honey and favorite hookup, John Walden, and one from Ezra, my second favorite hookup. John just wanted me to know that I was on his mind. Ezra wanted to let me know he'd be in town again in a couple of weeks to speak at another one of the boring plastic surgeon conferences and he definitely wanted to see me. He also assured me that his offer to bring me to Florida to get the free cosmetic surgery was still open, which was good news. I was glad to hear that. I had noticed that my butt looked like it had shifted down an inch or two, and I needed to get it taken care of before somebody else noticed (Ezra had already noticed . . .). Before I could respond to either one, I heard the front door open. I wasted no time turning off my computer. When I got to the living room, I was surprised to see Reed sitting on the couch staring at the wall. He'd just left an hour ago. This time his puppy-dog face was so long, he resembled a basset hound.

"Why are you looking so gloomy? What's the matter with you now?" I asked gruffly with my hands on my hips. I approached the couch and stopped in front of him. "And what did you come back home for?"

"Joan, this is going to be difficult, so you'd better sit down." His voice was so low and hoarse, he sounded nothing like himself. He lowered his head and rubbed the back of his neck.

"What's going on?" I asked, still standing in the middle of the floor with my hands on my hips. I stared at him and recalled something peculiar that he'd said to someone on the telephone last night. A few minutes before ten, I'd walked into the kitchen just as he was about to end a telephone call.

"Please pray for me," he told the person on the other end. A moment later, he hung up and turned around. He was surprised to see me standing in the doorway. "Oh, I was just talking to Dr. Shelby," he claimed.

"You asked your *podiatrist* to pray for you?"

"Yes, I did." He still had the phone in his hand and almost dropped it when he returned it to its cradle.

"The only thing wrong with your feet are your bunions, and they are not so bad that somebody needs to pray for you. And if they were, shouldn't you be asking a preacher to pray for you?"

"A lot of my patients ask me to pray for them—even for something as minor as a cleaning."

I'd laughed it off and put it out of my mind, until now. Something told me that I was not going to laugh about what he had to tell me this time—especially if he thought it was something I needed to sit down to hear. I eased down onto the opposite end of the couch.

There were tears in his eyes when he looked at me. "I . . . I . . . our marriage is a j-j-joke," he stammered.

I gave Reed a blank look and shrugged. "Our marriage has been a joke for a long time. I suggested we get a divorce years ago, but you made it clear that you would never give me one! I feel more like your hostage than your wife. You don't even have to threaten to commit suicide to make me stay with you anymore. You ought to know by now that I'm not going to leave you!"

"I know you're not going to leave me, Joan. But . . . but *I am going to leave you.*"

I blinked and shook my head. "What the hell—what are you trying to tell me?"

"I want a divorce. I'm in love with another woman, and I want to marry her."

Everything suddenly seemed surreal. I stood up and looked at Reed through narrowed eyes. I got so dizzy, it felt like I'd just been sucked into a whirlpool. A split second later, my head started throbbing and my thoughts were doing push-ups. Only a few seconds had passed since Reed's confession, but it seemed like hours. I had to respond before I lost touch with reality and slid into a deep daze. I didn't even think about what I said next. The words just rolled out of my mouth as if they had a life of their own. *"You're divorcing me so you can marry another woman?"* I clapped my hands together, shook my head, and slapped my ears because I could not believe what I was hearing. "You've got to be kidding!" I boomed.

"No, I'm not kidding. You ought to know better. Do you think I'd kid about something this serious?" he said sharply.

"Who is this woman?"

"Her name is not important—"

"You're leaving me to marry another woman—the hell her name is not important! When did this shit start?"

Reed rolled his eyes and gave me an exasperated look. "There is no need to use profanity, Joan. Your potty mouth is one of your biggest problems."

His words made my ears pop. "*You* are my biggest problem! I deserve to know when you started seeing a woman that you want to leave me for!"

"We've been seeing each other for quite some time now," he said in a very low voice.

"When and where?"

"I didn't go hiking with Dr. Weinstein a couple of weeks ago . . ."

"You spent that weekend with your whore?"

He nodded. "Joan, do not call her that." He was so damn brazen, a pensive smile appeared on his face as he continued. "She's a lovely woman."

I let his words sink in. When the full impact hit me, I got twice as angry. By now, my head was spinning so fast and hard I was actually afraid that I was in the first stage of a nervous breakdown. Somehow, I managed to maintain enough composure to continue speaking without babbling incoherently. Words spurted out of my mouth like a geyser. "Lovely women don't break up other women's homes! How dare you disrespect me by praising your bitch to my face!" I yelled, stomping my foot. "All this time, you've been breathing down my neck, accusing me of seeing other men, and threatening to kill yourself if I left you! And you were with another woman ALL THIS TIME?"

Reed held up his hands. "No, not 'all this time,' so you don't need to go there. It . . . it's only been a few months."

"A few *months*? So this shit was already going on when we went to that cookout at your parents' house back in March? In case you don't remember, while we were there you told me that I was the sexiest, most beautiful woman in the world and how lucky you were to have such a beautiful and sexy woman." I stomped my foot again and shook my fist at him.

"I'm still a lucky man. . . ."

"You won't think that by the time I get through with your ashy black ass!"

"What's that supposed to mean?" he whimpered.

"You'll find out soon enough!" I shrieked. "Tell me this, you no-good piece of shit! Why did you wait so long to come clean? Why are you telling me all this now? I never suspected that you were cheating on me, so you could have been with whoever the bitch is forever and I'd never have known!"

"Like I said, I'm going to marry her. I'm tired of lying and sneaking around." Despite me yelling as loud as I could, he kept his voice at a normal volume and so casual, it made his confession feel even more painful. Leaving me for another woman was the last way I expected Reed to betray me. I had truly believed that his suicide was the only way he could cause me as much pain as I was feeling now.

"Well, congratulations, you bastard! She can have your sorry ass! I can be out of here in fifteen minutes!"

Reed crossed his legs, held up his hand, and shook his head. "No, I don't want you to move out. I want you and Junior to stay on here. I've . . . I've already signed a lease for a house for me and my new lady friend."

"Oh really? And where is this love bird's nest?" I snarled.

"*Pffft!*" Reed gave me a snarky look and waved his hand. "None of your damn business!" He didn't sound so casual now. His brows furrowed and his lips quivered. "Do you think I'm stupid enough to give you my new address so you can bring your wild ass over there and show out?"

"What if I need to get in touch with you in an emergency or something?"

"You can reach me on my cell phone, at my office, and you have my parents' number. You can call any one, any time, any day, and I'll get the message." Reed snorted. "You'll be getting the papers soon with all my lawyer's contact information on it too. He'll know where to reach me at all times, so if you don't want to call any of the other numbers, you can call him."

"So you already had this all planned out, huh? How long have you been cooking up this shit?"

"It makes no difference!" he snapped. He gave me a look of

contempt and a dismissive wave. "I was afraid to tell you, so I had to work up enough nerve first."

"You were afraid of *me*? Why you dickless, punk-ass, shit-breath, funky black bastard asshole!" This was the first time I'd used so much profanity in the same sentence.

"You and your colorful language!" I was coming undone and Reed was so insensitive, he actually *snickered*. "One thing for sure, I am not going to miss your potty mouth!"

His words infuriated me. I had to move a few steps away from him because I was tempted to snatch his tongue out of his mouth. "Reed, I never thought you'd cheat on me."

"I never thought I would either. But it is what it is," he muttered.

"Does this have anything to do with me not wanting to have another child?"

Reed dropped his head and refused to look at me. I stomped my foot again. "Can't you even look at me and answer my question?"

He still didn't look at me when he announced, "She . . . she's also pregnant with my child."

"GET OUT OF MY SIGHT BEFORE I KILL YOU!" I roared. My chest was so tight and my mouth so dry, I could barely speak, so I didn't get to tell him that he was going to be potted meat by the time I got through with him.

Reed's eyes got big and his mouth dropped open, but he didn't say another word. He sprang up off the couch and ran out the door as if the building had just been bombed.

Chapter 46
Lola

*B*Y SIX P.M. FRIDAY EVENING, I HAD PUT AWAY EVERYTHING THAT Joan had bought for me, as well as a few other items I had purchased at Target on my way home from work. All I wanted to do now was kick back with a glass of wine, admire my new home, and fantasize about what I was going to do with Calvin when we got together again.

Just as I was about to fix myself a sandwich, somebody started pounding on my front door so hard it sounded as if they were trying to knock it down. I had not given my new address to Jeffrey or Elbert yet, so I knew it wasn't one of them. I had just spoken to my landlady a few minutes ago, so I knew it wasn't her either. I had seen some pretty scary-looking dudes going in and out of the halfway house next door, so I didn't know what to expect.

The door didn't have a peephole, and I was not about to open it until I knew who was outside. "Who is it?" I hollered, wishing I had grabbed a knife off the kitchen counter in case I needed to defend myself.

"It's Joan!"

I immediately let her in. "What the hell—" She didn't give me time to finish my question before she brushed past me.

"Thank God you're here! I've been waiting all day for you to get home from work!" she hollered. There was a wild-cycd look on her face. Her hair was matted, and her makeup was smeared.

"You look like hell! What's going on? Why didn't you call or come to the store?"

"I was too pissed off to come to the store, and I didn't want to tell you over the phone!"

"Tell me what?"

Joan took a deep breath and held it for several seconds. Her eyes were bloodshot and swollen, so I knew she'd been crying. "Reed left me!" she boomed.

If she had told me that somebody had just dropped a nuclear bomb, it would not have stunned me more. "You're kidding!" I shrieked. I followed as she stumbled to the couch. Instead of sitting down, she stopped and started shifting her weight from one foot to the other. "Joan, what the hell is going on? Why did Reed leave you?" I asked with my arms outstretched.

"He's having an affair!"

My jaw dropped. I was so dumbfounded I could barely talk. "How . . . how did you find out?" I stammered.

"He told me this morning!"

"This *morning*?" I glanced at my watch. "Where have you been all day?"

"I've been home most of the day trying to digest this shit."

"If you had let me know sooner, I would have left work early so I could be with you."

"I just told you I didn't want to tell you over the phone."

"You didn't have to tell me why you needed to see me. All you had to say was that you had a serious situation you needed to talk about, and I would have been there in a flash." I sighed and gave Joan a pitiful look. "Well, you're here now and that's all that matters. Sit down and let me get you some wine." I headed toward the kitchen with Joan right behind me cussing and fussing so hard, it felt as if the words were bouncing off the back of my neck. When I stopped at the counter where I'd set a half empty bottle of chardonnay, she stopped so abruptly she bumped into me.

"I could kill him!" She paused long enough to catch her breath. "Don't even bother with a glass!"

I handed her the bottle without pouring any for myself, and she started drinking immediately. I waved her to one of the four chairs at the kitchen table that the previous tenant had left. I sat down and dragged my chair closer to hers. "Who is the woman and when did he start seeing her?"

"I don't know all the details yet, but I will find out!" In all the years I'd known Joan, I had never seen her so angry. Her light brown face was rapidly turning red with rage.

"This is the last thing I expected to hear about Reed. Where is he now?"

"I don't know. When he saw how mad I was, he left the condo running!" She drained the bottle and set it on the table. "What else do you have in here to drink?" she asked before she let out a mighty belch.

"Nothing except soft drinks until I can get back to the liquor store. You want a Pepsi?"

Joan ignored my question. "He's probably at the house he'd already leased for them to shack up in." She grinded her teeth for a few seconds, and after a loud snort she dropped another bombshell. "And she's pregnant with his child!"

"Oh my God! Then there's probably not a chance that you and Reed will live as man and wife again, huh?"

"HELL NO! I'd rather be the bride of Satan! I wouldn't take that potbellied pig back if he came gift-wrapped with a halo above his head! Anyway, he's going to marry his whore."

"Joan, I'm so sorry. This is awful and so hard to believe. What are you going to do now?"

"I'm going to take everything from him except his American citizenship!" She had yelled so much, her voice had become hoarse, but that didn't stop her from yelling some more. "By the time I get through with him, he'll be so broke he won't even be able to pay *attention*!"

I gave her a sympathetic look and shook my head. "He accused you of cheating for years, as if it was the worst thing in the world. Now he's doing it. On top of everything else, he's a hypocrite too."

"Tell me about it!"

"Remember when you told me to look at Bertha's passing as a blessing in disguise?" I asked gently as I rubbed her shoulder.

"Yeah. What's that got to do with Reed?"

"Well, look at this as a blessing in disguise. Now you won't have to sneak around and tell a bunch of lies so you can spend time with other men. I always thought you'd be glad to get rid of Reed. So why are you so upset about him leaving you for another woman?"

Joan parted her quivering lips and exhaled. "What I'm really upset about is him manipulating me for so long when it wasn't necessary if he had another woman. He could have left me months ago, or whenever it was he started cheating. *That's* what I'm really angry about! I'm going to make him suffer!"

"Joan, I know you. You're just as angry about the other woman as you are about him manipulating you. Any woman would be angry if her husband left her for another woman. Even if she didn't love him."

"Yes, I am mad about that too." I was glad she had stopped yelling. She didn't even look as angry anymore. But she looked sad. "It means I wasn't woman enough for him."

"That's not why people cheat. One day I overheard my daddy tell one of his friends that none of his girlfriends were half the woman my mama was, but that didn't stop him from cheating. Some people need attention from more than one mate. I mean—now don't take this the wrong way—what about all your lovers?"

Joan's eyes got big. She looked at me as if I had lost my mind. "What's wrong with you, Lola? Why are you asking me such a ridiculous question? I had lovers because Reed was not the man I wanted to be with. You knew that."

"Yeah, I did." I hunched my shoulders and gave her a pensive look. I swallowed hard before I gazed at her sternly. "Now, I don't blame you for wanting to make him suffer, but don't do anything too bad to him."

"Like what? Right now I can't think of anything bad enough that'll really make him suffer!"

"Just don't do anything you'll be sorry for. Especially if it involves violence," I said.

Joan gave me a blank stare. Then she narrowed her eyes and a wicked smile crossed her face. "As long as he stays out of my way, I won't touch him. But if he provokes me, he's the one who's going to be sorry!" She fumbled with her purse, pulled out a small canister, and waved it in my face.

I gasped and blinked. "That's pepper spray!"

"Exactly. I picked it up on my way over here and I'm itching to use it."

Chapter 47
Calvin

Sylvia had been so frisky since we'd returned from San Ysidro a week ago yesterday afternoon, we'd made love every day since then. You would have thought that we had not had sex in years. All the attention I got from her did wonders for my already huge ego.

She told me almost every other day that she loved me, and I knew she meant it. I also knew that she was being faithful to me and believed that I was being faithful to her. Well, for a man, being faithful was easier said than done. I had more women available to me than I could handle. I was not always up to making love when Sylvia was, so our latest lovemaking marathon had really taken a toll on me. However, I tried to accommodate her as often as I could. Since she was going to be my bride in a few weeks, it was the least I could do.

"Calvin, you seemed distracted," she told me as we lay in her bed. It was eight p.m. We had eaten dinner at Red Lobster two hours ago. "I'd love to know what's on your mind right now. You've had the same Cheshire cat smile on your face since you got here."

My next run was coming up on Tuesday. I had to haul some electronic equipment from Portland, Oregon, to a new computer store in Burbank, California, in time for their grand opening at the end of the month. Time was going by too fast for me. I had to juggle my hours so I could find enough time to deal with my routine personal matters and Sylvia and keep Lola on the hook until I was ready to make my fatal move on her.

As anxious as I was to kill the bitch before Sylvia and I exchanged vows, it looked like I was going to have to delay it a little longer. Only a few more days, I hoped. Before I had arrived at Sylvia's house this evening at six-thirty after a brief haul I'd made from Sacramento to Berkeley, I'd made a call to Lola. Since the end was so close for her, it was important for me to keep up with her movements. She had sounded surprised to hear my voice when she answered her phone. I recalled our conversation with a smile on my face.

"Oh, Calvin! I am so glad you called! I was going to call you!" she'd squealed. "Another crisis has come up that I'll have to deal with before I can see you again."

"Oh? More problems with your stepsiblings?"

"Not this time. It's my best friend. I'm going to be spending a lot of time consoling her. I wouldn't feel too good about having some fun with you while she's so miserable, so it may be a while before I can see you again."

A while could mean anything from a few days to a few weeks. Maybe even longer! My brain felt like it was about to explode. I had literally been counting the *days* to the kill date! There was no way I was going to let this nasty skank string me along too much longer! "I hope it's not a long while," I whined.

"It could be sooner, but I can't promise anything right now," she'd told me with her voice cracking.

It took all of my strength to continue speaking in a normal tone. I'd wanted to shout every cuss word in the English language to let this bitch know exactly how disgusting she was. I silently counted to five and forced myself to remain calm. "I hope your friend is not in any serious trouble."

"It's pretty serious. Her husband left her for another woman and she's taking it real hard. The woman is also pregnant by my friend's husband," Lola said with a sniff.

"Damn! That is pretty serious. I can understand why your friend is so upset."

"Since I've never been married, I can't imagine how painful it must be to lose a mate to someone else. I hope it's something I never have to experience."

"Unfortunately, I've been in that boat so I know what it feels like. It's pain in its purest form. It took a long time for me to get over my wife leaving me for another man."

"What's so strange about my friend's situation is that Reed— that's my friend's husband's name—accused her of sleeping with other men on a regular basis for years."

"Hmmm. Is she the same girlfriend you told me about? The one who turned you on to the club?"

"She's the same one. Joan. Her club screen name is Hot-Chocolate."

"Oh yes. I read the club's reviews and the blog at least two or three times a week. HotChocolate is mentioned quite often. She has a lot of happy admirers."

"You're right about that."

"Since we're already on the subject, you're a very popular club member yourself." It was hard to keep myself from scream-ing obscenities at this slimy whore! "I saw your post about that real estate mogul from Ohio. . . ."

"Oh . . . well," she'd said sheepishly. "I read the reviews and the blog all the time too, so I guess you know I read what that woman in Mexico said about you."

"Oh . . . well," I snickered. "Touché." We'd both laughed.

Lola's voice had suddenly sounded extremely serious. "Joan is devastated, but she's a strong woman, so I know she'll be all right. In the meantime, I don't want to go on a date and have a good time while she's in so much pain. That would make her feel even worse, and I know she would do the same for me. I hope you understand. And I want you to know that I really am anxious to see you again."

"I do understand, and I respect you for letting me know in-stead of ignoring my messages."

"Calvin, I would never not respond to one of your messages," she'd assured me.

"Thank you, Lola, *honey*." I'd decided to throw her an occasional term of endearment to sweeten the pot. But I was not going to overdo it. "I'm glad to hear that. How are things going for you otherwise? There has been a lot of turmoil in your life lately."

She heaved out a loud, long sigh. "I'm doing all right, I guess. I'm still angry with my stepsiblings and I'm still sad about my stepmother passing. But I'm moving forward."

I had to ask a very important question next. "Did your landlady get the lock on your back door fixed yet?"

"Nope. The maintenance man got back from his vacation early, but now he's sick with some bug he picked up when he was in Mexico."

"Can't she find somebody else to come fix your lock?"

"I'm sure she could if I asked her to. I can live without a lock for a little while. This is a very quiet and crime-free neighborhood. But the sleeping bag I've been using is so uncomfortable. Starting tonight, I'm going to sleep on the living-room couch bed that the previous tenant left until I can get a bed to replace the one my evil stepsister gave to the junkman. Unfortunately, the living room is right next to the kitchen, so I'll have to listen to that leaky faucet, but I can deal with that for a little while too. It's so nice living by myself that I can put up with some minor inconveniences for a few more days."

Yes, a few more days. . . .

Sylvia pinched my cheek and interrupted my reminiscence. "Hello, Calvin. Come back down to earth," she said, giggling. "I hope I'm the reason that smile is plastered on your face, or something else just as nice."

I nodded. "It is," I assured her. "You have no idea how nice." And then we made love again.

Chapter 48
Joan

*L*OLA HAD INVITED ME TO SPEND THE NIGHT AT HER PLACE, BUT I was so angry I couldn't sit still for more than a few minutes at a time. I had to keep moving. I wasn't ready to go back to the condo. I needed to face my family soon so they could hear the news about Reed from me, not the gossip posse. That's how they heard about it anyway.

When I left Lola's place at six-thirty p.m., I went straight to Mama's house, and she was lying in wait. As soon as I walked in the door, she got in my face. "Well, Miss Prissy, you don't know what a good man you done lost," she said, looking disappointed and confused at the same time. "What done got into you, girl?"

"Nothing, Mama. Reed left me." I strode into the living room and stopped in front of the couch, where Elmo, my sad-eyed stepfather, sat with a beer in his hand. I sank down onto the couch like a lead balloon. Mama stood in front of me with her arms folded, shaking her head as I continued talking. "He wanted to leave me and I couldn't stop him. We're getting a divorce."

"Don't do it, girl!" shrieked my sister, Elaine, as she stumbled into the room and stood next to Mama. I was sorry to see that Elaine no longer resembled the glamorous swimsuit model she had been twenty years ago. Now she was just as frumpy looking as our mother. I was not the least bit worried about ending up like them. I was way too vain. I worked out when I could and I didn't overeat. And DrFeelGood had promised to perform all the cosmetic surgery I wanted, so I knew I'd be able to maintain my shape and looks a lot longer than most of the other women I knew. Especially since I would need to look good enough to land another husband now. "Baby sister, don't you let that man get away. You've stayed with him this long, what's another thirty or forty years? You want another woman to start getting all that dentist money?"

"Humph! Another one is already getting that dentist money. Reed told me he's in love with another woman." I paused and had to practically force the next sentence out. "He wants to marry her."

"I can't believe Reed ain't in the picture no more!" Elmo hollered. He gave me a hopeful look and lowered his voice. "I guess I don't need to worry about paying him back some of them loans I owe him, huh?"

"That's between you and Reed. Don't drag me into that," I said.

"What I want to know is, when did this thing between him and this other woman jump off?" Mama asked with a neck roll.

"I don't know exactly when it started. It took me completely by surprise. He went to his office this morning and came back home a little while later and told me that he wants to marry her." The words left such a nasty taste in my mouth, I had to switch gears and talk about something else for a while. "Where's Too Sweet?" I looked around, expecting to see my plump, elderly cousin waddling into the room.

"She's at Kandy's beauty salon. She called home a little while ago and told us about you and Reed," Elaine said. "Reed's mama got her hair done this afternoon and she's the one that broke the news to Kandy and she told Too Sweet. She called us on account of she couldn't wait until she got home to let us know. "

"One thing I know for sure, when it involves news, you can count on the telephone, a telegraph, television, and 'tell Kandy,' and she'll broadcast her head off." I was trying to lighten the situation. I laughed, but I was the only one who saw the humor in my comment. Everybody else looked so serious, you would have thought their faces had been carved out of stone.

"I'm surprised we didn't hear it from you before now, like right after he took off. You made us wait almost all day. It makes our family look bad to be among the last ones to get the news," Elaine complained.

I let out such a hard snort, my nose started throbbing. "I wasn't in the mood to talk about it this morning. I wish you would all consider my feelings for the next few days until Reed and I sort things out."

"Sort things out? Girl, according to what Reed's mama told them big-mouth heifers in the beauty salon, that sucker done already rented a house for him and this new woman!" Elmo hollered.

"And she's pregnant," I replied. By now my jaw twitched every time I spoke. Everybody in the room gasped. Mama's jaw dropped. "Didn't Kandy include that juicy piece of information when she told Too Sweet?"

"I guess she didn't know that part when she called," Elaine answered with an incredulous look on her face. "Basically, all she told us was that Kandy told her Reed's mama broke the news that you and Reed had called it quits. Losing a husband is bad enough, but it's doubly bad when you lose him to another woman."

"I can't wait to find out who the other woman is," I hissed.

"You mean to say you don't know? Lord have mercy!" Mama boomed with a horrified look on her face.

I shook my head.

"When you find out who she is, kick her ass and maybe your husband will bring his tail back home," Elmo suggested.

"The hell I will! I've never fought over a man and I'm not going to start now!" I shot back.

My sister blinked and gave me a look that was so full of pity, I wanted to cry. But I didn't want to shed any more tears for now, especially in front of my family. "I was on the phone with Rena

Henderson a little while ago. That big mouth knows everybody's business," Elaine said gruffly.

"What news did you get from Rena?" Mama asked, giving Elaine a sharp look.

From the grim expression on Elaine's face, I knew she was going to report even more bad news. "You know the psychologist that Reed plays golf with?" she said.

"Of course I know Lincoln Wheeler. He lived in a unit on our floor until he bought that big house in the hills last year. His wife used to be a Vegas showgirl back in the day. I heard she had a reputation that wouldn't quit—even after they got married. Reed told me a couple of years ago that Dr. Wheeler caught her in bed with another man." I stopped talking and looked from one face to another with my mouth hanging open. "Is that tramp the woman Reed left me for?"

"Naw! She ain't the one!" Elaine boomed. Then she sat down on the couch arm closer to me and lowered her voice. "Dr. Wheeler has three daughters."

Mama blinked and fanned her face with her hand. Elmo took another drink from his beer can. And then they all looked at me at the same time.

"I know. One married one of Reed's interns. The other two are students at UC Berkeley. Grace, the youngest one, used to babysit Junior a few years ago." I knew more devastating news was coming, so I swallowed hard and braced myself.

"Grace is the one," Elaine announced in a tone so harsh each word sounded obscene.

"What? Reed left me so he could marry a *teenager*?"

"You was just seventeen when he got you pregnant and married you," Mama pointed out. "Tsk, tsk, tsk. He was in his twenties then, so it wasn't too bad. He's in his forties now, and I can't imagine why a man his age would want to marry a girl that young."

I was so dumbstruck, I couldn't speak for a few moments. My head was pounding and my stomach was cramping. I didn't know what to say, and I didn't want to hear whatever my folks had to say next. I stood up and started backing toward the door. "I'm going home, but I'll probably be back tomorrow," I muttered.

"How is Junior taking the news about this mess?" Elmo asked in a gruff tone.

"He's upset, but he's holding up all right. I picked him up from school before I came over here. He told me that Reed had called him right after his math class and told him he was leaving me. Junior didn't even want to come back home with me, so I dropped him off at Aunt Becky's house to spend the night with his cousins." I exhaled and forced myself to smile as I opened the door. "Mama, I might call you later," I said. Then I couldn't get to my car fast enough.

My head was throbbing as I drove, cussing and slapping my steering wheel. Words could not describe how angry I was now, but I knew my anger was going to get much worse.

I cussed some more when I got to my block and saw Reed's Lexus parked in front of our building. I was afraid to go inside, more for his sake than mine. Knowing that he had been cheating on me with the same girl that I had thought of as the little sister I'd always wanted made me sick!

I parked behind his car and called his cell phone. I didn't like his tone when he answered. He sounded impatient. "What is it, Joan?" he barked.

"I'm sitting outside and I'm going to stay here until you leave," I said evenly.

"You won't have to sit out there long. I just came back to pick up some of my belongings. And you didn't have to dump my custom-made suits onto the floor! I'm surprised your ghetto ass didn't cut them to shreds or douse them with bleach."

"Humph! I have too much class to do something that tacky. I peed on your 'custom-made suits,'" I said with a smirk.

"Joan, there is nothing you can do that would surprise me. My only regret is that I didn't leave you sooner!"

"Why you . . . you punk-ass motherfucker! That's my regret

too! But I guess you had to wait until your little girl whore turned eighteen, huh?"

Several seconds went by before he responded. "You know about Grace?"

"Yes, I know she's the other woman. It's a damn shame you weren't man enough to tell me yourself."

"Whatever!" he snapped. "I'm glad you know. Come on in so we can talk like civilized adults about a settlement."

"Isn't that something we should be discussing in the presence of our lawyers?"

"Yes, but there are a few things we can sort out now."

"I'm not sorting out a damn thing until I talk to a lawyer!"

Reed groaned and mumbled under his breath. And then he started talking in a slow, patronizing tone. "I'm going to say a few things now anyway. You can have the condo, half of my stocks, and half of the money in our bank accounts. You'll receive a very generous financial settlement in addition to alimony. I'll continue to pay for the health insurance premium for you and Junior, and we'll have joint custody. That should be enough for you. Happy?"

"Hell yes! Are you?"

"Very much so. I'll have my freedom and peace of mind." He paused and sucked on his teeth. "And I'll be with the woman who really loves me. That's all I want."

"I don't want to continue this conversation here. Can you meet me at Mama's house after you finish packing your things? I want somebody to be present in case—"

Reed cut me off so fast, it made my head spin. "In case what?" He stopped and coughed a few times to catch his breath.

"In case things get ugly," I said calmly. I was tempted to cuss at him some more, but I wanted to deliver my best insults in person.

"Look, I am not going to stoop to your level and go off on a tangent, so if things do get ugly, it'll be on your end!"

"If you can't meet me at Mama's house this evening, I don't want to see your face again until we sit down with our lawyers."

"All right. I should be there in half an hour."

Chapter 49
Joan

*I*IMMEDIATELY TURNED AROUND AND DROVE BACK TO MAMA'S house. Elmo's old jalopy was not parked in the driveway, and Elaine's car was missing too. The lights in the house were on, but they were always left on when everybody was only going to be away for a short time.

I rushed inside and flopped down on the living room couch. I was in such a fog by now, I didn't realize I had removed my cell phone from my purse. Without giving it much thought, I hit Lola's number. "It's me," I muttered when she answered.

"Where are you? I was worried about you."

"Don't worry about me. I'm at Mama's house. Reed is on his way over here so we can talk about a few things. Guess who the other woman is?" I didn't give Lola time to answer. "Grace Wheeler."

She gasped so hard, I thought she was going to hyperventilate. "That cute young girl who used to babysit Junior?"

"Uh-huh."

"Isn't she still in high school?"

"She graduated last year. She's nineteen now and studying at Berkeley."

"I can't believe that she's the one!"

"You *can* believe she's the one, because Reed confirmed it," I said, squirting the words out like spit. "He even had the nerve to call her a 'lovely woman.'"

"I would have bet a month's salary that Reed had hooked up

with one of his staff or one of his patients. When and where did they get together?"

"I'm not sure when and where. What I do know is, he hasn't been hiking and having drinks with Dr. Weinstein, working late, helping people write speeches, and all the other alibis he's been claiming lately. Those were lies he told so he could be with Grace."

"Well, Dr. Weinstein is his closest friend, so he probably knows everything Reed's been up to lately. Dr. Weinstein drinks like a damn whale and drunks like to run off at the mouth. I'm sure he's blabbed a few things to his wife about his associates. Why don't you give Meg a call and pick her brain? She might be able to tell you a few things."

"What good would that do? Meg Weinstein is so desperate to hang on to that mule-faced devil, she'd lie to Jesus for him if he asked her to. And another thing—hold on! Somebody just drove up. I think Reed's here." I ran to the window and parted the drapes. He had parked in front of the house and was trotting up the walkway. "It's him! I'll call you later!" I turned off my phone and put it back in my purse. Then I sprinted to the door and snatched it open. He strutted in with a scowl already on his face. It didn't faze me, because next to mine his looked more like a smile.

"Start talking," I ordered with my arms folded and my foot tapping.

"Jesus Christ, Joan. Can't you at least give me time to get inside? And I'm thirsty, so I wouldn't mind a shot of vodka or anything else potent. Something tells me I'll probably need it."

"This is not a social visit, so you can forget about wetting your whistle with my stepfather's alcohol! Now you can sit your crusty black ass down and say whatever you have to say and then get the hell up out of here!"

Reed stared at me as if I was speaking gangster rap. I waved him to the couch, and he sat down with a thud and a loud groan. "I have a few more items to remove from the condo, and I'll try to get that done by next week," he said, looking around. "Where is everybody?"

"I don't know. The house was empty when I got back here."

"Well, I deserve—"

I wagged my finger and cut him off. "Deserve? Guess what, Dr. Booger Bear? You will definitely get everything you deserve."

"Humph! And so will you. One thing you won't get is another man who'll treat you the way I did."

His last comment almost made me throw up. "I sure as hell hope not! I don't want another cheating-ass punk in my life!"

He held up his hand and gave me a harsh look. "Slow down now before you say something you'll regret. Don't talk to me as if you've lost what's left of your mind. Be a real woman for once in your life."

"I will with the next man I get involved with. And I'm going to make sure he's more of a man than you are."

He raised his eyebrows and gazed at me from the corner of his eye. "What's that supposed to mean?"

"You weren't even man enough to tell your own son to his face that you were leaving me."

A pitiful look crossed Reed's face, which was now covered in sweat. "Well, I wanted to but I thought it would be less painful if I told him over the phone."

"Less painful for him or you?"

"Joan, I am a good father and you can't deny that. I've made mistakes, but I was good to you and Junior in every way! Yes, I was a little on the jealous side and I tried to keep close tabs on you, but we still had a damn good thing going!"

"Oh yeah? Then why did you cheat?"

He shrugged and took a deep breath. "I can't answer that, and I'm sure no other person can either. Maybe it's part of the game of life."

"It didn't sound like you thought it was 'part of the game of life' all those times you accused me of being with other men!" I shouted.

"Look, what's done is done. I fell in love with another woman, but I didn't mean for it to happen. I'm not perfect. I'm just . . . I guess I needed something different in my life and you couldn't give it to me. I tried to make do with you, but I couldn't keep up the pretense."

I did a dramatic neck roll and gave Reed a look of disbelief. "You tried to 'make do' with me?" I laughed so hard, tears pooled in my eyes. The next look I gave him was so menacing, he trembled. "Let me tell you what I had to make do with: lousy sex. I cringed every time you climbed on top of me."

If I had sprouted horns, Reed could not have looked more stupefied. "Oh really? Well, you sure never acted like I was bad in bed. If I was that bad, I would have figured out a long time ago that I wasn't satisfying you. You can keep that lie in your mouth, because I know you're just trying to make me feel worse. Other than our son, the only good thing we had left was a good sex life!"

"You're half right." This time I laughed so hard my lungs felt as if they were going to explode. *"I had a very good sex life and it wasn't with you!"*

Reed stood up so abruptly he almost fell. The blood drained from his face and his eyes bulged. "So you *did* cheat on me?"

"For years! One week I slept with three different men!"

There was so much rage in Reed's eyes they sparkled like glitter. "Why you despicable, deceitful, low-down, whorish little heifer!" he blasted with his nostrils flaring like a bull's. The next thing I knew, he lunged at me. He slapped my face so hard I hit the floor with the weight of a boulder. It hurt like hell, but I didn't even scream. I wobbled up and grabbed my purse off the coffee table. And then I pulled out the pepper spray that I had been saving just for him.

When he saw what I had in my hand, he yelped and shot across the floor toward the door with me right behind him, spraying the back of his head. "Oh shit! Get away from me, Joan!" He snatched open the door and bolted, and I was still right behind him. He was moving too erratically and covering part of his face with his hand for me to get a good aim. When he reached his car, he took his keys out of his pocket and ducked, but I managed to splatter one side of his face. "AARRGGHH!"

he screamed. His legs buckled and he collapsed. "Joan, please! Please stop!" He was kicking, farting, coughing, blinking, and fanning his eyes with both hands. I stood over him and gave him another hefty spurt. He covered his eyes again, so most of the spray landed on his chin and neck. "AARRGGHH!"

The pepper spray was so potent, I felt some of its effect. I had to hold my breath, blink my burning eyes, and cough a few times before I was able to speak again. "Get out of my sight before I call one of my brothers or uncles over here to finish what I started!" I threatened. "Compared to what they'll do to your ass, this pepper spraying episode will seem like a Baptism!"

Reed staggered to his feet, still wiping his eyes and gagging as he fumbled with his keys and opened his car door. Within seconds, he got in and started the motor. Whimpering and fanning, he took off like a bat flying out of hell.

Chapter 50
Joan

*I*DIDN'T WANT TO DEAL WITH MY FAMILY AGAIN WHEN THEY RE-turned, so I left right after Reed. My eyes and nose were still burning from the pepper spray fumes. I couldn't imagine how much damage it had done to Reed. As long as he got the message that he couldn't slap me and get away with it, that was all that mattered. I drove around long enough to cool off, and without giving it a second thought I went back to Lola's house.

She was horrified when I told her what I'd done to Reed. "You pepper sprayed your husband?"

"My soon-to-be *ex*-husband. He slapped me, so I was only defending myself."

"Why didn't you just slap him back? Pepper spray is nothing to play with."

"I wasn't playing. And I finally told him what a lousy fuck he is."

"I don't think it was a good idea to pepper spray him, but I'm glad you finally told him he's lousy in bed. You should have told him years ago. Maybe he would have found another woman and divorced you then and you'd be happily married to somebody else by now. Can I fix you a margarita or a glass of wine? I just got back from the liquor store, so there's plenty to drink." Lola waved me to the couch and I sat down with a thud.

"Thanks for asking," I said as I kicked off my shoes. I had to get comfortable, because I knew this was going to be a long visit. "You know that I'd love to have a few, but I won't. Because if I do, I won't stop until I pass out. I just want to sit here and talk for a while."

Lola sat down at the other end of the couch and gave me a pensive look. "You know I'm here for you, and I know you're here for me." She dropped her head, and when she looked up again she looked unbearably sad. "I'm feeling kind of shell-shocked by all that's happened lately. I never thought that Bertha and Reed would get out of the picture around the same time."

"I still can't believe what Reed did to me," I said, with my voice dropping almost to a whisper. "He'd better pray that I never bump into him and his whore in public! There might be a bloodbath!"

The sad look on Lola's face intensified. "I don't blame you for being so pissed off, Joan, but you need to get over it."

"That's easy for you to say."

"No, it's not. We're both going through a crisis right now, and I can't say mine is worse than yours or yours is worse than mine. At the end of the day, we're both in pain. Yeah, I'd like to beat Libby down, but what good would that do? And even if I did get violent with her, I might be the one to get beaten down. I'm not going to bother her, even if I run into her at the beauty salon or anyplace else we both go to."

"What if she calls you out in public? Are you going to stand there and let her whup your ass without defending yourself?"

"That's a different story. If she starts something with me in public, or anywhere else, I will defend myself. I've done it before and I'll do it again. I hope it never comes to that. Violence never solves anything."

I gulped. "Lola, I don't know how you do it. I could never be as calm about things as you are. You have the patience of Job, and not just with Bertha's kids."

"If you're going to mention that I'm still working for a low salary after all these years again, don't go there. I—"

I cut Lola off. "Let's talk about Calvin."

"Huh? Why? The way you roll your eyes almost every time I

bring up his name, I'm surprised to hear that you want to talk about him."

"He's on your mind seven days a week, right?"

Lola nodded and gave me a tight smile. "He sure is, and I can't do anything about it."

"You don't want to," I accused.

"Yes, I do. And I probably will eventually. After all that's happened lately, I realize just how short life is. We should never sit around again and wait for what we want to come to us. We should go after it."

"Isn't that what we've been doing all these years?"

"Not really. We're having fun in the club, but what are we going to have when it's all over?"

I wasn't sure how to answer Lola's question. I said the first thing that came to my mind. "We'll have some good memories."

"Will that be enough to keep you happy for the rest of your life? Do you want to grow old alone?"

"Hell no. And I'm not going to. My only regret is that I'm as old as I am now and still frustrated."

Lola gave me a puzzled look. "What do you mean by that?"

"I should have left Reed years ago."

"What if you had and he'd committed suicide like he kept threatening? Then you would have had to deal with the guilt."

"I would have grieved for him, but I would have recovered. And I would not have spent almost all of my adult life being so miserable. Can you imagine what the world would be like if everybody let somebody control and manipulate them by threatening suicide? I saw a movie about a woman who threatened to kill herself if her husband left her. He stayed with her for twenty years, miserable as hell. One day she got depressed about something unrelated to her marriage, stole a gun, and blew her brains out."

Lola blinked a few times and pursed her lips. "I think you're trying to tell me that I shouldn't have let Bertha control me, right?"

"I'm not trying, I am. You were so weak, you did almost everything she wanted you to do and look what it got you. I was just as weak. Reed manipulated me and I did almost everything he wanted me to, and look how I ended up!" I stood up and glanced around the room. "Damn! What I wouldn't give for a strong drink!"

"I can fix you one." Lola got up, yawning and stretching her arms. "I could use one myself."

I shook my head and sat back down. "I have to drive so I'd better take a rain check."

"Joan, this will probably sound corny, but I'm going to say it anyway. I'm glad I was the way I was with Bertha. I think that in the long run, you'll be glad you tried to please Reed. We both got screwed over, but it could have been a lot worse."

"That's for sure. Oh well. It is what it is. From now on, I'm not going to put off doing the things that might make me happy. I'm never going to allow another man to control me. If I'm not happy with the next man I have a serious relationship with, nothing is going to make me stay with him. If I see something or somebody else I want, I'm going to go for it. I'll worry about the consequences later." There was a curious look on Lola's face. "What I just said shocked you, didn't it?"

"Uh-huh. It shocked some sense into my bone head. I feel the same way you do. I'm going to go after what I want and not worry about the consequences."

I turned my head to the side and gazed at Lola from the corner of my eye. "Something tells me you're talking about Calvin *again*," I said.

"So what?" She pressed her lips together and gave me a defiant look. "You'll probably think I'm crazy, and don't bother trying to talk me out of it, but I'm going to let him know I'm in love with him as soon as possible. It's time for me to find out exactly where I stand with him."

Chapter 51
Joan

I LEFT LOLA'S HOUSE AT A QUARTER TO TEN. WHEN I GOT BACK TO the condo I saw that Reed had taken everything else he owned, even the unsweetened grapefruit juice nobody else drank.

I sat in the living room on the couch in the dark for fifteen minutes just thinking about the mess my life had turned into. Half an hour later, my cell phone rang. It was a club member who I had promised to spend time with on Saturday. I had forgotten all about him! Lawrence Thomas was a thirty-five-year-old tennis pro from New York. We'd had three encounters in the last four months. He had previously made several attempts to see me again during his frequent trips to California, but each time I had already made plans to see other members on the same dates. I was tempted to let his call go to voice mail, but I didn't. I was suddenly glad he had called. I was feeling pretty lonely and wanted to talk to somebody. With his bowl-shaped haircut and horn-rimmed glasses, he reminded me of an adult Harry Potter, but he had a great sense of humor. The corny jokes he had told on our previous dates and watching him dance around the hotel room with my panties on his head had kept me in stitches. I was glad that he had finally requested another date when I had no other plans because I could definitely use a few laughs now.

I called him immediately. "Hello, DickLicious," I greeted. He liked to be called by his screen name. "I was going to call you."

"That's good to hear. I sent you two text messages, an e-mail, and left a voice mail since I got into town six hours ago. I'm in a lavish suite in one of the poshest hotels in town and I've already stocked the bar with your favorite champagne."

"Thanks," I mumbled.

"HotChocolate, you don't sound too happy. Is there a problem?"

"Yeah, there is," I muttered.

"Oh hell! I was so looking forward to seeing you again, so I hope you're not going to tell me I won't. I even rescheduled one meeting and canceled another so I'd have some free time to spend with you. Now what's the problem?"

"My husband left me today and I'm feeling kind of down in the dumps," I blurted.

"Oh. That's a real bummer. Do you want to talk about it?"

I swallowed hard and continued. "He left me for a teenager. And she's one of the prettiest girls in town. I guess I'm feeling kind of old and homely. . . ."

"*Pffft!* You? Old and homely? Not by a long shot! Sweetheart, you have nothing to worry about. You're one of the hottest women on the planet and one of the most popular ones in the club. I am sure that that teenybopper your husband left you for is not even in your league!"

"Thanks," I said in a more cheerful tone. "I really needed to hear something like that."

"You'll hear a lot more when you get here tomorrow. I only wish you were here now."

"You do?"

"Hell yes! Otherwise, it will be self-service for me tonight. And I've never enjoyed pleasuring myself even when I was a teenager. I'd give my left ball to have you join me tonight."

I laughed. It felt so good I wanted to keep it going. "I'll be there in an hour or less," I said.

The bombshell that Reed had dropped on me didn't feel so painful now. I knew if I kept busy, I wouldn't spend too much time thinking about it. Right after I got out of the shower, my cell phone rang again. It was Lola. "I was just checking on you," she said, sounding extremely concerned. "How are you feeling now?"

"I'm fine. I'm going out in a few minutes. I was going to send you a text to let you know."

"Good! I don't think you should be alone tonight. I was calling to see if you wanted to spend the night at my place. Are you going back to your mother's house?"

"Uh, remember that Harry Potter–looking tennis pro from New York?" I didn't give Lola time to answer. "He's in town again and I'm going to see him tonight. I'll probably stay with him until morning."

"Hmmm. I'm glad to hear that Reed didn't slow you down too much. I was wondering when you were going to hook up with DickLicious again."

"Bye, Lola." I chuckled. "I'll talk to you tomorrow."

Lawrence's lovemaking was better than it had been the previous times, but it wasn't doing me much good. He couldn't have turned me on with twenty thousand volts. However, I had had so much "acting" experience in the bedroom—thanks to Reed—I was able to fake it so convincingly that Lawrence couldn't have been more satisfied. "Attention! You are too incredible for words. We *both* salute you!" He stood up in bed and saluted me with his hand and wagged a "salute" with his dick. I laughed and we made love again. I felt so much better, I spent the whole night.

We got up Saturday morning at eleven, yawning from exhaustion. "Let's order up some grub and before you leave we'll have a quickie to hold me over until we get together again," Lawrence suggested. I passed on the breakfast, and when I declined another lovemaking session, he pouted so much, I gave in.

I had enjoyed Lawrence's company, but by the time I got home at a quarter past two, I had slid back down into the doldrums. I had messages on every device. Mama had left one on my cell phone, chastising me for "acting a fool" in front of her house last night. One of her neighbors had witnessed my brawl with Reed and had called the cops! I was thankful that I had left before they showed up and even more thankful that the neighbor didn't know my address. I decided to avoid Mama and the rest of my family for a few days. I even sent her a text and explained that I needed some time alone and would call or visit when I felt better.

Kandy had sent me a text an hour ago. She told me that Reed's mother had returned to the beauty salon again earlier in the morning to get her toenails silk-wrapped. That old crow had bragged about how her "baby" was going to marry a psychologist's daughter. Two of my other regular club dates had sent messages to my e-mail address requesting dates for later in the month. The only person I wanted to communicate with was Lola.

I called her a few minutes after I'd checked the rest of my messages. I was glad she sounded so cheerful. "Good afternoon, Miss Thing. How was your date?" she said.

"Lawrence was a sweetheart and as funny as ever. But . . ."

"But what? Didn't he distract you enough to keep your mind off Reed?"

"He distracted me, but I kept thinking about that damn fool anyway. It's going to take some time for me to really get back into the swing of things. I know it sounds crazy, but I'm not going to accept another date for at least a couple of weeks. I don't want to be by myself the next few days, but I don't want to be around my family either."

"I'd love to have some company, and you can stay with me as long as you want. I went to Sears this morning and picked out a bed, but they can't deliver it until next Friday. So if you come, you'll have to sleep in the couch bed with me, or in that Spider-Man sleeping bag."

"Let me chill here in the condo for a day or so. I'll let you know by Sunday if I want to take you up on your offer." I cleared my throat. "But I don't want you to change or rearrange your schedule for my benefit. Unless it's for Calvin."

"I sent him a text an hour ago. I told him I have to talk to him in person about something very important."

"Has he responded yet?"

"Yeah, he did. That man's work schedule changes like the wind! He's got back-to-back runs for the next five or six days, but he's pretty sure he'll be back in town by Thursday or Friday. I texted him again and told him that I have to talk to him as soon as possible. I've waited long enough, so I insisted on it being no later than Monday. I can't wait to hear what he has to say when I tell him I'm in love with him."

"I can't wait to hear what he has to say myself. I'd give any-thing to be a fly on the wall—"

Lola cut me off so fast, I got dizzy. "Be serious! Don't you know how important this is to me?"

"Of course I know, but I don't know if it's a good idea to tell a man you met in a sex club you're in love with him. If he tells you that he wants to keep seeing you only for sex, will you settle for a relationship like that?"

Lola took her time responding. "I guess so," she muttered.

"You 'guess so'? You don't sound too happy about that."

"I'm not. The way things have been going for me with men, it may be the only kind of relationship I'm ever going to have."

Chapter 52
Calvin

MOTHER'S DAY WAS COMING UP IN A COUPLE OF DAYS. BECAUSE my estranged mother had passed before we could reconnect, this was the one holiday I dreaded the most. I was feeling sad about it, so I focused on other things to occupy my mind. I drank a few beers and watched a couple of TV shows Friday night. Before I went to bed around ten p.m., I read the latest text from Lola five times. I couldn't imagine what was so important that this beast needed to talk to me in person on Monday. Disturbing thoughts danced around in my head. What if it was something that would derail my plans? Maybe she wanted to tell me that she was no longer interested in seeing me! With all the negative things going on in her life lately, maybe she was going to relocate. If she moved to another city or state, it could take some time and a lot of effort for me to track her down. I couldn't put it off any longer. I had to kill her before Monday. . . .

One of the many mundane, idiotic things Lola had babbled about during our last hotel date was some shit about going to the Philippines to look for her uncle's ex-wife and her cousins. The most ridiculous thing she had told me was that she wanted to reconnect with one of her dead daddy's sluts. That sloppy whore had been brazen enough to move in and carry on her affair right in front of Lola and her mother. And Lola wanted to reconnect with an enema bag like her? That was the moment when I realized she was straight-up crazy. No sane woman would want to have a relationship with a woman who had disrespected her and her mother in such an unspeakable way! But when I gave it more thought, it made sense. *Like attracts like.* Lola was just as much of a slut as the slut who had fucked her daddy. And most of the others I had encountered. Were all women as bad as my ex-wife? I asked myself. Were there no decent women left? These were questions I didn't think anybody could answer. But I could answer one very important question: Was I doing mankind a favor by getting rid of so many whores? The answer was yes. Sadly, I could not do it all by myself, but I felt good knowing that I had already done more than my share. According to the statistics, there were dozens more, maybe even hundreds, like me at any given time, and for that I was grateful.

Because of that mess in Vegas with that Korean bitch and the meddlesome FBI's involvement in the murder of the racist hitchhiker, Melanie, I needed to quit while I was ahead. If Lola wanted to talk to me on Monday about ending our "relationship" or her moving away, it didn't really matter, because I'd never know. She wouldn't live to see Monday, so whatever it was she needed to talk to me about, she'd take it to her grave.

I couldn't kill Lola tonight because I was going to play poker with Robert next door and some of his buddies. And I couldn't do it Saturday. I had agreed to have dinner with Sylvia and some of her relatives at her place. Those people were not only excruciatingly annoying, they were the most long-winded people I knew, so there was no telling what time I'd be able to escape from them. If I could get away before too late, I'd kill her Saturday night after all. Otherwise, I'd have to wait and do it on Sunday. It would serve that beastly bitch right to die on Mother's Day. She had no right to even be thinking about having children! The bottom line was, Lola Poole had less than forty-eight hours to live.

I was sorry that I was not going to be able to have sex with that miserable heifer one more time. Especially since my lovemaking

made her so happy. However, I'd give her a few "happy" moments in the last hours of her life by texting her back and saying
something I knew she'd love to hear:

> **Will see you on Monday at same café where we met the
> first time. I'll call Sunday to let you know what time.
> Hope whatever it is you need to discuss, it's not some-
> thing that will cause you (or me . . . ☺) any discomfort.**

Saturday was one of the longest and most boring days of my
life. I woke up around nine a.m. with a headache that was so severe, even my neck and shoulders were in pain. I took some
Advil, stretched out on my living room couch, and remained
there for the next hour. I ignored Sylvia's noontime call, but I
couldn't ignore a call from my boss, Monty, that came in less
than five minutes after Sylvia's.

"Hey, Monty! What's up?" I greeted.

"Too much," Monty said as he cleared his throat. From his flat
tone, I knew he had something to say that I didn't want to hear.
"Cal, I hate to do this to you at the last minute, but would it be
possible for you to do a run to Long Beach tomorrow? Morgan
just called me from the hospital to let me know his wife went
into labor early. Things look pretty complicated, so he needs to
be with her until it's all over. This is their first child, so you know
how important this is to him and his wife. Even if she delivers
today, he wants to stay with her until she's out of the woods. We
have a shitload of furniture that he was supposed to deliver to
one of our most important clients. They're having a big sale
next week. The furniture has to be in their warehouse by five
p.m. tomorrow so they can inspect it and do all the paperwork.
If you can help us out, you'd really have to get an early start."

"Dude, I would love to help, but I have plans for tomorrow."

"Is it something you can postpone? Cal, I've called up three
other drivers and couldn't reach a single one. You'd be doing
me a huge favor if you can help us out. If you're not too tired
after the delivery, you can do a quick turnaround and be back
home in time to enjoy the rest of Mother's Day with Sylvia and
her mom like you do every year."

I took a deep breath and rubbed the side of my head, which felt as if it was about to spin off my neck. My thoughts were all over the place because my life had become so damn complicated! Well, it wouldn't be for long. I couldn't delay Lola's murder any longer so she had to die *tonight*. "Okay. I'll do the haul for Morgan," I said with a heavy sigh.

"Super! I really appreciate you always being so dependable, and I want to show my appreciation. You can take three additional days off with pay next month, so you can have more time to enjoy your honeymoon."

"Really? You just made the pot too sweet for me to pass up. Thanks, Monty."

Monty hung up and I immediately called Sylvia. Like always, she answered right away. "I just stepped out of the shower," she told me in an apologetic tone. "Can I call you back when I dry off and get dressed?"

"Baby, I just got off the phone with my boss. One of the other drivers' wife went into labor early so he won't be able to make an important run down to Long Beach tomorrow morning."

"Oh, Calvin! Did you volunteer to do it?"

"No, I didn't exactly volunteer. I was the only driver Monty could reach, and he practically begged me to do it. I'll come to dinner this evening, but I can't stay long. I have to be on the road before dawn tomorrow, so I need to get to bed at a decent hour."

"Mama's been cooking up a storm since yesterday and she's excited about introducing you to some of her friends this evening. I hope you can stay long enough to eat and get acquainted with everybody."

"I will, baby. I swear to God I'll make this up to you. Monty's giving me three extra days off so we can extend our honeymoon."

"That helps. Dinner is at seven, but I wish you'd come earlier," Sylvia said in a sad tone.

"I'll be there around six-thirty. Sylvia, look at it this way. This time next year, you might be the one in labor. Wouldn't you want me to be in the hospital room with you?"

"Yes, Calvin, I would. I can't wait to be a mother!" The sadness was no longer in her tone. Now she sounded downright giddy. "Just one thing. I don't want to disappoint Mama, so I'm not going to tell her you have to eat and run. A few minutes after we all finish eating, make out like you suddenly got seriously ill and need to leave right away. Will you do that?"

"Sure, baby. I'll do that. Your mama will never know the real reason I had to leave early. If I get back from my run in time tomorrow, I'm taking you, your mother, and anybody else you'd like to invite for a Mother's Day drink at one of the most elegant bars in town!"

"Thanks, honey. I know they will all enjoy that." Sylvia exhaled a loud breath. "I just hate to lie."

"So do I."

The next thing I had to do was case Lola's house.

Without her street address, I couldn't use GPS to find her. Her landline had not been installed yet, so I couldn't even get what I needed from the information operator either, but I was not worried. All I had to do was find the street she told me she had moved to and look for that halfway house at the corner with a yellow house next door.

At noon I made myself a sandwich and washed it down with a couple of beers. Afterward I put on a black knitted cap and one of my old camouflage jackets left over from my military days. I literally ran out to my Jeep. In addition to gloves, these were the same items I planned to wear on my mission in a few hours.

Once I got to South Bay City, it took only fifteen minutes to reach my destination. I circled her block twice before I parked directly across the street from the halfway house. I watched in disgust as several scruffy-looking dudes wandered in and out, scowling as if they wanted to cuss out the world.

Another reason I needed to complete my mission soon was because I didn't want to take a chance on one of Lola's new "neighbors" putting her on their radar first. She was just the type of juicy-butt young woman that a rapist, or any other criminal for that matter, would love to get his hands on. I laughed at the thought. Another thing that made me laugh was the fact that she was going to die in a yellow house, which was just as good to me as her fear of dying if she ever wore yellow clothing. Things couldn't have worked out better!

I whistled all the way back to my place.

Chapter 53
Joan

*I*T HAD BEEN A WEEK AND A DAY SINCE REED LEFT. THIS PARTICULAR Saturday seemed like it would never end. To kill time, around noon I did two loads of laundry, ordered a pizza for lunch, watched two episodes of *Judge Judy*, and then I took a long nap.

When I woke up at five-thirty, I noticed that Mama had left eight voice mail messages. Some had come in several days ago. I hadn't responded to any of them or spoken to her since last Saturday, and I still was not in the mood to talk to her today. Spending most of Mother's Day with her and some of my other family members tomorrow would be soon enough. In the meantime, I had a more important issue to address. I didn't know what Reed was up to, and I needed to know so I could be prepared for his next move. I hadn't heard from him since the pepper spray incident. He hadn't even attempted to talk to or come see Junior. That was probably because Junior had called him a "cheating scumbag" and hung up on him last Friday when he called him up at school and told him he'd moved in with his pregnant mistress.

I reluctantly called Reed's cell phone. I was surprised that he had not changed his number. I blocked the call so he wouldn't see my name and number on his caller ID. I didn't know much about pepper spray, and I had no idea if I had caused him any serious injury and I needed to know. On the third ring, a woman with a slightly hoarse voice answered. "Hellooo." She sounded like a drowsy, B-movie wannabe sexpot. I recognized her voice immediately. It was Grace, the scheming little heifer who had destroyed my marriage.

I altered my voice so drastically, I sounded like a gay man. "Is Reed there?"

There was a gasp on the other end of the line. The next voice I heard was Reed's. "This is Dr. Riley speaking. Who's calling?"

I hung up before he could say anything else. It was a relief to know that he was not stretched out in a hospital bed with injuries that had been caused by my pepper spray. I dialed Lola's number.

"Would you believe that he lets that bitch answer his cell phone?" I yelled as soon as she answered. "All the years we were together, he *never* let me near his cell phone!"

"You called Reed? Do you honestly think he wants to talk to you this soon after what you did to him?"

"Yes, I called that two-timing bastard! I wanted to make sure I hadn't blinded him or caused any real damage to his eyes with that pepper spray."

"Do you want me to come over?"

"No, but you know what? I think I'll come to your place and spend the night. I'd feel more comfortable there because I can still feel Reed's presence here and it's getting on my last nerve."

"That's fine, Joan. I sure would like some company and somebody to talk to. I'm getting kind of nervous about my upcoming meeting with Calvin on Monday."

"You suggested this meeting, so why are you getting nervous?"

"Telling him that I'm in love with him might scare him off."

"If you're worried about scaring him off, cancel the meeting. Or make up another reason you need to talk to him. You could even put this off until you feel more comfortable talking to him about it."

"I've waited too long already. I need to know now where I stand with him."

"Do what you have to do. We can talk more about this subject when I get there. I'll see you in a little while. "

The next person I called was Mama. "You called?" I said, when she answered.

"You know damn well I called, girl. And I done called more than once," she snarled. "How come you ain't called me back before now?"

"Mama, I told you I needed some time alone for a few days."

"Humph. I hope it done you some good and I hope you prayed that Reed don't have your tail arrested for pepper spraying him last Friday. That stuff can be real dangerous. You can mess up whoever you using it on, and you can accidentally get a dose of it yourself. You know how clumsy you can be."

"I wasn't clumsy enough to spray myself, Mama. I got him real good. Even so, I did have to hold my nose and close my eyes."

"You better be glad that's all you had to do. I don't know how Reed was able to see well enough to drive. And I can't understand why he didn't haul off and whup your behind. If I was in your shoes, I wouldn't let my guard down, because he still might do just that."

"Mama, whose side are you on?"

"I'm on your side and that's why I don't want you to get in no trouble. Believe me, you don't want to spend one night in a jail cell. I been working in the prison system for almost thirty years, and I still get nervous being around a bunch of frustrated female criminals. Thank God I don't have to use my pepper spray on them skanks too often."

"I pepper sprayed Reed in self-defense."

"Oh? Well, Carrie Rhine next door told us she seen you chasing Reed out the house. She said you was running like a snotty nose and didn't slow down until you got up on him real close. If he was leaving, how can you call that self-defense?"

"Because before he ran out of the house, he slapped me so hard I hit the floor."

"Say what? Why would a mild-mannered man like Reed do something like that?"

"I said something he didn't like and the next thing I knew, he slapped my face."

"Oh hell no! I didn't know he hit you! If I'd been here, I would have pepper sprayed him myself! I'm sorry, baby. Let me put on my shoes and I'll come keep you company—"

I cut Mama off as fast as I could. "Another time would be better. I'm going to spend the night at Lola's place," I said, already reaching for my keys on the coffee table. "It's going to take a while for her to get used to living by herself; especially with that halfway house full of ex-cons next door."

"Didn't you tell me she moved into a house with three bedrooms?"

"Yeah. So?"

"Tell her to get a couple of roommates."

"I don't think she wants to do that. She's always been a very private person."

"I don't know how she was so private with Bertha breathing down her neck. Poor Lola. She sure has had a miserable life since her mama and that skirt-chasing daddy of hers died. I'm surprised she ain't crazy as hell by now!"

"Lola is a very strong woman. She's too grounded to go off the deep end," I defended. "And anyway, she probably won't live in that big house more than a few months at the most."

"She won't? And why not?"

"Um, remember that truck driver I told you about? She's pretty serious about him, so she probably won't be single too much longer."

"Hogwash! Being 'serious' about a man don't mean nothing. I was serious about every man I was ever with and look how long it took me to get Elmo where I got him. Is this truck driver serious about her?"

"We'll find out soon enough. They're getting together on Monday so she can tell him how she feels about him. And she's going to ask him if he has feelings for her."

"Oomph, oomph, oomph. Something tells me she ain't going to like what he tells her."

Chapter 54
Calvin

WHEN I RETURNED TO SAN JOSE AFTER CASING LOLA'S RESIDENCE, I took a long, hot bath and drank two shots of rum. This was going to be the most memorable night of my life and I had to make sure everything went according to my plan. Now that I had the slut's new address, the most important thing I needed to know next was her plans for tonight. Without giving it much thought, I dialed her number. She was so anxious to speak to me, she answered less than a second into the first ring.

I could picture the look of euphoria on her face. "Hello, Calvin! It's so nice to hear your voice. I hope your day is going well," she chirped.

"My day is going just fine. I hope you're not too busy to chat with me for a minute or two," I said, trying to sound as giddy as she usually did.

"I'm not too busy to talk to you. I'm glad you called, because I was getting real bored. And I'm depressed because tomorrow is Mother's Day and this will be the first year I won't be celebrating it."

"I know just how you feel because it's a depressing day for me too. My siblings and I used to take our mom to brunch to celebrate the occasion every year since I was in elementary school. The first year after she passed was the hardest. The few days leading up to Mother's Day, I cried every time somebody mentioned it. Next year, and all the years after that, you won't get as depressed. And when you have your own children, you won't get depressed at all." I paused to give Lola time to think about what I'd just said. I had a feeling she'd say something corny and stupid, and she did.

"I can't wait to be a mother myself," she swooned. "That and being a wife are a woman's most important roles."

"I won't argue with that." I had to change the subject because listening to her rattle on about motherhood and marriage was making me even more nauseated. "What were you doing when I called?"

"I just used my new microwave oven for the first time and made some popcorn. Now I'm sitting here watching *Family Feud.*" I knew she was the type to watch one of the most idiotic programs on TV.

"That's one of my favorite shows! Um, I guess you have big plans for later tonight, huh?"

"Not really. I'll probably have a pizza delivered for my dinner. Other than that, I don't have any plans except to watch TV. "

"I'm surprised you don't have a date."

"I have several requests in my in-box right now, but I'm not going to respond to any for a while. I'd like to get my life back on track before I start dating again."

"Well, I hope you still plan to keep the date you have with me on Monday."

"Oh, yes! I still want to see you on Monday. Do you know yet what time we can meet?"

"Hmmm. How about seven?"

"That's fine. What I have to talk to you about won't take long."

"Lola, I know that whatever it is, it's very important to you. Otherwise, you wouldn't have made it sound so urgent."

"It is very important to me. It's something I've been putting off for a while. And . . . uh . . . I can't put it off any longer."

I was dying to know what she needed to talk to me about. I hadn't planned to ask, but now I was too curious not to. "Can you give me a little hint? The suspense is killing me. You don't have to go into all the details, but I would like to have some idea. I mean, if I've said or done something to offend you and you want to cuss my ass out, that's fine. If I've—"

She cut me off. "I'll tell you part of it and I'll tell you the rest on Monday." She let out a loud sigh and then said all in one breath, "Um . . . I . . . *I've been looking for a man like you all my life.*"

Her words were so irritating, I had to rub my ear. I never wanted to laugh so hard in my life! Did this nasty, stinking, stupid, gullible bitch think I'd settle for a washed-up, sloppy, used-up whore like her? I literally had to cover my mouth with my hand to keep from guffawing like a hyena! I coughed so I'd have an excuse to delay my response. "Lola, I can't tell you how pleased I am to hear you say that. I'm very insecure and I've never had much luck with women as beautiful and intelligent as you."

"I never would have guessed that. You're one of the nicest and most intelligent men in the club!" she exclaimed. "And you look better than any other man, black or white, that I've seen—including most of the movie stars. Your ex-wife must have been stone crazy to leave you."

Only an immature dingbat, which she was, would make such over-the-top, clichéd statements. I was pleased to hear that she had put me so high up on the social food chain, but I couldn't figure out why she found me so appealing. I was no gargoyle, but I was no Mr. Universe either. And I wasn't rich or unique in any way. "Thank you, Lola. You just made my day. Nobody has ever said anything that touching to me. I'm so flattered I don't know what to say." I sniffed and weakened my tone. I wanted to sound as sappy and romantic as she was making me sound. "I guess I look all right for a man my age, and I can carry on a decent conversation. But I know about the kind of dudes you're really used to—lawyers, and doctors, and whatnot. Last month I even saw a five-star review about you that some rock star from England posted."

"*Pffft!* I must not have impressed him that much, because I haven't heard from him since." She laughed. I didn't.

"Well, that's his loss. Believe me, you are not only the most beautiful woman I've ever been with, you are also the best lover I've ever had."

"Who, me? Um, thanks, Calvin. I hope I don't change. My main goal in life is to be happy and make other people happy."

I still found it hard to believe that I was talking to a woman in her thirties. This tutti-frutti nutcase was probably still playing with dolls. "I've kept you long enough, so I'll let you get back to your popcorn and your TV show."

"I don't have to go yet."

"I wish I didn't have to go. I have a busy day tomorrow and I just wanted to hear your voice before I turned in for the night. Maybe I'll see you in my dreams again."

"You've dreamt about me?"

"Oh yes. I have very pleasant dreams about you all the time." The profound gasp on her end told me that her jaw had dropped. I couldn't wait to see her reaction when I told her to her face that she'd been my worst nightmare from day one! Bitch, slut, whore, cow, pig, wench! There weren't enough loathsome English words to describe her completely.

"I . . . I . . . dream about you a lot."

As if I didn't know! "I'm glad to hear that."

I had a feeling she was going to let out another gasp, and I was right. "Calvin, I'm so glad you called." She answered my last question before I asked. "I'm in for the night." She paused. "In case you want to call me later on."

"I just might do that. Good night, Lola. Sweet dreams."

"Good night, Calvin."

I hung up and poured another drink.

It was a good thing I had a buzz when I got to Sylvia's house at 6:25 p.m. Her family and their friends were more annoying than I expected, especially her pie-faced mother, Gisele. "Calvin, you don't have enough food on your plate to feed a gnat," she complained as she piled a yellow meal-like concoction onto my plate. "You're way too thin for a man!" she added.

People stood around in the dining room with plates of food, chatting away about how happy they were that Sylvia was finally going to get married. "I been telling her all her life no man was going to marry her until she lowered her expectations," Aunt So-and-So said. Her statement confused and angered me at the same time. I couldn't decide if this withered old hag was implying that I met Sylvia's requirements or that she had "lowered her expectations" by settling for me. It didn't matter which one it was. I was not going to spend too much time with them in the future anyway.

All eight seats at the dinner table were occupied. I sat between Sylvia and her mother. Sylvia's sister, Sonia, sat directly across from me between her husband, a hatchet-faced Dominican with very dark brown skin and silver hair, and one of her brooding teenage male cousins. "Calvin, you don't look well," Sonia blurted out. Every eye in the room was suddenly on me.

"I . . . I'm sorry. I ate something this afternoon that didn't agree with me." I coughed and rubbed my chest.

"Don't worry. I have just the thing for heartburn," Gisele said. She gave me a pitiful look and started scooting her seat back. "I'll go get it."

I held up my hand. "I'm fine. Sylvia already gave me something for it. I left it at home, so I'll have to leave in a few minutes."

Sylvia whirled around to face me, but she confirmed my lie. "Uh-huh. I gave him some of the strongest charcoal pills we have in stock."

"It's so good to have a pharmacist in the family," Sonia's husband said. "We can all get sick for nothing. If we could get us a preacher in the family, we could all be good for nothing." Everybody in the room laughed, even me.

"Calvin, wouldn't you like to go lie down in the guest room for a while?" Gisele suggested. "I'd hate to see you leave so soon."

"I really wish I could stay, but I do need to get home and take care of myself. I have a very important haul down to Long Beach tomorrow and I can't afford to be sick," I said as I rubbed my chest some more.

"Well, fix yourself a plate before you leave," Sonia said. "You barely touched that flank steak I cooked."

"Thanks," I mumbled with a grimace on my face. To complete my performance, I wobbled up out of my seat and made a bee-line for the bathroom and stayed there for five minutes. When I returned to the dining room, I coughed again. Everybody felt so sorry for me, three people offered to escort me home. "I'll be just fine. I have only a couple of miles to drive," I told them.

Sylvia fixed a plate for me and walked me to the door. "I love you, baby," she whispered.

"I love you too. I'll call you later tonight or when I get to Long Beach tomorrow." I couldn't leave fast enough.

When I got home, I immediately turned on my laptop and pulled up Lola's profile. I stared at her picture for so long and with so much intensity, it began to look like it was in three di-mensions. "You filthy slut! You're finally going to get what you deserve!" I blasted. "This was a long time coming and I can't wait to see your face tonight when you see mine . . . *for the last time*! BITCH!"

Chapter 55
Lola

*I*T WASN'T EVEN COMPLETELY DARK YET, BUT I HAD ALREADY PUT ON my nightgown and stretched out in the couch bed with a glass of wine and the new issue of *Brides* magazine. I laid my cell phone on the coffee table so it'd be close enough to answer right away in case Calvin called. Before I could get comfortable, a call came in. I cringed when I saw Elbert's name on the caller ID. If I didn't answer, he'd call again. And he would keep calling until I talked to him.

"Hello, Elbert." It was hard not to sound annoyed.

"Hello," he mumbled. He rarely asked if he was calling at a bad time, but every time he called was a bad time as far as I was concerned. "I'm cooking dinner for Mama tomorrow to celebrate Mother's Day. Would you like to join us? I know you'll be thinking about Bertha not being here to celebrate one last Mother's Day with you."

"I have other plans, but thanks for the invitation," I muttered.

"If you change your mind, let me know." Elbert hesitated, and listening to his loud breathing for several seconds annoyed me even more. I knew that if I didn't end this call myself, he'd stay on the line fifteen minutes or longer. Before I could, he continued. "Guess what?"

I let out a loud sigh. "Elbert, I'm busy so I don't have time to play guessing games."

"Well, I had a manager's sale on my meat products today. Jeffrey came in a few minutes before I closed and bought some ox-tails. He's cooking dinner for his mother tomorrow too. He told me he moved out of Bertha's house and in with one of his cousins until he finds a place."

"Oh?" I suddenly got interested in whatever else Elbert had to say. "I didn't know that. Do you know why he moved?"

"He said he's going to divorce Libby because he's no longer happy being married to her."

"I'm so sorry for Jeffrey. He's such a nice person. Thanks for letting me know. I'll give him a call tomorrow. Divorce can be so traumatic."

"Tell me about it. I told Mama that when I get married again, I hope I stay married."

"I hope you will too, Elbert."

When he hesitated again, I knew he was about to say something I didn't want to hear. I was prepared to turn down another invitation to a bingo game or a pot-luck dinner with a bunch of his equally boring church friends. He said the last thing I expected. "Lola, you're the only woman I can see myself being married to."

I rolled my eyes and blew out an impatient breath. At the same time, I felt a churning sensation in my stomach. "Me?"

"Don't act so surprised. I've been grooming you for months to be my wife." He laughed, but I knew he was dead serious.

I liked Elbert, but he was the dullest man I knew. He could bore me to tears, so being his wife was out of the question. "I'm flattered, but I don't know if I'm ready to take such a big step."

"Not ready? You're the only woman our age I know who has never been married."

"You don't need to remind me of that!" I snapped.

"Is it that you're not ready to marry *me*?"

"Don't put words in my mouth."

"Then tell me why you don't want to be my wife. I know you have feelings for me."

"I do have feelings for you, but I have feelings for several other men I know and I don't want to marry any of them either."

"I see. So basically what you're telling me is that I'm competing with 'several other men'?"

"I didn't say that," I said sharply. Now would have been a good time to tell Elbert that I was in love with Calvin, but first I had to find out how Calvin felt about me. "I have to be honest with you. I know I couldn't live with you and your mama and be happy. I would end up taking care of her and then I'd be tied down just like I was with Bertha. And that's one thing I never want to go through again."

"Is that the only reason you don't want to marry me?" Elbert didn't give me time to respond. "You won't have to. Mama's been seeing a man since last year who's been badgering her to marry him and move into the senior citizen facility where he lives. She told him to give her a little more time to think about it."

"Do you think she'll marry him?"

I didn't expect his long-winded response. "I know she wants to. I overheard her tell one of her friends that she'd love to be married again. My four siblings live in Philadelphia, but they don't want to be bothered with Mama, so the whole burden is on me. I love her to death, but living with her is no picnic. She recently told me she feels the same way about living with me! She also told me that I'm the only reason she hasn't moved on with her life. She blames me for her missing out on things she'd rather be doing with her boyfriend. I can't tell you how that made me feel. Not only that, she told me years ago that she didn't want to be a burden to me in her old age. She had to take care of her mama and she admitted that it was such a bad experience, she ended up hating my grandmother. Mama was actually glad when she passed. A couple of her friends had similar experiences, and they eventually dumped their parents into the first old folks' home that had room for them, where they got abused and neglected. Mama doesn't want that to happen, and neither do I. I didn't know how she felt until we had a long talk the day after Bertha's funeral. So you can forget about having to take care of another old lady. Now that I know how Mama feels, I realize *I'm* a burden to her." Elbert finally paused. "So what's your next excuse? Is it because you don't have any feelings for me? Love isn't the only reason for two people to get married. Marriage is a partnership, and love is just one of the aspects. We both want children so—"

I cut Elbert off in the middle of his last sentence. I couldn't stand to listen to him for another minute. "You picked a bad time to bring up such a serious subject. I'm still grieving Bertha's passing and my personal life is in an uproar. I'm not in the mood to discuss a marriage proposal tonight—especially over the telephone."

"I can come over right now and do it in person if you'll give me your address!" I couldn't believe how eager he sounded. "I'm surprised that you haven't given that information to me already."

I was so exasperated, it was hard to remain composed. I had to end this call before I started screaming. "I have to go. We can finish this conversation at another time. I'll give you my address then."

"When?"

"I don't know."

"Okay. We can discuss marriage later. In the meantime, will you still let me take you out?"

"Elbert, we can still go out and we can still be friends. If you don't mind, I really need to get back to what I was doing. I still have things to unpack."

"Will you give me a call soon?"

"Yes, I will. Now you have a blessed night." I hung up before he could say another word.

I turned off my phone and for the next five minutes I stared at the wall and thought about Elbert's clumsy proposal. Now that I knew how serious he was about me, I was glad I hadn't told him about Calvin. I didn't want to hurt his feelings any more than I already had. And I didn't want to sever my relationship with him completely in case I needed to fall back on him someday.

Joan showed up half an hour after my conversation with Elbert. I decided not to tell her about his proposal for the time
being. With her life in such a mess, she probably would have
said something I didn't want to hear.

After a few minutes of small talk, she poured herself a large
glass of wine and flopped down on my couch. "Let's take a
Caribbean cruise or fly first class to Mexico and party for a couple of weeks. We could leave next week. I know this rowdy bar
on the beach in Puerto Vallarta where we can really let our hair
down."

"Joan, you know better."

"What?" She took a drink and belched.

"I have a job to go to. I've missed several days since Bertha
died, so taking off two more weeks this soon is out of the question. And with all my unexpected new expenses, I can't afford a
vacation right now.

"*Pffft!*" Joan gave me a dismissive wave and took another
drink. "You'll be my guest, so I'll pay for everything."

I shook my head and gave her an apologetic look. "I can go
with you later in the year, but for now I need to get my affairs in
order. And that list keeps getting longer."

She must have been reading my mind, because what she said
next was exactly what I was thinking. "I'm sure that Calvin is at
the top of that list."

I nodded. "Like I told you already, I'm going to find out
where I stand with him this coming Monday."

Joan hunched her shoulders and gave me a skeptical look.
"Good luck. Do whatever you have to do if it'll make you happy.
That's exactly what I'm going to do. Before I start partying like a
rock star, I'm going to get in touch with DrFeelGood and tell
him to set up a date for me to come to Palm Beach for the breast
implants and all the rest of the surgeries he promised me. The
next time Reed sees me, he'll realize what a fine-ass, young-looking
bitch he gave up." Joan finished her drink, stood up, and yawned.

"You're drunk and you look sleepy. You can have the couch
and I'll sleep in the bedroom in the sleeping bag," I said, rising.

"No. You sleep out here and I'll take the sleeping bag. Good night, Lo . . . la. Sleep tight," she slurred as she staggered out of the room.

I left the end table lamp on and stretched out on the couch. I eventually dozed off and probably would have slept through the night if I hadn't felt my comforter being tugged. "Joan, cut it out and take your drunk ass back to bed," I scolded. A split second later, I felt a tap on my shoulder. When I turned over and opened my eyes, I saw the last person in the world I expected to see hovering over me: *Calvin!*

Chapter 56
Lola

*C*ALVIN WAS ON MY MIND SO OFTEN NOW, I DREAMT ABOUT HIM almost every night. But tonight's dream seemed so real! I assumed it was because we'd talked about us dreaming about each other earlier tonight. It took only a few seconds for me to realize I was not dreaming this time.

I sat up, rubbed my eyes, and stared at him. "How did you know where I lived? How did you get in my house?" I asked with my voice cracking. He ignored my questions. "Would you please tell me what is going on?" All kinds of strange thoughts were swimming around in my head. Had Calvin died and I was looking at his ghost? He was not an apparition, because his body was flesh and blood and as solid as mine. What I saw in his hand didn't make any sense. My next question slid out of my mouth like vomit. *"Why are you pointing a gun at me?"*

"It's judgment day, BITCH!" he snarled.

I could not believe what I was seeing and hearing. What the hell was going on? My head was throbbing like it had never throbbed before. Either I really was dreaming after all, or I had lost my mind and was having a delusion. Maybe Calvin had lost his mind. "Have you lost your mind?"

"No! I'm as sane as you are! And a lot smarter! You are the stupidest bitch I have ever met!"

Except for Libby and Marshall, no other human being had ever spoken to me in such a disrespectful and hostile manner.

Now here was the man I had hoped to marry talking to me like I was a dog. "What are you talking about? Why are you calling me those vile names?" I held up my hand. "I know you have a great sense of humor, but if this is your idea of a joke, you're scaring the hell out of me!"

"Humph! You should be scared. Because tonight you're going to get everything a skanky whore like you deserves!"

The gun in his hand kept me from reaching for my cell phone. Without another word, he pulled something out of his pocket and moved closer, holding it up to my face. It was a picture of *me*! "Where . . . when . . . I never posed for that!" My first thought was that he had photoshopped one of the pictures I had posted on the Internet. But why? I squinted and stared at it a few more seconds. When I looked back at his face, his eyes looked as cold and empty as the eyes on a dead man. "Why don't you tell me what the hell is going on?" I wailed. "You break into my house dressed like a burglar and point a gun at me and I have no idea why! Was that story about you being a truck driver a big lie and you're really a criminal who befriends women so you can rob them? If so, why did you choose *me*? What do I have that you'd want to take? You know damn well I don't have much now! And . . . and . . . now you're showing me a picture of myself that I don't remember taking."

"That's because this is not a picture of you," he said calmly. "She is . . . *was* my wife."

I gulped. "That's Mrs. Ramsey?"

"Yes and no. Her name was Glinda Price. She refused to take my last name because she claimed it would interfere with her independence."

This information hit me like a thunderbolt. Glinda Price was one of the three missing black women I'd read about in the newspaper! Calvin's eyes darkened as he continued. "I was pissed because she didn't want to take my last name, but I'm glad she didn't. A lot of the people who read about her disappearance didn't even know I knew her. She left me for a fucking career criminal. That sucker had been accused of making other people disappear, so nobody who knew she was my wife suspected me when she went missing." He leaned forward and waved the picture so close to my face, it brushed my nose. "I loved Glinda. She was my world and I would have died for her," he added in a weak tone. Tears began to roll down his face as he sniffled and cleared his throat. "I couldn't let her go."

"What's that got to do with me?" I whimpered, sounding like a sick kitten.

"Look at this picture some more, BITCH! You thought it was you! The first time I saw the picture you posted online, I realized Glinda was still very much alive."

"She's . . . she's dead?" I stammered.

"Very dead, and has been for several years." Calvin blinked and shook his head. "But she's still with me." He narrowed his eyes and gave me the most menacing look I'd ever seen on a man's face. "I killed that whore the night she tried to walk out on me. She's in a freezer in my garage."

"You killed your wife and stuffed her into a freezer?" I asked in stunned disbelief.

He nodded. "And she's not alone. Two other sluts, who looked enough like her to piss me off, are with her. And guess what? It's a big freezer, the kind they use in restaurants and hospitals and whatnot. And guess what else? There's room for one more body. Do you want to know whose body that's going to be?" He laughed.

"Calvin, I wish you would hurry up and tell me what's really going on. Are you punking me?" After all I'd seen and heard so far, this was a very stupid question. I knew I was not being punked, but I had to ask anyway. In the back of the whirlpool in my head, I still thought there was a chance that I was dreaming. His explosive response removed that doubt.

"YOU STUPID COW!" he roared. "Do you want me to pull this trigger and show you this is not a fucking joke?" He raised the gun and pointed it at my head.

Everything seemed surreal, and my body felt as light as a feather. I was surprised that I hadn't floated up off the couch by now. I sat with my trembling hands in my lap and my blood pressure rising. "Calvin, I can't believe you've killed three women."

He laughed again and shook his head. "*Three?* The number is a lot higher than that. I've been doing this so long, I've lost count. And each one had it coming—hitchhikers, hookers, and other skanky women like Glinda. Most of them didn't look like her, but at the end of the day all whores deserve to die. The only thing I was sorry about after I killed my wife was that I could kill her only one time. Then I got the notion that I could relive the experience by killing whores who looked like her. You look more like Glinda than any of the others, and that's why you're so special."

"I don't believe what I'm hearing!"

"Then you're dumber than I thought! You told me you'd read one of the newspaper articles about those three missing women. You can't tell me you didn't notice how much they resembled each other."

"I . . . I . . . I did notice that," I stammered. My head felt as if it were going to disconnect from my body.

"Missing hitchhikers don't get too much media attention, because their bodies usually end up in places where they'll never be found. But I know you read about that hooker they found in an alley a few weeks ago. They pinned the murder on her pimp and he's doing time for it, but I'm the one who did the crime." He laughed some more. It was an eerie, high-pitched cackle. This time he sounded like the maniac he was claiming to be.

"Are you telling me that the only reason you contacted me in the first place was so you could kill me because I look like your wife?"

"That was the main reason, but since you're such a fine-ass bitch, I wanted a piece of ass too. I call that my bonus."

"You won't get away with this!" I sobbed.

"No body, no crime. Now stop boo-hooing and get your filthy ass up! You're coming with me—"

"The hell I will!"

"The hell you won't! I've been planning to murder you for a

long time. My plans changed from time to time, but I knew I'd never rest until you were dead. Believe it or not, you'll be my last victim. Then I can begin to heal from the pain Glinda caused me and go on with my life. By the way, I'm getting married next month. The day I called you while you were having lunch with some asshole, my fiancée and I had a nice engagement party in Vegas. Tonight I had dinner with her and her family. And next weekend my boss and some of my buddies are having a bachelor party for me. While I was in Vegas, just thinking about you caused me to take out my anger on a sleazy little Korean whore. That bitch actually recovered, but not enough to finger me. Jail is not on my agenda, so I have to make sure I do the job right on you! Even though your body is going into my freezer, and I'll eventually have the damn thing dumped in some remote loca-tion, I might chop off a few of your body parts just for sport!"

I was so numb by the time Calvin ended his long-winded rant, I thought I had had a silent stroke and was now paralyzed. I was surprised that I was still able to speak. "You've killed a bunch of women and you're going to kill me, and you think you're going to go on and live a normal life?" My voice was so low and raspy, nobody would have recognized it.

"Nothing is 'normal' anymore, baby. Normal is the new crazy, and if you ask me, *every* human being on this planet has a dark side, some much darker than others, of course. And if that's true, and I believe it is, if there's a hell below, we're all gonna go. Now get your ass up and get dressed! I don't want to have to tell you again!" He glanced at his watch. "I have a run to do to-morrow, so I have to get up early."

I wanted to cry some more, but I was in such a state of shock and disbelief, so I couldn't. I was barely still able to speak. "Wh—why don't you just shoot me now and get it over with?" I choked.

"*Pffft!* That would be too quick and easy. I've spent too much time and energy planning this event. I'm going to make you suf-fer as much as you've made me suffer. You're going to curse the day you decided to hook up with me. When we get to where we're going tonight, I'm going to take my good old time so you'll have plenty of time to think and pray about everything. And then I'm going to strangle you! Any questions?"

"You bastard! I'm not going anywhere with you! If you want to kill me, you'll have to do it here! And I'm not going down without a fight!" I was trying to think of everything I could say to stall him. I glanced around the room, but I quickly returned my attention to his face. I couldn't let him know that Joan had tiptoed into the room and was creeping up behind him. Her cell phone was in her hand and she was recording everything! And I was so glad to see her holding that can of pepper spray I'd advised her to get rid of.

Chapter 57
Joan

I HAD NOT BEEN SLEEPING WELL SINCE REED LEFT ME. NO MATTER what time I went to bed, I usually stayed awake for an hour or longer. On top of that, I had suddenly become a very light sleeper.

I had just dozed off when I heard a man's voice coming from Lola's living room. My first thought was that it was her oafish stepbrother, Marshall. It would not have surprised me if he had come to teach Lola a lesson for blowing the whistle on Libby's affair. It didn't take but a few seconds for me to realize it was not Marshall's voice. It was one I had never heard.

At first I was too groggy to understand what the man was saying. Since it was not Marshall, or that pesky Elbert, the most logical conclusion I could come to was that one of the ex-cons in the halfway house next door had gotten loose and broken in. Lola and I were both in danger of being raped, beaten, and maybe even murdered! The reality of the situation hit me like a ton of bricks. I crawled out of the sleeping bag and crept closer to the door. What I heard made my flesh crawl. Calvin had broken into the house and was holding Lola at gunpoint! I grabbed my cell phone, crept into the closet, and dialed 911. I had to whisper, but the dispatcher heard all she needed to hear. I ended the call and eased out of the closet, praying that the cops would get to us in time. I got the pepper spray out of my purse and started moving toward the door. When Calvin told Lola the reason he had come to kill her and about the women he had already killed, I started recording them on my cell phone.

There was no telling what would have happened if I had not decided to spend the night with Lola. Had Calvin kidnapped and killed my best friend and put her body in that freezer, I probably would have never known what happened to her.

Ironically, Reed was the main reason Lola was not going to die. It was because of him that I was too depressed and angry to be alone in my own home tonight. I was still mad as hell and I was not through with him yet. But tonight I was glad he was such an asshole.

I always thought that Calvin sounded too good to be true, and I never would have guessed that he was a psycho serial killer all along. The boogeyman responsible for the missing women we had read about, plus the murders he'd confessed to Lola, had been hiding in plain sight all this time. This sucker had finally met his match. His butt was mine!

Lola looked right in my eyes as soon as I entered the room with the can of pepper spray in one hand and my cell phone in the other. She quickly looked back at Calvin and he continued talking. Right after he ordered her to get up and get dressed, I jumped from behind him and started spraying his face. I held my breath so I wouldn't inhale too many fumes. The look of surprise on his face was priceless. "YOU—YOU BITCH!" he blasted. He dropped the gun and fell to the floor wiping his eyes, kicking like a wild bronco, and screaming like a banshee.

"The cops are on the way!" I yelled to Lola. "Get his gun!"

She scrambled up off the couch, ran across the floor, and picked up the gun. "Motherfucker, if you try to get up, I will blow your head off!" she hollered. It was so hard to believe that this was the same man she had been fantasizing about marrying. The whole situation was hard to believe, period.

"Now I'm going to send both of you whores to hell!" Calvin roared. He was still wiping his eyes and writhing in agony.

"Oh yeah? And you'll be going with us!" I kicked his side as hard as I could with my bare foot. Then I leaned over and sprayed his face from ear to ear.

"AAARRRGGGHHH! STOP!" he screeched hysterically as he

covered his face with his hands. He was still kicking when Lola got closer to him. The next thing I knew, he tripped her. She didn't fall, but she dropped the gun. He felt around until he got his hands on it. And then he staggered up. I was out of pepper spray by now, but my cell phone was still recording.

Even though Calvin couldn't see us clearly, if he started randomly firing his gun, he could hit and *kill* one or both of us!

Lola and I had been in tight spots before. We had always been lucky enough to wiggle our asses out and land on our feet.

Our luck had finally run out. This time we were in *real* trouble.

Chapter 58
Lola

WHEN WE WERE IN ELEMENTARY SCHOOL, JOAN AND I HAD VOWED that we'd be BFFs until the day we died. That prediction was about to come true because we were going to die together tonight. My prediction that something yellow would be associated with my death was too. I had been diligent about avoiding this color for decades. Here I was now in a yellow house with a self-confessed serial killer pointing a gun at my head. I believed that the mysterious chill I'd felt when I saw the house for the first time had been an omen that something really bad was going to happen to me.

Once the whole convoluted story got out, the gossips would have a field day, but only if somebody found our bodies and Calvin got caught. The thought of being put into a freezer with the corpses of three strangers turned my stomach. When I thought about how I'd made a fool of myself wallowing around in bed with this monster, telling him all my personal business, I actually got sick. Hot, slimy puke landed on my bare feet. I hopped and screamed, and when I did, Calvin fired the first shot. The bullet whizzed so close to my face, I smelled the gunpowder.

He stopped wiping his eyes and started blinking real hard. He was coughing and cussing and calling us every nasty name in the book as he stumbled in my direction. "This is one fucked-up night, but I'm going to make it right again!" he wheezed. Tears were oozing from his bloodshot eyes. I couldn't tell if he was crying because he was upset or because of the pepper spray. His face was so contorted, he didn't even look like a human being anymore. His face looked like a mask, and in a way he had been wearing one all along. I was staring at true evil. And I had nobody to blame but myself. But I was going to delay my soul's one-way trip to hell as long as I could. When Calvin got within a couple of feet of me, I kicked his leg hard enough to make him fall back to the floor, but he held on to his gun and was back on his feet within seconds.

"Calvin, please put the gun down!" Joan pleaded. "Think about what you're doing! I have a son to raise!"

"Bah! Don't make me laugh! Whores like you should not even be allowed to have children. Your son will be much better off without you in his life. Shit. If he finds out someday that I was the one who finished your ass off, he might thank me," he taunted. Then he let out that eerie laugh again. "Now, I want both of you skanks to get dressed. We're going to take a ride over to San Jose." He wiped his eyes and coughed some more. The fumes from the pepper spray were making me nauseated, so he had to be in extreme distress. "Okay, you bitches from hell! I'm . . . I'm . . ." His voice trailed off and he swayed from side to side. I thought he was going to hit the floor again, but then he stopped swaying and stood as straight as a pole, glaring from Joan to me. "I'm going to make—" He stopped. Somebody had kicked open the door!

"DROP THE GUN!" a loud voice boomed. It was the sweetest sound I had ever heard in my life. The burly Hispanic cop standing in the doorway clutching his gun with both hands looked like an angel. Before I knew it, several more cops holding guns rushed in. "Drop the gun and put your hands in the air!" the first officer told Calvin.

"Fuck you!" Calvin scowled at the cops and held on to his gun. When he pointed it at the officer, all hell broke loose. I had no idea how many shots were fired and how many of them struck Calvin. But before he went down, he managed to shoot one of the officers in the head. That poor man was dead before he hit the floor.

Joan stumbled over to one of the cops and threw herself into his arms, crying hysterically. I was so stunned, I just stood still and stared at Calvin lying on his back. He was still conscious, and so combative, it took four officers to hold him in place. Despite all the chaos, he still managed to look up at me. I had never seen so much hatred and anger in another person's eyes. If his glare alone could have killed me, I'd have dropped dead on the spot. Even though I stood at least five feet away from him, he hawked gobs of spit in my direction several times.

The cops treated him for chemical exposure and they took care of his wounds as well as they could. Five minutes later, two ambulances arrived. One group of EMTs loaded the dead policeman into a body bag and hauled him away. The others treated the gunshot wounds Calvin had sustained, but it did no good. He died a few minutes later.

After Joan and I had composed ourselves and got dressed, we were ushered out the door, surrounded by half a dozen cops. A caravan of police cars was parked on both sides of the street. Dozens of looky-loo neighbors lined the sidewalk, and a local TV news van had just pulled up.

We were transported to the police station to give our statements. Joan's horrified parents were in the lobby when we came out of the interview room, and they made her go home with them. She was almost delirious by now, so she was in no shape to resist. From the dirty looks I got from Pearline and Elmo, I was not surprised that they didn't extend the same invitation to me. I had nobody to turn to, and I felt lonelier than I'd ever felt in my life.

I didn't want to wait around for the police to take me home, so I walked the quarter of a mile back to my house. All of the neighbors, the news van, and most of the police officers had left. Joan's car, which had been parked in the driveway next to mine, was gone. There was yellow crime scene tape wrapped around the house, but a very sympathetic policewoman escorted me inside so I could get some clothes and other personal items. She even helped me load everything into my car. I knew that if I didn't remove the rest of my property in a timely manner, the landlady had the right to keep or dispose of everything I'd left behind. But I didn't care. I didn't want to spend another minute in that house, not even to collect the rest of my stuff.

It was the worst night of my life. While I drove around looking for another cheap motel, my chest heaving and my heart pounding, disturbing thoughts buzzed around in my head like killer bees. My brain felt like scrambled eggs, so it was hard for me to process everything that had happened in the last few hours. I felt like a zombie and probably looked like one too.

While I had been floating around on cloud nine fantasizing about marrying Calvin, he'd been planning to kill me! I was glad he was dead, because I could not have faced him in a court-room. If he had survived and gone to prison, I would have lived in fear for the rest of my life. I knew it would be a long time be-fore I trusted another man, and I'd probably never fall in love again.

A sudden panic attack forced me to pull into a vacant lot. While I was trying to catch my breath and hold back my tears, my cell phone rang. It was Elbert. "Thank God you answered!" he hollered. "When they interrupted the late-night movie with the news about what had happened to you and Joan, I couldn't believe what I was hearing! Are you all right?"

"I'm fine," I managed, choking on a sob. I had to take a few deep breaths before I could continue. "I packed a few things so I'll be checking into another motel as soon as I find one I can af-ford."

"Motel? Sweet Jesus, Lola!" Elbert wheezed so hard it sounded as if he was sitting right next to me. "You don't have to go to a motel. How many times do I have to tell you that you're wel-come to move in with Mama and me and stay as long as you want? In the first place, if you would have taken me up on my offer when you got kicked out of Bertha's house, you wouldn't be in the mess you're in now."

There was no doubt in my mind that even if I had moved in with Elbert, Calvin would have found me. He had been determined to kill me and would have tonight if the cops had not killed him first. I wasn't going to say too much to people about him and our relationship because I didn't want them to know the whole story and how reckless and immoral I'd been. Despite Elbert's steadfast holiness, I didn't think even he would want to associate with a vile, stupid, whorish fool like me if he knew I'd been having sex with strangers I'd met online and that Calvin had been one of them.

"Elbert, thank you again, but I don't want to stay in your house." I was in such a vulnerable state, I was afraid that if he proposed to me again while I was under his roof, I'd be too helpless to turn him down.

Chapter 59
Lola

*T*WO HOURS AFTER I HAD CHECKED INTO THE RED DOG MOTEL, I turned on my laptop. It was seven a.m. and I had slept less than an hour since the night before. I had received e-mail messages from a dozen people I had not heard from in years and four from people I couldn't even remember. My daddy's estranged brother in Anaheim had even left a message for me on Facebook. He advised me to get back to him as soon as possible so he could "pick my brain" because he wanted to sell a story to a tabloid! My uncle had had nothing to do with me since I was a little girl, and now he was trying to make money off my pain. I was so appalled I didn't even reply.

Calvin had changed my life forever, just as I'd predicted he would.

I returned to work on Monday, and reporters were all over the place. I refused to talk to them. After they left, almost every customer in the store came to my counter to say something stupid or snap pictures of me with their phones. I almost lost my cool when one brazen woman asked, "Was Calvin good in bed?"

I threw up my hands, but before I could say anything, one of my elderly employers rescued me. Mrs. Cottright beckoned for one of the other cashiers to take care of my long line of customers and she ushered me to the back of the store. "Honey, if you want to clock out and go back home right now, that's fine with me.

And you can stay off until things settle down. I'm surprised you ain't lost your marbles by now."

I had five more hours to go before my shift ended. I knew that if I tried to finish it, I'd be mincemeat by the end of the day. "Thanks, Maisie," I mumbled, wiping sweat off my forehead.

Mrs. Cottright gave me a hug. "I'll pray for you and Joan, baby. Now go home, where you can have some peace of mind."

I left work immediately. The Red Dog Motel would be home until I figured out what to do next.

I didn't give my landlady a thirty-day written notice to let her know I was moving like I had agreed to do when I signed the month-to-month lease. I told her in a voice mail message. I didn't even care if she sued me for breaking the lease. That nice lady called back and told me not to worry, because she didn't want me to say anything negative and discourage other prospective tenants from moving in. "It's going to be even more difficult now to attract people who are not afraid to live in a house where such a bizarre crime occurred *and* is next door to a halfway house," she told me. She blamed herself for not being more proactive in having the back door lock repaired. I blamed myself for letting Calvin know about it. I had practically opened the door for him myself!

The cops had located his Jeep Cherokee parked in an alley two blocks from the scene of the crime. When they searched it, they found a duffel bag that contained duct tape, handcuffs, garbage bags large enough to hold a petite body like mine, a bottle of chloroform, a claw hammer, and a set of brass knuckles. The sales receipts from the two stores where he had purchased these items were in his pocket. My assumption was that once he got me into his vehicle, he planned to duct tape and handcuff me, then use the brass knuckles and claw hammer if necessary. I knew that he had intended to kill me, I just didn't know how. I had seen a lot of horror movies, so my imagination flew off the charts.

Within days, there was a full-blown media circus, and Joan and I were the main attractions. It was the biggest crime story involving people connected to Northern California since the Jim Jones mess back in the 1970s. Somebody who knew my cell phone number passed it on—probably for a profit—to the media. Black serial killers were so uncommon, people all over the world wanted to know more about Calvin Ramsey. Joan and I received several voice mail messages from a pesky reporter in Japan. She refused to return his calls. I called him back after he had left four messages, and that was only to tell him to leave me alone.

The story kept growing. Four days later, an escort who called herself Heidi was interviewed on the local six o'clock news. Between sobs, she claimed that Calvin had invited her to his house. "Since he was a regular with the service I work for, I didn't mind doing a house call. He was real nice at first. Then all of a sudden he went off on me. He roughed me up a little, but when I told him I was pregnant, he backed off and I hauled ass," she said with tears streaming down her face. When she gave the date of the encounter, I was flabbergasted. It was the same night that I'd met him at the pizza parlor! It was also the same night that Bertha died. Recalling those two events made me shudder.

Several escorts from other dating sites came forward. Unlike the pregnant Heidi, none of them had anything negative to say about Calvin. One woman even called him "one of my nicest tricks." So far, none of the women from Discreet Encounters who had dated Calvin had been identified or come forward.

When a local reporter tracked me down, I moved to a motel on the other side of town.

My cell phone rang constantly, so I turned it off for the next two days. When I turned it back on, my voice mail was full. When my caller ID identified somebody from the media or some other busybody, I deleted the message without listening to it. Elbert had called eight times, but I had no desire to talk to him anytime soon. Jeffrey had left five messages, so I called him back right away.

"I'm sorry it took so long for me to call you back, but I didn't want to talk to anybody," I apologized. "I am so damn tired of all the media bullshit and everything else."

"I understand. I was just concerned about you. How are you holding up?"

"I've had better days," I said, surprised that I was able to chuckle. "It gets a little better each day."

"Lola, I'm glad to hear that you're okay. I hope you come out of this mess in one piece. That might be hard to do as long as you stay around here. If you want to disappear for a while, I'll buy you a ticket to anywhere you want to go. But I have to warn you, there is probably no place you can go to get away from this. Not for a long time."

"Thanks, but no thanks. I'll have to go back to work soon so I can afford to eat and pay rent."

"My father owns an apartment building on Bellflower Street. A young dude who's been living in one of the units for the past two years just accepted a job in Oakland. He doesn't want to commute, so he's going to be moving to the East Bay soon."

"How much is the rent?" I asked.

"It's within your price range. The guy was also the apartment manager, so Daddy let him live there rent free."

"Oh. You think your daddy would let me take over that responsibility so I can live there rent free too?"

"He owes me a few favors, so I promise you he will. After all you've been through it's the least I can do."

"I left a lot of my property in that house, but I'll never go back inside that place again. I can't stop thinking about how scared I was that night, and all that blood the dead cop and Calvin left on the floor and—"

"Stop! I know it's not easy, but you need to put that shit out of your mind and move on. Don't worry about your stuff. I'll hire somebody to pick it up and haul it to a storage facility until you're ready to retrieve it."

"Jeffrey, that's the best news I've heard since . . . well, in a long time."

"I can believe that. By the way, I bumped into Joan's stepfather at the flea market last Sunday. He told me that the whole family knew you'd be Joan's downfall someday. I was tempted to set him straight, but I didn't want to upset the old dude." Jeffrey laughed.

I laughed for the first time since the night Calvin came to kill me. "They think I was a bad influence on Joan? If they only knew the half of it." I laughed some more. "I'm glad Joan doesn't feel that way. We talked this morning and she's about to go stir crazy being under the same roof with her family again. She moved back into her condo today and she's cooking dinner for me tomorrow."

"I'm glad to hear that. I always liked Joan. Do you have plans for dinner this evening?"

"Other than a few crackers and some potato chips, I haven't eaten a decent meal since . . . since *that night.*" The words left a bitter taste in my mouth. I was still having trouble wrapping my brain around what had happened. Never in a million years would I have thought that anybody—other than Libby and Marshall—would attempt to kill me. The pain of knowing that the person I thought was going to "rescue" me wanted to kill me was so excruciating, I didn't know if I'd ever date again. I had already deleted my profile from the Discreet Encounters website.

"Well, I'm sure you've heard by now that Libby and I are separated," Jeffrey said in a low voice.

"I know. Elbert told me. I hope you and Libby can work things out."

"No way. I'm done with her. I ignored a lot of red flags over the years, including mysterious phone calls in the middle of the night when she thought I was asleep. And I don't want to go into the details, but I have other evidence that she was cheating on me. I'm divorcing her. I've already filed the papers."

"How is she taking it?"

"Oh, you know her well enough to answer that question yourself. She's fit to be tied."

"Oh well. That figures," I said, forcing myself not to snicker.

"And she blames you for breaking up her marriage."

"The hell I did! She did it herself by being careless enough to get caught with another man. I'm glad she knows I'm the one who put the bug in your ear. She caused me pain for years, and it was a pleasure to finally give her a taste of her own medicine."

"I hear you. And I hope it makes you feel better."

"It does." A wicked smile crossed my face, and I was glad Jeffrey couldn't see it. Despite what I'd just said, I didn't want him to know just how overjoyed I was about the outcome of ratting Libby out. "Now, what time are you coming to pick me up for dinner?"

Chapter 60
Joan

MY NEIGHBORS WERE VERY UNDERSTANDING AND SUPPORTIVE. They mentioned the incident as little as possible. A couple whom Reed and I used to socialize with brought me home-cooked meals for a week. Another neighbor did my laundry and grocery shopping. The airline pilot who lived in the condo next door offered to let me and Junior stay with him and his fiancée for a while, but I declined his invitation.

Dr. Weinstein, Reed's so-called best friend, checked in with me every day to see how I was holding up and to ask if I needed him or his wife to run any errands for me. I was surprised that he never brought up Reed's name, and neither did I. I was convinced that if he had helped Reed hide his affair with Grace, he regretted it now.

My landline rang day and night. Because my number was listed in the telephone book, I was a sitting duck for sick puppies all over the country. Some called just to do some heavy breathing. Others called to bombard me with profanity. Last night a man accused me of being the prostitute he had contracted HIV from. A local woman called and swore that Calvin was the father of her three children and she wanted the name of the cop who had shot him so she could file a lawsuit. Another man accused us of luring Calvin to the house and "setting him up to be killed by the cops" because we hated black men. A woman with a German accent, who claimed to be a psychic, told me that another man was going to "finish what Calvin had started."

After the cops had viewed what I had recorded with my cell phone, somebody on their end leaked the video to the media. It went viral and was shown all over the Internet and on TV news programs almost as much as the Rodney King video. Now everybody knew the reason Calvin had targeted Lola and that he had been killing women for years. Pictures of the three dead women in his freezer, as they had appeared in life, were in every newspaper, as well as TV and the Internet. My likeness was too, but Lola's was the one that got most of the attention. Everybody agreed that she resembled the women in the freezer. A lot of people couldn't tell Lola from Calvin's wife. They looked that much alike. One reporter nicknamed him the "Look-Alike Killer."

Producers from three national TV talk shows invited us to appear to tell our side of the story. We both refused. The same people kept calling until we had our telephone numbers changed and unlisted. We deleted our profiles from the Discreet Encounters website, but a few members sent messages to our e-mail addresses, not to ask for dates but to beg us not to mention their names. None of the prominent men we had dated came forward and revealed their connection to me or Lola. And I was not surprised. They all had too much to lose by telling the whole world that they belonged to a sex club. I was so glad that Lola and Calvin had never posted any reviews about each other on the club's review board.

The Discreet Encounters staff remained quiet about Calvin, Lola, and me being members of their club. I assumed it was because they thought it would be bad for business. But I didn't think most lonely people cared one way or the other, because even after the TV movie about the craigslist killer and other bad publicity about online dating, Discreet Encounters membership had *tripled* since I'd joined two years ago.

*　*　*

Reed never ceased to amaze me. Instead of showing the mother of his child some sympathy, he ignored me completely. He was quoted in the newspapers left and right, and he wasn't saying anything nice. He had the nerve to tell one reporter that he always knew I was going to end up in something over my head. He claimed I'd been "sneaky" for so many years, he didn't know who he was married to anymore. And even though he knew damn well that I had never pepper sprayed anybody before him, he told another reporter that it was my "style" and that I'd recently used it to assault him. He didn't mention that he had assaulted me first.

It really hurt when I heard that Reed told some of the people we used to socialize with that he had been trying to get away from me for years because I was so unpredictable, deceitful, and unstable. He claimed that he had stayed with me only because of Junior but that I'd become so volatile he feared for his safety and had had no choice but to leave me. I was so glad that lying bastard was out of my life! I never wanted to see him again, so I planned to have him pick Junior up from Mama's house when he wanted to see him.

My family got on my nerves big-time the short time I stayed with them. They seemed to be in such awe, you would have thought that Lola and I had parted the Red Sea. No matter how much I balked, they wouldn't let up. Our dinner table had always been like the hood version of *The View*, so that was the venue for most of the discussions.

Sunday afternoon, two weeks after the incident, the subject came up again at Mama's dinner table. I was glad that she and Elmo were the only two present with Junior and me. My stepfather loved true crime stories, so he was in his element. "Girl, this is the biggest news involving black folks since the O.J. Simpson thing. If cops in this town was as smart as they want people to believe, they should have put two and two together and looked into this case better when them three women that looked alike disappeared without a trace. And they should have looked into the killing of them hitchhiking women along the same route that Calvin drove. It took you, a run-of-the-mill, PTA-meeting, everyday housewife, and Lola, a dead-end-ass, low-paid cashier, to bring down one of the most dangerous men in the country!"

Elmo stopped talking, and Mama started spooning collard greens onto her plate and talking at the same time. "I got a feeling them big studio hotshots down in Hollywood will be calling soon about making a movie about y'all! Or one of them Discovery Channel true-crime show producers. This story is right up their alley. Lord, I hope they don't get no ugly actress to play me," she said with her eyes sparkling like wet diamonds.

"You don't have to worry about an ugly actress portraying you, because there is no way I'm going to let the whole world see my life on a screen. And Lola feels the same way."

Junior sat across from me with an exasperated look on his face and his hands covering his ears. "Do we have to keep talking about that crazy Calvin? I'm sick of hearing about how he almost killed my mother," he snarled.

"Shet your mouth, boy! Shet it up right now and take them hands away from your ears," Mama ordered, giving him a menacing look. "We'll be talking about that crazy sucker from now on. I been a prison guard since Joan was a baby, and I ain't never been caught up in a situation with a serial killer until now." With a pat on my shoulder, Mama added with tears in her eyes, "And to think that one almost took my baby girl away from me!"

"I feel the same way Junior feels. I wish everybody would find something else to talk about," I complained. "I'd like to forget about what happened. Lola and I are fine, Calvin is dead, end of story."

No matter how much I protested, my folks refused to let up. They kept me up until midnight asking all kinds of questions, some that they had asked already several times. They asked me for the tenth or eleventh time when and where Lola had met Calvin. She and I had agreed to tell everybody that they'd met back in February in the food court at one of our favorite malls.

"Humph! I wonder how many other maniacs Lola done picked up in food courts," Elmo sneered. "Joan, you need to put some distance between you and that sex-crazy woman. Associating with her is too dangerous. Calvin might not be the only serial killer after her with her nasty self! Y'all might not be so lucky the next time."

"There won't be a next time," I said firmly.

Chapter 61
Joan

*I*T SEEMED AS IF EVERYBODY IN TOWN WANTED TO HAVE THEIR FIF-teen minutes of fame by piggybacking off Lola and me. A former classmate I couldn't even remember told a newspaper reporter that Lola and I had been two of the most promiscuous girls in South Bay High. The boy that I'd given my virginity to claimed that I'd pestered him for days on end to have sex with me. Patty Baker, a former bully that Lola had helped me beat up in grade school—and hadn't spoken to since—bragged that she had been one of my best friends back in the day. One of the worst mean mouths was Reed's mother. "I am so glad my son got rid of that woman! She's been a thorn in my family's side since the day we met her," Mother Riley said during a local TV news interview.

My son was taking everything in stride. "Mama, I don't care what people are saying about you. I think you're the world's greatest mother. And Lola is just as cool as you are in my book." Junior was the most important male in my life. I was glad that he had "forgiven" his father and resumed their relationship. How-ever, Reed had to pick him up from my parents' house when-ever he wanted to see him.

Libby and Marshall had the longest and most vicious tongues of all. In one of Libby's newspaper interviews, she made Lola sound like the stepsister from hell. "She had the temperament of a shark, so I kept my distance. I was afraid of her. When my mama married her daddy, Lola was still in middle school, but she was already as loose as a goose." She told another reporter, "Lola was such a sex addict, she started throwing herself at my husband when she was a teenager, but I put her in her place." Libby never mentioned that Jeffrey had left her because he found out she had cheated on him. Marshall, one of the homeliest men in town, even claimed that Lola had repeatedly come on to him. "I didn't like to be alone with my stepsister because she made me nervous. She was too affectionate, if you know what I mean." Those two jackasses' lies, delusions, and exaggerations didn't faze Lola, but it pissed me off. I prayed that I would never run into those two scumbags in public, because I was afraid of what I would say, or do, to them.

In one newspaper article, a reporter implied that Calvin's experience in the war in Afghanistan may have had something to do with his breakdown. Another referred to him as a bad seed who'd had evil festering in him from the day he was born. I didn't buy that, and neither did Lola. From what we'd been able to determine from all the things we'd read about Calvin's background, he had been a model citizen until the night he killed his wife. His worst known "crime" was a speeding ticket when he was seventeen. The only bad seeds I knew of were Libby and Marshall. I honestly believed that their evil ways started when they were still in Bertha's womb. Other people felt the same way. At the end of the day, Calvin had still been a monster and got what he deserved. And I *knew* that someday Libby and Marshall would also get theirs.

Everybody felt sorry for Sylvia Bruce, Calvin's clueless fiancée. Well, not *everybody*. When she appeared on a local live TV talk show, one mean-spirited female audience member insisted that Sylvia had to know something about Calvin's murderous activities. Sylvia emphatically denied it, but the woman wouldn't let up until the host stepped in. By then it was too late. Within seconds, Sylvia had a complete meltdown. She started crying and spewing gibberish, and had to be helped off the stage.

Calvin's family refused to talk to the press, but a man named Robert, a neighbor who also claimed to be one of his closest friends, couldn't stop talking. Almost everything that came out of his mouth was negative. "I always knew something wasn't right about my homeboy. When his wife went missing, he didn't seem the least bit concerned. And another thing, he was real particular about who he let in his garage. One time when I asked if I could store some frozen goods in that big-ass freezer he had in there, he got nervous and told me some cock-and-bull story about the freezer being on the blink. He never let me near his garage again."

Pictures of Calvin, the one that appeared in his high school yearbook and one of him in his marine dress blues, were splashed all over the newspapers, right above the ones of the three dead women he'd hidden in his freezer.

When the investigators searched his house, they found a box in his attic that contained IDs and other personal items he had collected from some of his victims. These items eventually helped identify most of the murdered women. I was glad that the families finally knew what had happened to their loved ones.

After I left Mama's house and went back home, I talked Lola into staying with me until the tenant had vacated the apartment Jeffrey's father was going to let her have. She cried off and on every one of those days. One night she ran out of the guest room screaming and jumped into bed with me. It took an hour to calm her down. "I still can't believe that the only reason Calvin was interested in me was because he wanted to kill me and put my body in his freezer. What did I ever do to deserve something that awful?" she sobbed.

I was still just as rattled as she was, but I was better at hiding it. I cried in private. "The only thing you did was meet the wrong man," I told her, as I handed her a shot glass filled with vodka that I had set on my nightstand a few minutes earlier. "Drink this and go back to bed."

One mighty swallow was all it took for Lola to empty the glass. After a loud belch, she continued. "Thanks for letting me stay with you. I'm sorry I almost got you killed. I wish you hadn't been there."

I rolled my neck and eyes at the same time. "Shut your mouth! What's wrong with you, girl?" I scolded. "Be thankful that you're still alive *only* because I was with you."

"I am. I really am thankful to be alive." A frightened look suddenly crossed Lola's face. "What if I had married him and then found out what he was planning to do?"

"Don't even think about that," I said with a shudder. We remained silent for a few moments.

There was a gleam in her eyes that I hadn't seen since the last time she fantasized about marrying Calvin. I couldn't wait to hear what she was going to say next. In a deadpan tone she told me, "When you buy some more pepper spray, get a can for me. With people like Libby and Marshall, not to mention all the potential Calvins, running around loose, I may need it."

"I'll pick up several cans," I said.

Epilogue
Lola

Two years later

SOME PEOPLE WERE STILL TALKING ABOUT THE NIGHTMARE THAT Joan and I had survived. Last Saturday afternoon, a middle-aged white woman I'd never met stopped me on the street. "You look like one of the women that Look-Alike Killer almost killed a couple of years ago," she told me, giving me a sympathetic look.

"I know. I hear that all the time," I replied.

"You're lucky the cops stopped him from killing women who looked like the wife he'd murdered, because you look just like her. Ted Bundy also went after women who resembled a girlfriend who'd dumped him. A friend of mine was one of his victims. She and I looked a little like the girl who had driven him to kill." The woman's voice cracked, and tears pooled in her tired blue eyes. "I was supposed to hang out with her the day Bundy got her, but I bumped into a boy I liked, so I decided to hang out with him instead. If I'd met up with my friend, we'd both be dead. You and I were lucky, huh?"

"We sure were, ma'am," I muttered. The woman gave me a hug. It pleased me to know that people who didn't even know me cared about me.

And a lot of people cared about me.

Last year Elbert proposed again and I accepted. All those

months that I'd wasted fantasizing about Calvin, my true soul mate had been right under my nose the whole time! I didn't know what true love was until I realized what a good man Elbert was. It didn't take long for me to fall head over heels in love with him.

The day after we returned from our two-week honeymoon in Tahiti, Joan called me and asked if he was good in bed. "He's the best lover I've ever had. We can't keep our hands off each other. If we had slept together before I got caught up in that sex club, I would never have joined. But I'm glad Elbert had enough respect for himself, and me, to stick to his principles. He is every woman's dream."

"Do you still think about Calvin?"

"Only when the media mentions him or when somebody else brings up his name. The night before he came to kill me, I had had a very nice dream about the lavish wedding we were going to have. I had been having nice dreams about him almost every other night for several weeks before that. I haven't dreamt about him since."

Elbert purchased a beautiful house for us near the meat market he managed. Two weeks after we exchanged vows, I quit my job at Cottright's and went to work for Elbert, and not just because he made me his head cashier and doubled my salary. I wanted to work for him so we could spend as much time together as pos-sible.

Our son, David, will be three months old in two days, so we must have created him on our wedding night, the very first time we made love. Unfortunately, Elbert's mother didn't live long enough to see us get married. Six months after the Calvin incident, she and her new husband died in an automobile accident.

Despite the massive grief I'd endured and the dangerous choices I'd made, I finally had everything I ever wanted.

Joan didn't date again until a year after her divorce. She started a relationship with the son of one of her stepfather's friends, a nice, quiet man who treated her like a queen. She sold the condo and bought a smaller, much less expensive one located in the same neighborhood where we had grown up. She is very happy now and anxious to remarry and have more children.

Ironically, Grace deserted Reed less than a year after he married her for a man closer to her own age. Grace received a huge settlement and full custody of the daughter she had with Reed. The last time I caught a glimpse of him walking down the street, he looked like a man who had lost his will to live. And maybe he had. He had done enough to bring it about.

Joan and I eventually stopped mentioning the sex club and Calvin, but I thought about each one from time to time. One day last year, I got lost trying to find a new discount store. I ended up on the same street where I'd almost lost my life. I slowed down as I drove past the yellow house. A couple in their thirties occupied a glider on the front porch. There was a fussy toddler in the woman's arms. A teenage boy was in the driveway bouncing a basketball. I was pleased to see that the house had new tenants, because it was a nice place. I probably would have stayed in it for a long time if it hadn't been for Calvin. I didn't know why, but after that night I no longer feared anything yellow. A few months ago while I was shopping in one of my favorite boutiques, I saw a skirt with a matching jacket that I just had to have, but the only one in my size was yellow. I purchased it, and when Elbert saw me in it, his jaw dropped and he couldn't stop staring. "That color makes you look even more beautiful. If I had better legs I'd get the same outfit for myself." I promptly added several more yellow pieces to my wardrobe. Joan was pleased to hear that I had gotten over my fear. She had several yellow frocks in her closet that she'd outgrown, and when she offered them to me, I accepted every single one. I wore the color so often, she told me that I had begun to remind her of a sunflower, which was my favorite flower. It was one of the nicest compliments I'd ever received.

After Jeffrey divorced Libby, he joined Match.com and met the woman he married last month. "Lola, if things don't work out with Elbert, check out a few dating sites. The Internet is the best place to find a suitable mate these days. Food courts, like the one where you met Calvin, are as bad as bars. They attract a lot of beasts," he told me. Even though millions of people had positive experiences with Internet dating, I couldn't bring myself to tell him that that was where I'd met my "beast." He had always held me in such high regard, I hoped that he would never find out I'd already tried online dating, but only to have casual sex. Realistically, I knew I couldn't keep my dirty little secret forever, especially from my husband.

Last week when I heard that a very famous true-crime author was planning to write a book about the incident, with or without cooperation from Joan and me, I panicked. I had read a lot of true-crime books, so I knew that those authors found all kinds of ways to get the information they needed. Sometimes they even paid their sources. Most of the greedy people I knew would sing like a Christmas choir for enough money. I didn't want Elbert to read about my misadventures; I wanted him to hear it directly from me. I told him while we were having dinner yesterday, and I left no stone unturned. It took more than an hour to tell him everything, and the whole time he remained silent.

"Sweet Jesus," he murmured when I stopped talking. With a blank expression he reached for another pork chop and cut it in half before he spoke again. "It'd take an eggbeater to beat a story like that." He took a deep breath and then he looked at me with his eyes glistening. "Baby, whatever you did before I married you is your business."

"You mean you don't care that I was a . . . a . . . that kind of woman?" I asked, holding my breath.

"All I care about is the kind of woman you are now. You made one hell of a bad choice, and you paid a very high price for it. We all do at some point in time. I sure did."

"Huh? What did you do?"

Elbert took another deep breath and continued. "I cheated on my first wife with her best friend."

If he had told me that he had once been a hit man for the

mob, I couldn't have been more flabbergasted. "You did?" I was so taken aback I almost fell out of my seat. "But I didn't know—"

Elbert dropped the pork chop onto his plate and held up his hand. "A lot of people didn't know me that well back then. When I came home from the military, and even before I went in, my two best friends were cocaine and alcohol." He paused and gave me a pensive look. "And I loved the ladies."

"You've got to be kidding me—"

He immediately cut me off by snapping his fingers. "Let me finish. Anyway, I lost my wife, I disappointed my mother, and I lost respect for myself. It took a drug overdose, and what I believe to this day was a near-death experience, for me to come to my senses. When I got out of rehab, I promised God, my mother, myself, and everybody else who cared about me that I would turn my life around. And I did. That's why I don't drink, do drugs, sleep around, or do any of the things most people our age are doing in three shifts. And I've been very happy ever since."

"But I never heard anything about you doing drugs, drinking, or chasing women while you were still married! You had me, Bertha, and everybody else in town fooled!"

Elbert nodded. "I sure did. I was just as sly and deceitful as you and Joan were. I had no idea what you were doing, and I'm not about to judge you. Everything you just told me will stay with me." He took my hand in his and gazed into my eyes. "The man you married is not the one he used to be. The woman I married is not the one she used to be. Let's leave it at that."

And we did.

Joan eventually told her family everything. After they had talked about her like a dog and called her a nasty buzzard, a shameless hussy, and a Jezebel (and a few other choice names that she was too embarrassed to tell me), they forgave her. It didn't even faze her son. All Junior cared about was that his mother was happier than she'd been in years. Joan decided not to tell Reed about her former secret life. She was still so angry with him, she wanted him to find out when that author published his book. "I want him to know what all I was up to when we were still married. And I want him to see it in print. It'll have a bigger impact and will last longer than it would if I told him," she told me with a snicker. I thought she was being cruel, but if Reed didn't deserve to be treated cruelly, who did?

One of the best things that happened in the past two years was that Libby and Marshall finally got a visit from karma and it made up for lost time. According to Kandy's House of Beauty grapevine and other reliable sources, six months after Libby's divorce, she met a "between jobs" musician in the same casino where she had lost a huge portion of her inheritance. He was handsome and so slick, within a month he had sweet-talked her into letting him move into the townhouse she had purchased. Kevin hated his mother's new lover, so he moved in with Jeffrey, but Libby was so hopelessly in love, all she cared about was pleasing her new man. She gave him power of attorney, so he handled all of her finances. Four months into the relationship, she returned home from an all-day shopping spree and got the shock of her life: Her sweetie had packed up and disappeared. He had helped himself to the large collection of expensive jewelry she had purchased with Bertha's money, a set of heirloom silverware Bertha's family had owned for three generations, and *all* of the money she had left. To add insult to injury, he'd also taken a large ceramic piggy bank she had been putting loose change into since she was twelve.

Libby's lover had also maxed out all of her credit cards and left her thousands of dollars in debt. She was so furious, she approached a couple of local thugs and asked them to find her a hit man who'd be willing to do a job on credit. They laughed in her face. It wouldn't have done any good if she had found a contract killer, because the man she had trusted with everything she owned had been using an alias. None of his associates even knew his real name or where to find him.

Creditors stalked Libby so aggressively she had to file for bankruptcy. She had no marketable skills or work experience, so she had settled for a housekeeping position in the same sleazy motel I had moved into when she evicted me. Her salary was so low she couldn't make the payments on her new Jaguar, so the repo men paid her a visit. A week later, the bank foreclosed on the townhouse she'd purchased and she had to move in with Marshall. He had also made a mess of his life, so his situation was almost as bleak as hers. He had squandered most of his inheritance on two luxury cars, high-end prostitutes, bad investments, and numerous trips to the casinos in Vegas and Reno.

Shortly after Libby moved in with Marshall and started throwing her weight around, his meek, long-suffering wife threw in the towel, moved back in with her mother, and immediately filed for a divorce. The icing on the cake was, all the years Marshall had been fooling around with other women, his wife had had a lover. She married him four months ago. I didn't like to gloat, but when it came to Libby and Marshall, I made an exception.

Last but not least, Shirelle Odom, the brazen mistress my daddy had moved into our house when I was in middle school, was back in my life. I still thought of her as "my other mother." Three days ago, she waltzed into the store five minutes before the end of my shift. I was glad she was the last customer in my line so we were able to chat for a few minutes.

"Oh my God," I said hoarsely when she placed the new issue of *People* magazine and a bottle of wine on the counter. Except for a few wrinkles on her face and about thirty extra pounds, she looked as glamorous as ever. Elbert was helping another customer two counters over, so I lowered my voice. He knew about Shirelle and Daddy, and he was one of the few people who had never said a mean word about her. But I still didn't want to talk loud enough for him to hear, because I had no idea what Shirelle was going to say. "What a surprise to see you again!"

"I hope it's a nice surprise and you're glad to see me," Shirelle replied with a woeful look on her face. "Lola, I . . ." She stopped and began to fidget.

I could tell she was having a hard time talking, so I jumped in and said, "I'm so happy to see you after all these years! I thought you'd forgotten all about me."

"I could never forget you, Lola." She cleared her throat, and the look on her face intensified. "I'm sorry I didn't reach out to you when all that serial killer mess was going on. But my family and friends were making so many ugly comments about you and Joan, I just couldn't get caught up in it and risk losing their respect again. I don't care what people say or think about me now. My life has been so wonderful these past few years, I can afford to have a few setbacks." Shirelle laughed and then she suddenly gave me a serious look. "I felt so guilty about not reaching out to you when I first heard about Calvin Ramsey. It bothered me so much, last week I decided to do something about it. None of the folks I contacted knew where you lived or worked. I got so desperate, I finally gave Libby a call and . . . uh, I stopped using profanity when I found Jesus, so I can't repeat what she said about you."

I held up my hand and shook my head. "You don't need to go there. I have no contact whatsoever with her and her brother. I hear all the gossip about how bad off they are now, but I haven't even seen them in public since the day of Bertha's funeral."

"I even tried to get in touch with Joan and Jeffrey, but they have unlisted telephone numbers too. I got lucky yesterday when I ran into Jeffrey at the gas station. He shared all kinds of information with me. He told me everything about Bertha leaving you out of her will and Libby kicking you out of the house and giving your stuff to the junkman! I couldn't believe my ears when he told me Libby and Marshall had had you chased out of the church during Bertha's funeral! Poor Jeffrey. I was happy to hear that he'd divorced Libby. He's such a good man and deserves a much better woman. The best piece of information I got from him was that he told me where to find you."

"What about your husband? I thought you didn't want him to know about me."

"Right after I heard about you and Calvin, I told my husband about my past. I told him everything. He wasn't happy to hear that I'd lived under the same roof with my married lover and his family, and it caused a little tension between us, but he got over it. If I had known years ago how he'd react, I would have told him a long time ago. And you and I could have resumed our relationship before now."

I gave Shirelle a pensive look. "I'm glad to hear that. It would have been nice if I could have called or visited you from time to time."

She nodded. "I was happy when I heard about you and Elbert. I never got to know him well, but from what I've heard, he sounds a lot like the wonderful man I married."

"Elbert is a wonderful man. It took me a long time to realize that, and I'm glad I finally did. He is a great father and we are very happy. I finally have another family of my own again."

"Well, if it's not too late, I'd like to be part of your family."

There was nothing Shirelle could have said that would have made me happier. "I'd love that," I replied with my voice cracking.

"My husband is doing so well, last month we sold our house in San Diego and bought a new one in San Francisco. We moved in last month. I'm so happy to be living in the Bay Area again! I'm hosting my family's annual reunion next week. Would you like to come?"

"You know I would! Thank you!" I squealed. It was hard to hold back my tears. I had attended several of Joan's family reunions. Even though I'd always enjoyed myself, I had still felt like an outsider because so many of her relatives made me feel like one. I knew I wouldn't feel like that at a reunion with Shirelle around.

She gave me one of her dramatic neck rolls and then she slapped her hand on her hip. "You won't have to worry about any of my folks bombarding you with questions and comments about that serial killer. I know you're sick and tired of that subject by now."

"I hope I never hear Calvin Ramsey's name again as long as I live," I said, choking on a sob.

"I'll pray that you won't." Shirelle took a pen and a small scratch pad out of her huge leather purse, scribbled down her telephone number and address, and handed the page to me. And I gave my contact information to her.

I felt so much love for this woman, I could barely contain myself. Tears rolled down my face. I was happy that "my other mother" was back in my life. This time she was my *only* mother.

THE DEVIL YOU KNOW

Mary Monroe

ABOUT THIS GUIDE

The suggested questions that follow are included to enhance your group's reading of this book.

DISCUSSION QUESTIONS

1. Lola barely knew Calvin, but he was such a good liar and she was so in love with him, she believed everything he told her. Do you think she was a little too gullible for a woman in her thirties?

2. Joan's relatives knew she was miserable and wanted to end her marriage. But they didn't want her to divorce Reed, because they cared more about the money and gifts he gave them than her feelings. Do you know people as greedy and trifling as Joan's family?

3. Reed kept Joan under his thumb by behaving like a love-struck fool and threatening to commit suicide if she divorced him. Were you surprised when he left her for another woman? Did you suspect that he had been fooling around all along?

4. Joan had numerous online lovers and was desperate to end her marriage. Did you expect her violent reaction to Reed's betrayal, or did you think she'd be happy that she was finally going to be rid of him?

5. Do you think the argument between Lola and Bertha caused Bertha's fatal heart attack?

6. Do you think Bertha's daughter Libby crossed the line when she accused Lola of "killing" her mother and then slapped her in front of Bertha's doctor and preacher? Lola didn't want to make matters worse, so she didn't hit Libby back. Do you think Libby treated Lola the way she did because Lola was so passive?

7. Libby had the locks changed so Lola could not return to Bertha's house. Then she hired a junkman to haul away

some of Lola's property before she could retrieve it. Did Libby's actions surprise you?

8. How did you feel when Libby and Marshall had Lola kicked out of the church during Bertha's funeral?

9. Despite Lola's devotion, Bertha left her house and everything else to Libby and Marshall. Neither one had ever shown Bertha any love or respect, not even in death. To keep from paying for her funeral, they wanted to donate her body to science! Lola felt slighted, but she took it all in stride. Would you react the same way?

10. Calvin was anxious to marry Sylvia, but he wanted to find and kill Lola first. She unknowingly made it easy by revealing enough information for him to locate her residence and that the lock on the back door was broken. Would you ever give out this much personal information to anybody other than family and close friends?

11. If Calvin had succeeded with his plan to murder Lola, do you think he would have finally stopped killing women who reminded him of his ex?

12. Were you shocked when Lola finally accepted superstraitlaced Elbert's marriage proposal? Did she do the right thing by telling him that she had been leading a double life as a member of the online sex club where she'd met Calvin?

13. Lola was stunned when Elbert told her that he had also once led a double life as a drug addict, a womanizer, and an alcoholic. Do you think he did the right thing by telling her?